# THE DRESDEN TANGO

KEVIN O'REGAN

PUBLISHED BY CORE BOOKS
ISBN-13: 978-1-7392206-0-0

*To my parents and Nen,*
*successful migrants to another country.*

*"I read the manuscript in less than two days. This wasn't due to any urgency but because I found the stories of the two main characters so compelling."*

Fred Lockwood (author of the Jack Collier series)

*"The book is very readable. I found the voices of the two narrators convincing and I cared about them. The minor characters are very well drawn; Canon Peter is a wonderful creation. There were many superbly narrated scenes, such as the rolling of the dice in Chapter Seven."*

Patrick Sanders

*"I love this book, Kevin. I felt so many emotions on reading it: tears, sadness, anger and something close to the power of Spirit even in the worst moments."*

Brenda O'Neill

*"Patrick is a very powerful and convincing narrator of the epic sweep of the novel. I think you understand his psyche inside out. The journey for both [characters] is a very dark one – shades of Thomas Hardy. But I did find the conclusion redemptive and their separate journey of suffering made them suitable partners in the aftermath."*

Mark Kenny

*"Rose has a convincing female voice and the reader cares about her."*

Jane Wilkinson

*"I found the historical and cultural detail and the migration story fascinating, and this kept me reading to the end. Using the two narrators was effective in expanding the perspective and works even better when the characters' views of the same moment are subtly different."*

Caroline Browne

# CONTENTS

# ACKNOWLEDGEMENTS

This book started life as a song called *The Dresden Tango*. I had a rhythm that I could not clear from my mind, then a chord sequence but I needed the subject matter. The rhythm was an Argentine tango but I wanted to write more songs with an Irish connection. Whilst exploring that connection, I came across the web-site of *The Society for Irish Latin American Studies* and on it an article from *The Buenos Aires Herald* of 17th March 1999 by Michael John Geraghty in which the story of *The City of Dresden* expedition was told. I am indebted to the Society and Mr Geraghty as, without them, this book would not have been written.

I am extremely grateful to those who read the book in an earlier draft and gave me very valuable feedback, suggesting changes and, above all, encouraging me to continue to publication by the warmth of their responses. Thank you to Fred Lockwood, Caroline Browne, Patrick Sanders, Brenda O'Neill, Mark Kenny and Jane Wilkinson.

My thanks also to my publishing team at Kindle Book Publishing who have brought my book to the World and, finally, to my wife for her patience and encouragement.

# NOTE TO READER

In early 1889, a ship called the *SS City of Dresden* arrived in Buenos Aires with nearly 1800 Irish migrants on board, mainly from poor areas in and around Dublin, Cork and Limerick. Several hundred were sent to Naposta, an area about 400 miles south of Buenos Aires, where they attempted to establish a colony. Some young women were tricked into prostitution. Although based on an historical event, all characters and situations in this novel are fictitious.

# OVERTURE

## EASTER SATURDAY, 28TH MARCH 1891

My hand is trembling; I grasp the door knob more tightly. I force myself to look back at the room. The first grey light of dawn is filtering through the threadbare curtains and, for a few seconds, I watch the figure under the sheet. She is sleeping soundly, her chest rising and falling, rising and falling. Molly. She has been no friend to me these last two years, two years in which I felt myself becoming hollow, empty, a shell, no longer able to feel even anger, let alone love.

Except this ache in my heart.

I move like a ghost down the stairs from our attic and then on down the grand stairs to the ground floor, my eyes and ears alert, like a wild animal sensing a predator. The house is still asleep but I peer through the crack of every door left ajar. No one. I take some bread, cheese and water from the kitchen, quietly, and put them in my bag, the same carpet bag I had brought with me on that journey from Ireland two years ago.

My lips form a silent, automatic prayer: Hail Mary, over and over again as I close the outer door and glide along the street, hurrying in the direction of the port. My mind tells me they cannot be following but fear compels me to snatch furtive glances behind.

The streets are busy with workers: the day starts early for most in Buenos Aires. As I near the docks, there are men with carts, whistling in the cool of the morning, getting as much done before the sun rises too high and too hot. Head down, I make my way to St Joseph's

Church. I can wait there unseen for the two hours I need before moving to the place we have agreed. I stop in the porch to lift my veil over my head, letting it fall over my face. It seems to offer some protection.

The handle is heavy and the door swings slowly open. It creaks and I hold my breath. I slip in and close the door, turning the handle back carefully so the big metal latch will not clank as it falls. Silence. I sense no human presence but that feeling … it's always there in churches … the great space reaching upwards to fractured light, the sense of being watched, the lingering fragrances of incense and candle wax, smoky and cloying.

I move softly to the rack of candles in front of the side altar. No candles are burning. I drop a small coin in the box, hearing it chink on those already there. Holding a candle in one hand and a match in the other, I hesitate. For whom do I light this candle? For myself, perhaps, to light me to a better life, an escape from the horrors I have endured? For Patrick who wants to save me? For the hundreds of souls who were brought out here with promises of riches and freedom? Or for that little lost soul whom even now I cannot name. I wish I could cry, but I am drained.

The match flares and shrinks to a steady flame. I light the candle and watch as it takes hold, shedding a small halo of light in the dark church. "God help us all," I whisper. Perhaps God is listening … perhaps …

"My name is Rose … Rose Kelly," I mouth, trying to remind myself who I am, that I have a family, that I was once loved. I left Ireland full of hope for a better life here in Argentina. Now I dare not let myself hope that this attempt to escape today will happen … yet here I am trying anyway, a sickness in my stomach I know to be fear … fear of being captured and of him not coming, and being abandoned to continue suffering this hell.

I sit for a long time, the church clock striking the slow passing of the quarters, until I hear the door handle clanking. A few old people hobble up the aisle ready for the nine o'clock mass. They say nothing, but kneel in the pews, most clutching rosary beads, their mouths fluttering soundlessly as they pray. I envy them their belief. The church clock strikes nine, the altar bell tinkles shrilly and the priest enters the chancel.

Tip-toeing down the side aisle, I open the church door a little, furtively checking the street outside for watchers, my whole body clenched with fear. The bustle and noise of the docks hits me. The air is already warmer and the workers seem cheerful, calling to each other as they push the heavy carts along the street.

"¿Quieres que te lleve al barco? Al barco?" The man, holding the reins of his pony in one hand and waving to me with the other, startles me. He grins, revealing a set of yellow teeth with several missing. I shake my head and hurry away – I cannot afford a ride to the boat.

It is not far to the spot we have agreed to meet and I see some crates there as if they have been positioned for my use. I would like to find somewhere to sit in the morning sun, to bask in it as if already free but of course I cannot take that risk. Therefore, I stand just at the end of the crates, enabling me to see out but ready to melt back into the shadow if I need to. I've learnt that over the last two years – the ability to be invisible, melt into the background, hearing nothing, seeing nothing until I'm called. It has been a question of survival.

And so I wait, searching the busy street, in fear that he will not come, in fear that one of my captors will. It's like the space between life and death, death and life, limbo and purgatory.

# ACT 1

# CHAPTER 1

# SALIDA

**Patrick**

Saturday 26<sup>th</sup> January 1889, a date now etched in my memory.

A bitter wind from the East, searching, chill; I pulled my overcoat tight around me. I'd arrived at Queenstown in good time. I paid the driver, being sure to add a tip, and he touched his cap. "Thank you, Father, thank you, sir." He nodded his thanks several times before stepping backwards and climbing up into the trap. I could see the smile on his face and I was pleased that I had been able to give something to an honest man doing his job. I have to confess that in my naivete back then, I was also pleased by the deference he had shown to my clerical collar.

Along the road to the docks, we had passed a straggling line of people with suitcases and bags, heading for the boat. I would have liked to offer them a lift but that was impractical. Most of them wore threadbare coats and a few had only battered jackets to keep out the cold. Guilt loitered in my mind that I should be riding, well-dressed, in a trap whilst they walked, wearing old worn clothes against the biting wind but it strengthened my resolve to make sure, in whatever way I could, that these people would find better lives.

The terminal at Queenstown was bustling, the air of excitement palpable. There were families, friends, single people, others seeing loved ones off. I stood, somewhat bemused, amongst the throng.

Suddenly, there were voices shouting.

"Don't go, son, don't go and leave me lonesome, a poor old woman with no one." The elderly woman's faded black shawl was slipping from her shoulders as she clutched the arm of a young man.

He shook her off. "I've got to. There's nothing for me here. Can't you see that? You'll be alright … our Mary and Joe will look after you." His dark features were a scowl, unsoftened by any gentleness in his voice. Perhaps it was not hardness but a stifling of what he was feeling.

"But Arthur, you're my son, me own flesh and blood. I'll never more see you coming home from the field, watch you atin' a dinner I've cooked for you. What's over the sea for you?"

My heart surged at this opportunity so soon to exercise my calling. I approached her, now sobbing into her shawl with Arthur looking embarrassed beside her. I laid my hand on her shoulder and she looked up. "I'm sorry, Father, but 'tis hard for an old woman to lose her son."

"Take heart. Your son will come home to you, bringing riches to keep you in comfort. God will take care of him and yourself. Trust in him. Now will you pray with me?" The words I spoke were laden with certainty, my faith absolute.

The two of them, mother and son, bowed their heads and I said a Hail Mary. The mother was quiet and I made the sign of the cross on her forehead, softly, to give a blessing. Arthur looked as though he may refuse a blessing but he did bow his head again for it.

Almost immediately, I was approached by a man probably in his late fifties, if not sixties, whom I took to be another parent. He was stooped, his head already receding between his shoulders, telling of a lifetime of drudgery.

"Ah Father, would you be after knowing where I'd get the boat to Hargentina?"

"Right here," I said, startled that he was starting a new life at his age. "They'll call us soon and we'll go to that table over there I think, and they'll have your name if you're booked on her."

As I spoke, I looked over to the table and saw two well-dressed gentlemen there who looked as though they were organising things. Two younger men sat at the table and were ticking people off on their lists, the one with a great flourish each time, the other with a face of faint disdain. After the formalities were complete, they directed them to the throng of passengers on the quay waiting to board the ship. There was quite a queue at the table, too.

"Are you able to wait in the queue?"

"Oh, I am right enough."

"And your name is?"

"John Connolly, Father. I'm from Limerick way."

"I thought it would be only young people emigrating today."

"Ah well, there's nothing for me here and they said there would be work for me out there. I've nothing to lose, I s'pose."

"Well let's join the queue together."

We joined the queue that snaked around the building. One of the two men standing by the table spotted me there and approached.

"Hello, Father. Are you travelling in steerage?" He sounded concerned.

"No. I have a second-class berth."

"Ah well, this is not the queue for you then. Come with me and I'll show you. My name is Michael Duggan and myself and my colleague Charles O'Grady are in charge of the expedition."

His voice was clipped, a man who enjoyed being in charge. He was slightly taller than myself, six feet I'd say, and he held his large frame erect to give himself an air of authority. He offered his hand which I shook.

"Father Patrick Gilligan," I responded, and then he turned to lead me across to the hallway. "Come now John, we'll be sorted over here."

Duggan stopped and turned to face me. "Ah no, Father. This is just for second-class passengers." He looked at John, distaste evident in his face, as if poverty might be contagious. "You'll need to join the queue over there."

I was shocked by Duggan's response. "But surely he can come with us? A man of his age should not have to stand."

Duggan held up his hand. "You must understand, Father, that we will deal with everyone more efficiently if we hold firm to the procedure we have."

"I'll be right enough now, Father. Don't you worry about me." John's face broke into a wide grin and so I allowed myself to go to the hatch where I presented my ticket. With the boarding papers duly stamped, Duggan showed me out of the building to the boarding ramp.

"Here she is, the *SS City of Dresden*." He waved his hand in a proprietorial manner at the ship towering above us. "She's almost brand new … only launched in December last year."

She was an impressive vessel and my eyes roamed approvingly over her gleaming paintwork, the black hull and white superstructure reflecting snatches of sun when it broke the clouds. "Will you and your colleague be sailing with us?" I asked.

"We will of course. We'll see you safely landed on the other side and then we'll be returning here. I'll see you on board I'm sure, Father Gilligan." He turned away and strode back the way we'd come.

A sailor took my suitcase and led me, stumbling clumsily, up the ramp and onto the deck where a steward checked my ticket and led me to my cabin. The steward, German like the rest of the crew, explained in broken English that I would have it to myself as there weren't many first- or second-class passengers on this trip. His white jacket was clean and crisp and spoke of meticulous attention to detail. He explained meal times and pointed forward to where the second-class dining room was situated. I thanked him and, when he had gone, sat down on one of the bunks.

It was soft; I'd sleep well on it, provided the passage was not too rough. I'd never been outside Ireland before, never been on a ship, though in my later childhood I had helped on small fishing boats that worked out of my home town of Schull. The cabin walls were varnished wood, a rich, warm, golden colour, and red curtains hung at the large porthole which looked out over the harbour. Soon we would be sailing out through those waters and would not know when we might return. What would we find across that wide ocean? What difficulties would we face? My stomach fluttered with nerves.

Reaching into my jacket pocket, I felt for the little wooden cross that Monsignor O'Rourke had given me, its smooth contours a comfort as the old priest had said they would be. He had given it to me the day he asked me on behalf of the bishop if I would be part of this migration to Argentina.

"I don't want to put any undue pressure on you, I hope you understand that, but it is something you may want to do. You're a young man – twenty-five you said – that's good in many ways but perhaps not in others." His lean frame was draped in his chair, his hands folded on his stomach as he awaited my answer.

The clock beat an insistent rhythm on the mantelpiece and the room wrapped its comfort around me. Sitting there, cup of tea steaming on the table, it was easy to agree to go. I felt I was up to the challenge. I became increasingly sure as he spoke that I was being called to this ministry. A thrill of excitement gripped me: this was why I had been called to God's service, to do something great in a faraway place. It would mean rolling my sleeves up and getting my hands dirty, which I much preferred to living in comfort in some sleepy parish as I had been during my curacy.

"I think I am being called to this ministry," I said, looking him directly in the eye.

He nodded slowly. "It'll not be easy Patrick, you know that. 'Tis a long way from Ireland and a long way from your home, your family, everything you've known so far in your life."

"I know that, Father, but I am sure I am destined for a ministry that will be demanding."

He smiled. "The bishop will be pleased." He took a folded newspaper from the table beside him and handed it to me, pointing at an article. "You should read that though before you finally agree."

The article was from the Cork Examiner which raised concerns about the promises being made for the expedition. Doubt began to seep into my mind. I read it through several times, all the while trying to make a decision. The article suggested the promises of excellent agricultural land, equipment, seed, the eventual opportunity to purchase a holding may not be fulfilled. But, I reasoned, that made it even more important that a priest should be part of it, to bring God to those who were trying for a new life.

I put the paper down carefully on the coffee table. "How much of this is to be believed? There's no evidence, just a suspicion that the promises are empty."

"That's right, but ... the source is from people on the ground out there who know the situation." Monsignor O'Rourke leaned forward. "I don't show you this to deter you but so you know what you might be letting yourself in for. If people go, there may be even greater need for ministry and it may be even more challenging than you think."

I said nothing, taking this in. I felt a twinge of fear, like a hand gripping me inside, but then I thought, why should I shrink from the difficult? Did Jesus run away when he knew he had been betrayed? "I will go, Monsignor. I'm sure I'll be able to do some good."

He didn't reply immediately. He held his hand out and I shook it.

"You're a good man, Patrick, and a brave one, but perhaps you demand too much of yourself. Always remember that you are doing God's work and he is always with us, even in those moments when we feel abandoned." Then he took from his pocket the small wooden cross. "Take this," he said, "and hold it in your hand whenever you feel God is not with you."

I took the cross and felt its smoothness, caressed by years in his hand. I had often wondered why he kept one hand in a pocket. It was carved olive wood and shaped like a cross but not quite symmetrical so it would fit comfortably into your hand.

"Thank you, Monsignor. I will treasure this."

Remembering that moment, I felt a surge of love for the old man. He seemed to understand so much. He was not one who sought his own comfort and would visit the poor in the parish every day, often giving them his own food and what little money he had. If I could be half as good, I would be fulfilled.

The following day would be Sunday, a very different one to what I was accustomed to. It reminded me I needed to find out quickly what arrangements there were for mass, whether there were other priests on board and where a service could be held. I found the steward again, who led me down a narrow staircase and into a corridor adorned with pipes and cables to see the purser. Fortunately, he too spoke English well.

The purser, a dark-haired stocky man, had just left his office when the steward called him. He turned and ambled back towards us, flat-footed, like a duck. Taking a list from his desk, he ran his eye over the sheet labelled first- and second-class passengers. "You are ze only priest as far as I can see," he said, his voice heavily accented.

"But you don't have the complete passenger list there, do you?"

There was a slight amused pity in his face when he replied. "Zere are no priests travelling in steerage so I need to look at only first- and second-class. We have only fifteen passengers in zose two classes together – ze rest are steerage. One zousand seven hundred and fifty-nine," he added, pronouncing the numbers carefully.

"How many does the ship hold?"

"Zere are cabins for zirty-eight first-class, twenty second-class and one zousand seven hundred and fifty-nine berths in steerage."

"Steerage is completely full then?"

"Zat is correct, Fazer Gilligan." His tone was that of a parent or teacher patiently explaining something to a dim child. I ignored it.

"If I am the only priest on board, I would like to say mass for everyone tomorrow morning. Shall we say ten o'clock? Where would be best to hold the service and how do we let everyone know?"

The purser thought for a moment. This had obviously not been considered. "When we go furzer south and it is warmer, ze best place would be on ze main deck amidships but tomorrow, wiz zis wind, your words will be blown away. I zink you had better use ze mess room in steerage zough zere will not be room for everyone."

"Perhaps I could do two or three services?"

"As you vish." He seemed to have lost interest already.

"Will the first- and second-class passengers join the rest of us in steerage for the service do you suppose?"

He looked surprised, then he smiled. "You can ask zem but …"

I had brought no communion wafers with me so I had to ask him for bread, cut into small pieces, which I would bless. He would arrange for a bottle of wine and I had my chalice with me but no chasuble nor surplice, just my stole. I was partly disappointed that arrangements would be so makeshift but mainly I felt a surge of joy. This was my ministry, to bring God to people whatever the limitations of place, time and facilities.

## Rose

The quay was stifling ... the press of bodies, the babble of voices, so much grey humanity, the smell of sweat. I tried to calm myself, to breathe deeply, holding my hand before my nose and keeping my bag on the ground tight between my legs for safe-keeping. The hull of the ship loomed black before us and I looked above it to where the top parts, though barely visible, were a ghostly white. Only a little of the sky could be seen but it was enough to calm me.

The question that had gnawed at my mind over the last few weeks could not be completely dispelled. Was I doing the right thing? Both apprehension and excitement boiled within me, a rise of hope like sunlight amongst autumn leaves before a tight grip on the stomach and a sudden plunge into darkness. I fought to suppress them. One minute, I felt like running back to my home, the next I wanted to board the ship as quickly as possible.

The crowd shuffled forward and then it was my turn to step onto the ramp. This was it, this was the first step to a new life. A sailor put his hand on my arm to steady me and then I was staggering up the ramp, clutching my bag. As I climbed, I glanced down – it was so high and the heads of those still on the quay looked smaller with each step. I felt a little dizzy and so I looked up instead. The two high masts that reached skywards on top of the ship seemed to scrape the speeding clouds, the funnel huge and black above the white superstructure. Gulls were wheeling overhead, screaming and calling, effortlessly riding the wind, as if they felt the excitement of our imminent departure as much as me.

When I stepped off the top of the ramp onto the deck, a sailor asked me in a foreign accent which class I was in. He pointed to a door in the middle of the ship through which the people ahead of me were disappearing. I was about to move forward when I felt a push in my back. I stumbled.

"I'm so sorry, miss, I'm sorry. I lost me balance."

Turning, I saw an old man being supported on the deck by the sailor who hoisted him upright. The sailor looked annoyed but said nothing before turning to the next passenger.

"God, sure, I fell off the top of the ramp. What'll I be like when the ship is on the wide sea, bucking and rolling? I'll have to sit down all the time."

His eyes twinkled in a heavily lined face. He was certainly old … as old as my father if not older. His jacket looked threadbare at the elbows and his trousers hung on him, held up with a belt that looked like it might give way at any time. He stood slightly stooped, his shoulders sagging. Had he been more upright, he'd have made a fine scarecrow. I immediately reprimanded myself for the unkind thought.

"Are you alright? I didn't push you over I hope?"

"No, no … I'm fine."

"Ah sure, 'tis great to be young … and so pretty." I blushed at the compliment. "John Connolly at your service, miss." He made a little bow, lifting his cap as he did so.

"I'm Rose Kelly, from Cork city. Are you heading over to that door?"

"I am right enough. Sure, 'tis a fine head of hair you have. Is it from your mother you have that?"

"I think it came from my father's side … he has a little trace of red still though he's going grey now." I relaxed, feeling he needed my help more than I needed his and touched by his compliments and courtesy.

I slipped my arm through his as we crossed the deck, his body rocking forward and back with every step. I thought with a pang of guilt of my father. He would grow old like John but I may not be there to see that, to steady him when he stumbled. My eyes watered and I shook my head to dispel any tears that might form. I must look to the future but could not help feeling my father's arms, warm around me, as he hugged me awkwardly in the early morning darkness before I had left that day.

A sailor at the door directed us where to go when we went below. The single men were in the forward section, us single women were in the family section amidships. I wished John well then, and holding the door open, watched him descend the stairs carefully into the bowels of the ship before following him down.

Gloom, the faint smell of bodies, and bunks, rows and rows of bunks stacked three high. No cabins. Light entered only from a couple of portholes on the port side, long shafts stabbing the dullness, revealing the floating dust but, when the sun slipped behind a cloud, it was as if a light had been doused. I noticed a few unlit oil lamps hanging from the iron beams as I carried my heavy bag through the passageways, treading carefully to avoid belongings already littering the floor. At last, I found the family section, a part of which was designated for the use of single women. I hoped we wouldn't have a rough passage; the idea of lots of young children being sick and wailing all night did not appeal!

I hoisted my bag onto the middle bunk of a stack of three. It barely sank in the straw mattress – not much comfort on that. I fought the sense of disappointment that overcame me, flushing out any excitement I had been feeling. This was not what I had imagined. Foolish I know but I had allowed myself to create a different picture … cabins with perhaps two people, a porthole through which one could see sunlight dancing on the water as the great ship cut a path through the sea.

It brought back that day four months ago when my employer had told me she was closing her dressmaking shop and there was no longer a job for me. I had stared at the Waterford crystal vase adorning the windowsill, a present to her from some grateful customer. The late September sunlight sent shards of light around the room and then it seemed to shatter into a thousand splinters. What would I do? I had expected to continue working at her shop, even convincing myself that I would take it over one day. In one sentence, my hopes, my expectations, had been smashed.

She'd looked over her glasses which, as usual, had slid down her long nose. "Therefore, Rose, my girl, you'll have to find a new position, I'm afraid. I will of course be happy to write a reference for you but … I fear …"

I looked up, startled. "What were you going to say Miss O'Leary?"

"There are few jobs to be had in Cork for dressmakers these days. The trade is dropping for the small shops. Ladies want to shop in the big stores in the city which source their dresses from abroad. You may have to think about domestic service. Sure, 'tis a good thing I have you well trained in keeping house, is it not?"

"Yes, Miss O'Leary," I answered mechanically. I dreaded having to tell my parents, watching their eyes sink in disappointment and worry. I had been able to send a good amount of money home in the last year or two since I had earned a wage. They would miss that and, of course, they would have another mouth to feed unless I could find work.

"I'm sure you'll find something suitable, Rose. You're quick and willing, you have developed good skills with your needle and that will always be valued by an employer. You can read and write — that's a great asset. If you can't find anything here in Cork, you could always think about going to England. There's plenty of work in service there I'm told."

And so here I was, heading for Argentina rather than England, sitting on a hard bunk, the enormity of the decision I had made threatening to send me scurrying back to shore.

This will never do, I told myself sternly. It was my mother's voice I heard. "You must make the best of it," she would always say at any difficulty. Yes, I must. There was no other option. I had made my decision and must embrace whatever was in store.

I started to explore the dark world of steerage, threading my way slowly through the labyrinth of bunks. The sense of confinement was almost overpowering, making me want to get back on deck, to light and air. Already people were lying or sitting on bunks, no doubt exhausted from the long walk to the ship from God-knows-where. Buckets were positioned at every stack and my stomach heaved at the thought of the smell as they would be filled.

"I wouldn't go in there if I were you." A young man was lounging against a stack of bunks. He smiled at me – a handsome fella sure enough. His weathered face was set off by the sweep of his dark hair and bright blue eyes. His hands had clearly seen hard work and he was dressed probably in his best clothes, a rough tweed jacket and trousers, with a thick woollen jumper over a cotton shirt. His boots were heavy, made to last.

I tried to sound confident. "Oh, and why is that?"

"This is the section for single men." He pointed to a sign hanging from the ceiling.

"Oh … I see." My eyes flashed to the sign.

"Unless of course you're looking for someone …" He smiled again.

My face burned. "No … no, I'm not. I'm just looking around. There are so many bunks down here."

"There are … one each I'd say!" He laughed. "James O'Neill is my name." I said hello and was about to move on when he asked, "May I know your name?"

"Rose … Rose Kelly."

"Well, 'tis nice to meet you, Rose. And this here's my friend Will." At the mention of his name, another young man rose from his reclined position on a nearby bunk and stood beside James. He was dressed in the same manner but was taller with a tangle of fair hair perched on his head.

"Pleased to make the acquaintance of such a beautiful young woman," he said, smiling directly into my eyes. "I hope you'll excuse me; I need to lie down for a bit as I'm nearly destroyed with the walking. Your man here had us nearly running all morning so as not to miss the boat."

"Ah don't talk so daft."

"I'll maybe see you later, miss," said Will, ignoring the comment. He turned and flopped on the bunk.

"And what brings such a pretty girl on a voyage like this?" James smiled at me.

"I lost my job and there was nothing I could find at home. Then one Sunday I met this fella – O'Grady was his name – who told me about this trip."

"That's the fella I met. God, sure you couldn't resist it, your own plot of land to farm … He stopped suddenly. "Not that you'll be farming, of course."

I smiled. "No. I hope to get a job as a seamstress or maybe in service." He did not respond immediately and I turned to go.

"Are you going up above to watch the ship sail?"

"Yes, I will … in a bit."

"I'll maybe see you up there then, Rose." His smile was warm, genuine, his eyes looking directly into mine, not, like many men, roving unwelcome over my body.

As I wove my way back to our section, I remembered that Sunday last September, the very same day that Miss O'Leary had dropped her bombshell, that I had met O'Grady. As usual, I had joined the strollers through Cork along St Patrick's Street to the river. I was leaning on the bridge parapet, gazing at the boats on the River Lee, trying to dispel anxiety by dreaming of faraway places and the exciting life that might be had on the other side of the sea, when I became aware of a man stopping beside me.

"And how are you today, miss?"

I turned and smiled as I would to any stranger. "I'm very well, thank you."

He returned my smile and said nothing for a while, looking around him. "You seem, if you don't mind me saying, lost in thought. I wonder what those boats there are making you think of?"

I glanced at him. He was not the usual type of young man out for a Sunday stroll to chat up the girls. He was older, probably in his forties, well dressed – not flashy – but a suit that cost more than a poor man could afford, and shoes that were more elegant than the clumpy boots working men wore. His eyes seemed restless, shifting this way and that.

"I often wonder where they'll be going," I said. "I know these ones don't go far but it always makes me think of faraway places, warm sunshine, an easier life."

"I know what you mean. I've often dreamed of that. What do you do, may I ask?"

"I'm a dressmaker but … my employer has just told me that she's closing the shop. I've to find a new job if I can. God knows that'll be hard enough."

"I should introduce myself. My name is Charles O'Grady. I'm working on something at the moment that may interest you. Have you heard of Argentina?"

"Of course. South America, is it not?"

"That's it. Myself and a colleague have been employed by the Argentine Government to invite people to go to Argentina to start a new, prosperous life. It may suit you. We're looking for people who have skills and, if you're a seamstress, there's a good living to be had, I can promise you. You may start in domestic service but you'd soon be able to put enough by to start your own dress-making business. How does that sound?"

I had felt a rush of excitement as I took the proffered bill which contrasted now with the dismal surroundings of steerage. As I sought my way back to my bunk, I found a bathroom near the family section. There must be others, I thought. Even if this was only for the family section, it was very small, just half a dozen cubicles and half a dozen sinks, each with a single tap. It would be a long wait in the morning, what with so many emptying the slop buckets.

When I found my bunk again, there was another girl sitting on the one above, swinging her legs, eyes closed. She had lovely dark hair falling in luxuriant curls to her shoulder. You'd not call her face pretty but it was handsome enough, sharp featured with heavy dark eyebrows.

"Hello," I said.

She opened her eyes and smiled. There was a real spark in her brown eyes and I liked her instantly. "I'm Annie, who are you?"

"My name's Rose."

"And where're you from, Rose? I'm from Dublin. God what a journey. It took me three days trying to get lifts off carts and such, and fightin' off the fellas." She jumped down from the bunk.

"I'm from Cork city, well, I grew up just on the edge of Cork, but I've been working in the city."

"Will we go up above to watch the ship leave?" She grabbed her coat and turned without waiting for an answer.

# CHAPTER 2

# CAMINATA

**Patrick**

The brass handle was solid, speaking of expense, and the heavy wooden door swung closed behind me with a clunk. I was the first to arrive for lunch in the second-class dining room which was most agreeable: the same wood panelling as in my cabin, a large table in the centre, set for four and positioned on a carpet into which my shoes sank. A crystal glass vase with a large base was the centrepiece of the table but it held no flowers. The air was rich with the scent of beeswax and linseed from the furniture polish, speaking of age even though the ship had only very recently been built, and bringing memories of the library at the seminary in Cork where I trained for the priesthood.

I had loved my time there and especially the library. I would spend hours reading the lives of the saints, the great deeds they had done and also of the brothers of the order who had worked in the four corners of the Earth, bringing God to the people who lived in darkness. The monks who taught us fired our enthusiasm to emulate them. They were days of belief, belief that we would bring great comfort to the people of Ireland with our preaching and our deeds, belief that we would achieve great things in far parts of the world, belief that we had been chosen by God for this special work. My heart surged with joy: here I was setting out to do just that.

My fellow second-class passengers entered the dining room. There were only three: an engineer called Stephen Hogan with his wife Sheila who were returning to Buenos Aires, and a clerk, I suppose you'd call him, who worked for an agricultural merchant in Buenos

Aires, also returning. His name was Frank Butler. His face in profile looked like a crescent moon and his body when he walked seemed hollowed out into the same shape.

"She's a fine ship," said Hogan, slurping soup from his spoon. "Launched on the first of December last year only, built in Glasgow for the Norddeutscher Lloyd company with the purpose of carrying migrants. She's just over three hundred and ninety feet long and forty-seven feet in the beam." Hogan's balding head shone in the new electric lights that adorned the walls.

"She's a good size to be sure," offered Butler eagerly, ingratiating himself with Hogan. His lank, brown hair flopped across his forehead which was creased with earnest enquiry.

Mrs Hogan said nothing, concentrating on sipping her soup with as much elegance as possible. She had the appearance of a bird perched on the edge of a pool of water, her head dipping towards the soup bowl each time she drank. She feigned boredom, or perhaps it was not feigned. How many conversations had she sat through with her husband boring listeners with tedious technical details?

"Her gross tonnage is four thousand, five hundred and twenty-seven and she's powered by a single screw that'll drive her along at thirteen knots. Not bad at all." Hogan had the air of a man who was very satisfied with himself. I wondered whether he ever showed interest in another person.

"So, given reasonable weather, we should be in Buenos Aires in … what …about twenty days?" Butler was working hard at being interested.

I let the two of them talk for a while and tried to engage Mrs Hogan but she seemed reluctant. I was not sure whether that was shyness or something else. Her carefully made-up face, adorned with meticulously brushed hair, darted like a bird's from my face to the table, occasionally tilting as if selecting a morsel of food. When the dessert was served, I broached the subject of mass the next day. At first, she seemed politely interested but as soon as I mentioned the service was to be held in steerage, there was a sudden change.

"Well, I think, Father, I'll need to see how I feel tomorrow morning. I'm not a great sea traveller, you see."

"Ah well. I hope you will feel right enough to join us," I said, knowing none of them would. I felt like saying something stronger but thought there was little point. Mrs Hogan asked me then why I was going out to Argentina. It seemed less like curiosity than a challenge. I told her briefly about the request from the bishop but said nothing of my desire to do good in the world, to make my life count. I didn't feel she would understand that.

After the rare treat of a cup of coffee, I took a stroll on deck, braving the wind to watch the preparations for our departure. The deck on which my cabin was situated was marked for second- class passengers. It did not run the whole length of the ship but, leaning against the rail, I had a good view of Cork city in the distance. I looked down, watching the stream of passengers struggling up the boarding ramp with bags and suitcases. I looked out for John, the old man I had spoken with in the departure hall, but I didn't see him. As I had expected, nearly all were young, probably in their twenties, thirties and a few in their forties. There were quite a few families with young children but many looked to be single young men with only a few single young women.

None of the passengers were being directed up to the deck I was on, but were shown through a door on the main deck. I assumed they would then be shown to their cabins. Some who had probably boarded earlier were doing the same as me, leaning on the rails, observing those still boarding. We are all fascinated by the activity of others. I suppose it was also the prospect of going to sea and heading for a new land, chasing dreams.

Voices, loud with excitement and perhaps apprehension, occasionally reached me. "I'll be in the first-class section," a tall young man with a mop of fair hair joked to the sailor at the top of the boarding ramp. "That'll be the section for first-class idiots," his companion replied. The sailor's expression remained blank and he pointed to the door where everyone else was disappearing.

We were due to leave mid-afternoon with the outgoing tide. Smoke was already belching from the funnel, immediately torn away by the wind, and a dull throb reverberated through the ship. The stream of passengers boarding came to an end and I saw a port official walk up the ramp and say something to the sailor before returning to the quay. The gangplank was then moved away with much clanking and shouting from the men on shore and most, if not all, of the passengers, it seemed, were there to watch our departure. A tug boat pulled us away from the quay, slowly, so slowly, the gap widening between the ship and the dock. I felt a twinge of apprehension again; too late for regret now, I told myself, and I tried to dispel the cowardly thought.

But the figure of my mother formed in my mind. She had stood open-mouthed when I told her that I'd agreed to go to Argentina. Her body had seemed to slump and she had turned away to the range, mechanically lifting a pot and replacing it.

"I thought you'd be pleased," I said softly. "You were very pleased when I said I wanted to be a priest."

She turned to face me then and I saw she was fighting back tears. Her voice was strained, sharp.

"I suppose if you've been called to it by the good Lord, who am I to complain? But you'll leave us lonesome here whilst you go off to save the savages."

"Argentina is a civilised country, Mother. 'Tis not like I'm going to the depths of Africa." I spoke curtly, unable to allow the doubts she was creating infect me.

"I'm sure Patrick will be fine. The Lord looks after those he has called." My father, God bless him, ever the mediator, tried to calm her fears. And it was of course fear that had produced her bitter tone.

I held her then and she sobbed. "Sure, I'll be back in no time at all and you have the rest of the family around you."

I'm sure I was not the only one grappling with such thoughts; that young man – Arthur – whose mother I had calmed in the port building, for example. I wondered how he was feeling now about leaving her, though no doubt he was glad to be leaving a life of poverty and toil.

There was a moment when all on board fell quiet, the only sound the gulls above us, calling and keening as if in warning. We watched the dock buildings move away from us, realising that this was real at last: we were leaving.

Then suddenly everyone was cheering and calling, waving hats and scarves to the people on shore. I looked up and could see Mr Duggan and his colleague O'Grady standing magisterially on my deck but further for'ard in the first-class section. A shrill whistle from the funnel announced our departure and the rhythmic thump of the engine grew in intensity, a rhythm that would be a constant companion. What glimpses there were of the sun between the scudding clouds showed it to be sinking low in the West already and I thought of the people in other parts of the world seeing the same sun, feeling its warmth, saddened by its departure each night, perhaps. In South America, it would be only late morning, the day not yet at its hottest.

The city of Cork was already shrinking in the distance, the imposing building of St Colman's Church, not yet complete, on top of the hill above Queenstown, calling the faithful from the sea. I looked down onto the main deck, thronging with the passengers from steerage. They looked a grey lot in coats and jackets, the men in flat caps. There were just the few women amongst them, some keeping children close, others on their own or with a companion.

Two in particular caught my eye. One had dark hair, falling beneath her bonnet in curls to her shoulders, and the other had hair of a beautiful shade of gold which blew about her face, catching the late sun. Was it then, as Canon Peter so much later said, that the golden-haired girl entered my heart? I would have been shocked by such a thought at the time, seeking only to fulfil my ministry as I was, but I'm not so sure now. I'm no longer sure of anything. The dark-haired girl looked up, said something to her companion and then with a broad smile, waved at me. I waved back. The golden-haired girl looked embarrassed. Such a tiny incident but one that revealed two very different personalities.

By the time we passed Rams Head, the deck below was almost empty, and the amber underbelly of the clouds had intensified to crimson. One of the two girls I had seen earlier was still by the rail, taking her last look at her homeland, I supposed. Her hair no longer looked gold but was auburn, no less beautiful. Who or what had she left behind? Perhaps some sweetheart, probably a mother and father who would already be mourning her departure, wondering would they ever see her again.

Soon after we slipped past Roches Point with its lighthouse stroking the darkening sea in great sweeps, a young man joined her at the rail and they talked. I could tell he was not yet well-known to her but he clearly wanted to be. I could not describe nor explain the strange, shadowy feeling that crept deep into my breast, a loneliness, a sense of disappointment, a longing, but for what I could not fathom. I went in from the cold wind which burned my face.

I have sometimes wondered would I have set out, would any of us have set out, on that bitter January day, knowing what we know now? Probably not. I would not have had the courage. But would I endure it all again? That's a different question. I have no hope of any sainthood when I say I would — not willingly — but my life would be worthwhile if I could alleviate the suffering of just one person.

## Rose

As we threaded our way back to the narrow stairs that led up to the deck, I couldn't help noticing Annie's clothing — you always do when you're a seamstress. Her tweed coat was worn and her boots badly scuffed. In fact, it looked as though they might fall apart. Her linen skirt — surely a hand-me-down — was grubby around the hem, telling of a winter journey. She did not seem to care.

There were crowds of people, mainly young men, on the deck but Annie pushed her way through them, dragging me behind her until we got to the rail. One fella protested and she gave him a huge smile saying, "Ah, we're only little so we can't see a thing from here." He smiled and offered to lift her up. "And have you feeling my private parts! Not likely fella." She punched him playfully and pushed on.

At the rail, Annie slipped her arm through mine and we looked down, silently watching the space between the ship and the dock widen a few inches. "That's it. We're off. The adventure begins." I coughed to cover the choke in my voice while all around cheers broke out.

Annie looked at me and smiled. "Let's hope it'll be a good one." She looked up and nudged me. "Look at the priest up there, like he's God himself."

I turned and looked. "Sure, you wouldn't expect a priest to be down here, would you?"

"Now, I call that a waste of a man."

"What d'you mean?"

"Well, look at him. A fine figure of a man, handsome face. But he's totally wasted as he's not available. I bet he'd make a fine husband." I was shocked – it seemed disrespectful – but Annie waved and gave him a big smile. He returned both and Annie tittered. "Maybe one of us'll have him for a husband yet." There was no doubt about it, he was a good-looking man but that clerical collar marked him out as different. He was beyond reach.

We stood on the deck watching the land slide by as the ship slowly threaded a path southwards towards the open sea. Annie decided it was too cold and went below but I stood at the rail, sheltered a little from the wind by the superstructure of the ship, thinking about leaving my homeland. I had never been away from Cork city before, let alone away from Ireland. Until now, it had held all my hopes and dreams, all the people I loved and who loved me. The enormity of the decision I had made settled like a weight on my heart.

The sun was setting, occasionally flashing a golden ray of light across the water but mainly obscured by cloud. The ship slipped past Roches Point and I watched as the distance grew, our wake trailing behind us like a cord linking us to the shore. The wake would fade as the sea settled once more and that link would melt away. The light on Roches Point was flashing, a lonely beacon in the fading twilight and, with a twist of anxiety, I wondered how long it would be before I saw it again.

I was startled by a voice very close to my ear. "Now, I wonder what you're thinking. Are you regretting the decision to come away or are you glad to be leaving the place?"

It was the fella I'd bumped into down below – James. "Oh … I don't know … probably a mix of the two."

"I know what you mean. It was hard leaving my Ma and Da the other day. As I walked away, I wondered if I'd ever see the hills of my home again."

"And where is your home?"

"Not far from Limerick. It's a small farm my folks have but 'tis not big enough for all of us. My youngest brother will likely take it on in time so the rest of us must make shift some other way. There's no work round there."

I nodded. "The ol' story, I guess." I told him of my family, my work in Cork as a seamstress and we began to share our hopes for the future. The sense of a new adventure overcame my usual shyness.

He pulled a folded sheet of paper from his jacket pocket; I recognised it as the same bill that I had been given months ago that had led to my joining this expedition. He intended to take up the offer of land, seed, machinery and the rest of it and hoped in time to be able to buy the land he farmed. "Sure, in a few years, I'll be a rich man and I'll come back to Ireland and give my parents an easy life." He laughed then. I think neither of us knew whether that would be possible but I suspected it was the secret hope of everyone on board the ship.

My life, I realised, had been very comfortable. One could see hardship in the tattered clothes worn by most of the other passengers, in the stooped shoulders of that old man, John. Many had worked on the land or perhaps in labouring jobs in the big towns, scratching a living on meagre pay and rations. And James's story was so common – the older siblings in a family having to move away to get work and the youngest boy taking on the farm when his parents were too old to work. It was not something people complained about; it had happened for years and one accepted that, for the likes of us, that was the way of the world.

I warmed to James. He was an easy person to talk to; no side to him, just a pleasant, optimistic young man with a passion to better himself. For a while, I forgot the cold wind as we stood in the growing darkness, the last light streaking the western horizon. Then I shivered and he noticed.

"Sure, what am I doing, keeping you out here where you'll catch your death of cold? Let's go down below and get something t'eat and warm up."

Down below, they were serving the evening meal from big cauldrons set on wooden tables. The place was crowded and, despite the cold outside, was warm with human bodies. The smell of boiled cabbage was overpowering. There was not enough room for everyone to eat at once at the wooden trestle tables so the families ate first and then us single women. James had to wait with the single men but I found Annie again and we sat together. Annie lapped up the thin gravy, mashing some spuds into it. It was tasteless. "Sure, I hope the food gets better," I said.

"Ate it while there's something to ate, that's what me mother always says. You never know when you'll get the next meal."

The food did not improve. Gradually, over the voyage, the amount got less. The men in particular were hungry all the time and complaining. They even started to ration the drinking water but I'll come to that.

That night, some of the fellows produced musical instruments and started playing in the area where they had served the food. It was wonderful and it became a nightly occurrence. I suppose that night we were all in high spirits despite the food and so there were lots of jigs and reels, and some of the young women danced in the traditional Irish way, their feet clacking on the wooden deck. There were a couple of fiddlers, one fella on a whistle and a couple playing bodhrans.

John, the old man I had met when boarding the ship was sitting on a bench, tapping one heavy boot on the floor in time to the music, puffing on a clay pipe and blowing occasional clouds of delicious smoke into the air. "Are you enjoying the music, John?"

"Ah, 'tis grand. There's nothing like a good jig or reel to lift your spirits. Are you not dancing?"

"Oh no … I'm not good at dancing."

"Sure, I'd lay a bet that's not true. Go on out there and let's see that beautiful hair flying around." The lines around his eyes creased like gathered leather. Such a lovely old man.

After a bit, they started to play waltzes. I saw James on the other side of the room and he caught my eye, motioning with his head to the centre where people were dancing. I shook my head and flushed. He was not going to be deterred by that, though. I saw him weave his way around the room until he was at my side.

"Come now," he said, sliding his arm around my waist. "I bet you're a great dancer."

I had learnt to dance of course, but with other girls. I allowed myself to be taken onto the dance floor if that's what one could call it. There was very little room to move but we managed and I loved it, being held by him, feeling him close to me, his strength, his youth, his vitality. We danced to the slow waltzes and the faces of those watching floated before my eyes as I turned gently in his arms, his warm body close to mine. Lightness, grace, elegance – these were mine as we danced. He was respectful, holding me only as he should to dance and not like some would, allowing hands to wander where they had no business. All regrets about this adventure evaporated from my mind for those precious moments.

I saw Annie out on the floor with a fella. She was having a wonderful time, throwing her head back and laughing, her hair flying out as she was whirled around, those eyes of hers alive and bright like diamonds. Oh, to dance with such abandon, such freedom; it was a thrill to watch her.

The next day was Sunday. There was a mass after the breakfast in the dining place taken by the priest we had seen the previous day. To my surprise, Annie decided not to go – I had assumed everyone would. The priest introduced himself as Father Patrick Gilligan. He seemed to be uncomfortable, not being in his usual church, I suppose, and wearing only his suit and a stole. The place did not lend itself to a holy atmosphere, the stale smell of last night's meal and sweat lingering in the air. He gave communion, blessing some little pieces of normal bread that had been cut up and giving us a sip of wine from a chalice. The words of his final prayer are scratched into my mind. "Dear Father, bless all of us who travel on this ship. May we find the comfort and happiness we seek in the new land to which we go."

People started to file out, negotiating the narrow corridors to return to their bunks, and I was one of the last to leave on the starboard side. Father Gilligan was finishing a conversation with John who negotiated his way around the edge of the floor, steadying himself with his hands on anything available.

Father Gilligan picked up his bible and chalice and joined the shuffling line at my side. "May I ask where you're from?" His voice was quiet, rounded, rich when heard so close.

I told him and asked about himself. He was chatting about how he had been asked by the bishop through another priest if he wanted to be part of the expedition. When he said the name, Monsignor O'Rourke, I gasped. "Sure, he's the parish priest of my parents. He arranged for me to be trained as a dressmaker in Cork city, a different parish to his. Such a lovely man."

It seemed to create a bond between us and we chatted about his parish, the city, my work and his family near Schull, a place I knew of but had never been. In truth, I had never been far from Cork city before. And I would never have believed that I could talk so freely with a priest. I had always been in awe of them – everyone in Ireland was. Priests were close to being God and some made sure you thought of them as such. But Father Gilligan was different. Perhaps it was his age – he was still a young man – but also his character. He would never be one to look down on people.

"What are the conditions like down below? In truth," he said, leaning his head closer to me so he could speak without being overheard, "I thought there would be cabins down here, perhaps shared, but not such a cram of bunks. I cannot believe how many people are pushed into this space."

"You're not the only one, Father. 'Tis a bit like being cattle."

He wanted to know about the food, washing conditions, sleeping arrangements, space for stowing personal property, privacy. I laughed at that. "There's precious little of that down here."

He nodded slowly, looking worried. "I will have words with the organisers." He took his leave then, a shy smile forming on his face. "It is a pleasure to meet you, Rose. God bless you and keep you safe."

There being no privacy to speak of, I had decided on the first night to sleep in my chemise. On the Sunday night, I had just let my dress slip to the floor and stepped out of it, when suddenly there was a voice, hoarse, quiet, male, close to my ear. The smell of drink was strong.

"Sure, you're a fine looking colleen." The man was standing behind me and then I felt his hands slide around my waist. One started to travel up my body and I gasped as he cupped my breast. I was so stunned, I couldn't speak though my mouth was open, no doubt a wild, frightened look in my eyes.

"What the feck are you at?" The hands left my body and I whirled round. It was Annie, advancing on the man as if she would punch him, her eyes blazing. "Where did you come from?" She looked him up and down. "You're from the family section, I'd say."

The man said nothing but leered at both of us. The motion of the ship and the drink made him unsteady on his feet.

Annie put her face close to his. "You can just feck off back to your family. If you need to get your cock out, you can feck yer wife or better still, feck yerself." She pushed him away and he shambled off.

"Thank you, Annie," I gasped, still reeling from the shock both of the man and her words.

"That's no problem. Yer need to tell these fellas straight. Where I come from, if yer don't do so, you'd be prey for every Dick in the city." She smiled then. "You alright?" I nodded. "Did you see his nose? It looked like he had his dick on his face." I laughed as much with embarrassment as anything. "Time for bed, then, I think." She put her arms around me and kissed me on the cheek. "We'll stick together. I'll keep you safe and you can keep me pure … " she laughed, "… well, you can try, anyways."

# CHAPTER 3

## CALESITA

**Patrick**

It was two days after the second Sunday that I was made aware of the sickness in steerage. Of course there was sea sickness, plenty of that, especially as we sailed across the Bay of Biscay. It's notorious apparently for storms, the Atlantic throwing itself against the French coast, and goodness we were flung about. But this was different. Some women and several children were taken ill and then a couple of men. They were packed into the ship's hospital, far too grand a word for such a rudimentary place, and attended by the ship's nurse, a ferocious German woman who seemed to have no trace of the sympathy one expects from someone of her calling.

I visited and tried to alleviate their distress, holding a cup of water to the quivering lips of children. No one knew what was wrong with them. I prayed with them and tried my best to offer some kindness.

After one such visit, I went again into steerage to see if there were others falling ill. As soon as I went below, a tall, tousle-haired young man called Will said that there was someone very sick in the section for single men.

"He's an old 'un, Father. Why on earth he came on this trip, I've no idea." I followed him through the labyrinth of bunks, stepping over belongings that spilled onto the floor and almost stifled by the smell of vomit, sweat and God knows what else. It was the old man I had spoken to on the day of our departure, John Connolly.

He was gasping for breath, a rasping in his throat each time he inhaled. I had been there only a few moments when Rose, the young woman with the lovely auburn hair, brought water. I watched her lift his head gently with one hand and offer the glass to his lips carefully with the other, murmuring to him in her soft voice. He breathed a thank you and she lowered his head slowly to the pillow. He closed his eyes and seemed to relax. I have no medical knowledge but I had seen enough people in the final stages of life to know John was not long for this world.

I signalled to Rose to move away a little. "Why is he not in the ship's hospital?"

"That nurse, the German lady, said there's no room."

"But he can't stay here. We don't know what ails him. If he's infectious, the whole ship could catch whatever it is."

"I know, Father, but where else can he go?"

Two young men, Will, the tall, fair-haired one, and James, the dark one I'd seen on the deck with Rose, were standing there. "Lads, help me carry him."

"Where will you take him, Father?"

"There're empty cabins in second-class, and in first-class for that matter. We'll take him to one of them."

"They won't like that, will they – the captain and so on, I mean?" Rose looked startled.

"Frankly, what they like or dislike is of no concern. This man should not be left here. Even if it is not infectious, he should be able to spend his last days in peace and dignity."

"His last days, Father?" The concern, fear perhaps, was evident in her voice.

We lifted him carefully, the three of us, while Rose brought his bag of belongings. It was a struggle carrying him through the narrow spaces and up the companionway, and I was glad to get out onto the deck. The weather was warmer now we were further south but too cold still to leave John on deck, though the fresh air would have done him good. We carried him up the stairs to the second-class section and into the empty cabin next to my own where we laid him carefully on the bunk.

"I'll sit with him awhile," Rose whispered so as not to disturb John. "James, will you ask Annie to come up and take over from me? She said she would but she won't know where we are."

James nodded and the three of us went out of the cabin. I had hardly closed the door when the steward came at speed down the corridor towards us.

"Father," he called. "Father, I'm told you've brought one of the steerage passengers up here."

"That's right. He's sick and there's no more room in the hospital."

"But Father, steerage passengers are not allowed in this section of the ship."

"What harm can it do? There's nowhere else for him and we don't know what's caused the illness. He may have something infectious. If he stays down there, he'll be passing it to everyone and then we'll have a whole ship sick."

"I'm sorry, Father, it is not allowed. I need to tell the purser."

"You go and do that. There are empty cabins here. Should we have put him in first-class? Would that be better?" I could feel my anger rising. He turned on his heel and strode back the way he had come. I smiled at the two young men. "You'd perhaps better make your way back to your quarters."

It was only a few minutes before the purser came to see me. I had gone into my own cabin when there were two sharp raps on the door signalling that he was in a mood to put his foot down. The conversation was much the same as with the steward but I kept my voice controlled, speaking very clearly, my eyes on his. The result of the conversation was that he would have to consult the captain. I said I would accompany him and the two of us walked in silence to the captain's cabin where we ran the conversation again.

The captain thanked the purser and said he would handle the matter. When the door had closed, he invited me to sit. There was room for only two chairs and we sat close together. "You see, Father," he said slowly with a heavy German accent, "the other passengers in second-class have paid a great deal extra to be in more … shall we say exclusive surroundings. They will not be pleased to see someone from steerage in their section."

"Captain, the man is old and he is dying. He will not be going anywhere and the other passengers will not see him. They may see the two young women who will take it in turns to sit with him but I'm sure they will not cause any offence. They will simply go in and out of that cabin."

He nodded slowly. "Fine, Father. But no more."

"That will depend on what happens down there. 'Tis a disgrace that so many people are crammed into that section. The arrangements are unsatisfactory … and this is a new ship."

"The arrangements are the same on all ships of this kind."

"Well, they should be better. I'm told that the rations are insufficient, too, and there's not  enough water to drink. There's growing anger about that. We're not yet halfway, Captain. I sincerely hope you've enough food and water for the whole journey."

"It has been calculated carefully. I'm sure there will be enough." He stood, my signal to go.

I went back to the cabin and found Annie with John. "It is kind of you," I said.

"Oh, 'tis fine. There's nothing else to do anyway."

I'm not sure how one measures kindness. Annie gave up her time to sit with a sick old man, perhaps putting herself in danger though she did not seem to have Rose's gentleness of manner. Her accent suggested Dublin, which she confirmed. I asked her about herself and the life she had just left. She shrugged her shoulders and said she had no regrets about leaving it but gave no details. I wondered what her life had been that she could shrug it off with such apparent disregard.

I divided my time between visiting those in the ship's hospital, talking to people from steerage and visiting John in the cabin next door. He was failing, his breathing laboured, short breaths that hardly made his chest rise at all. Rose was spending a lot of time with him, mopping his brow with a wet cloth to cool him. We had opened a window in the cabin during the day as the temperature was rising.

One evening, I think it was the second day he had been in the second-class section, I went into the cabin and she was there as usual, sitting on a chair by his bedside, watching him with troubled eyes. I stood beside her and looked down at John. I knew then that he had little time left. From my own cabin, I brought my bible and the small phial of holy oil I had with me. Rose looked at me in some alarm when I returned.

"It is time now for this, Rose," I said as gently as I could and then began the prayer for the anointing of the sick. Wetting my finger with the holy water, I drew the sign of the cross on John's forehead. "Through this holy anointing, may the Lord ..." And so to the Our Father and the Apostolic Pardon as John could neither make a confession nor take communion in his frail state. "May God bless you and his angels carry you safe to a better life."

Rose sobbed, just once and I put my hand on her shoulder. "Rose, you must rest. Let me take over now."

She turned her face to mine, its paleness beautiful against her hair, and I could see the fatigue in her eyes which she struggled to keep open. "I'm fine," she said softly.

"Now, we don't want to lose you as well, do we? So rest. You can do nothing for John at the moment. See, he sleeps."

She turned away to look at the old man lying on the bed and then stood up, slowly, almost painfully. She took one step from her chair and her hand went to her head. She faltered and I thought she would fall. I put my arm around her waist and held her up. "Come, lie here for a while." I supported her to the other bed – it was only two steps away as the cabin was not large – and lowered her gently onto it. "Lie down now and sleep. I'll be here."

"Thank you, Father," she breathed and her eyes closed. I watched sleep take her into its arms and slipped off her ankle boots so she would be more comfortable. I felt a huge tenderness towards her – that brief moment of contact, the slightest intimacy. And so I watched the two of them, the old man and the young woman. Both looked peaceful as they slept. With a guilty pleasure, my eyes were drawn to Rose. Her face was hollow from long hours of watching by John's bedside but she looked beautiful, her gorgeous auburn hair spread across the white pillow, her neck so smooth and long.

Of course, I dozed off in the chair and once woke with a start as I felt myself falling. I returned to my own cabin for a few hours of fitful rest. My head was filled with images of the sick and the cramped conditions down below. *I must do something about the food* became an endlessly repeated chant in my head to the rhythm of the pounding engine.

The early morning light woke me and I rose from my bed. I had slept in my clothes, expecting to go into the other cabin during the night. The door made a soft swish as I opened it and stepped in. All was quiet … too quiet. It was a stillness I had felt before. A great fear suddenly clenched my stomach. "Please God, no," I whispered to myself and I looked first at Rose. Relief flooded through me when I saw she was breathing, slowly, regularly, still wrapped in sleep. I turned to John, knowing what I would find. His body was still. I felt his neck for a pulse and, as I expected, there was none. His skin had the unmistakable pallor of death.

Gently, I shook Rose until she stirred. I sat on the edge of the bed and waited until she was properly awake. "How's John?" she asked immediately.

"He's well now, Rose, he's at peace."

It took her a few seconds to realise what I meant. She sat up and looked across to the other bed. Her face crumpled and a tear ran down her cheek. She stood beside the bedside and looked down at John, kissing her fingers and laying them on his forehead.

"You and Annie were a great comfort to him in his last days, Rose. God will bless you for that. He makes provision for all of us."

She looked at me. "What do you mean?"

"God brought you and Annie to this ship to be with John in his last days and give him the love that his family could not. Never doubt His wisdom and His care."

There have been many times when I have regretted saying that. My words were hollow, born out of the things I had always been told about God, about Him controlling everything. I could see doubt on Rose's face as I said those words; she had perhaps a deeper understanding at that time than I.

The captain said we could not keep John's body on board until the ship docked in Buenos Aires as, in the heat, it would start to fester, creating the risk of disease. For the first time in my life, therefore, I prepared to carry out a burial at sea later that day. The passengers and many of the crew stood in silence on the main deck as I said prayers over John's body. Even Hogan, his wife and Butler from the second-class section as well as the two agents, O'Grady and Duggan, stood on the upper deck, looking down.

The day was calm, the slightest breeze on our faces. "We may well ask why sickness has visited us, why John was taken from us. But the ways of God are unfathomable and we can never know the answer. But one thing that this event does reveal is the love that can be shown to a stranger and surely that is part of God's purpose. As Jesus said, when someone does this for another, they do it for me."

John's body had been laid on a board and wrapped with a sheet. Only a few of us knew that it had been weighted with some pieces of ironware. The purser had said that crew members would lift it and slide it into the water but Rose had organised some young men from steerage to fulfil that function. Only four of them lifted the board for John was not a big man. They carried it to the ship's side, resting the outer end on the rail.

I said the final prayer in English so everyone would understand. "In sure and certain hope of the resurrection to eternal life through our Lord Jesus Christ, we commend to Almighty God our brother, John Connolly, and we commit his body to the waters, earth to earth, ashes to ashes, dust to dust."

I nodded my head and the two men closest to me – James and Will – lifted their end of the board. For a terrible moment, I thought John's body would not move but, as they lifted the board higher, it slipped over the rail and the empty board was lowered. A sudden shrill blast from the ship's whistle startled us and we looked up to the great funnel towering above us, trailing wisps of smoke, a spirit departing.

I did not know then that John would not be the only one we had to cast into the waters. Later, I berated O'Grady and Duggan for the hopeless lack of provision on the ship. They did not even express concern. "We just have to hang on until we reach Buenos Aires," Duggan said. "There'll be ample food and accommodation for everyone and they can recuperate until they are ready to move on."

Lies, lies, lies.

**Rose**

The voyage was about halfway through, ten days past and ten to come, when John died. There had been no dancing for several evenings and, that night, we stood quietly in the food room, listening to the sad old songs we knew so well. I wondered how many more of us would follow old John into the watery depths before we reached Argentina.

As the familiar strains caressed us, my thoughts were full of my home, the familiar streets of Cork city, my mother and father sitting by the fire at the day's end and the realisation that I may not be able to tend them in their last days as I had cared for John. The enormity of my decision to leave Ireland hit me. I felt again my father's breath on my cheek on the morning I left and my mother's fixed smile, desperately trying to hide the loss she felt. Perhaps I would never see my parents again.

I cried softly. James had his arm around me and, were it not for that, I would have been desolate.

"I hope … I hope nothing happens to you."

He looked at me with puzzlement. "What do you mean?"

"Well, you know, if you … went the same way as John."

"And why would I do that?"

"We're always fearful for those … for those we … we cherish." He pulled me closer and I nestled my head against him.

Annie stepped forward. She spoke quietly with the musicians who nodded and then she sang *The Parting Glass*. Her voice surprised me, clear, strong, soaring when it needed to be. We joined her in the final line of each verse, singing quietly so as not to detract from the sound of her solo voice. It was a song of leaving this life and filled us with sadness. I knew many were also angry. John's was an unnecessary death. He had been weakened by hunger and thirst because O'Grady and Duggan had not furnished the ship with sufficient food and water for the voyage.

Our rations had reduced. They said it was because some food had been ruined in the hold but we suspected that was another lie. There was never enough of it. When we were nursing John in the cabin next to his, Father Gilligan brought in some much better food for John. He said he'd 'acquired' it from the second-class kitchen but I think it was his own lunch and dinner he brought. There's many a priest would have left us to our fate, stewing down there in the hold.

At least now the days were warm enough to be up on deck but, with so little shade, it was difficult to stay out of the sun which blazed down and made all the metal on the ship ferociously hot so you'd burn any part of your body that touched it. The sun shot up from the sea in the morning, climbing quickly until it was directly above our heads at mid-day and then plunging rapidly into the ocean in the West. Twelve hours of darkness and twelve hours of searing heat. The word went round that we were about to cross the equator.

Annie and I still visited the passengers in the hospital and brought what comfort we could. The place was always full, new faces replacing those well enough to leave. In truth, had there been more room, there would have been more people in there. As it was, they had to stay in their bunks, sweltering during the day and often shivering at night.

We would meet Father Gilligan there. He looked more and more worried as time went on. When a child died, he looked angry. I wanted to ask him why God had let that happen but I waited until his anger had subsided. He looked at me before answering. "I don't know, Rose. I don't know."

I thought that he seemed less sure about God than he had even a few days before. I felt a little stab of fear; if a priest was unsure about God, how could the likes of me be sure? "Will it not be part of God's plan, Father?" That's what we had always been told.

"God asks us all to love our neighbours and that is how he cares for us. But some people …" he appeared to fight within himself for a moment, "… some people do not have that capacity, it seems. This death did not have to happen."

It was a pitiful sight, the small body wrapped in a sheet lying on the board before being slid into the sea. The parents and siblings were distraught. How can anyone deal with the loss of a child, especially when it could so easily have been prevented? How can anyone leave a child out here in the endless ocean, nothing but sea all around us for mile after mile? Where would one go to grieve, to leave a posy of flowers for remembrance? So lonesome, this vast emptiness.

As we left the equator behind us, we looked forward to some relief from the heat but for several days, there was no noticeable difference. The rations continued to decline and most of us had parched throats and cracked lips because there was so little water to drink. The atmosphere on the ship was increasingly tense, people worrying who the next casualty would be, who would next be slid over the rail. We all retreated into ourselves, unable to do anything but sit and wait for the journey to end.

Then one night, it exploded. We were eating in the food area and the young men had started to file in after us single women. Annie and I always came in at the end of the families so we could sit with James and Will. A fella called Arthur, who always scowled from a lowered head, was at the serving table and the usual gruel was slopped into his mess tin with one potato.

"What d'you call this? How's a man supposed to live on this? It wouldn't keep a child alive!" He slammed the mess tin on the table and glared at the crewman serving the food. "Give me a decent amount or

I'll go up to the captain and tell him what you're doing to us."

"I have my orders," the crewman said, spreading his hands wide. "One potato for each person is all." He turned to the next man and prepared to slop the disgusting liquid into his mess tin.

"Take your fecking filth and ate it yerself!" Arthur shouted and he leaned over the table, thrusting his hand behind the crewman's head and pulling him forward. For a moment I thought he would push his head into the cauldron and I jumped up, sending my chair tipping backwards.

James leapt behind Arthur's back, holding his arms, and shouted, "Stop! Stop!" Will darted behind the table and tried to pull the crewman away from Arthur's grasp. There was much shouting and swearing and finally they dragged Arthur away.

"This is not the way!" shouted James to Arthur.

"Not the way, not the way? What way is there? We've been complaining long enough and things are still no better!"

The crewman recovered some composure and from the relative safety behind the table waved his ladle at Arthur. "I get you arrested! I get you arrested!" He thrust the ladle at the other crewman who looked petrified and then stormed off, shouting in German.

"Come on now," Will said quietly. "You must eat whatever there is. Shouting won't bring more."

Eventually, Arthur calmed enough to sit at a table and eat but he was still seething. We expected crewmen to come mob-handed to arrest Arthur but it was Father Gilligan who came. A replacement crewman crept behind him and stood nervously behind the table helping to serve. The other crewman pointed at Arthur, and Father Gilligan came to our table. "May I sit with you?"

"Of course, Father." James pulled out a chair for him and the priest sat down.

"I thought I'd find a riot down here from what your man said," he smiled.

"Every day they serve us this muck. That's bad enough, but there's nowhere near enough to keep us fed. Look at us. We're wasting away!" James leant back and pulled the waistband of his trousers out.

"Sure, the cows at home are fed better!" Arthur was still smouldering.

Father Gilligan's knuckles were white where he gripped the table. He looked at the mess tins being carried by other young men past our table. "It's getting worse, then?"

"It is Father. And water … there's never enough. More are going to die unless they give us more water."

Father Gilligan nodded. "It's a disgrace." He thought for a moment. "The crew are not at fault here, though. They can only give you what the purser has provided and, as far as I can see, the purser can only distribute the provisions that were laid in by the two agents. Those two are responsible for this. They simply miscalculated or … maybe there was another reason." He left us, moving amongst the other tables listening carefully to the tired voices of the men.

Next day, James and I were sitting in a square of shade on the deck. He was, as usual, talking about the great plans he had for the future in Argentina. "This journey will end soon and then we can start to live again and I'll be able to create the farm of my dreams."

"I'll probably have to stay in Buenos Aires … there'll be no work in the country for me."

"Sure, that'll be fine … if you can live without me for a year or two. And when I've got things sorted and a nice house ready, I'll come and whisk you away with me."

I laughed. "You're making assumptions, aren't you, James O'Neill? What makes you think I want to spend me life with you? I may meet a wealthy fella in the city who has a fine house and servants and a carriage to take me to church on Sunday."

"Oh, of course you might … but will he be handsome and charming like me?"

"You're rather full of yourself, James O'Neill." I hit him playfully on the shoulder and we kissed. It was wonderful to think of this hell ending soon. Another week or so and we'd be off the ship … if we lived to see it. We became aware of raised voices on the upper deck. Looking up, we could see the captain, the purser, the two agents and Father Gilligan standing at the rail.

"It's not good enough," Father Gilligan shouted, shocking us, his voice usually so gentle and calm. "These people are starving and the need for more water is urgent. What happened last night in the food area was just a spark. But let me tell you, it won't take much for there to be an explosion. They are angry and they have very good cause to be."

"Now, Father, don't exaggerate," Duggan replied, holding his hands palm outwards in front of him. "There will be enough food and water and 'twill not be long before we're at Buenos Aires and then there'll be food and accommodation for everyone." He looked totally unconcerned.

Father Gilligan took a step forward, his hands clenched into fists at his side. "More promises! How can I be sure that there will be food and accommodation? How can I believe a word you say?"

O'Grady shuffled his feet. "What Mr Duggan is saying is right enough. Things will be fine in Buenos Aires." Despite his words, he seemed less sure than Duggan, his eyes flicking from face to face.

"But they're not fine now and that's what I'm concerned about! You *must* increase the rations!" The exasperation, the rising anger was clear in Father Gilligan's voice.

Duggan hesitated. "We need to be careful, Father. 'Tis no good giving out more now and finding we run out altogether before we get there."

"What you're saying, then, is there's not enough to last the voyage. In that case, we need to go into port, Salvador perhaps, to stock up."

O'Grady and Duggan were trying to come up with reasons not to do so. "They don't seem to want to spend any more money, do they?" James said to me.

"That's the way of it, I'm sure."

It was the captain who spoke next, his strong German accent coming to us clearly as we sat on the deck below. He was an imposing man, neither large nor tall, but he exuded authority, competence. His voice was calm, measured. "Look at the sky ahead of us. What do you see?"

Everyone on the upper deck, as well as James and I on the lower, looked where the captain pointed. The sky was hazy, very high cloud starting to veil the sun though it still shone through.

"That," continued the captain, "is the start of a storm being brought from the south-east on the trade winds. It will hit us as we pass the coast of Brazil. It is not possible I think for us to get into Salvador port. We would have to ride out the storm at sea, waiting perhaps for one or two days for the sea to settle to allow us to go in to the harbour."

There was silence on the upper deck for what seemed like several minutes, though of course it was not that long. Finally, Father Gilligan spoke. "So we go into Rio de Janeiro, further south. The storm will have passed by then."

The captain shrugged. "Maybe it will, maybe not. We have to wait and see. But at Rio we are only a day or two from Buenos Aires. Perhaps by then it will not be worth delaying."

There was a long pause. Father Gilligan looked at O'Grady and

Duggan. When he spoke, his voice sounded tired, almost defeated. "If any other passengers die, it will be on your heads. 'Twill be on your consciences for the rest of your lives ... if you have a conscience, that is." He turned away from them and headed for the steps that led down to our deck.

"I thought God's forgiveness was infinite," Duggan said, grinning.

Father Gilligan turned at the top of the steps, slowly, controlling himself. "Oh 'tis ... but to be forgiven, you have to repent, genuinely repent, and then you have to make good the damage you have done, if you can." He came down the steps slowly, deep in thought, his face creased with worry. I wanted to go to him then and comfort him but what comfort could I bring? He was a man who sought a solution and I had only words, only an ache in my heart for him. What could a mere girl do to ease the pain of a priest?

But as he was about to pass us, I stood up. He stopped and looked at me. "Father, we heard the conversation ... you tried, Father, you tried. We are all grateful for that."

"Thank you Rose ... but is it enough to try? Surely we must succeed and I ..."

I saw then that he demanded of himself more than anyone, more than God, could reasonably ask.

# CHAPTER 4

## BOLEO

**Patrick**

Needless to say, we did not go into Rio de Janeiro. The captain said the sea was still too rough after the storm to enter the port. Waves still rocked us but I'm sure he could have put in had he wanted to – or had O'Grady and Duggan requested it. As it was, the passengers in steerage endured more hardship and sickness as the ship bucked and rolled in the huge waves; we slid one more over the side, another soul lost to those grey waters.

We watched the coastline crawl past. At last, the ship turned to starboard towards the land and we entered a huge bay. As we approached, the skyline of Buenos Aires became clearer. I could see church spires and towers thrusting out of the mass of buildings. People crowded the decks but this time there was no mood of celebration, just a desperate desire to get off the ship that had brought so much misery. They stood in silence, watching the place slowly growing in size and definition. The plunging and rolling of the ship ceased and she was steady as she cut through the waters of the bay.

I saw O'Grady and Duggan on the first-class deck and paced towards them. "Gentlemen, we've arrived."

"You see, Father, I told you we'd get here alright." Duggan looked smug.

"Oh, we're here right enough … most of us, that is … though I don't think you can say anyone is alright, apart from yourselves and the other first- and second-class passengers."

"Well, Father, the provision for steerage passengers is standard for all ships of this type." O'Grady's jaw jutted forwards in an attempt at defiance.

"It may be standard but it is completely unacceptable to cram over seventeen hundred souls into that space and deprive them of sufficient food and water to keep them alive."

"Well, 'tis done now, Father, and they can start to enjoy a better life than they had back in Ireland."

"What are the arrangements for providing food and accommodation? You'll no doubt have people to guide them to where they are staying?"

"We'll sort all that out when we arrive."

"It may have escaped your attention, Mr Duggan, but we are arriving very soon. I hope you're ready."

"You can leave it to us, Father. No need to worry about it."

I had not noticed it before, but did then. Another ship was following us into harbour though she was some way behind. With all the usual shouts and clanking of gear, casting of mooring lines and so on, we were eventually berthed. The other ship was berthed soon after just a little way along the quay. I had my case all packed and I stood by the gangplank to wish people well as they left. The relief on their faces told its own story.

Rose and Annie were leaving together with the two young men, James and William. They all shook my hand which surprised me. "Thank you, Father," Rose said quietly as she did so.

"God bless you," I replied. "God bless all of you." They managed to summon smiles despite their weariness. It amazed me then and has done ever since how resilient is the human spirit.

"And you, Father," Annie chirped, that slightly cocky smile in her eyes.

"Where are you all heading?"

"Oh, Rose and I will be looking for a job in a grand house where we'll be paid a huge barrel of money for doing nuthin'."

"And we'll be looking to take up the offer of the house and land, wherever that might be."

"Right enough, James," William slapped him on the back, "but we'll get a good fill of food before we go and a comfy bed to sleep on that doesn't toss you about all night."

"Sure, I'm longing to put me feet on solid ground that doesn't try to throw you into the sea every second." Annie looked down at the bustling quay, the hunger to get started on her new life obvious.

And then they were off down the gangplank. I watched briefly as Rose and James embraced, lingeringly, longing in every move of Rose's body as she left him. Annie led the way through the crowd on the quay, Rose hanging on to her with one hand, the other clutching her bag. I felt a strange loneliness, an emptiness, a yearning, as if colour had drained from the sky.

Then they were lost to me.

I stayed on deck bidding everyone farewell. I could see the quay clearly from the height of the deck. The other ship was also disgorging passengers and the quay was becoming crammed with people. When I myself walked down the gangplank to join them, I had to weave between them and carts and dockers and crates of cargo that had been hoisted down by the cranes. It was pandemonium.

Monsignor O'Rourke had told me there would be a bed for me at the Catholic Presbytery where Canon Peter Flynn lived. Like the others, I was longing for a static floor and, frankly, to be free of the noise and bustle of the harbour. On board, I had felt as though I had been in a noisy factory, the endless thumping of the engine pounding through the hull and the constant babble of voices, press of bodies, smells …

Yes, it would be good to have a day or two out of that before starting my ministry. But it was not to be. The crowds were not diminishing. There was no sign of O'Grady and Duggan, no sign of any organisation, no officials marshalling people to their accommodation. Men, women and children milled around, asking each other where they should go. I asked Arthur if they had been told anything.

"Nuthin' at all!"

Anger was seething inside me. I went back to the gangplank and told the sailors there that I needed to speak to someone on board. They were reluctant to let me back on the ship but I think being a member of the clergy was my passport. Leaving my suitcase and coat with the crewmen near the boarding ramp, I strode up it, along the deck and up the steps onto the upper deck. I barged straight through the door into the first-class section and stunned a steward who was cleaning the dining room. The opulence of the saloon – more extravagant than the second-class dining room – was not lost on me.

"I'm looking for Mr O'Grady and Mr Duggan."

"I go look for them," he said and walked through a door on the opposite side. He was back very quickly. "They not here, sir. Already left ship."

I had my doubts but I marched back to the quay. They were nowhere to be seen there, either. I jostled along the crowded quay towards the other ship, lugging my suitcase which seemed heavier than ever. It was early afternoon and the day was hot. I carried my heavy coat over my free arm and longed to be able to put both suitcase and coat down. Irish accents gave way to Italian and occasionally Spanish from locals working at the docks; all were milling around directionless. A carriage pushed through the crowd and, when it had gone past, I thought I saw Rose and Annie riding in it – a flash of auburn hair – but then thought I must be seeing things.

Two policemen lolled against the wall, apparently completely unconcerned by the throng on the quayside. I supposed they were used to such scenes. "Excuse me. Where should the travellers go for food and accommodation?"

One looked away along the quay; the other looked me up and down slowly. I could see him register my clerical collar and he stood up from the wall – some mark of respect, I suppose. But that was the only concession to my calling. He clearly did not speak English and I had no word of Spanish. He shrugged and babbled something but I could not make anything of it. I thanked him and walked back the way I had come towards our own ship.

Some sort of official was in heated conversation with a group of passengers I recognised from the *Dresden*. He was speaking in broken English. "I know nothing about food, I know nothing about house. You must go to Hotel de Inmigrantes. Is this way." He thrust his arm out along the quay towards the city centre. "Not far … you can walk."

I established after several misunderstandings the directions to reach this place and I suggested to the group and everyone around that we head there. The word seemed to spread like fire amongst the passengers and, when I looked back, there were hundreds of people following. I hoped we had been given the right directions; if not, frustration would boil over. The Hotel de Inmigrantes was where we had been told but the people there seemed completely unprepared for new arrivals. I had thought as we walked that it would need to be a huge place. It wasn't.

The manager was called. He looked out over the sea of people and threw up his hands in disbelief. "No room, no room for all these people. Only room for a few."

"Where should the others go?"

"I not know. Not my problem. You ask at Immigration Office."

"Wait here," I said to the people closest to me, "and spread that word to everyone while I go to the Immigration Office."

It was not far but I feared it may be closing for the weekend. The foyer was quiet after the bustle of the streets. A young man in a smart uniform sat at a desk; he said he spoke English. As I explained the situation to him, he looked increasingly worried, then embarrassed and finally angry. He asked me to wait and disappeared through a door. He returned in a few minutes with another, older man, short and podgy. He's seen it all before, I thought, looking at the resigned expression on his face.

"Where are all these people now, Father?"

"I left them waiting at Hotel de Inmigrantes."

"That is the right place."

"But the manager said they can't possibly take all the people. There were over seventeen hundred souls on our ship and there is an Italian ship docked too."

The official shook his head and sighed. He looked at the clock on the wall. "I come with you. Wait one moment."

He disappeared again and returned with a hat. He said nothing as we retraced my steps to the Hotel de Inmigrantes. He came to a sudden halt when we turned the corner and saw the massive crowd in front of the building. The people parted to let us through and we went inside where it was cooler. The manager was again summoned, and the immigration official and he began a conversation in Spanish that quickly became louder and more heated. At the end of it, the manager stomped off, gesticulating and shouting.

"Ok," said my official. "For tonight, things will be difficult but we will squeeze as many as possible into the hotel. Some to sleep in courtyard. They will try to arrange food. Tomorrow, we need to find other places. You came on boat today?"

"Yes, on the *City of Dresden*."

"And where you go for tonight?"

"I am to stay at the Catholic Presbytery with Canon Flynn."

"We are not ready for so many people. You must ask Canon Flynn to help find places for them to stay. Perhaps at the Covent of St Joseph, perhaps in houses around the city."

"We were told that food and accommodation would be ready for everyone."

He shrugged. "We are not ready," he repeated. "Go now to Canon Flynn and see what can be done."

That put me in a quandary. I thanked him but what should I do? I did not want to leave these people to a miserable night. They had had enough of that on the ship. I spoke with some of those waiting and explained what would happen. I told them I was going to the canon to see if I could get help but it probably would not be possible to arrange anything until the next day. I think it was only utter exhaustion and starvation that prevented a riot. They were too drained physically and emotionally to create a fuss. And thus it is that the poorest can be exploited.

The presbytery was not far from the docks and I was soon ringing the bell of a substantial house next to St Joseph's Church. A Spanish maid opened the door and showed me in to a sitting room – comfortable but not extravagant, with armchairs that were well used. Here I waited, pacing, for Canon Peter to come. He came into the room softly while I was striding towards the window. When I turned, he was there, smiling, his hand out to take mine.

"Father Gilligan, I presume." The smile did not leave his face as he spoke and his handshake was firm, warm. He was a little shorter than me and was filling out in the manner of most middle-aged men. He had the appearance of softness in everything, his skin, his body, his manner. "I'm Canon Peter … Peter Flynn."

"Hello, Father. I'm pleased to meet you."

"You look tired, Father. Was it a bad passage?"

"It was … but not especially rough. I'm afraid the arrangements …" I could say no more for a moment. I sank onto a chair.

"Father, I think you are unwell."

"I am … sick at heart. Those poor people …" I turned to him in silent appeal for I could not speak.

## Rose

Excited, terrified – I veered from one to the other. I was glad to be with Annie. She seemed to take it all in her stride. There were hordes of us from the *Dresden* mingling on the quay, calling to each other, parents shouting at children, trying to keep them close, the sounds mingling with the calls of dockers and locals shouting in Spanish and lots of people babbling away in another language which someone said was Italian.

I held tight to my bag with one hand, my coat slung over that arm, while I held onto Annie with the other hand. "It feels as though the ground is moving. I thought we would be alright once we got off the ship."

A man clutching a suitcase in one hand and a child in the other laughed drily. "That's because you gained your sea legs on the ship and now you need to get your land legs back again."

"Oh, I see. Thanks." I turned to Annie. "If we get parted, meet by the ship's gangplank." I shouted to her even though I was right next to her.

"Hold on tight and we'll not be parted. You and me will stick together always," she laughed. She was in her element, I think, looking around, her bright eyes taking it all in.

"We need to find somewhere to stay." I did not want to be sleeping under the stars in a strange city and there seemed to be no one organising things or telling us where to go.

"Just wait a bit. There's no rush." She clambered onto a crate that was lying nearby and looked around her. Then she leapt down and grabbed me. "Come on … over here."

I had no idea where she was going but I made sure I stayed with her. A little further along the quay was a carriage with two horses eating hay from bags tied round their necks. There was a couple of fellas telling people they were not for hire. Sitting up in the carriage were two young women, both attractive, in well-cut linen dresses, whom I did not recognise – not from our ship.

Annie led me to the taller of the men who smiled broadly, his white teeth flashing beneath a jet-black moustache. His English was not bad but spoken with a strong Spanish accent. "Ladies, how you do today? You look for work?"

"We need somewhere to stay first of all." I could not keep the pleading tone from my voice, hoping he would know somewhere we could go. He wore a smart suit and his face was handsome, tanned, with playful eyes – a practised charmer – which made the fluttering of nerves in my stomach worse.

Annie went straight to the point. "We're looking for work right enough. Do you know of anything?"

"What kind of work you look for? Perhaps you like to work in big house … bed and food provided, of course."

"That would be ideal," said Annie while I nodded. Relief flooded through me that everything might be sorted out straightaway.

"Alright. You like ride in the carriage and I take you to some big houses where you might get job."

The other fella took our bags and hoisted them onto the rack at the back of the carriage while the first one handed us up. I felt like a lady sitting up there above everyone, looking around. People were looking at us with envy and wonder. We said hello to the young women already seated who smiled and replied in Italian.

"God, I feel like a rich lady," I whispered to Annie. "I've never been in a carriage before … an omnibus is the best I've been in.

"It's great, isn't it? If only the folks back home could see us now."

The carriage jolted as the horses took the strain and it clattered over the cobbles of the dockside, parting people who drew back to look at the fine ladies riding in style. Annie waved occasionally, nodding to the people as if she were a rich lady out for a drive in her carriage. It made me laugh, partly from relief, I suppose.

Once clear of the dock, the horses trotted and I was in awe of the great buildings we passed, much grander many of them than those in Cork city. The carriage turned into a huge square surrounded by several imposing buildings. The Charmer brought the carriage to a stop and, turning, he pointed to a beautiful pink building. "This the customs house," he said proudly. "Was designed by a man who was part English, part Argentine. Is beautiful, no? And this square we call the Plaza de Mayo."

I marvelled at the colour and the grand design. The two Italian girls seemed to get excited when looking at the building. I think it may have reminded them of home. The trip seemed quite long and I wondered if we were going out of the city. I felt a sudden twinge of fear again but dismissed it. Annie was completely unconcerned, enjoying everything.

"I think we're going back the way we came," she said suddenly. "Look at the sun. 'Twas on our right when we started for quite a way, then behind us, then on our left and now in front of us. I hope he's not just going to dump us back at the dock."

I hadn't noticed but she was quite right. Before I became alarmed, though, the carriage pulled into a wide street that I guessed was not far from the docks. The horses slowed to a walking pace; the Charmer turned again and with an expansive wave of his arm said, "What you think of our city?"

"Very nice," replied Annie. "Aren't we nearly back at the docks?"

"Not far but I wanted to show you city. Is lovely in the summer sun, no?"

Then the carriage stopped at a big house, set back from the road just a little, with some flowering bushes growing in front. There were steps in the centre, leading to a porch with pillars and a large door. The Charmer jumped down from his seat at the front of the carriage and ran lightly up the four steps. He rang the bell and then returned to the carriage where he handed the four of us down in turn. The big door opened and a young woman – Molly, as I would soon discover – asked us to come in. She spoke in an Irish accent and her eyes, which bulged slightly, were a hard, icy blue. Her dress was a good quality linen and well made from what I could see at a glance. This must be a fine house for a servant to be dressed so well.

Molly led us into the hall and then left us in a sitting room. The Charmer had come in with us, the other fella staying out with the horses. I looked around the room and wondered why we had been brought somewhere that was clearly not for the use of servants. The armchairs and settees were covered in a plush red velvet, and rich red curtains with gold fringing dressed the large bay window. There were some fine-looking small tables against the wall, a glass-fronted cabinet with drinking glasses and some ornaments. I looked at Annie and she smirked.

After a minute or two, Molly brought a tray of glasses and a jug of water which we drank gratefully. A minute or two later, a large, older woman entered the room. I stood up and pulled Annie's sleeve for her to join me.

"Ah sure, there's no need for that. Sit you down." The lady's voice was deep and hoarse, almost like a man's, and her Irish accent was strong. "I'm Mrs O'Shaughnessy and this is my house. Now, I'm looking for a girl to help with things here. Maybe I might take two but probably only one." She dominated the room, standing as she did almost in the centre with her hands on her hips. She was tall and full of figure, her ample bosom straining at her bodice which was trimmed with lace.

She looked at the four of us, smiling at her and hoping we would be the one chosen. At the mention of the possibility of two of us being employed, my heart lifted. Wouldn't it be great if she took both Annie and me? She started talking to the Italian girls but that didn't last long. She could not speak Italian and they could not speak English. They kept saying the same thing, sounding more desperate as they failed to make themselves understood. I don't know what they were saying and nor did Mrs O'Shaughnessy. In the end she said, "I don't think you'll fit in here, girls, though you look well enough."

Why had she commented on their appearance, I wondered? I supposed it was because she wanted to know that anyone she might employ would take care of how she looked and not show her up when visitors came. She then asked Annie where she came from and which part of Dublin was it and what did she do before coming over and was she able to cook and so on. The questions came more rapidly as this went on, as if being fired from a gun, but Annie was not thrown by it. She looked back at Mrs O'Shaughnessy, not defiantly but as if challenging her to ask whatever she wanted.

And then it was my turn. I could not look the lady in the eye as Annie had done but I think I answered well enough. When I said I was a dressmaker, she looked very interested and seemed pleased that I had done plenty of housework whilst employed as a seamstress. I was a little alarmed when she stepped forward and put her hand on my hair but she was complimentary, saying, "That's a fine head of hair you have – the gentlemen will love that."

I felt that her keen gaze during questioning would allow her to detect any lies. She was someone who knew what she wanted and would soon tell you if your work was not good enough. "Right. I think it will be just the one today. Rose, would you like to work here? The pay is good and, as you see, 'tis a nice house."

I looked at Annie. She must have seen the disappointment, perhaps fear in my eyes. She smiled. "Take it, Rose, you may not get another offer as good."

"But … but what about you?"

"God, sure I'll be fine." She turned to the Charmer. "Are you taking us to other places?"

"Yes, yes … lots of places. There be work for all attractive young women." He smiled broadly and I noticed how he caught Mrs O'Shaughnessy's eye.

"As Miguel says, there's plenty of work here for … young women."

"There now," Annie said to me. She stood up as did I and hugged me.

"We'll see each other sometimes, I hope …" I looked at Mrs O'Shaughnessy.

"You'll have time off right enough to see your friend."

I felt better then. "I'd love to work here, Mrs O'Shaughnessy," I said, giving a small curtsy, before turning to Annie. "Thanks Annie … for everything. I'm so glad we met. Look after yourself."

"I will, don't you worry. And you must, too."

And then she and the two Italian girls were being shown out to the carriage. Miguel called to his mate to bring my bag and coat and I waited in the hall for them to be brought in. Molly was hovering in the hall, too, and Mrs O'Shaughnessy stood on the doorstep. Miguel had handed the other girls into the carriage and returned to the porch. Mrs O'Shaughnessy handed him money. I could not see how much but it looked like several notes. It seemed a lot to pay for a carriage ride but, at that time, I had no idea what the money was worth. She shook his hand very warmly and he took his leave.

I went to the door and stood on the porch, waving to Annie until the carriage had rumbled some way down the street. Relief at being employed so soon mingled with a sense of loss. I had felt protected, safe, when with Annie and wished she could be with me still.

Mrs O'Shaughnessy called me in and closed the door. "Well now, you must be tired. You certainly look it. Molly, take Rose up to the room now and let her rest."

"Thank you, madam. I'm afraid it was hard to sleep on the boat."

"Oh, I remember right enough, though for me it was a long time ago."

Molly stood at the foot of the big staircase. She did not smile and I felt some hostility in her manner, her direct, appraising stare. She said nothing, though, and I followed her up the stairs to the first floor and then up the second flight which was much smaller. I noticed how the decoration was much poorer as we ascended and realised we were going into the servants' quarters. By the time we reached the attic room, I was puffing. The poor food, the fitful sleep and the lack of exercise on the boat had put me out of condition.

Molly opened the door of a room and pointed to a bed. "That's yours," she said and then she pointed to a wardrobe and a small chest of drawers, "and those are for your things."

"Thank you, Molly. And whose is the other bed?"

"That's mine. I hope you don't snore."

I was a little thrown by the directness of the statement. "No ... no

I don't think I do."

"I'll soon let you know if you do. Now you want to rest."

"Yes, but … d'you think there would be a chance of something to eat? I'm afraid the food on the ship was terrible and we had nothing since breakfast." It was the middle of the afternoon and I was hungry. I suppose being on dry land had restored some appetite.

"Come with me, then." Still unsmiling, she led the way back to the ground floor and into the rear part of the house where the kitchen and scullery were situated. "There's some bread and cold meat in the pantry there."

The pantry seemed to be well stocked with food. I took the plate Molly handed me and served myself with bread and meat. Molly poured me some water from a big jug and told me to sit at the large kitchen table. The food was delicious compared to the appalling stuff we had been eating for the last three weeks. I was still swimming a little as if the ground was swaying but was better sitting down. Molly leaned against the dresser, watching me. I felt uncomfortable under her gaze.

Mrs O'Shaughnessy came into the kitchen and I started guiltily. Here I was, eating already, and I'd done no work.

"Hungry is it?"

"Yes, Mrs O'Shaughnessy. I'm sorry but …"

She held up her hand. "That's alright. I suppose they gave you nothing on that ship but some filthy gruel and the odd potato?"

"That's about it … and bread at breakfast."

"You look a little on the skinny side, I'd say. Stand up and let me look at you."

I did so and she stood beside me. She pinched my cheek, not hard, but to test how much flesh was there. Then her hands were on my waist, feeling my body and I froze a little. I almost jumped when she put one hand on my breast and squeezed gently. No one had touched me there before – well, apart from the fella on the boat that night.

"You need feeding up I'd say. A bit more flesh on your bones would do a power of good."

Looking down at myself, I realised that my dress hung on me limply. I had not noticed how much weight I'd lost during the voyage though I should not have been surprised given the conditions and the lack of food. I sat down to finish eating. When Mrs O'Shaughnessy left the room, Molly followed her. She did not close the door fully and I could hear their voices outside. They talked in whispers so I did not catch everything but I knew they were talking about me.

Molly said something first that I did not hear. Mrs O'Shaughnessy's deep voice was more audible. "She'll be popular with that lovely hair and pretty face. And besides, there'll be good money paid for someone young and fresh."

"Did you see how she jumped when you touched her breast?" hissed Molly. "How's she going to be …" I think Mrs O'Shaughnessy had silenced her but then I heard her voice again. "That dark-haired one would have been ideal."

"Ah yes, she would have plenty of experience I'd say but you know many a man likes a girl to be less forward. Anyway, do I detect some jealousy? Afraid you'll be knocked off your perch, is it?"

Molly was suddenly back in the kitchen. "Have you finished yet or what?"

"I have, thank you. I'll just wash up."

"Good. You can find your way back to our room if you want to rest."

"I can, thank you. Thank you for looking after me. I suppose you came on a ship like me? How long have you been here?"

"Too long. Go up now while I prepare the dinner."

I was glad to get out of there; Molly's hostility was like gunpowder and I was afraid lest I would set it off by saying something that offended her.

# CHAPTER 5

## PASADA

**Patrick**

Concern darkened Canon Peter's face. Emilia, the housekeeper, brought tea and cake. Once I had started my tale, the words tumbled from me, spat with anger. He did not try to stop me nor remonstrate but nodded slowly at various moments.

"Previous immigrants have been well served. The government here in Argentina is encouraging immigrants to come. They have set aside one million dollars a year to support them – to set up new farms in areas that are not yet developed but of course … there's corruption. Much of that money will have lined the pockets of officials all the way from the top to the bottom."

I stood up, anxious to do something. "We need to find accommodation, food and water for those poor people."

"You must rest now, Father Patrick. You cannot do anything for them in your present state. You are exhausted. You will eat something later and then you will sleep. Tomorrow, you and I will make sure relief is given to those poor souls. Now, I must pay some visits to start that process."

I slept, but fitfully, and woke early. I was thankful that those sleeping outside had not had a cold night, that we had arrived in summer, not quite the hottest part but still warm enough. At breakfast, Canon Peter told me what he had been able to achieve the previous day. He had not been idle. He had visited the Mother Superior at the Convent of St Joseph and she would make provision for the single young women. He had spoken with an influential parishioner who would activate the church's charities immediately to provide food and water. I was impressed. This gentle man had done more in a few hours than I would have done, venting my anger and no doubt making enemies.

We walked together through the streets to the Hotel de Inmigrantes. Along the way, we passed several people I recognised from the ship, sitting at the edge of the road, staring vacantly before them. They had slept on the street and were weak with hunger and thirst.

"Come," Canon Peter said gently, "come with us if you can. We'll take you where there is food and water and then sort out somewhere to stay until you get settled."

And so we walked at the head of a growing number of desperate people to the Hotel de Inmigrantes; the scenes were horrific. The courtyard was full of people, some of the children naked and everyone sprawled on the ground as though life was seeping from them. I found James and Will slumped against a wall.

"Hello, Father. So much for the promises of food and accommodation."

"No sign of O'Grady or Duggan I suppose?"

"None," said James, so weary there not even a trace of resentment in his voice.

"Did you say Duggan?" Canon Peter looked at me keenly.

"I did."

"I've recently taken over from Canon Duggan who is too sick to carry out his ministry here. I wonder if there is a connection? Canon Duggan did great things, starting the newspaper and so on but now he is to spend his last days in Ireland."

"If there is a connection, he will be ashamed of his relative, surely.

He and his fellow agent have told nothing but lies."

"The house and land and so on will be there though, won't they, Father?" Will looked anxious.

"I hope so," I said but I could not look him in the eye.

"House and land. Who told you that?" The doubt in Canon Peter's mind could be read clearly on his face.

"I have the leaflet here." James reached into his bag and produced a folded piece of paper. He handed it to Canon Peter who scanned it.

Slowly he lifted his eyes to me. "It says here that it is all to be funded by a bank set up by Canon O'Farrell. But he's been dead these twenty years. Perhaps the Immigration Department has this arranged."

We spent the day doing what we could, making sure that everyone was fed by the volunteers who brought food and water. The single women went to the convent and some places were found for others. Some went to stables to sleep. The words of Arthur came to mind, how the cows at home were better fed. That's what these poor people were … just cattle.

The next day was Sunday. I said the early mass and Canon Peter the later one. The church was full on both occasions and communion took a long while. It was a sorry sight, the trail of weakened people shuffling up the aisle for the bread and wine. We were able to give food for their souls but I wondered how long it would be before some of those departed the bodies that contained them. I prayed that some of our number at least had found a safe place: Rose and Annie came to my mind, weaving through the crowds on the quay, long hair flowing behind them; Annie was a survivor and Rose would be safe with her.

There were more deaths, of course. It was inevitable despite the actions of so many providing support. Canon Peter and I launched a massive charity drive to raise enough money to support the immigrants. I went alone to the offices of the Southern Cross newspaper and spoke with the editor, relating the whole sorry tale; I asked him to put a notice in the paper asking for donations.

"We'd be happy to do that, Father. Our founder, Canon Duggan, would have been very keen to do whatever he could."

"I understand he is returning to Ireland."

"He is." The editor coughed.

"Tell me. Is there a connection between Canon Duggan and the man who was one of the agents on the *SS City of Dresden*. His name is Michael John Duggan."

"There may be a connection." The editor shifted in his chair and shuffled some papers on his desk. "The canon has been told of the situation already by Canon Peter. He is dismayed by these events. I fear it may worsen his condition. He will certainly be anxious to get back to Ireland as soon as possible."

We talked some more and I left, asking him to do whatever he could. "These people are desperate and need the wherewithal to start new lives; they have nothing."

I spent several days visiting the companies and influential people that Canon Peter suggested and he, of course, visited others. The response from most was positive though some were reluctant. Hogan, the engineer I had met on the *Dresden*, listened to my reminder of the dismal way the migrants had been treated with a coldness that surprised and angered me. At last, he reached into his inner jacket pocket and pulled out his wallet. He took a note from it, fingered it carefully as if reluctant to part even with that, and placed it slowly on the desk in front of me. "I hope that helps and now, if you'll excuse me, I must get on." I suppose he thought it was a price worth paying to get rid of me.

He was, I'm pleased to say, the exception. Most looked increasingly concerned as I told my story. Perhaps I became better at telling it, focusing on the details that evoked most sympathy but I felt no guilt about that. Between myself and Canon Peter, we raised a good sum that would keep hunger at bay for a week or so. Each day, Canon Peter and I shared our successes as we ate our evening meal. I found it hard to swallow the food which was good, varied and tasty because I could not remove from my mind the way so many of my fellow countrymen and women were living.

One evening, Canon Peter suggested we should visit Canon Duggan before he left for Ireland. "I've told him about you and … I've told him about the situation."

Canon Duggan had been spending his last few weeks in Argentina in the visitors' wing of St Joseph's Convent, being cared for by the nuns. We were shown by a sister into his room. He was huddled in an armchair by the open window which looked out over a part of the city and the docks.

"Forgive me if I don't stand," he said, holding out his hand to us. I took it and felt the limpness in it, the pale skin blotched with brown marks stretched over the bones. "I sit here and look at the dock, thinking will I be strong enough to make the journey back to Ireland?"

"Ah you will, Edward, you will. Once you know you're going, you'll feel better."

"The ship is supposed to sail in a few days' time. I'm packed and ready to go … not that I have much." He turned his tired eyes to me. "So, Father Patrick, you've come to Argentina to do great things?"

"I don't know about that but I'll do my best."

He nodded. "That's all any of us can do. Sometimes 'tis not enough but we must keep trying." His words hit me. I had already discovered the truth of them on board. "Canon Peter tells me things are not good for those who came on the *Dresden*."

"That's an understatement, I'm afraid. Things are terrible. Everything was promised but nothing arranged."

He nodded. "So I heard." I sensed he wanted to say something else. "Did you meet the men who were the agents in Ireland?"

"I did, Father – Charles O'Grady and Michael Duggan." I watched his face carefully.

"You know, I suppose, that the latter is my younger brother."

"I was not sure but I had made the connection." Again, I watched his face. My eyes flicked up to Canon Peter who looked concerned.

"If only I had the time and energy to put right what he has done or rather failed to do. But I have neither. I can see you're wondering how he could have acted like that with his brother in such a position as mine. Money, I suppose. Oh, 'twill have started out honest enough but as they found it harder to recruit people, the promises will have become more extreme."

"Now, Edward, you must not distress yerself. No one can lay any of this at your door."

"I know, I know but all the same … one feels a responsibility. He will meet his maker one day and then he will be judged, as will we all. God only knows how we have fared. Did we always do the right thing, did we use the gifts we were given fully? I don't know about that but I hope for forgiveness if I did not."

He stared out of the window and I wondered how much his eyes actually saw. His focus was on that inner world that would determine his place in the next life. Surely a man who had given so much to others, who had devoted his life to the service of God would have a place in heaven? I know now, of course, motive is everything. A man may do a good deed but he may do so to make himself feel good, for his own pride and only God knows that. Or perhaps we do, too, if we have the honesty to admit it to ourselves.

Before that visit, I had wanted to vent my anger at O'Grady and Duggan. I had not been able to find them since landing in Buenos Aires and I wanted to confront them. I had thought that Duggan's brother would be the next best person to receive my condemnation. But how could I do that to this sick old man? He was not to blame. We are not our brother's keeper after all. We wished him well for the journey and for the days left to him in Ireland.

I had already turned to leave the room, when his frail voice stopped me. "Father Patrick. May God bless you in your work but remember this – he does not expect us to solve all problems. All he asks is that we try."

Over the next week or two, having obtained temporary but far from satisfactory accommodation and a good supply of food, I put pressure on the Immigration Department to find situations for everyone. Gradually, offers started to come, mainly from landowners who were keen to start new colonies. Many had acquired the rights to large tracts of land in the areas the Government was keen to develop and were now wanting tenant farmers to work it. Gradually, the numbers of migrants who had come on the *Dresden* reduced as some left for those new places. I prayed that they would not be faced with further disappointment.

An offer came through from a landowner at a place called La Viticola in the area Naposta, near Bahia Blanca, a city on the coast further south. It was to be a big colony and three hundred people said they would go. They would travel on the railway which had been finished only a few years before; there was only one service per month and it took twenty-four hours. Now, at last, the promises of a new and better life were to be realised. I told Canon Peter that I felt I should go with them. This was by far the largest group that had been formed for any one place and I felt it my duty to minister to them. He gave me his blessing.

"You must expect some hardship, Father Patrick. Write to me and let me know how things are going."

It was a ragged group of people who assembled at the railway station the following week but they had now at least been fed reasonably well and had slept. Hope was in their eyes, laughter on their lips, and energy in their step. I walked among them, trying to remember as many names as possible. There were many families with young children but several were single young men, hoping to start farms before taking a wife. I came across James and Will and stopped to talk with them. They both had great plans and were excited by what they had been told. "The land there is amongst the best farming land in the world, they say."

There seemed to be no doubt on Will's face, though there *was* in my mind, but I couldn't dampen that enthusiasm. I said a silent prayer that all would be as promised as I listened to their talk.

"Anyways, in two year's time, I'll have a better farm than you, Willie boy."

"No chance! I'll be driving in a pony and trap while you're still breaking sods in the field."

I could not avoid a nagging feeling of disappointment. "I think I saw Rose and Annie drive off in a carriage. Would I be right?"

"You would, Father. I've no idea where they went but I'll find her when I come back in me own carriage."

Will laughed and pushed him playfully on the shoulder. I thought of Rose then, the natural grace of her movement compared to Annie's rapid energy; her gentle voice, her watery green eyes. I forced the image from my mind as I left the two young men and wove my way along the platform, trying to avoid stepping on little children who were running about and shouting noisily. The people did not have much luggage, just what they had brought from Ireland and food for the journey provided by the nuns.

The train pulled in slowly, blowing smoke from its funnel, steam from its pistons and a fierce shriek from its whistle which startled many, especially the children. I suppose most of them had never seen a train before, especially so close. The guard was shouting and waving everyone on board, occasionally helping with a heavy suitcase or bag. "Todos a bordo del tren," he called, shooing people off the platform as if the train was about to leave. It did not, of course. There was plenty of time for everyone to get settled.

I waited on the platform to make sure everyone boarded. One young man stood holding his suitcase, looking at the train suspiciously with lowered head. "Are you getting on or what?" I called cheerfully. He said nothing so I approached him. "Are you alright?" He nodded. "Then you must get on board. I stood at the side of the door until he had climbed up before ascending the steps myself. We stood in the passageway at the end of the carriage. "We'll need to find seats now." There was still no audible reaction and he would not look me in the eye. "What's your name?"

"James … Jimmy."

"Where're you from, Jimmy?"

"Limerick – nearby."

I managed to coax a little more information from him. He had been on the *Dresden,* though I had not noticed him. There was no one else he knew from Limerick so he was on his own. What misery must he be enduring with that level of shyness and no one to call a friend? "Come now, Jimmy, and let's find you a seat." I found one for him a few carriages along.

The carriages were spartan, the bench seats hard. Canon Peter had suggested I travel second-class but this time I insisted I would go third-class with the rest of the passengers. I would be sharing whatever trials they endured at the new colony and I wanted to make clear that I did not see myself as better than anyone else. I have to confess, there were times on the journey when I regretted that decision. Despite putting my coat on the seat to act as a cushion, my backside became sore and twenty-four hours with no break from noisy children and that press of humanity was difficult.

Hardship, though, is, like everything else, relative.

## Rose

Treading softly as I did not feel I belonged, I climbed the stairs again to the room. I was able to look around more carefully without Molly. It was by no means luxurious – you'd call it functional, I suppose. There was little that spoke of comfort, just the necessaries, and it seemed faded. The curtains were flimsy cotton with a pattern of flowers that was pastel with age, though surely more vibrant when new. The bedclothes were not expensive and my bed sagged a little in the centre. But I was grateful – for the job, for a roof over my head even on the first night, for the food in my stomach and for a safe arrival after such a horrible passage.

I decided to sort my things and unpacked my suitcase, setting aside the under garments that needed washing. I did not have much but I had packed two other dresses that would need to hang for a few days before the creases would come out. When I opened the wardrobe door to put them away, there were three dresses hanging there and two calico shifts, soft to my touch. I took out one of the dresses.

It was a rich, satin fabric, green, with a cuirass bodice, the kind that the most fastidious customers at Miss O'Leary's would no longer have regarded as fashionable. The sleeves of the bodice were finished just below the elbow with cotton frills and panels of taffeta had been sewn in with princess seams. I imagined them iridescent in candlelight. It looked like a natural form day dress except the neckline, which was fringed with white lace ruffles and plunged alarmingly low.

I held it up in front of me, running my hand longingly down its silky smoothness. It was about my size though it would have been made for someone with a fuller figure. I hung it back in the wardrobe and fingered the other two; one was a bright red and the other blue, both silky and elegant. I wondered whose they were. Perhaps Molly's? I peeked inside her wardrobe and there were several dresses in there; either she had a lot or they belonged to someone else.

I lay on the bed in my clothes and, in no time at all, I was asleep. I woke only when I felt myself being shaken. Molly was standing over me. "Get up now and come down for some dinner." I did so, rubbing my eyes and feeling worse than before I had lain down. The prospect of food enticed me, though.

We ate in the kitchen, seated around the large table in the centre of the room; I was surprised that Mrs O'Shaughnessy ate with us. There were two other girls – women, I should say – and a man (in his late twenties, I guessed) as well as Molly and Mrs O'Shaughnessy. She introduced them as Maggie, Sheila and Michael. The two women had a brash, hardness about them and Michael seemed dark, brooding, almost dangerous. He said nothing throughout the whole meal and I asked Molly about him later. "He's a bit simple" she said but did not elaborate.

"Welcome to Placer House," Maggie said and she looked at me with a knowing, pitying smile. I felt like a schoolgirl amongst women.

"Placer House?"

"It's the Spanish word for pleasure. That's what we specialise in here." Sheila laughed and I noticed the look she shared with Maggie. I was not sure what to make of it.

The food was good and I ate hungrily, though of course remembering my manners. Maggie and Sheila were chattering about what and whom they'd seen on their walk that afternoon. Molly seemed to be watching me carefully and once I caught what looked like a sneer on her face. I knew then that I would have to work hard to win her over. But I was confident I could do so. I had found with my employer, Miss O'Leary, that being reliable, keeping your head down, getting on with things without a fuss won approval, albeit grudging.

In a lull in the conversation, I asked Mrs O'Shaughnessy what she would like me to do first thing in the morning. "Well, first of all, you can call me Ma. Everyone else does. In the winter, there'll be fires to clean out and light but at this time of year, 'tis a matter of cleaning the downstairs rooms. We're not up early in this house as we retire late at night."

Molly smirked at the other women. Ma then explained that there were dresses in my wardrobe that would need adjusting to fit me. She said that I should make a start on those tomorrow and told me where the needlework box was. "Now don't be taking them in too tight as we need to get some flesh on your bones. And tomorrow afternoon, you can have a bath in the scullery there after Molly."

I thanked her, delighted to be using my needlework skills and quite breathless that I would be wearing those dresses. The prospect of a bath was appealing, too, having been a rare event in my life so far.

"I've a petticoat that needs repairing. It got ripped the other ni—day. I'll bring it down for you," Maggie said.

I offered to wash the dishes after dinner but Sheila and Maggie said it was their turn and there'd be time enough for me to do those things when I had rested. Suddenly, all the others except Michael seemed to be brisk and business-like. "Rose, you may spend this evening in your room. I suggest you get as much rest as you can for you'll have plenty to do from tomorrow. We must get ready for this evening."

As I passed through the hall, I looked into the other grand room that opened off it. It was much larger, two big bay windows and furniture around the edges of the room. The floor was, like the sitting room, dark, polished wood and the central part was covered with a huge carpet with a design of flowers and swirls. I had never been in a place that looked so grand.

I climbed the stairs again to our room. There was a washstand with a bowl, and a jug which was empty. I would need to fill that to wash in the morning so I traipsed downstairs again to fill it. Sheila showed me the pump out the back to get water. I certainly felt tired by the time I had carried the heavy jug back upstairs. I took off my dress, stays and petticoats and slipped under the sheet. As I did, the door opened and Molly came in. I watched her undo her dress and let it fall to the floor. She stepped out of it and hung it in her wardrobe. She then changed her petticoat for another and put on a different dress.

"That looks lovely." My admiration was genuine. She sat at the small dressing table which had a glass attached to it and she put her hair up. It had looked nothing remarkable when it had been hanging down, simply tied at the back but it was transformed when she gathered it into a bun at the back of her head. She pinned it in place and pulled a few strands out so they hung in wisps each side of her head. She then took a box from under her bed and applied her make-up. I was fascinated. I had never used make-up before – it was too expensive and too flighty as my mother said. Molly finished the picture by putting on large earrings, a necklace and a huge butterfly pinned to her hair.

She stood up and turned to face me. "Now, what do you think of plain old Molly?"

"You look like a princess," I said. She was pleased, I could tell, but I was not just saying it. She certainly looked like a lady, older, more sophisticated. "Are you away out?"

"Not a chance. We've to entertain gentlemen who come in of an evening. They have a drink, perhaps a cigar and they chat. We serve drinks and make them feel good. Most of them are older men with a good bit of money. They like having attractive young girls around them. Makes them feel young I s'pose," she added with some contempt. "Still, why should I care? They pay well." She turned away. "Sleep well," she said over her shoulder as she left the room.

I was tempted to get up and try to see the activity downstairs but sleep got the better of me and I drifted off very quickly. Before doing so, I thought how lucky I had been to land in a place like this. The food was good, I had a comfortable bed and it sounded as though the work would not be hard. There was the added attraction of entertaining the gentlemen in the evenings so things would not be dull. If the pay was good, as Ma had said, I should be able to send a good bit home. I said a prayer of thanks before closing my eyes and conjuring up a picture of James and his smiling face. I hoped he had been as fortunate and had already found a place where he could establish his farm. He would still be in Buenos Aires, of course, but as long as he had found a place to head for, that was the main thing. I wrapped my arms around myself as if it were his arms around me and I smiled to myself, thinking of his playful eyes and the way he had kissed me.

When I woke next morning, Saturday, I could hear movement in the street outside. Molly was sleeping soundly in her bed, wheezing each time she breathed out. She would be the one who would snore, then! I slipped my legs out and went as quietly as I could to the washstand where I splashed water on my face. There was a clean towel for me on a rod at one end of the wash stand; Molly's was at the other end. I dressed and went downstairs, passing through the kitchen and scullery and outside to the toilet. After the one on the ship, it was quite reasonable; at least it didn't move about the whole time. The big old long case clock in the hall showed it was not long past eight o'clock. That would have been considered a very late hour to rise at Miss O'Leary's. This was clearly a very different establishment. No one was up and about at all.

The smell of stale smoke and drink hung in the big room I had seen yesterday so I pushed up the sash on each of the two windows. It was quite a struggle as they were large and didn't run freely but it was enough to let some fresh air in. There were used glasses left around and ash-trays with the stubs of cigars. I brought them all into the kitchen and found a bin for rubbish where I emptied the ash. I made sure the furniture in the room was arranged nicely and found a dustpan and brush in the scullery to sweep up a few places where ash had fallen on the floor. I then set about washing all the glasses and had done so by nine o'clock.

Being hungry again, I could have done with a bite to eat but I thought I had better wait for someone else to come down. It was half past by the time I heard steps on the stair. Ma walked slowly into the kitchen, looking still half asleep.

"Ah, 'tis you is it?"

"Yes, Madam."

"I told you, call me Ma."

"Sorry Ma. I've tidied the big room and washed the glasses. Is there anything else I should do?"

"That's good. I like a girl with initiative. No, there's nothing else at the moment. Let's have some breakfast and then you can have a look at one of those dresses."

We ate at the kitchen table and one by one the others joined us. They all seemed tired and said little but gradually they began to look more lively. After breakfast, I cleared the table and washed the few dishes we'd used. I then went into the back room beside the kitchen where the needlework box was kept. There was everything I might need there, plenty of needles, cotton thread of different colours, thimbles. It was the green dress I decided to bring down to work on first as I thought it would set off my hair well and was close to the colour of my eyes. It was a joy to be working with a needle again; it seemed an age since I had sat in Miss O'Leary's making and mending the customers' fancy dresses. But here was a very fancy dress which was for *me* to wear! I could not help feeling excited at the idea of me wearing it and entertaining the gentlemen.

Later that day, as Ma had promised, we took baths out in the scullery. I was after Molly so I had to use her water but it had been heated enough and was still warm. It was luxurious, sitting back in the tub and letting the water seep into my skin. The soap had the smell of roses or some such flower and was so much more exotic than the rough old stuff I was used to. The lather produced was lovely, creamy, soft, and felt so smooth when I rubbed my arms. After I dried myself and started to dress, Ma came in.

"I've brought you a bottle of scent. Here, try it." She held out a bottle to me and I unscrewed the top. "Put a little on your neck and your wrists."

The sweet smell from my wrist brought a smile to my face. "Thank you very much, Ma. 'Tis lovely."

"Well, good, but don't use too much. You don't need to smell like a perfume factory. Just a hint is all you need. That gives a man pleasure if he passes close to you. You managed to alter one of the dresses?"

"Yes, Ma. The green one. 'Tis lovely."

"Good. You can join us tonight in the big room and start to learn how to be a good hostess."

I was excited but … there was some doubt gnawing at the back of my mind which I tried to suppress. It was as if I could hear the nuns who had taught us at school standing at the front of the class declaring "pleasure is wrong" in voices that conjured the day of judgement. So much seemed to be wrong in their eyes, the world full of temptations to trap the unwary into sin. I fought to suppress those sentiments as I know Annie would have encouraged me to do. Why had I deserved such good luck? Fine dresses to wear, not much work to do and entertainment in the evening. I was determined to enjoy it.

# ACT II

# CHAPTER 6

# VOLCADA

**Patrick**

The last stretch of the railway line was across a vast, flat, grassland plain with scrubby bushes, stumpy trees and no sign of any agriculture. It seemed to promise only disappointment but I thrust that thought from my mind. The train slowed before coming to a halt, blowing steam and screeching brakes. I could see nothing in the way of houses or development. The station was a small hut with a low platform and seemed to be in the middle of nowhere. Jumping down, I saw the guard near the rear of the train. As with our arrival at Buenos Aires, there seemed to be no one organising things, just a fellow with an ox and cart outside the station fence. I therefore asked the guard where Naposta was.

"Sí, la naposta está muy cerca," he said. It was not his words I understood but his head nodding and his arm pointing outside the station, sweeping around.

The air of excitement amongst the passengers had, of course, abated on the long journey but it revived as they tumbled off the train, stretching limbs in the late morning sun. Some women and most of the children had to be helped down and the luggage had to be unloaded. The crowd soon filled the little platform and there was much shouting to children to keep back when the guard blew his whistle, climbed up into his van at the rear of the train and, with a ghostly howl and slow bursts of smoke and steam, the monster began to draw away. We watched it gather speed, become smaller and smaller, the smoke dissolving into air, before we were left in silence.

I approached the man with the cart. He spoke a little English and said he worked for Signor Sanchez, the owner of the La Viticola estate. He was short and wiry; his name was Faustino. His eyes were wide with horror at the sea of people standing before him, gathered around the cart. He explained that he could only take luggage and directed us away from the station along a track. "Is not far," he said encouragingly, waving a brown arm, bare almost to the shoulder. It would take at least two trips to transport the luggage, he said; I asked James and Will to stay with the luggage that was left until he returned.

"Alright, everybody. Faustino here has shown me where to go … it's only a short walk, he said." I then explained about the luggage and said I would lead the way to our destination. "Let us start with a prayer. Dear Father, we thank you for bringing us safely to this land and we place ourselves in your hands whilst we do your work here. May our endeavours be blessed and our trials so far earn us rewards in the future. In nomine Patris, Filii et Spiritus Sancti." The chorus of "Amen" was resounding and cheered me as I set off at the head of the straggling line. Warm sunshine fanned my hope, the tall grass whispered like spirts in the light breeze. What stories were being told, what welcomes being voiced?

Someone started to sing *In Dublin's Fair City*, and others took it up. It was perhaps not the best song to choose, given the final verse, but no one seemed to worry about that. Our walk was across a level, scrubby plain. Behind us was the railway line but it soon disappeared from sight in that featureless expanse. We were left walking into a nearly deserted land. On both sides of the stony track were open plains of grass.

As we walked, we could see in the distance the dust raised by Faustino's cart. It was not long before we could see a building which, when we were closer, turned into a large house, a smaller building and a barn. I wondered where all the houses were. Cattle grazed the grass as far as the eye could see. I halted in the dusty courtyard in front of the house and waited until everyone had joined me. A man in his mid-forties walked slowly towards us from the house. He was swarthy, muscular and sported a bushy moustache. He stopped several yards in front of us and looked from left to right.

I stepped forward. "Signor Sanchez?"

He took two steps to meet me and held out his hand. "Sí. And you are?"

"My name is Father Patrick Gilligan and I have accompanied these people as their priest."

Behind him, four others walked slowly forward from the house, a woman of about Sanchez's age, a young woman, a girl of about seventeen and a boy of about thirteen.

Signor Sanchez shook his head slowly and then spread his hands wide. "So many people."

"About three hundred souls, including the children. They said there was space enough for everyone who wanted to come here."

"Is space, yes. But food, tools, seed …"

My heart sank. I did not dare turn to look at the faces of my fellow travellers. The picture I had formed of happy faces in a well-run estate disintegrated.

"We need food and water." He looked horrified but asked that some of them helped his wife and maid to prepare a meal.

"Where are all the houses, Signor?"

His reply was blunt. "No houses … they must be built."

Some of the women volunteered to help cook and I went with them to see what the state of affairs was. There were sacks of flour and potatoes stored in a shed that leant against the house and the women set about baking bread and scrubbing the potatoes under the direction of Signora Sanchez and their maid, Paloma, an attractive young woman in her twenties, I guessed.

I asked to speak to Signor Sanchez privately and he took me into a pleasant sitting room. It was not opulent, the furnishings being ordinary and there being no expensive ornaments and such around, but it was comfortable. A faint smell of cigar and wood smoke lingered. I declined the offer of brandy but he helped himself to a generous slug, swallowing it before splashing more into the glass.

"I say we could take a lot of people but this too many. I do not have stores for so many. The ground needs to be dug and is too late now to sow seeds until spring. I think some must go back."

"There's nothing for them in Buenos Aires and they have no money for the train fare. We must find a way to make it work. We were promised good agricultural land, houses, seed, tools and equipment …" I stopped as my voice was rising with the anger that was flooding me again.

He looked at me but said nothing. I wondered what he was thinking. I suppose he saw in front of him a naïve young man who knew nothing of the land and the issues to be faced. He would have been right to some extent but I was determined that this colony would be a success.

"Where will the people sleep tonight?"

"We have tents and we can make space in barn. I have to find more fabric in Bahia Blanca to make some cover. We need more food, too. This will cost much money before these people are able to grow enough to sell and earn money."

Looking back, I wondered why I didn't telegraph Canon Peter and ask him to send enough money to get everyone back on the train. Sanchez was right. The preparations were completely inadequate for so many people. But hindsight is a great thing and, in truth, I was driven by my need to succeed. I did not want to lead a group of tired and hungry immigrants back to the city and see their spirits crushed with disappointment. I set about organising.

That first day, I made sure that families with children were properly provided for with shelter, as many in the barn as possible and the rest in tents. The single young men slept four to any tent that was available but of course there were many who slept under the stars for the first few nights. Signor Sanchez offered me a room in the house but I declined. I could not consider my own comfort when everyone else was enduring hardship.

On the next day, my limbs aching from a night spent on the ground, I stopped Juan Sanchez as he left the house and asked him about timber for houses and the water supply. I know I was more aggressive than I would normally be; it was not just the discomfort of the night but my determination to get things sorted out. He waved his arms around indicating the area. There was hardly a tree to be seen.

"Where will we get timber to build houses?"

"There is a forest but it is many miles. We can get some in Bahia Blanca but we will need to order more."

"And water?"

"The well is good at moment but for so many we need more wells."

"Do you have tools?"

"Some."

"Right, we'll need picks and shovels to dig wells, axes and saws to fell trees, nails and hammers to build houses and ploughs to start preparing the ground for crops."

I stomped off and gathered the men in the space in front of the house. I explained the situation and said we needed to create work parties who would do different things. God bless them for their willingness. There was no grumbling or argument. Those who had some skills with woodwork would start building using whatever timber we could get from Bahia Blanca, others would go to the nearest woodland and collect suitable wood for fires and others again would decide where the best land would be for growing crops and start turning the soil.

"There is one thing I ask of you. No one, no one must be left out. Let us work together for the good of all. We need to see our work in these early years as being a shared endeavour. Some men will build houses, some will dig wells, others will work the fields so that all may flourish with the help of God."

Those first few days were a nightmare. I had to put pressure constantly on Signor Sanchez to spend money, to send Faustino and a couple of the men into Bahia Blanca to get more provisions, bedding, tent fabric, tools. It was a two day round trip in the cart, some fifteen miles. Juan Sanchez constantly grumbled about the expense and said he would soon run out of money.

Reluctantly, I borrowed a horse from Sanchez's stable and went into Bahia Blanca about a week after we had arrived. It was many years since I had been on horseback but it is one of those things you don't forget. Sanchez sent one of his men with me and there was a pleasure in riding across the open plain like a cowboy. It would have been a joyful few hours had I not been burdened by anxiety. I was able to send a telegraph to Canon Peter asking him to send staple foods such as wheat grain and potatoes on the next train. I said money would help too but the food would soon be in short supply in the area and we needed to ensure we had sufficient to last the coming winter.

There was only one train each month but the next brought a great number of sacks of grain and potatoes with salted meat in barrels. "God bless you, Canon," I said aloud and that night I gave thanks to God in my prayers for Canon Peter. I remembered Monsignor

O'Rourke's words then that God can only work through people. He had surely put it in Canon Peter's heart to raise the funds for the food.

In the midst of our adversity, there were some lighter moments. On the second day, I was discussing the construction of the first, communal building with a group of the men when one of the women asked to speak to me. It was Mary McCarthy whose young child, Ellen, clung to her apron and looked at me shyly with a finger in her mouth.

"What is it ... it's Mary, is it not?" Her face was ashen and I feared a terrible revelation.

"It is Father, Mary McCarthy. Father, I wonder would you come and look at the water. We think there's something wrong with it and wonder if it's safe to drink."

As we walked together to the well behind the big house, my mind was racing. What would we do if the water was contaminated? Mary scooped up her daughter who was unable to keep pace with us. She set her down again when we got to the well and joined a small group of women with anxious faces. "You see, Father," stammered Mary, "when we pour the water from the well bucket into the bucket we're using to carry it, the water goes round the wrong way. At home it goes round the same way as a clock but here it goes t'other way." She pulled the well bucket over the parapet and tipped the water into the empty bucket standing there.

I had to keep myself from laughing, with relief as much as anything else. "Sure, there's nothing wrong with that at all. You see, at home we're in the Northern Hemisphere and water always drains from a sink in a clockwise direction but here in the Southern Hemisphere, it goes the other way."

The relief all round was touching. "Thank you, Father," Mary said, putting a hand to her chest.

"Sure, may all our troubles be as simply resolved." That was my hope but deep down I knew they would not be and that incident was to be disturbingly prophetic.

Looking back at my journal, it is full of hope and gratitude for the strength and drive of those men and women. We were united in adversity and I could feel God's presence among us. The men on building duties decided that it would be best to start with one large building in which several families could sleep, food could be served for everyone and we could meet for such things as mass. I was delighted with that decision of course because it cemented the unity that was growing.

It was several weeks before that building was ready and that first Sunday, I said mass out in the courtyard. We had had very little rain and we could depend on being dry outside. But, of course, very little rain meant there was a risk that the well would run dry. There were two groups of men digging wells. They had to go a good way down to find water and the first two attempts yielded nothing. I feared for their safety as the holes became deeper and deeper. They took it in turns to work down the hole, swapping then to work on the surface, hauling up buckets of shale and tipping it. Had we had an ox or a horse spare, we could have rigged a pulley system and lifted bigger buckets.

"Sure, there must be water down there somewhere," said Pat, a huge hulking fellow with a heart of gold and always a ready smile.

The men digging the ground on which crops would eventually grow made good progress though the soil was dry and looked poor. Sanchez had acquired another ox and a plough which speeded things up a little but it was to be a long process to prepare enough ground to feed so many. Of course, we had plenty of time before seed could be sown but we did need to be ready. Someone suggested gathering kelp from the shoreline by Bahia Blanca as a fertiliser, as we did at home at times. It was too far, though, and we used what animal and human manure we had.

My conversations with Signor Sanchez were always strained as I was constantly after something that we needed. He resisted as much as he could but I was persistent. I persuaded him to give us a few of his cattle and to buy goats, hens and a couple of pigs. "You must pay," he grumbled but he agreed.

"Consider it a loan. It'll be paid when money starts coming in." Had I been in a different situation, I would have been appalled at how I was bullying the man but I had no misgivings. It was a case of survival. The grass was scrubby and not great for cows but the goats had no problem putting on weight. They would, God willing, have kids in the spring and provide milk, as would the cows. We started collecting eggs fairly soon and I ensured that they went to those who were most frail. Mary McCarthy was one. She had become pregnant with her second child soon after we arrived and it was important she had good nourishment.

It was a great day when the first, large building was finished. We had an opening ceremony where I blessed it and the work of those who had built it. Everyone filed in, looked around wonderingly at the space and then filed out, a stream of people marvelling at its construction. I say everyone; it was not *quite* everyone. I saw a few of the men who had been digging the fields and wells standing aside.

"Are you not going to look at the new building? 'Tis wonderful," I ventured.

"To be sure 'tis a wonder," snarled Arthur who had been angry about the food on the ship.

"I gather you're not impressed."

"Sure 'tis fine for them, building a great shed for everyone t'admire. But you can't grow food in it nor drink it and no one cares that some are out digging from morn 'til night under the hot sun."

"Arthur, Arthur … the time will come when we thank you and the others for your work. Did I not say so at mass only last Sunday?"

"Oh, yeah, you did. But how many people come out and see what we're doing – they're always hanging around that shed saying how wonderful it is."

I felt a chill in my heart at this dissent. I could not allow it to grow. "We need to be thankful for the contribution *everyone* makes. Each must serve as they are most suited. When we are drinking water from the wells you have dug, you will be the ones everyone turns to in gratitude. Be content, share in the enjoyment of your fellow men and women, be happy for those who have succeeded in their task as they will be happy in yours."

His jaw clamped tightly shut, the muscles in his cheek working. He scuffed the ground with his boot but said nothing and I knew he was not convinced. That was the first example of discord in our community and by no means the last. I wondered for a time if it was because of the pressure we were all under but then I thought of the jealousies and squabbles that arise in every community, however rich or poor. It seems to be one of the curses of human kind, the stain of Cane's murder of his brother, Abel.

I made sure of course that at mass the following Sunday, I suggested we take a walk to view the dug ground and the wells and I blessed them all. I thought Arthur was mollified but he was difficult to read; he had a brooding presence and I felt, if dissent were to arise, he would be at the forefront.

As summer faded into autumn, I realised with foreboding that this land would have more challenges than expected. We did have enough food thanks to Canon Peter and we did have enough shelter but, on several days, wind and rain swept across the plain with nothing to provide protection. There was none of that golden light that I remembered so well from my home in Ireland. There were no trees, no wonderful changes in the colour of leaves to delight us, no softening of the days, no morning mists lying in the valleys. As April gave way to May, I longed for the rich fields of home, the cows occasional lowing from the pasture, the call of departing birds.

Ash Wednesday had been on the sixth of March, less than a fortnight after we arrived at La Viticola. I had to make do with burning wood to make ash for the service. Everyone filed up to the front where I made the sign of the cross on foreheads with the ash. In my sermon, I told them they should not worry about giving something up for Lent as was the custom at home. "You have given up so much to be here and, frankly, when you have so little, God would not expect you to give up anything. This is a time which is about preparing to receive the holy spirit when Christ rises from the grave at Easter. For us, this year, it is as if we are sharing Christ's time in the wilderness. I pray that next year things will be different."

It was strange being in the lower half of the world. At home, we would be looking forward to the coming of spring, the days lengthening, life returning, lambs being born, flowers bursting from the dead ground. But here, the sun was struggling to rise into the sky, a cold wind blowing across the empty plain and life retreating to prepare for winter. Easter Sunday, which was late that year – the twenty-first of April – was not the glorious celebration that we enjoyed each year at home. I made sure all the children had an egg to eat, but otherwise, we had nothing special and rain dampened our already failing spirits. I said no one should work on buildings, fields or wells. Easter Sunday should be a time to rest and enjoy each other's company though it was difficult in such poor conditions.

It was after Easter that frustrations started to boil over into heated disputes and I spent much of my time trying to resolve issues and calm tempers. The first came when we divided the land into lots. I had wanted to leave that for at least another year, to be sure everyone had a share of whatever was produced, but some of the men were eager to get started on their own small farms. Most would have plots that had not yet been dug but at least I gained agreement that we should all help to do the first dig of every plot. There was a slight rise in the ground in one area of the estate and there was reluctance to have a plot on it because it meant hauling water from the wells. It could hardly be described as a hill but when people have been worn down by hardship, the slightest thing can become a bone of contention.

Predictably, it was Arthur who started the complaining. I went out on the estate, not exactly supervising but intending to make sure things were done fairly, when I saw a knot of men at the base of this slight rise. Heated voices reached me as I approached.

"Why should you fellas get the best land? We've been working just as hard, stuck down holes in the ground to find water for everyone." It was Arthur.

"What makes you think we've got the best ground?"

"It's obvious. That bit of hill there will be enough to make the land dry out completely in the summer months and we'll never haul enough water up there for the crops."

"Ah, don't talk so daft," Michael Rooney shouted back. "There's hardly a hill there at all so it won't be any drier than the rest of it. We'll help you dig it so what's the problem?"

"You're the fecking problem, Rooney." Arthur advanced towards him, his chin thrust forward and his fists clenched.

I arrived at the group just at this point, pushed my way into the circle and stood directly in front of Arthur. He stopped, uncertain. For a moment, I thought he was going to raise his fists to me. I'd be no match for him but I stood my ground and looked him in the eye. He glared back at me but, as I had assumed, my position, my clerical collar was enough to make him back down. He pushed his way out of the circle and started to storm off.

"Arthur ... Arthur ... come back here, please!"

He muttered something that I did not hear but I think it was offensive. I knew I had to stop him walking away. Trouble would escalate if he did. It's not seemly for a man of the cloth to shout but I knew I had to do something to stop him. To run after him would be undignified so I roared, "Arthur O'Brien, come back here this instant!"

Mouths fell open all around me and Arthur stopped. He turned slowly and glared at me. My mind was racing. What would I do if he turned again and walked off? What would I do if he came back at me and hit me? The men around me would surely stop him raising a fist. "*Now*, please, Arthur," I called, not as loudly but with authority. Slowly, he walked back towards us. I waited until he had joined the group. Anger lurked in the tension of his body and his eyes were fixed on the ground. I wanted him to look at me but he would not.

"Michael, please tell me what is going on here. You, Arthur, must remain silent while he talks and then we'll hear your side of the argument."

"Well, Father, we're dividin' up the land as you know and giving a plot to each of us. Arthur was given a patch on this rise of land here and he thinks it won't be any good as he thinks 'twill dry out in the heat of summer. I don't think it'll be any different to the rest of the land."

"Thank you, Michael. Now Arthur what have you to say?"

"If there's no difference, then Rooney can have the f ..." His eyes blazed and his fists clenched.

"We'll have none of that language please, Arthur. I'm a priest not a tavern keeper," I interrupted, holding up my hand.

"I was saying, if there's no difference then someone else can take the plot on the rise."

"But, Arthur, everyone will help dig the plot and will help haul water in the summer if you need it."

"They say that now, but will they do it when they're busy with their own plots? I don't think so." He spat out his last words – clearly not someone who would easily be mollified. I hesitated. What should I suggest? Perhaps I should just insist that he took the plot – I didn't like the way he seemed to want to bully his way to get what he wanted.

"Father?" Big Pat said. "I'll be quite happy to have a plot on the rise and Arthur can have mine down on the flat."

"Are you sure, Pat? 'Tis very generous of you. Arthur, will you help Pat with the digging and watering."

Arthur looked at Pat, somewhat shamefaced. "I don't want to put another man out. Are you sure, Pat, you want to do that?"

"I really don't think there'll be any difference in the land so I am happy to do that if it will sort things."

They shook hands and I made sure that Arthur and Michael Rooney did so too. "Gentlemen," I said, "things are very difficult for everyone. We are in a terrible situation. I understand that differences will arise but we must try to resolve things in friendship. If we fall apart, we're finished." I looked around the circle. They all knew that was a real possibility. We were living on a cliff edge; one slip and many might perish.

That night, as every night, I said my prayers. I wondered if I had bitten off more than I could chew. I kept Monsignor O'Rourke's wooden cross in my pocket during the day and held it often. As I prayed, I laid it on the ground in front of me and looked at its smoothness, reminding myself of what Jesus had suffered on our account. Surely I could deal with this situation when he had been garlanded with a crown of thorns, made to carry a heavy cross to Golgotha and crucified on it? And after our suffering, there would surely be deliverance even if that was in the next life. Most nights at that time, it was enough to calm my fears and restore my strength for the next day's endeavours.

I lay on the straw in my tent. They had insisted that I had a tent to myself, saying I needed some privacy. I felt guilty about it but they were right – I did need those few hours of being apart. Though exhausted every night, my sleep was fitful, no doubt due to the pricking of the straw and perhaps the feverish thoughts and plans that never left my mind.

There was another reason of course and one that unsettled me. Unbidden and despite my efforts to dismiss it, an image always came to me. It was John on his deathbed on the ship and, beside him, Rose. She turned her head towards me and there was the faintest smile on her face, a deep warmth in her eyes. I noticed the few freckles across her nose, something I had not remembered before, and I wanted to reach out and touch her rich, golden hair.

# CHAPTER 7

# GANCHO

**Rose**

I stood before the mirror in the green dress I had altered, admiring myself though very self-conscious of the low neck revealing the white of my chest. "That's grand," Molly offered. "Still a little room for some flesh as Ma said and then it'll be perfect."

"What about the top, though Molly? Is it not a bit low? People may see my ... bosom."

She laughed. "Not a bit of it. That's the idea." She leaned forward and whispered, "The gentlemen like to see a hint of flesh – it excites them."

I was not sure what to make of her comment and thought I must remember not to lean over in front of anyone, to hold my hand on the bodice if I did.

It was the first Saturday, after the bath and dinner, when Molly had come with me to our room to supervise my dressing. She dressed herself again and I watched her applying her make-up so I'd see how 'twas done. She looked gorgeous and I told her so. Again, I saw a faint smile and thought I would be able to soften her manner towards me over time. Then Molly helped me with the make-up, using her box.

"Ma'll get you some of your own soon, I'm sure." She showed me how to put my hair up and pull out a few wisps. Then she looked at me in the mirror. "Quite the lady, aren't you?"

I was amazed at the transformation. I did look like a lady and I felt like one. I turned around in front of the mirror, feeling the petticoats under my dress sway around my legs. "Do I look alright?"

"You'll do fine." Molly's words were kind enough but that feeling of slight hostility had returned and her eyes betrayed darker thoughts. I dabbed a little of the perfume on as Ma had shown me and we walked down the two flights of stairs to the grand room. Michael was lighting candelabra to supplement the light from the gas mantles. The room had a warm glow. Comfort, wealth and pleasure seemed to be promised and I felt a flutter in my stomach of excitement and nervousness.

Ma and the others joined us. Ma told me to watch what the other girls did, to smile and to be pleasant if any of the gentlemen spoke to me. It was approaching nine o'clock when the first arrived and the rest came soon after, so they had eaten dinner and were now relaxing with a drink. There were six of them that first evening. I noticed how Ma and the other girls were very welcoming to the gentlemen, making them feel special, saying how well they looked, how glad they were to see them. They sat them down, made sure they knew the gentlemen sitting nearest to them and brought whatever drink they had ordered. Most seemed to drink brandy. They all smiled at me and I saw several whispering with Ma. It was obvious they were asking who I was.

I was surprised when Ma made a point of introducing one gentleman to me. "Signor Ramirez, the Chief Superintendent of Police," she said pointedly. She asked me to show him to a chair and pour him a drink. When I brought it to him, he asked me about myself. His English was good. He was quite a good-looking man, probably late-forties or early-fifties, I'd say. He had a small moustache, a mere line of dark hair above his lip which, together with sharp and darting eyes, gave him an air of shrewdness. He would need to be, I was sure, given his work.

His eyes flicked frequently to the top of my dress and I felt uncomfortable. Fortunately, another gentleman needed a drink so I was able to escape. I couldn't help feeling that Signor Ramirez's eyes followed me around the room. Once, when I had to pass close to his chair, he put his hand out and laid it on my bottom. I pushed my hips forward quickly to move myself away from his hand, but it followed me until I had stepped away. He looked at me, his eyes twinkling and he laughed.

When I was able to catch Molly for a second, I told her what he'd done. She laughed, too. "He's a man to keep on the right side of." She said no more and continued pouring a drink. I did not know whether I should tell Ma but then I saw Maggie sit on a gentleman's knee and drape her arm around him. Next thing, Sheila was doing likewise with another man. Soon after, they both left the room leading the gentlemen out. The men said good night to the other visitors and knowing smiles passed between them. Maggie and Sheila were gone a good time, perhaps half an hour or more, so the three of us entertained the other gentlemen.

Then Molly left with another gentleman. Maggie and Sheila returned but they were alone and they began to flirt with two more of the gentlemen. Then they left with them. Molly came back again after about thirty minutes, again alone. She crouched beside Signor Ramirez, pushing her chest out so he could not fail to see down her bodice. I watched as she laid her hand on his knee and rubbed it slowly up his thigh. She whispered something in his ear and then she stood and led him from the room.

"Nearly done for tonight," Ma sighed. "Not a good night for a Saturday. Still, you have to take the rough with the smooth and 'tis summer. They have more to do in nice weather like this."

"Did I do alright, Ma?"

"You were fine, girl." She lifted an empty glass and poured herself a drink.

"Signor Ramirez… touched me …"

"Well sure that didn't do you any harm, did it?"

"No, but …"

"Rose, you're not a young girl anymore. I think you've had a sheltered life, have you not? There's no harm in a little fun. These men have difficult jobs, perhaps are unhappy at home. We give them a little pleasure and if they do something the nuns told you was not right, it won't hurt you, believe me." She took a long pull from her drink and set the glass down on the occasional table beside her. "Signor Ramirez liked you, that was clear … as did all the others. You're a pretty girl and the sight of you would cheer a man. Be pleased that you've been blessed with such looks." She drained her glass and asked me to refill it. "Many men admire a girl like you, one who has a little shyness about her, some gentleness. They don't all want hard bitches like Molly."

I was shocked at her use of that word for one of her household. Molly did have a hardness about her but I thought that was just to me and that it would soften. I wanted to ask her about the way the other three had disappeared but I decided not to. My sheltered upbringing was already very obvious and perhaps I did not want to know – I wanted to enjoy this new life and not think of what may be in store. I told myself that I would not be required to do what the others were perhaps doing.

We were late to bed but I was still up earliest the next morning. I cleared the main rooms again as I had done the previous day. It was Sunday and when Ma made her sleepy way into the kitchen, I asked her about going to church. She said she and the others did not go. I was shocked. She drew me a little map to show how to get there and said I had missed the early mass but could make it for the eleven o'clock service at the nearest church, St Joseph's.

I left the house quite cheerfully, hopeful that I would see James or at least Annie at Church. I saw neither of them, nor Father Gilligan who had been on the boat over. There had been an earlier mass and perhaps they had gone to that one. There were lots of other people from the boat filling the pews. It was a Canon Flynn who took the service. He seemed like a nice man, older, with an air of wisdom about him. He would be a good priest to hear confession, I thought. That was something I needed to find out about.

I talked with a few of the people from the boat and was horrified at what I heard. There had been nothing arranged for them and many slept out in the open that first night. I looked at the weary faces in front of me and thought how lucky I had been to have found a place like Ma's. I walked back, sorry for those people but determined that I would not complain about such things as an occasional hand on my bottom. There were worse things to be endured: hunger and no shelter. I suppose that thought may have lowered my resistance to subsequent events.

That night, there were different gentlemen and slightly more of them. Maggie, Sheila and Molly disappeared with different ones throughout the evening. It was as though I refused to acknowledge it. As Ma had said, I had lived a very sheltered life till then but even I, deep down, must have known. Signor Ramirez was not there but another man called Signor Calvo was. They all seemed to speak quite good English. He told me, laughing, that his name meant bald and he rubbed the smooth top of his head to make the point. He fingered the wisps of my hair that were loose, twisting them around his finger and then stroking my cheek gently.

"Tan bonita," he said softly, "so pretty."

"Thank you, sir." I flushed slightly with his praise and he patted his lap. I was not sure whether I should and I glanced across to see if Ma was looking. She was not; I smiled and sat down. He slipped his arm around me and pulled me gently but quite firmly closer to him. I tried to sit up straight but it was difficult. His hand began to rise from my waist and I put my own on it, holding it firmly in place.

"You no like?" He smiled and allowed his hand to drop so I was not alarmed at all.

And so the evening passed and the next and the next. More gentlemen came during the week and one or two even called in the afternoons. That happened more often in winter according to Molly; she said we needed to be ready to entertain them at any time of day or night. The first time it happened, she told me to take the gentleman into the salon as it was called and get him a drink. She quickly ran upstairs and changed into one of her evening dresses. She walked like a princess when she came downstairs and into the room. It was a gentleman she knew and she sat on his lap immediately, slipping her arm around his neck and leaning close to him. I had work to do in the scullery and when I went into the salon to return some glasses, they were gone.

On the Thursday, I asked Ma if I could go to church on Saturday afternoon to make my confession. She looked at me strangely. "If you want to, that's fine." She looked away and said, "Rose, when is the time-of-the-month with you?"

I was surprised, embarrassed at the directness of the question. It was not something ever spoken of, even with my mother, after the first few times. "Well, it started on Monday and I should be alright tonight."

"And are you regular?"

"I am. Why do you ask?" I wondered if I had spoiled something without realising it.

"Oh just …'tis always good to know these things. You know how 'tis with some women. You take Sheila … she's awful crotchety when 'tis her time. But you were fine, were you not?"

"Yes … I was."

Saturday afternoon was bright. The sun had passed its highest and hottest by then but it was plenty warm enough and I didn't need a coat. I wondered whether I could find out where Annie had gone, whether she had been as lucky in finding work and, of course, to have a friend in a strange place is a great thing. We had not spent a long time together but, in the confines of that boat and the awful treatment we had received, we had formed a close friendship. I thought she might be at confession, too, but she was not there. I knelt in the pew, waiting my turn. There were a few people from the boat, but not many. I supposed by then they had left the city for the places they would be living.

The priest was Canon Peter Flynn according to the sign on the confessional box – the one who had said mass on the Sunday. His voice was soft, slow, gentle and I felt a great warmth and understanding. Though I had little to confess, it felt like a cleansing, as though I was free again. My penance was light, a few Hail Marys and an Our Father. I often wondered what kind of penance you'd get if you'd murdered someone. That wouldn't be cleared with a few Hail Marys. Walking back through the busy streets, I looked around me at the people I passed, some honey-skinned, others fair-skinned like me. I could hear different languages I didn't understand. This was a real melting pot of people.

I had a strange feeling as I walked that I was being watched, followed. I kept turning round but could see no one. Then one time, as I drew closer to Placer House, I thought I caught a glimpse of Michael darting under an arch, strange Michael from the house. I tried to catch sight of him again but did not so I thought it was my imagination.

I had my bath as the previous week and then we had dinner. I was surprised when Ma poured us all a glass of wine. I had never taken drink before and sipped it cautiously. It tasted nice, though a little bitter on the tongue. "Sure, you need to drink it up," said Sheila, "there's plenty more." I continued to sip the wine to start with, but as the meal went on, I found myself drinking it as I would a glass of water. I began to realise that I didn't feel quite as usual … strange …

lightheaded. I remember thinking this was what it was like to be drunk.

There seemed to be an air of excitement amongst Ma and the other girls. "Is there something special happening?" I asked.

"Ah, you wait and see. Just make sure you look your best tonight." I saw Ma wink at Molly who smirked but said no more. Maggie asked me how I'd got on at confession and I told her the priest seemed very nice. "He had a soft, forgiving voice … I'm sure if you told him something bad, he'd understand."

"You can't depend on that!" Sheila's voice was hard, almost bitter.

Michael sat throughout the meal hunched over but often I caught him looking at me, his eyes furtive in his lowered head. He seemed to have a permanent leer on his face or perhaps that was just when he looked at me. I sensed menace in his looks, a slight threat that put me on edge whenever he was around. His black mop of hair, thick eyebrows and slightly darker skin suggested a mixed parentage. I felt guilty. He was obviously not quite all there but yet he was one of God's creatures and I knew I should not harbour such feelings towards him.

After washing up, we went upstairs to change. I was amazed when Molly put on a suspender belt around her waist and sat on her bed to pull on black stockings. "Molly, are those stockings silk?"

"They are … are you jealous?"

"No, of course not. But … how did you buy …?"

"I didn't buy them and I didn't steal them in case you're wondering. They were a gift."

"Goodness. Do you have an admirer, Molly?"

"I hope I have several." She slid her hands over her stockinged legs, feeling the smoothness. "D'you want to feel them?" I sat on the bed beside her and put my hand carefully on her leg just above the knee. "Go ahead … slide your hand up my leg. Just don't dare catch them with your nails."

I had never felt such smoothness before. Molly put her hand on mine and drew it up her leg until it reached the top of her stocking. "It's so smooth," I whispered.

"And tonight I'll have a man do that instead of you." She pushed my hand away. "Smooth as silk they say, don't they? These were a gift from one of the gentlemen. He'll be here tonight and he likes to see me wear them. You see, there are some very nice things we get doing this job … if you're good to the gentlemen that is." She stood up and put on one of her dresses.

"He'll not see them under your dress."

She looked at my pityingly. "Oh, he will, believe me!" She arched her eyebrows and pulled her dress up her leg slowly, revealing the black silk. "How could any man resist that?"

I was not sure what to make of that so I laughed awkwardly. "What dress shall I wear tonight?"

"Put on the green … that looks best on you."

I felt flattered. She was right, the green dress did look best on me. I left my hair loosely tied at the neck. I'd maybe let it down as the evening went on. I was proud of my hair. I know I should not have been but, when you're nineteen, you take pride in such things.

That evening, it was even more exciting than it had been all week. A fella turned up with a violin and another with a bodhran and another kind of drum. They were Irish, they said, and had come to Buenos Aires a few years before. They'd be playing during the evening so we could dance. Michael came and rolled up the big carpet in the salon which gave a good-sized dance floor. I was glad of the little bit of practice I'd had on the boat, reminding me of some of the steps.

There were more gentlemen that night than any of the previous occasions. I supposed they had heard about the music and the dancing. None of the four of us girls were able to sit down at all, what with fetching drinks and dancing. As soon as one dance finished, there'd be another gentleman waiting with his arms wide, ready to spin you round. They played waltzes to start with and then some faster tunes. They even played jigs and reels but I had never learned the traditional dancing so I improvised. I loved to feel my hair swaying out around me as I whirled round or bouncing when I skipped and jumped in the jigs.

Both Signor Ramirez and Signor Calvo were there and they each danced with me several times. At one point they appeared to argue as to whose turn it was but I think it was good humoured. I had no time to see what the other girls were doing but we smiled at each other as we passed on the dance floor. Molly called to me once; "Are you enjoying yerself?"

"Of course. Why wouldn't I be?" I was surprised that each time I stopped dancing to fetch a drink for a gentleman, there was one of the other girls at the table and they always poured a drink for me. I tried to refuse but even Ma told me to drink it. "Ah 'twill do you no harm. Tonight we're enjoying ourselves." I was feeling distant from everything, remote as though this was not really happening to me.

A little later, I noticed Molly had gone. I assumed she was seeing a gentleman out. The music stopped and all the dancers sat down. It was as if there had been a signal. Perhaps there was but I missed it. Then the drummer began to play a strange rhythm unlike anything I had heard before. He was using his other drum, not the bodhran. It was a heavy single beat, a pause and then two beats together. There seemed to be an air of expectation in the room. One gentleman stood up and walked to the centre of the dance floor. His head was high and his face was deadly serious, like a great general looking down at everyone. He pulled his shoulders back and put his hands on his hips, standing tall and straight like a statue.

The beat continued and all eyes turned to the door into the salon. I saw her first on the last steps of the stairs but not properly until she strutted into the room, standing just inside the door. It was Molly, in a short, bright red dress. The stockings were clearly visible. She stood facing the gentleman in the same pose, the same expression of disdain on her face. And then the violin started, a rhythmic, pulsing sound before it began to climb and became a tune, graceful, swooping, soaring over the pulse of the drum.

Molly and the gentleman moved together, their steps jerky, strange, like wild animals. Suddenly they were clasped together and moving as if joined. Molly was weaving herself around him while his hands slid over her body. She whipped her head to the side, she arched her back, she lifted a leg, wrapping it around him and sliding down to sit on the knee he pushed forward. It was as if they were in a battle, a battle but also a passionate love affair. They seemed drawn together like magnets and yet despised each other. I can't remember everything they did but it was mesmerising, shocking, exciting.

My eyes were fastened on them as they moved. I did not care that Molly's legs were visible above the top of her stockings through the split in her dress. I did not care that this was behaviour that I, brought up by strict parents and the nuns, would never have thought permissible. I felt that beat in my own body. I stood absolutely still but, in my mind, my body was making the moves that Molly made, my face was like hers and I realised that my hand was sliding up and down my upper leg, slowly, slowly …

And then it was over. We all clapped and cheered. Molly and the gentleman took a bow and turned to the musicians to applaud them. We filled the glasses and excited chatter broke out in the whole room. Before the dancing started again, I had the chance to catch Molly.

"That was brilliant, Molly. I've never seen dancing like it."

Her smile was triumphant and so it deserved to be. "It's called the tango … it's a new dance, started here in Buenos Aires. They dance on the street sometimes and they are much better than us. I'll take you to see them if you like … sometime."

"I'd love that. And the dress – it looks wonderful. I could never wear something like that."

She laughed. "Ah, you will one day if you stay around here." She moved away and left me thinking hazily to myself that I could never wear a dress like that, however long I stayed.

After a few more dances, the musicians had a break. I was not sure if they were finished for the night or no. Ma was in great spirits. "Now," she called, "we have a little matter to settle. You gentlemen know what I'm talking about. Those of you who have an interest, come round this table here now." She had moved a small table into the centre of the room and on it laid a pair of dice. "You know how this works. You'll each throw the dice and the person with the lowest score has to drop out. We then throw again and so on until we have the last man."

There was a lot of fun as each man stepped up to throw the dice. A great cheer rose in volume and pitch until the dice clattered onto the table. I noticed both Ramirez and Calvo were amongst the seven men who were taking part. I had no idea then what was at stake, why they were casting the dice, what the winner would achieve. The excitement in the room grew again as the lowest scorers dropped out and fewer men were involved. At last, it came down to just two: Signor Ramirez and Signor Calvo.

Ma stepped forward. "Now, gentlemen, from this point, the winner will be the best of three throws each."

The two men looked at each other across the table, again without anger or enmity. This was a good-natured battle. Ramirez gestured for Calvo to throw first. He picked up the dice and shook them in his hands, at last releasing them onto the table where they rattled to a stop. One read five and the other four. There was a small cheer and shouts of "Nine!" Then Ramirez picked up the dice and shook them in his cupped hands, the faintest smile playing in his eyes which he kept on Calvo. The dice skittered across the table and stopped just short of the edge. A four and a two. A bigger exclamation from the gentlemen.

"First throw to Signor Calvo," announced Ma.

The second throw went to Ramirez. There was an excited tension in the room as Calvo picked up the dice for the third time. He cupped them in his hands which he drew to his lips, blowing a kiss between his fingers. He released the dice. A five and a three. Ramirez was absolutely cool as he picked up the dice and looked heavenwards. He rolled them in his hands a long time before releasing them with a flourish. A six and a five. There were cheers all round, slaps on the back for the two men who then shook hands.

"You first and me second," said Calvo graciously.

Throughout this, I could feel myself becoming more tired and my head woozy. I had sat down on the arm of a chair and realised that I had taken far too much drink. Cigar smoke hung thick in the room like fog that caught in my throat. When I stood up, I staggered and had to sit again. Molly came beside me. "Are you alright?" she said but it was amusement in her eyes, not sympathy. "I think it's time for you to lie down. You're not used to the drink I s'pose."

She helped me up and I saw Ma look at us. I expected her to be angry but she smiled and nodded. I stumbled up the first flight of stairs with Molly holding me under the arm. I could barely stand up by myself. When we reached the top of the first flight, Molly guided me a short way along the corridor and opened a door into one of the rooms. "But Molly, this isn't our room."

"God, sure you'll never make it up the next stairs in this state. Besides, something interesting might happen." She laughed.

In the room, she lit a single candle which gave a soft light. She helped me take off my dress – well, she took it off really as I seemed incapable of doing anything. Then my stays and petticoats were taken off and she doubled a sheet and laid it on the bed; I supposed that this was so I didn't dirty the other bedclothes. She told me to lie down and I was grateful to do so. "Molly, how long will it take …?"

"Oh, it won't be … how long will what take?"

"For me to be right again."

"Oh that. You'll be fine by tomorrow morning – maybe a bit thick-headed but you'll not die, don't worry."

I closed my eyes and then sensed her sit on the bed beside me. "Now you just lie there and dream of your young man coming to you. He may kiss you like this – I felt her lips briefly on mine – and he may lay his hand here – I felt a hand on my breast – or here – and then her hand was gently moving up the inside of my thigh. I tried to sit up but she pushed me down. "Relax," she said. "Enjoy it. Your womanhood needs to be woken. I'll leave you now. Just relax – don't fight it and you'll be fine."

She left the candle burning. I remember thinking I should put it out but was too sleepy to do so. I heard the door swish closed and felt myself sink into the soft bed. James came to me then, his eyes bright and loving, his hand stroking my hair and moving down my face, tenderly, gently travelling down my neck to my body. I vaguely heard the door again but did not relinquish my dream.

# CHAPTER 8

## SACADA

**Patrick**

All through that first winter, the work continued building houses and digging the ground. The houses were very simple, just one room with an earth floor, though, as the poor weather besieged us, I suggested the soil should be covered so people would not be living in the damp. We spread stones on the floor as a temporary measure until we had enough houses built and wooden floors could be fitted.

I say "we" because I worked with the men on the houses. I was not, of course, skilled but I could hold timber while it was fixed in place and could carry the lengths of wood from the stacks to where they were needed. There was amusement at first from the men and indeed some of the women.

"You'll soon be the strongest priest in Christendom," James called as I hefted a pile of planks onto my shoulder.

"Sure, he is already," shouted Maggie O'Keefe hanging ragged clothes on a makeshift washing line.

Being timber, it was too much of a risk to light fires for cooking inside the houses and so these were lit in front of each one. At night, the embers glowed red in the darkness and silhouettes huddled around them, squatting on the ground like primitive people, faces spectral in the flickering light. A black and white pile of ash with a thin coil of smoke greeted the occupants when they ventured out each morning, an image of something destroyed.

Though many still slept in tents, by the start of June when the cold night air crept around us, no one was sleeping outside exposed to the elements. I was thankful for that; they would have been in a poor state had they been out in the weather we experienced. It was not just the rain, we Irish were used to that, it was the north westerly wind that came with it, driving the drops into your face, stinging. There was no shelter from it for the men and women out digging. They turned their backs to it and laboured on.

The women had hard lives too, hauling water from the wells, cooking over open fires, washing clothes in the few tubs that Sanchez had supplied, trying to keep children happy and fed as well as doing what they could in the fields. Nothing was easy and there was no relief. Every day was the same grind, the same meagre rations, the same bleak view of that endless plain. I had already come to hate its starkness. There was no beauty in our natural surroundings, only the occasional flight of a buzzard or hawk, hovering, seeking its next meal. They seemed to be almost like vultures and I had to remind myself that they also were God's creatures.

One day in early June, Juan Sanchez asked me to come to the house. He took me to the store room and opened the door. "See, Father." He spread his hands wide. There were only a few sacks of grain and potatoes left and one barrel of salt meat. "This no be enough to last whole winter."

I felt a burst of anger. What did he expect me to do about it? "You'll need to lay in more provisions," I said carefully.

"Me? Me lay in provisions? I already fed you people for months."

"That's not quite true, Juan. We had a very large shipment of food sent by Canon Peter from Buenos Aires."

"And you must send for more."

"You invited people to come here. It is your responsibility to provide for them until they are able to provide for themselves."

He exploded. "My responsibility? *My* responsibility? I no ask three hundred peoples to come here! I never make any promises. I knew it would be hard."

"Whose fault is it?" I struggled to keep my own voice calm. I wanted to shout, to tell him what these people had already endured, on the boat, in Buenos Aires, the lies, the broken promises.

"I not know. The immigration people, I think, maybe the agents who brought them from Ireland."

"Oh, they're definitely at fault, there's no doubt about that." I looked at him and he stared back with silent hostility. "This will get us nowhere, Juan. This is a problem that you and I have to solve. I must go to Bahia Blanca to telegraph Canon Peter again for more food. Is there anything else we can do?"

He shook his head. I knew he was not an evil man. He wanted to improve our lot but he was overwhelmed by the scale of the problem, the huge number of people, the drain on his resources. Far from being the expansion of his empire he had hoped for, this could ruin him.

A picture came to me of my grandfather, huddled in an armchair, thin wisps of grey hair streaking his head, who every time we saw him would tell us about the famine of the 1840s. It haunted him, the bodies lying in the street, the gaunt faces, the skeletal frames and he told anyone who would listen. I felt a chill of fear; I must prevent that happening here. *The fishing kept us alive*, he would always conclude, nodding his head slowly to confirm it.

I faced Sanchez again. "Is there any fishing from Bahia Blanca?"

He looked up surprised. "Some … not much but plenty fish in sea and, how you say, crust … selfish."

"Shellfish." I corrected him absent-mindedly "We could catch fish then – I know it's a way to the sea but it's a thought."

"You need boat. I no have boat."

"We could buy one perhaps."

"More money! Father, I not have money to buy boat for you." Exasperation was in every slow word.

"Maybe Canon Peter would send money. I'll see what a boat costs when I go to Bahia Blanca."

He looked doubtful but as long as it was not costing him money, he did not oppose the idea. I was on a mission again, initially to get more food and money and then to try to establish another source of nourishment and, perhaps eventually, income. I needed to be cautious as raising expectations was to be avoided. My casual enquiries found that the brothers Frank and Mike Keenan, from an area fairly close to Cork, used to fish but the boat had been damaged and they could not afford the repair. I invited them to come with me when I went into Bahia Blanca a couple of days later.

When we arrived, after trudging the long fifteen miles, I suggested they go to the harbour and see what kind of fishing there was. I went to the Post Office to telegraph father Peter and to the bank. There was money sent by Canon Peter still in the account. I suspected it would not be enough to buy a boat but my busy mind was seeking a way round that.

When I met the brothers, they seemed more cheerful than any of our number had for several months. "There's fishing right enough, not many boats and all quite small but there was one landing a good catch," they said as they exchanged excited glances.

"We couldn't find a soul who could speak English and tell us what fish they were landing but there were fellas on the shore bidding for it and it looked good. About a foot long, nice shape, something like a pollock I'd say."

"Were there any boats for sale?"

"Not that we saw. We need to find someone who can speak English."

"Come on then. Let's do that." We strode back to the harbour and looked around to see if we could find any kind of official who might speak English. There seemed to be no one about but the quay was spread with the usual trappings of a fishing port: lobster or crab pots, nets heaped up and the unmistakable smell of the sea that reminded me of my home. Even the gulls were quiet, gliding smoothly through the air, waiting for the next boat to come in to feast off the scraps. I walked purposefully to a small shed on the quay to dismiss those homesick thoughts and I knocked on the door.

"Adelante!" a voice shouted from within. We opened the door to find a rotund man, probably in his forties, sitting at a desk. He was picking his teeth with the sharpened end of a matchstick.

"You speak English?" I ventured.

He smiled. "A leetle."

I spoke slowly and clearly to help the communication. "We would like to know if there is a boat for sale for fishing."

He lowered the matchstick and thought for a minute. "No … but there may be. One of the fishermen is old and wants to stop. Maybe he sell boat."

"Where would we find him?"

"You come." He hoisted himself up from the chair, took a jacket from a hook behind the door and ushered us out of the shed, locking the door behind us. We followed him along the quay, his feet splayed wide with his bulk, to a larger shed, and he pushed open the door. "Carlos," he shouted and shook hands with each of the three fishermen inside. The third was the elderly Carlos, a wizened but wiry man with white hair. He stood up and smiled, the few yellow teeth he still owned projecting forward at the front of his mouth.

The harbour master and he had a conversation, speaking rapidly in Spanish while we stood and wondered what was being said. Finally, he turned to us. "Carlos interested in selling his boat and nets, pots, other equipment if price is right."

"How much would he want?" There was another rapid conversation and the harbour master again turned to us.

"He wants 30,000 pesos." The harbour master saw me trying to calculate that and smiled. "About 330 United States dollars."

That was well out of our range. "Would he be willing to negotiate? We cannot afford that."

The harbour master consulted Carlos who put his head on one side and then said something to his fellow fishermen. One shrugged and spread his hands, the other I think gave a figure which when translated was still too much. I managed to get agreement on 25,000 pesos, just under 280 US dollars. That was still too much but I had another plan. I explained to the harbour master that I would like to pay Carlos 15,000 pesos now and that Frank and Mike would pay him something each week when they had landed a catch. Again, after translation, he nodded.

"Now I need to discuss this with my companions before we finalise the deal. Can I find Carlos here tomorrow morning early, say eight o'clock?"

That was agreed and, as we were leaving, Frank asked the harbour master about the fish they had seen landed. "Ah … whitemouth croaker, I think, a delicious fish," he said holding his index finger and thumb together and making a kissing sound as he put them to his lips. "You can catch plenty shellfish and shrimps also – they jump in the pots and the nets," he chuckled.

Outside, the afternoon was waning into evening, the brittle aquamarine of the winter sky cracking with amber, and I suggested we find a cheap boarding house for the night. After a very basic supper, I leaned forward conspiratorially and explained my thinking. "We will use the money we have in the account from Canon Peter's fund-raising to buy the boat and equipment. If you two are willing, you will live here in Bahia Blanca and become fishermen. You will have to pay Carlos something each week and you will have to supply us at La Viticola with fish. We can probably send someone on a horse to collect it on a set day each week, say Thursday. If that is not possible, you could salt it and put it in barrels so we can collect it in the cart maybe once a month. There's plenty of salt to be had … you just need to look around the shoreline."

Mike was nervous. "Sure, it's a big responsibility. If we're not able to catch enough fish, we'll never pay Carlos, supply you at La Viticola and make enough to live on."

Frank was more optimistic. "What do we have at La Viticola? There's not enough for all of us to live on and probably won't be for years. This way, it will be two less mouths to feed and we'll be helping by supplying food."

In the end they agreed and the following morning we returned to the quay. We shook on the deal and took Carlos to the bank where, after much explanation, he was able to open an account to which the money was transferred. He was of course sceptical. Money he could not see did not exist in his view but, eventually, the clerk persuaded him it was safer than keeping such a sum at home where it might be stolen.

The two brothers were ebullient and I suggested they should find somewhere to live. They, however, said they would sleep in the shed on the quay until they had sold enough fish and could pay for a small place. They set off in good spirits for La Viticola to collect their belongings and would return to Bahia Blanca as soon as possible. I would follow the next day but I had more to do. I needed to find the office which dealt with employment.

Eventually I found it, just off the main street. It was a small dingy office with an officious clerk whose moustache seemed to occupy most of his face. As I made my request, I wished I had learnt Spanish and wondered how I should set about that. Fortunately, the clerk spoke good English. No doubt, he had been recruited for that reason as several Irish immigrants had come to Bahia Blanca in past decades. He listened silently to my explanation of the community at La Viticola.

"I need to find work for more of our people. We simply cannot support so many. It will take years to develop the farms to a point where they can provide for that number."

The clerk nodded and began to shuffle through cards in a box. "Women or men?" he asked, his face blank.

"Mainly men but there could be some women. If women come, they will have husbands and some may have children."

He took out a batch of cards and laid them on the desk. "Here is one for a woman in a big house. There may be work for a man too. And this one is for two men to work on a farm just outside Bahia Blanca."

He wrote those addresses on paper together with some more. I was disappointed. I needed to find places for perhaps fifty but he said I should ask at likely places. "We no have all work here ... some no tell us."

I thanked him and turned to leave when he said, "There is of course work at Balcarce, not far from Mar del Plata. Is maybe 100 kilometres from here."

"What kind of work?"

"Farms. They give you the land and you pay over time."

"That's what they said would happen at La Viticola but it didn't. Nothing was ready."

"I know. This place is much prepared. Has been running for many years."

I thanked him and tramped around the town visiting the addresses he had given me. I asked in boarding houses, workshops and picked up a few more vacancies, adding the addresses to the list. I came away from Bahia Blanca with a few possibilities but nothing like the number we needed.

There was a degree of excitement back at La Viticola generated by the return of Frank and Mike and the account they gave but, as usual, there was some resentment. It was Arthur again, this time at the head of a group of men who stood behind him, scowling.

"Why them?" he demanded as soon as he saw me.

"Because they have been fishermen and know what they are doing. We will all benefit from the fish they catch. It will be an important addition to our diet."

"They'll be living it up down there then while we're slaving here."

"They'll not be living it up, Arthur. They'll be working hard, paying off the debt and supplying us with fish. They'll not have time for fun and games." I was angry and I let him know it. "What would you do? What's your suggestion for keeping all these people alive?"

"But that was our money. 'Twas given to help everyone, not just two." Behind him, the men stirred, muttering agreement.

"I've explained. We will get a weekly supply of fresh fish which will be an important part of our diet."

"And what happens if they don't catch anything? Wouldn't it have been better to spend that money on some decent food?"

"There's plenty of fish in the sea but if it doesn't work out, we'll sell the boat again and we'll have the money. If we had spent it on food, what would we do when that food was gone? This way, we have a continual supply."

"That's if they keep their side of the bargain." It was one of the others – Tom O'Mahony – a small, usually quiet man in his forties who had a very attractive young wife called Kate.

"I see no reason at all why they would not. If they don't, we'll claim the boat back again and sell it." I paused. "I can see you're not happy with the decision to buy the boat but I have to do something to keep people alive. The poor food we have every day is going to produce weakness and, if we're not careful, death. I must do something to prevent that."

"It's you who must make all the decisions then?" Arthur's voice was a growl and he stared directly into my eyes. His jaw was clamped tight shut and the muscles in his cheeks twitched.

As they walked away, I was left with a sense of guilt that I had not called a meeting but I had not wanted to raise hopes. Arthur's accusation prompted me to call the adults together in three groups to explain what I had arranged in Bahia Blanca and to tell them of the few opportunities I had found there. A small number, two families with children and four single men, thirteen in all, decided to go and try their luck there. I gave them the addresses, explaining that they could ask someone for directions as I knew they may not be able to read. Two days later, that small group left us, following the Keenan brothers to seek their futures in the town.

Those few were followed by twenty others who decided to try their luck at Balcarce, the place the clerk had told me about. They would have to walk there. Juan Sanchez allowed Faustino to take their belongings and the women and children in the ox cart some of the way but it would still be a long walk.

With a heavy heart and a deep sense of failure, I watched them leave along the track to the station. I had wanted to build a community here for everyone who travelled on that train from Buenos Aires. That dream was evaporating.

What would a new employer see? Tired and hungry people in shabby clothes and disintegrating boots. I barely noticed such things any more. There was little money left after the boat purchase, but I gave them some and made sure they left with enough food for the first two days at least. "God be with you," I said to each one. I stood at the entrance to the homestead and watched the figures grow smaller, disappearing from sight.

My steps were heavy as I trudged back towards my hut. I needed to spend time with my prayer book and collect my thoughts but that was not to be. Mary McCarthy was waiting for me by her house, her face creased with worry. She came forward as I approached. "Oh Father, 'tis my Ellen … she's sick. Would you come and see her? I don't know what's wrong."

The little girl was lying on the straw mattress, pale and limp. Her eyes were closed but she opened them as I approached the bed. They looked sickly. She coughed, a weak cough with no energy behind it. I crouched down beside her. "I hear you're not well, Ellen."

"I feel tired, Father."

I laid my hand on her forehead. It was burning. "I think you have a fever. You rest and your mammy will take good care of you." I signalled to Mary to join me outside. "How long has she been like this?"

"It started yesterday, Father."

"We must get her good, nutritious food. Go and get eggs and milk and make an egg custard. If we have sugar, put some in. She needs energy to fight this … whatever it is."

Mary walked hurriedly to the store room and I turned away. I feared that little Ellen might be the first of many. If whatever she had was contagious, it could run through our community like a wild fire. I prayed that would not happen. It didn't … not then and not in that way.

In the evening, I went back to Mary's house. She had been given candles by Signora Sanchez so she could comfort Ellen if she woke in the night. The flickering yellow light looked warm on the timber of the walls, though shadows of the roof beams flitted like spirits on the ceiling. Ellen was lying on the bed, still, apart from the slightest movement of her chest. Her breaths were short and rasping.

"Is she any better?" I whispered.

"Not really, Father."

Mary's husband, Finbar, had stood when I entered. His head was lowered slightly and he looked at me. I was not sure whether it was the candlelight on his eyes that made them look fierce or whether he was angry. "Why, Father?" he said simply. "Why must we be punished like this?"

"It's not a punishment, Finbar. 'Tis simply nature. We must trust in God to bring her through it."

There was the faintest "Huh" and he left the house, his boots loud on the wooden floor. I went and crouched beside Ellen. So young, I thought, so innocent. Why should she have to suffer? The thought was dangerous for a priest. We were taught that suffering is part of the human condition and that the reward for enduring it would come in heaven. I was no longer sure about that. Ellen's face was paler, more so than earlier, and she was so thin. She should not have been so thin. This was a clear sign of the inadequate diet we were enduring and the very young had no reserves to sustain them. How could she grow strong on the meagre rations we gave each person?

Ellen opened her eyes, not wide but enough to see me crouched beside her. "Hello," I whispered, smiling at her.

"Hello, Father." Her voice was faint. Had I not been so close, I may not have heard her.

"How are you feeling now?"

There was a pause before she replied. "I'm worried, Father."

"Sure, you mustn't worry. What are you worrying about?"

"Am I going to die?"

Her directness jolted me. "I don't think so, but 'tis only God knows when each of us has had our time on this Earth."

She thought for a minute. "Father, if I die, will I go to heaven?"

"You will, of course. I put my hand on her head. Sure, why would you not go to Heaven? You've not done wrong and God loves children. Didn't Jesus himself say that the children should be brought to him and that if we want to go to heaven, we must become like children? When it is your time, you'll go there, but it probably won't be for many years yet."

Back then, I had not realised how the dying, even young children, know they are slipping away, often sooner than those around them. I smoothed her hair gently. "I'm afraid, Father," she said softly.

"What are you afraid of?"

"When I die, I won't know how to get to heaven. I don't know the way."

"Ellen, darling, you don't need to worry about that. God will send his angels to show you the way and carry you there safely."

"But … but I've never seen an angel."

I chuckled. "Of course you haven't – none of us have. But sometimes you can feel them. Close your eyes now and concentrate and you may feel your guardian angel above your head." I was sure then that it was permissible for me to pretend, to give that little girl some comfort in her final hours but I've often wondered since whether the deception I practised on her was sinful. When her eyes were closed, I moved my position and blew very softly on her fair curls. One moved just the slightest amount. "Did you feel anything?" I whispered.

She opened her eyes again and the faintest smile crossed her face. "I felt my hair move. I think the angel flew over my head."

"That's probably right. Your guardian angel would be around your head."

"But I don't feel him all the time."

"Ah no. Most of the time, he won't be close enough but he'll be there nonetheless."

She closed her eyes again but I did not repeat the deception and I stood to let her rest. Mary followed me outside where Finbar was leaning against the wall. "I think I need to give her the last rites."

Light from the dying fire burned red in Finbar's eyes. "I asked you back then, Father, why would he take a little girl like Ellen?"

"I don't know, Finbar, why some die so young and others live to a great age. I cannot know the workings of God. All I can say is that heaven can't wait for those God loves. Ellen is loved more than any of us can understand."

He stayed where he was, smouldering against the wall. I knew my answer was inadequate but what else could I say? I was trying to give him some comfort. Mary had glided back into the house and we stood in silence. I felt my relative youth then as I had felt it on the ship when we had buried old John and the others at sea. "Will you pray with me?"

He shrugged but bowed his head just a little. "Dear Father, bless this little child Ellen and bring about a speedy end to her suffering. Bless your servants, Mary and Finbar, and give them the strength to bear whatever may come to pass. We trust in your great mercy and your infinite wisdom and know that Ellen will be safe in your care and the care of your angels. In nomine Patris, Filii et Spiritu Sanctus." We crossed ourselves and stood again in silence.

The door opened and Mary joined us. I could tell instantly that something was not right. Her face, in the glow from the fire, looked hollow, as if she had become a spectre. "Will you come Father. I think ... I think ..."

I went into the house, followed by Mary and Finbar. I did not have to go close to Ellen to know that she had departed; I could feel it instantly, the stillness unmistakeable. I did go to her though and crouched once more beside the bed. Her eyes were closed and I felt her little neck for a pulse even though I knew I would find none. I started to say the prayers for the dead, speaking softly the Latin words and the English version so Mary and Finbar would understand. I could hear Mary sobbing behind me. Finbar made no sound.

When I had finished, I stood up. "Her suffering is over. She is with God now." I could feel tears starting in my eyes and was thankful that Mary had plunged her face into Finbar's shoulder. "I will leave you now and ask the women to prepare Ellen's body."

But before doing so, I walked away from the houses along the track that lead to the railway station where I knew I could be alone. Then I let my tears flow. "What do you want from us?" My voice was hoarse. I looked up to the grey sky above and shook the tears away. I was angry. How could this be a loving God? How could he allow such suffering?

In the morning, Ellen was brought outside the house so everyone could file past and pay their respects. Mary and Finbar stood silently either side of her and, as each person passed, he or she whispered, "I'm sorry for your trouble." When the long file had passed, I draped a sheet over her, an old one donated by Signora Sanchez, before Finbar, James, Will and Arthur lifted the board on which she lay onto their shoulders. The procession filed away from the house to the patch of land that I had hurriedly consecrated that morning as our graveyard. Two men had dug a grave and a third had made a rough cross.

After the prayers, she was lowered slowly into the grave. Finbar picked up a fistful of soil and let it fall on her tiny body. "I'm sorry," he said gruffly, "for bringing you to this terrible place, far away from our homeland."

I laid my hand on his arm. "You're not to blame, Finbar. You did what you thought was best." I could say no more. Suddenly, Mary's knees buckled and she sank upon the ground, a wail coming from her that froze my blood. Her body was convulsed with huge sobs and other women started to keen, the sound filling the air in that desolate place, blown away by the wind, carried God knows where.

# CHAPTER 9

## ATRAPADITA

**Rose**

I felt his hands on me … one creep up my chemise and settle on my breast. Drowsily, I put my own hand on it to move it away but it remained there, massaging me. I felt my nipple harden. And then his hand was on my thigh, travelling upwards and resting between my legs.

"Tu cuerpo es tan hermoso." The hoarse breath of his voice startled me from my stupor. When I opened my eyes, it was not a dream … it was not James … it was Ramirez. I tried to wriggle away from him but his weight was on me. He held my arms down on the bed and laughed. "You are awake now." Dimly I realised that my underwear had been removed – by Molly or by him, I did not know.

"What are you doing? Leave me alone!" I gasped. I could hardly struggle I was so drowsy still and the attempts I made seemed to excite him more.

"I wait a long week for this and now I fuck you."

One hand went to my chin which he pushed down hard and the other was between my legs. I felt a stab of pain there and his member entering me. I gasped but could not cry out. I lay in fear as he pushed and withdrew, pushed and withdrew, heaving and gasping. There was a faint smell of sweat from him. I kept my eyes tightly closed … I could not look at him. And then he gave a big heave and shuddered.

He was panting. "I see you again soon." I looked from half-closed eyes as he put on his trousers. He did not look back as he walked to the door and left.

I lay still. I could not move. Was this a nightmare? Would I wake? In my head I pleaded that it had not been real. Even in my drunken state I felt the pain of the violation, the physical pain and the mental horror. I heard the door open again and instantly I was more alert, sitting up. It was Molly.

"Now then. How was that? Not so bad, was it?"

She had a bowl of water with her and she instructed me to lie down while she washed me down below. I needed to ask her. "Molly … did you know … did you know that would happen?"

"Of course. What did you think was going to happen when I brought you in here? Did you not realise what the dice game was about?" She finished washing me and dried me with a towel. "There now, you can go back to your own bed now."

I felt a sob forming and I tried to keep it out of my voice. "But Molly, he … he put his thing in me."

She gave a short, harsh laugh. "That's right – you're a whore now just like the rest of us. Not so high and mighty now, are you? Not such a good little girl doing what the nuns want, eh?" There was no sympathy at all in her voice, just a hard satisfaction in telling me what I was. When she pulled the sheet off the bed, I noticed it was stained with blood. She saw me staring at it. "Yep, that's yours, but don't worry, that only happens the first time."

She left the room. I gathered up my clothes and climbed the stairs wearily to our own room where I slumped on the bed. I felt like crying but I could not. It was as if my insides had been frozen. Slowly, I lifted the sheet and covered myself with it. I heard Molly come in and go to bed. I said nothing and turned to face the wall so she could not see me. My mother's face filled my mind but her eyes were hard, seeming to hold no sympathy; they became Molly's eyes, mocking, callous. You have only yourself to blame, they seemed to say. Then I could not help it. I tried to stifle them but sobs escaped.

They came from deep inside me, seeming to well up and shake me uncontrollably.

"For God's sake, stop that noise, will you? What's wrong with you? You're a woman now … you should be pleased."

The harshness of her voice struck me like a slap across the face and I held my body rigid, determined to make no sound. It is possible to cry silently, to cry inside. I learnt that then. I did not sleep but gradually as the drink wore off, I was able to think. Everything I had tried to deny over the last week now fell into place, the visiting 'gentlemen' as they called them, the way the other girls disappeared not once but several times in the evening, the way Ma had felt my body and talked about needing more flesh, the things she said about some gentlemen liking a shy girl, not a hard bitch like Molly. And she *was* a hard bitch, I had just discovered that.

Why did she hate me? Was it because she saw me as a goody-goody, like a teacher's pet? Was it because she was jealous of me? I remembered the conversation I had overheard that day I arrived, how she thought Ma had made a mistake. Well, she had made a mistake. I was not going to stay here to be a prostitute. When I thought of that dice game, I was filled with anger. They had rolled dice to see who would have me first. What had Calvo said? "You first and me second." He thought he would be next, then.

I decided I would leave this place. I would pack my bag and leave before they had risen. I had no idea where I would go but I'd worry about that when I got away. I think then I must have slept a little but I woke early and the nightmare returned. Molly was sleeping, a wheezing sound accompanying each outward breath. As quietly as I could, I put my things – only *my* things – into my big bag. I put on the dress that I had worn on the boat over and I crept down the two flights of stairs.

Reaching the big front door, I turned the key to unlock it. It made quite a clunk. I drew back the bolts, which again I could not do silently, and lifted the latch, the final barrier to my freedom.

"Where d'you think you're goin'?"

I spun round, startled. It was Michael. "I'm … I'm leaving this place. I'm not working here any longer."

He grinned at me and walked forward. I realised that I had not heard him speak before. His voice was thick and rounded, his words slightly slurred. "No … you're not to leave. Ma said so. She said I have to stop ya."

He was standing right next to me now, his hand on the door. "I'm sure Ma would not want me to stay … you'll let me out, won't you?"

The grin appeared again and he shook his head. "You're staying." Suddenly, his face scrunched with malice and he grabbed my arm, pulling me away from the door with such force I nearly fell. He slammed the bolts home and turned the key in the lock. It was only then that I realised how powerfully he was built, a hulk of a man, and I realised that my thoughts about him being dangerous were absolutely right. He was an uncontrollable animal.

"Alright. If that's how you want it. I'll speak to Ma when she's up and then I'll leave." I marched through to the kitchen and sat down at the big table, quivering with a strange combination of fear and anger. Michael stood leaning against the dresser, a leering grin on his face. A couple of times he stood up and walked slowly around the table as if stalking me. I kept my eyes on him, ready to jump up if he tried anything and, when he passed behind me out of my sight, I tensed with fear.

We both waited until Ma's sleepy steps brought her flopping into the kitchen in slippers. She looked from one to the other of us and then at my bag and coat beside me on the floor. "Thank you, Michael, I'll manage it from here." He looked disappointed. "Go along now … I'll call if I need you." With another leer at me, he sloped off to do his jobs outside.

I had stood up when Ma came in the kitchen. "That man stopped me leaving this morning but I am leaving. How could you do that to me?"

She turned to me and smiled. "And where will you go?"

"I don't care as long as it's away from here."

"The city can be a dangerous place for a young girl on her own."

"And this place is not dangerous to me, I suppose?"

"No, 'tis not. For God's sake, Rose, what happened last night is what happens to women every night of their lives. That's our lot, to keep the menfolk happy, give them relief. It just means that now you're a woman. You're one of us." She paused, looking at me with her shrewd eyes, no doubt trying to work out if she could convince me. "Oh, I know the first time is hard, it hurts, does it not? But you'll not feel a thing after a few more. Just relax, enjoy the attention and the money you're earning."

"Doesn't it worry you that it's a sin … to do that outside of marriage? You've ruined me."

She put her cup on the table slowly. "You've a lot to learn Rose. Making some vows and having a priest shake holy water on you makes a difference, does it? A husband still wants the same, to stick his dick into you."

I flinched at the crudity. "I am not going to allow myself to be used like that … like a cow being serviced by the bull."

She laughed briefly without humour. "That's a nice image. I suppose that's what it is, except we do what we can to avoid pregnancy. Did Signor Ramirez use a rubber?" I stared at her blankly. "We ask our gentlemen to use a rubber so the girls don't get pregnant." I opened my mouth but no words came. I did not know what she was talking about. She smiled at me pityingly. "You've a lot to learn, Rose, but you're bright and you'll soon get the hang of things. A rubber is a tube that we put on the man's dick so when he releases his juices, they don't stay inside you … then you don't get pregnant."

The fear of pregnancy loomed in front of me, the condemnation of everyone for the girl who became pregnant outside of marriage, the way they'd disappear suddenly and you'd hear they had been taken to a Magdalen laundry. "I … I don't know …" Tears were starting in my eyes and the anger that had kept me together evaporated, leaving only fear.

"Well, I think we'll have to show you a few things. I'll get the girls to do so. Now you're properly one of us, you need to know all the secrets of the trade."

"I am not staying here." I wanted to sound firm, determined, in control but I could hear my own voice wavering.

"I asked you where you'll go."

"Anywhere. I'll go to the convent."

She laughed. "The convent? You think they'll take you in when they find out where you've been for the last week?"

"I'll find somewhere else."

"Oh, you will. Probably another house where the kind of man is a good deal rougher, where they pay less, where they don't care about looks, they just want to feck you and there's a queue of sailors or such like waiting for their turn. Is that what you'd like?"

"I'll get a proper job in service. Not all the places in the city can be like this."

She filled the kettle and set it on the range. "Let me tell you about a girl from another house who decided to leave. She was reported for stealing from the house. The police arrested her and slung her in jail where the officers took their pleasure in turns." She turned to me a face that was hard, her eyes steely. "Signor Ramirez likes you. He would not want you to leave so soon. I think he may find it convenient to have you arrested and put in jail where he could have his pleasure for nothing … and then let his men have theirs."

I was horrified as she knew I would be. "But … but … you can't do this! I've never stolen anything in my life."

"You're a long way from Ireland now, Rose. What you have been counts for nothing. The magistrates just see another poor immigrant who would steal because they all do. Oh, we're at the bottom of the heap you know, to be used as they see fit. You'd never last a minute out there. Better to be here where we can look after you, where there's dancing some evenings and nice gentlemen who'll maybe give you expensive gifts if you please them … no worries about where your next meal is coming from. And all you have to do is give those men a little pleasure. You just lie back, open your legs and let them do their business. 'Tis them that are the victims, you know … governed by an insatiable need to have sex. Poor bastards."

She said nothing for a while and I sat down, my mind a mess. She was not right but I had to recognise she had the power. Ramirez, Chief Superintendent of Police. Would he really have me arrested and use me as she described? I thought of the line of his moustache, like a scar, the eyes always flicking around taking everything in, the force of him pumping inside me. Oh yes, he was capable of anything.

Ma sat at the table. She reached her hand out and placed it on mine. "Rose, I promise you, 'twill become easier each day and I'll pay you good money at the end of each month. You'll be able to send a good bit home and you needn't tell your mother how you earned it. You stay in your room tonight and I'll have Maggie talk with you about things. Now, you must eat something."

I couldn't eat but I did sip some tea. I then trudged back up to the room and unpacked my bag, changing into the day dress I had made for myself. It was Sunday but I couldn't face church. When I had a moment to myself, I knelt by my bed and prayed … for forgiveness. I had sinned even though unwillingly and my fear of the city would lead me to sin again and again, every day probably. What had I done to deserve this? That priest on the boat said that God determined where we should be, what we should do. I had been brought, he said, to give comfort to old John in his dying days. How could God have chosen this life for me … the life of a whore?

Ma had said I was a long way from Ireland. I felt it then, an unconquerable distance, a vast ocean to cross. It was not the physical distance that caused the feeling of sickness but the change in my life. I thought of the parish in which I had grown up, not really part of Cork city, a village where I knew everyone and they knew me, where there were trees and sunlight in summer, where I strolled through a carefree childhood. Even when I started working for Miss O'Leary at fourteen, there was safety, my family not far away, familiar things, ways one lived and ways one did not. And I had abandoned all that for this. Tears streaked my cheeks and I lay curled on my bed for a long time.

In the afternoon, Maggie took me into one of the rooms and started showing me where the rubbers were kept and the other 'tools of the trade' as she called them. I was reluctant, frosty, distant but she persevered with a pleasant smile. She took a rubber and showed me how to put it on the neck of a wine bottle. She then made me try. As I stretched it to go over, it leapt from my hands and flew across the floor. I laughed, I couldn't help it. Maggie laughed too and then I couldn't keep up the coldness towards her. She talked to me about how to please a man, how to make him feel special, how to make sure he had a good conclusion.

I listened without saying anything. Maggie realised I had gone quiet. "Are you alright, Rose?"

I shook my head. "No … this is not the life I want." I tried to stop tears squeezing from my eyes but could not.

Maggie gently brushed a tear from my cheek with her fingers and then her arms were around me. "Ah come now, Rose. You mustn't cry. We all felt the same way at first but … you get used to it and then you start to enjoy it. The rest of us do. You know the men think they have the power but it's us has that. We can play them along, make them beg even. We have good fun, we earn good money and one day, when our attraction is not as great, we'll be able to buy a house of our own and live as we want. You know, I've sent enough money home for Ma and Da to buy their own plot of land. Can you imagine that? No more rent to pay and a small farm to hand on to one of me brothers."

"But 'tis wrong, Maggie. 'Tis sinful."

"Ah yes. That's what they tell you. But look at the priests and the nuns. Sure, aren't they just frightened of the other sex? They do what they do because they're afraid of sex and they make everyone else afraid too. There's nothing to fear. Sure, didn't God create sex? So how can it be bad?" I was not convinced of course but I warmed to Maggie. She could be like an older sister. I felt that she would not dismiss me if I went to her unhappy as Molly would.

As Ma had said, I did jobs in the scullery that evening – washing the dishes and so on – before going to our room. Any thoughts I may have had of leaving were dispelled by the sight of Michael bringing a chair from one of the other attic rooms and placing it noisily opposite our door. His gave me his usual leering grin as he sat on it and folded his arms.

I would have liked to lock our door but there was no lock and besides Molly would have to get in later. I did not trust him and lay on my bed fully clothed for a long time. I summoned James's face to my mind. He was the only comfort I had, his lovely eyes, his boundless optimism. I could feel his arms around me but I did not allow the vision to touch me anywhere as he had done the previous night. I was always alert, too, for the sound of the door in case Michael were to enter. I cried a little when the thought crossed my mind that James would not want me now, a fallen woman. What decent man would? Eventually, exhaustion allowed sleep to overcome me.

Next day, Monday, there was a huge and pleasant surprise. Mid-morning, Ma found me where I was mending clothes and said I had a visitor waiting in the lounge. I approached the room cautiously. It was the room we had been shown into on that first day. I thought it was probably Ramirez, come back for more or maybe to make his peace. I peered around the open door and saw a woman in a dress. I knew instantly, even before she turned to face me, who it was.

I rushed forward and flung my arms around her. "Annie! Annie, I'm so glad to see you!"

She hugged me and then we released each other, looking into the other's eyes as if we had been apart for years. It felt like half a lifetime but had been only a little over a week. "Rose, you look troubled."

"I am, Annie. This place … I've got to get out but … but …" I could feel my lip quivering.

She hugged me again. "Ah now, 'tis not so bad, is it? Come and walk with me in the city."

"They'll not let me out. They're keeping me a prisoner. If I leave, the police will arrest me."

She smiled. "No, they won't. Not when you're with me." Suddenly she turned and called. "Ma, we're going for a walk for a bit. That'll be fine, won't it?"

Ma must have been listening at the door for she appeared almost straightaway. "Of course. Rose will need to be back for lunch, though. She needs feeding up … she's still a little on the skinny side." She laughed pleasantly.

The day was warm and there was no need for a coat. The sun hit me like a steel blade, making me feel exposed, vulnerable. Had I not been with Annie, I would have gone back inside. I couldn't believe that Ma had agreed so readily to this but soon I realised why. Michael was following us, making no attempt to stay hidden. Annie asked me why I kept turning round and I explained.

She turned to look at him. "God, he looks a right ape, doesn't he?"

"He's a bit simple but he's dangerous and very strong."

We walked on some way, passing the house where Annie worked. It looked dilapidated, paint peeling from the window frames and the front completely uncared for. It was quite close to the docks. We soon came to a small square with a church at one end. We sat on a bench in the sun while Michael lurked in the shadows of the buildings watching … watching. I felt everyone would be looking at me, condemnation in their eyes if not their mouths.

As soon as we sat down, the flood gates opened and I poured my misery out to Annie. She said nothing but held my hand. When I had at last subsided into sniffles, I thought to ask her how things were for her.

"Oh, you know … they're fine."

"The place you showed me looked a bit run down."

"Ah, 'tis right enough. We get a different class of customer there … closer to the docks … sailors, working men and the like."

"Customers?"

She looked at me surprised. "I'm a working girl too, you know. That's what that fella was doing on the docks … picking up young women and taking them to the whore houses."

"But Annie … and here's me going on about myself and you … you're in the same position!"

"Well, not quite. I know about Placer House. You have a better class of client there, probably not as many each day."

"There's more than one each day?"

"Of course … your face! You've been very sheltered in your life."

"I have. I can't do this Annie and nor should I have to. You shouldn't have to. We need to get away."

"Oh yes, and where would we go? We'd be picked up, taken to somewhere worse."

I looked at her. She seemed resigned to it. "Annie, you mustn't let this happen to you. You're too good for a life like this."

"Hah! Too good? Let me tell you about meself, Rose. I didn't have the safe upbringing that you had. Where I lived, all sorts of things happened. Women were beaten by husbands, daughters fecked by fathers and brothers."

I stared at her, horrified. "Fathers and brothers? Did that happen to you?"

"It did surely, lots of times from the age of about twelve. My Da said it was all I was fit for. I used to make a few pennies from the boys in our street and later the men."

"But how can you do that, day after day?"

"You get used to it and … the way to deal with it is to get them excited quickly. The sooner they come, the sooner they've gone. That's the secret."

"Twelve years old and having that happen. Annie …" I put my arm around her and held her tight. She shook me off, not roughly but she did not want sympathy.

"It started when I was ten actually … with the local priest."

"The priest?"

"You're sounding like an echo, Rose." She looked at the shock on my face and laughed. "Oh yes, the priest. A priest is just a man with his collar on back to front, no better than any other man. He said he wanted to help me be a good catholic so I had to go to the house once a week, then more often. It started with him touching me and kissing me and then he wanted me to touch him and then rub his scrawny dick 'til it became hard and he spurted. He told me I would be damned to hell if I told anyone. Then he would stick it in between my legs or in my mouth."

There was no anger in her voice, no sadness. How could she be so matter-of-fact about such horrors? We sat in silence for a while, the sun crawling slowly up the sky. "I'm sorry, Rose, you've not ended up where you want to be but you've a roof over your head, you've good food, you'll get paid well so you can send money home and all you have to do is switch off inside and spread your legs."

"I wish I could see it that easily."

"You will, Rose. That's the sadness of it, I suppose."

"I'll never be able to accept it, Annie. I'll be off the first opportunity I have. If I could find out where James has gone …"

She smiled at me with pity in her eyes. "James, yes. He'll make a fine husband but …"

She left the sentence unfinished and when the clock struck midday, we stood together without speaking and walked back the way we had come. As we were approaching Annie's house, I felt a clutch of fear in my stomach. "Will I see you again, Annie? I go to confession each Saturday afternoon – after lunch – and we could meet if you can …"

"We'll do that surely." She stopped and faced me. "Now, Rose, remember what I said. The sooner they've come, the sooner they've gone." We hugged each other and she went inside. I watched her walk down the side of the house and through a door near the back. My heart ached for her. What sort of childhood must it have been?

How could someone of such spirit tolerate such daily abuse? And the priest! What kind of priest could do such things to a young girl?

Michael was standing a little further down the street where we had just walked. I'd never get away while he was watching. I would need to convince Ma that I had accepted my lot so she wouldn't have him watch me all the time. I walked slowly back to Placer House, my mind pulled every which way. Annie seemed to think I was lucky to be there, a better class of customer, plenty of food, a roof over my head, money. I could not feel lucky at all. And then there was the feeling of stupidity. Had Annie realised straight away what kind of place it was I wondered?

That evening, I was required to be in the salon with the others. I tried to be pleasant, to cover up the anxiety and anger but I was in a state of fear. I felt like a lamb amongst wolves, wondering which one would be taking his pleasure and dreading the encounter. Tonight, there was no drink or whatever else they used to trick me and to deaden whatever pain I would suffer. Tonight, I had only my wits and they would be no protection.

Signor Calvo arrived a little later than the other men. There were only half a dozen again – Monday evening was not the most popular. Calvo approached me, his bald head catching the light from the candles as he leaned in towards me and slipped a hand around my waist. "Is nice to see you again Rose. We have a meeting later, I think."

I said nothing. There was nothing I could say. I felt like smacking the smile from his face and shouting at him to leave me alone. I felt, God forgive me, like fetching a knife from the kitchen and stabbing him if and when he came near me. But I knew I could not and when the time came, I walked with him up the stairs to the same room in which Ramirez had destroyed me. I tried to remember what Maggie and Annie had said. I tried to smile but think it was a grimace. When he started to undress me, I couldn't help it, I pulled away and ran to the other side of the bed. He chuckled and a look of delight flashed in his eyes. He came after me and I tried to push him away. We struggled for a while but he was far stronger and he held me around my body with one hand while undoing my dress with the other.

I realised then that my attempts to resist were inflaming his desire. He was enjoying it. For him it was a game, me resisting, he overcoming me. I stopped fighting then and let him undress me. I let his hands travel over my body, closing my eyes so I would not see the desire on his face. He picked me up and lay me on the bed where his mouth explored me. The quicker they come ... I could hear Annie's voice in my head, over and over, and I lay back. Suddenly, I remembered the rubber. "You must wear a rubber," I said to him, pushing him away.

He looked stunned and then angry. I leaned over to the bedside cabinet and took a rubber from the drawer. Please God it won't fly off round the room I thought as I stretched it over his huge member. Then I lay back and let him do his business.

"Was wonderful," he said between breaths as he lay beside me. "Thank you, Rose. We do it again soon."

I said nothing and was glad when he rolled off the bed and began dressing. I pulled on my chemise and went to the washstand to wipe myself. I wanted to soak in a bath. I felt dirty, used, cheap but, looking back, I did at least feel something. The worst thing is that, eventually, you feel nothing, as if inside you there is a block of ice.

# CHAPTER 10

# GIRO

**Patrick**

That winter was hard but our weekly supply of fish always raised spirits. I think it was one of the main reasons we survived and most stayed fairly healthy. We were still having to ration food so the fish was welcome, even when some weeks we could not send anyone to collect it and we had some salted from the barrel.

I went to Bahia Blanca myself to collect the first delivery. I quizzed the Keenans on how the fishing was going. "Oh, 'tis grand, Father," Mike said enthusiastically. "We're able to sell all we catch and we're out sev – six days a week."

I smiled. "You know, Mike, the Lord will forgive you if you have to work on Sunday, too. The men at Viticola dig the fields on Sunday and the women cook and clean."

Frank laughed at his brother. "It is a great thing to have the boat, Father. We're giving Carlos a sum each week and, even with that and the fish we put by for La Viticola, we'll be able to save a bit. We hope to rent a small house soon and, who knows, one day we'll maybe buy one."

"Hark at him." Mike jabbed Frank playfully in the ribs. "Let's take it one step at a time."

"We've just given you fish today, Father, but would you want some shrimp next week? We may get crab too but they fetch a good price so perhaps …"

"Give us whatever you can spare. As long as you can keep letting

144

us have some of your catch each week, the others will accept the arrangement." I wondered whether to say more and decided they may as well know. "One or two were not happy that I spent money on the boat and gave you two the chance to fish."

"Well, 'tis hard work. 'Tis not as if we're lazing in the sunshine all day."

I held up my hands. "I know, I know but … there'll always be some who resent, you know."

The brothers looked at each other. "Don't pay it any attention. They'll come round as soon as I take this fish back, I'm sure."

There was much excitement when I rode into our compound and opened the bag, releasing the fresh smell of the sea. I suggested we make a big fish stew so it would be easier to share and nothing would be wasted. The women who volunteered to make it sang as they stirred the big pots and children played nearby, sticking noses into the air and shouting, "Ah … lovely" in imitation of myself when I had first smelled the cooking. It was like a feast and we had singing and dancing afterwards as if it were Christmas. I was filled with joy and hope. This community of ours could be a success despite all the broken promises and hardships.

I watched with satisfaction as everyone ate and chattered. There had been precious little of such joy in our time so far and I revelled in the optimism that seemed to be everywhere. I noticed Arthur tucking in to a bowl of stew. For a moment, I felt like walking over to him and asking if he thought the boat was a good idea now but I dismissed the temptation. It would not have been becoming for a priest to crow over success.

That spirit of hope was revived each week when the fish came. It became a tradition to have a communal meal each Friday and that brought people together in a way that we had not been able to do thus far. As the days lengthened and the sun climbed in the sky, we set about sowing grain, vegetables and potatoes in the dug ground. The first few shoots of growth added to our hope, even though our supplies of food were diminishing. Each day would see many of us out in the fields checking for growth and praying there would be no setbacks.

It was time for me to make a start on teaching the children. My aim was to teach them all to read and write and to make sure they heard the Bible stories. If possible, I would teach them the Catechism too. Oh, I had grand plans for how our children would be well educated. I taught lessons in the large communal building. Of course, with nearly a hundred children, I had to have four classes as there was not room for more than twenty-five. I divided them by age but even the oldest couldn't read and write and we had very little in the way of books and paper.

At last, things were picking up and I thought our troubles were over. It is strange but as things improved, disagreements increased. That seems to be the way with people. When things are hard, we work together but as soon as things get better, we start to argue about who should have what. There was still plenty of work to do though. We would need more land dug, there were the animals to tend to, the growing fields to be weeded, the higher ground to be watered, vegetables to be nurtured.

Although each man had been assigned a portion of land, some strips had not by then been dug so there was still a need to share labour and what would be produced. The animals were all communal property and everyone had a share of eggs, milk and the dung to spread on the land. None of the animals was ready for slaughter and consumption so we did not have that to fight over. A dispute arose again over the watering of the higher ground. Big Pat and the others who had strips on it needed help with watering. It was a huge task to carry water in buckets from the wells to pour on the dry ground.

And the land was already becoming dry. The sun had not reached its hottest but the skies produced less and less rain. The lower ground was still moist enough from the rain that had fallen in the winter but the higher ground was, as we anticipated, drying out. Thankfully, it was not Arthur who started it this time; he did his share of the watering without complaint, keeping his word when he had swapped the strip with Big Pat. It was Mikey O'Riley, a wiry little man who was married with four children.

"Jasus, that's enough water for you lot up there," he shouted belligerently when he was asked to help. "We've got work to do on our plots. We need water as well."

"That was the arrangement," Big Pat said calmly.

"Arrangement? Arrangement? It may have been yours but it wasn't mine."

"Shut up, Mikey. We all agreed," Will said, picking up the bucket that Mikey had flung on the ground.

"Shut up yerself, ya long streak of piss."

I was not there to witness this but it degenerated from there with others joining in on one side or the other. It came to a drastic head when Mikey picked up a shovel and went at Will, intending to belt him with it. Apparently, Mikey was swearing and shouting threats but none of the men would tell me exactly what he said. As he lifted the shovel over his head to swing at Will, a huge hand grabbed his arm and he was held from behind. Big Pat lifted him off the ground with one arm and James took the shovel from him.

"Leave me go, you big ape!" yelled Mikey but Pat held him in a bear hug until the fight went out of him. He walked him back to the homestead, gripping his arm, followed by a large crowd of men. I was in the building teaching a class. Some of the men were still arguing and I could hear the rumpus approaching until it was right outside the building.

James came in. "Father, I'm sorry to interrupt, but we have a problem."

I followed him outside and saw the large crowd. I could sense the anger. James explained to me what had happened. Others tried to join in but I raised my hand and silenced them. Thank God for the respect that priests command. I could feel my heart racing but knew I had to maintain a calm exterior. I said a quick silent prayer for just a little of Solomon's wisdom.

Finally, I spoke and the restless scuffling of feet ceased. "In the beginning, after the fall from grace and the expulsion from the Garden of Eden, Cain slew his brother with the jawbone of an ass. We all carry the stain of that sin on our souls. It means that we are always vulnerable to the temptations the devil places in our hearts, the desire to have more than our neighbour, the desire to consider only our own needs. This place is as far from the Garden of Eden as one could get. It is a hard, unforgiving land, punished by a climate that in winter is too wet and in summer, too dry. That is the lot of humankind, cursed as we are by original sin. We have to struggle every day against it as you well know. Will we succeed? I don't know, but I am sure of one thing: if we do not work together, we will surely fail."

I paused. None of them looked me in the eye. I dropped my voice, a terrible sadness overwhelming me. "If the land on the higher ground is not watered, the crops will fail and we will not have enough food to last the next winter." Several of the men looked up at me with understanding and fear in their eyes. "I will therefore leave the children I am teaching and go out with a bucket and water the high ground myself. I will do so all day and every day that it is needed."

None of them looked me in the eye except one. Arthur's eyes held the slightest amusement as they met mine in passing.

I went into the building and told the children there would be no more lessons. I wish they had shown some regret but they dashed out shouting and cheering before I could change my mind. I took off my clerical collar and hung it on a nail on the wall. Outside, without another word nor a look at anyone, I strode towards the well. I did not turn back. There was only a few seconds pause and then I heard the scrape of boots on dry ground. There was no other sound. At the well, I hoisted the bucket and tipped the water into one I could carry. I lifted it and headed for the higher ground. Only when I had arrived, did I turn to Big Pat and ask him where to tip it.

All the rest of the day, there was a silent procession of men carrying water to the higher ground. At the end of the day, Big Pat and the others said that would be enough for several days. I called all the men to gather round. "Thank you for your labours today. I wish to tell you a story. There was a man who died and went to hell. He was shown a big room where everyone was seated around a sumptuous feast. Each person held a huge long spoon but could not put any food in his own mouth. They were starving and unhappy. He then went to heaven where he saw the same sort of room again with people seated around a huge feast, each holding a long spoon. They were feeding their neighbours and were gloriously happy. 'Why do they not feed themselves?' he asked. 'Because they cannot reach their own mouths with the spoons but they have learned that if they feed their neighbour, their neighbour will feed them.'

Again, Arthur's eyes held mine for a moment, amused, perhaps mocking. I said no more but turned to head back to the homestead. Mikey O'Riley stepped in front of me. "Forgive me Father."

I looked at him. He looked wretched, his eyes cast down and his brow creased with anxiety. He knew he had done wrong. "Mikey, I will hear your confession when you have asked forgiveness of those you have wronged."

He nodded and I saw him approach Big Pat who was walking slowly with the other men from the higher ground. They listened to him and then Big Pat put out his hand. What a lovely man. I stopped and waited until Mikey came back. He looked at me but said nothing. Then he dropped to his knees. "Father, forgive me for I have sinned against my brother and I am truly sorry."

It seemed rather staged and I wondered how genuine it was but I said the words of absolution and gave him a penance. I told him to stand. "You know, Mikey, you nearly did today what Cain did. Had you not been stopped, Will might be lying dead now waiting for burial and we would be waiting for the police to come and fling you in jail. How would that help your wife and children?"

He nodded. "I know, Father. I just got angry ... all the work to be done and ... you know."

"Oh, I do know, Mikey. I do know how we are being tested. But we must not fail."

Despite my doubts about Mikey's confession, I was feeling pleased with myself as I walked back to the homestead. God would judge him – no need for me to do so. James fell into step beside me. "That story you told, Father ... sure, you'd think in heaven God would provide a decent length of spoon."

I turned sharply to look at him, wondering if there was criticism in the remark. His eyes were twinkling, the corners of his mouth twitching. I laughed then and released the laughter from him. Later, I heard him telling others what he had said and how I had responded. As I knelt to pray that evening, I reflected on the goodness of some people, their ability to bring lightness when things became dark. Big Pat was a good man, James was a good man and there were many others who were equally good. They deserved success and I vowed I would make sure they gained it. But lurking somewhere in my mind was the look in Arthur's eyes, prompting the thought that I had been pompous, taking upon myself a role that was not properly that of a priest. It was hard to decide what was appropriate and what was not. "If I have been proud, Lord, I ask for forgiveness," I whispered.

Later, as I drifted towards sleep, she came to me again, her lovely soft hair brushing my face. She looked down at me and bent close to kiss me lightly on the cheek. It was the merest touch, like breath, and I reached up to put my arms around her. I sat up, shocked, ashamed. I was trembling. My vows! I had made my vows of celibacy and here I was, dreaming of the touch of a young woman. I tried to think of what they had told us in the seminary – how to deal with temptation. But that vision … it was exquisite, gentle, alluring.

And then I thought of James's smiling face. His trust, his support of me, his steady hard work. I thought of him lying in a hut not far away, feeling Rose's soft arms around him and here was I, entertaining the same vision. It felt like I had sinned against him as well as against Rose and my vows. It felt like a betrayal, especially of James. This was temptation. This was what it was like to taste the forbidden fruit but I knew the fault was mine. It was not Rose's doing. Her loveliness, her gentleness were not temptations. They were the gifts of God and not to be abused. The fault was in me.

I stood up quickly and lit a candle. Searching for my bible, I fumbled through the pages until I had found the Psalms. The page fell open at Psalm 31 and I read, whispering secretively when I reached verse three:

*Bow down thy ear to me: make haste to deliver me. Be thou unto me a God, a protector, and a house of refuge, to save me. For thou art my strength and my refuge; and for thy name's sake thou wilt lead me, and nourish me. Thou wilt bring me out of this snare, which they have hidden for me: for thou art my protector.*

*Into thy hands I commend my spirit: thou hast redeemed me, O Lord, the God of truth.*

I read on, mouthing the words, concentrating on them, dispelling the temptation from my mind. When I returned to my bed, I thought hard about the words of the Psalm, but I could feel that image, somewhere in the back of my mind, calling me, drawing me. I prayed until sleep at last ferried me to safety.

As the sun climbed higher each day and the eager youth of spring became the strong adult of summer, we watched the crops growing. We knew it wasn't going to be the best harvest as the soil was newly worked and the small amount of manure we had been able to put on it would not give the ground the fertility we hoped it would eventually gain. But it would be enough, we were sure, and our hopes for the future rose with the sun.

It was strange to celebrate Christmas in the heat of summer. The carols we loved seemed completely out of place here with their references to cold and snow. We sung them just the same and thought of the people we had left behind in Ireland, celebrating the birth of Christ, cosy by their firesides, out of the wind and rain. As none of our animals were yet ready for slaughter, Signor Sanchez donated a fine pig for our Christmas day meal. A couple of the men butchered it some days before. Many people gathered to look at it hanging by its hind legs on a rope from a beam in the barn, blood dripping into a pan beneath it. It was cooked over a big fire in front of our communal building. Children danced around it, enjoying the delicious smells filling their noses.

There was no working that day. In the morning, we had mass outside; communion as always took a long time with so many to receive but everyone was used to that. The pig had been set to roast early in the morning and the smells taunted us throughout the service. As I gave my sermon, I could see eyes straying in its direction. I kept my sermon short as a consequence; there was no competing with a roasting pig!

The Keenans had arrived on Christmas Eve, carrying a big bag of fish and shellfish. There were even a few crabs so we were going to have a huge feast. We ate dinner in the middle of the afternoon, mostly sitting on the ground though we had some benches to sit on. It had been agreed that the children would eat first. I said grace and they ran to line up, clutching plates and bowls, their eyes open wide with anticipation. There was a strange focus, a quietness that descended on them. The usual boisterous behaviour was replaced by solemnity. This was a meal that needed full concentration.

There was plenty of meat for everyone, fish and shellfish too. I looked around at the satisfied faces. Those who had come first had finished well before the last were served. "Father, come you now for your dinner," Maggie O'Keefe called.

"Have you all eaten?"

"Not yet, Father. We will now, after you."

I walked close to the table from which the women were serving. "Now, ladies, please serve yourselves and then I'll take some myself." Maggie started to protest but I held up my hand. "No, I insist. You have been working hard and you must eat. And don't serve seconds until you have finished your dinners."

They served each other and went to join their families. I helped myself and walked to the end of a bench beside James and Will. "God, sure that's the best meal I've had since leaving Ireland!" Will licked his lips loudly and rubbed his stomach.

"It is surely," James agreed. "If we ate like that every day, we'd be in heaven."

"But with a sensible size of spoon, I hope." I smiled and they laughed.

After the dinner there was singing and dancing. The men whom Signor Sanchez employed joined us, as did the maid, Paloma, and Sanchez's daughter, Gabriela. Both were never short of partners, though one of Sanchez's men seemed to spend much time with Paloma. Gabriela was the centre of attention, her dark hair flying out behind her as she spun, her eyes flashing with pleasure from her honey-skinned face and her laughter a rich, unreserved, siren song. But there was also something else that troubled me: she flirted, she was coquettish, her eyes were knowing. She was young, carefree, as yet unmarried and I hoped she would retain her zest for life without courting danger. I looked at the women from our community, in good spirits today to be sure and lifted by hope, but tired, drawn, bowed down with the burden of poverty.

Hope … it's a blessed thing. But how fragile it was, how soon it was to be dashed. It started the day after St Stephen's Day with a child vomiting. His mother said he had been suffering with diarrhoea since the day before. Another child fell ill with the same symptoms and then one of the women. Others followed – children, men, women. Within two days, we had some thirty souls ill. We gave them lots of water but they could not retain any solid food.

On the second day of illness, the face of the first child took on a bluish hue, his eyes were sunken and his skin cold to the touch. There was an unmistakable fishy odour to the vomit and his mother showed me the bowl of diarrhoea he had produced. It was a thick, pale substance like nothing I had seen before. I had to force myself to look at it; every fibre in my body wanted to recoil from the sight. The same symptoms were soon evident in the other sufferers.

I went to Signor Sanchez. "We must get a doctor. We have about thirty people suffering and they're getting weaker. Please send one of your men to Bahia Blanca for a doctor."

He threw up his hands. "And who will pay? Tell me that! Who … will … pay?"

"When you are facing God on the day of judgement, will you want to be told that you allowed people to die for the want of a doctor's fee?"

"Always the threats. Always God will punish. What will a doctor do? Charge a high fee and tell us they are ill? We know that."

Suddenly I felt tired. "A doctor might be able to give us medicine." Forcing the issue, however, seemed pointless. "I may have enough to pay him."

"May? And if not enough, who pays?" He thrust his jaw forward. "Me! More money." He turned and went into his house slamming the door behind him. I stood feeling foolish on the doorstep. I would need to send one or two men to Bahia Blanca and we would have to offer what money I had left to any doctor willing to come out. I heard a horse being walked from the stables at the rear of the house and then Faustino was mounting in front of me.

"I fetch doctor quick," he said.

"Bless you, Faustino. Could you please also go to the harbour and find the Keenan brothers? Ask them if they have been ill after eating the fish or the shellfish."

"I will." He spurred the horse which galloped out along the track.

I prayed then for his safe, speedy journey and for Signor Sanchez. I hated myself for having to be mean to him but I knew I had no choice. As I stood there, I could hear Sanchez shouting at his two children; I went round the corner of the building. He looked up at me. "I tell them they no be with your people until this sickness go." There was no point in arguing.

When I returned to our collection of huts, there was a group of men and women gathered in the morning sun by the communal building. They fell silent as I approached. Then one stepped forward: Arthur.

"Father, 'tis the fish surely that's caused this. You can smell it."

I knew behind the remark was a criticism of me. He may as well have said plainly that it was my doing, that I had brought this upon our community. "Just because there is a fishy smell, Arthur, does not mean the fish was responsible." As I said it, I hoped the doctor would confirm a different cause. "Signor Sanchez has sent Faustino to Bahia Blanca to fetch a doctor. Let's see what he says."

By the time Doctor Mendes arrived, the number who had fallen ill was closer to fifty. He looked at each of the patients, examining the first thoroughly but giving the others no more than a glance. I followed him, anxiety gnawing at me. Finally, he looked directly at me.

"There is no doubt. Is cholera. There are cases across much of World and we have cases here in Argentina."

"What has brought it here, Doctor?"

"Most likely, is in water you use."

"We draw water from wells. Surely they would be free from disease?"

He shook his head. "It may get in the water some way off and run here underground. You must dig new well, I think, long way from the present one."

My heart sank. "We had fish and shellfish brought to us from the sea at Bahia Blanca which we ate on Christmas Day. Some think that may be the cause."

"Is possible but … I think many people in Bahia Blanca eat fish and shellfish from the sea and we have had no cases there. Change the water supply."

I thanked him and took out my money bag to pay him. He looked around the collection of huts, the bedraggled people standing there and I saw for the first time what a stranger would see: poverty, want, despair. It was in the haunted eyes of those waiting for the diagnosis, in their gaunt frames, their ragged clothes.

He looked at me. "There is no charge, Father. Give them clean water and food when they can eat it. Other than that, you must pray."

I thanked him and called everyone who was there to gather round. The sun was falling but the air was still warm. I explained what the doctor had said. "For tonight, we must ask Signor Sanchez to use water from his well. Tomorrow we must find a site for new wells."

Arthur checked again about the fish but I repeated what Doctor Mendes had said.

The first death occurred on the following morning and, by evening, there had been five more. Fear now gripped the community. We had new wells to dig – Sanchez advised where we should try – and now we had graves to dig too. I knew there would be other deaths but I never imagined there would be so many. Every day brought more. It was the children who seemed most vulnerable, failing quickly, their small undernourished bodies offering little resistance to the unseen killer. I was saying the last rites several times a day and, on one day, twelve times.

All of us were sick and the digging of graves and the new wells was carried out by men who were weakened with illness and lack of nourishment for they could not keep food in their stomachs. The hollow eyes of the adults were wide with fear or cast down with sorrow and silence hung like a dark fog over us all until broken by the keening of women when another soul had departed a frail body.

I kept a record in my journal of the numbers we had lost. We had arrived in La Viticola with exactly three hundred people, of whom one hundred were children. Before the cholera descended on us, five children had gone with their parents to Bahia Blanca and, including the two Keenans, ten adults. In addition, twenty of our number had left for Balcarce of which seven were children. We had lost little Ellen and we were two hundred and sixty-four in number before the cholera. We lost fifty-eight children to cholera, leaving only thirty in our community. Forty adults succumbed to the illness leaving us with one hundred and sixty-six.

The cholera passed with the clean water from Sanchez's well and we hoped the new wells we dug would be free of contamination. I told the men digging them that whenever they reached water, they should call me. I would drink the water first. James protested. "Father, you should not do that. I'll do it."

"No James, no … I'm not risking anyone else."

"But Father, what becomes of us if you …?"

The question hung in the air. I smiled, touching my clerical collar. "I have special protection, James."

I drank the water from the first well when it was finished. It tasted cool and pure but so had the water from the other wells we had been using. "I'll drink some of this several times today and tomorrow. If I don't get ill, perhaps others will try it the day after – those who are strong and were not badly affected by the sickness before." After three days, we were confident the water was clear of contamination. We repeated the process with the other new well which was also clear.

In the cool of each evening, most of us gathered in the graveyard. I said prayers, tried to give comfort to the bereaved, but I felt my words were inadequate. It was the parents of the dead children that had the deepest sorrow. Such a cruel blow to take those short lives, lives that would never be lived. These parents would not see their children grow strong towards adulthood, they would not see them take sweethearts, be married, have children of their own. Each evening, I counted the crosses we had erected: ninety-nine including Ellen's, ninety-nine thorns of guilt on my head.

As I walked back from the graveyard to my hut, I saw the wheat swaying in the gentle breeze, the ears fattening and turning from green to gold. It seemed a bitter irony that the harvest would now be sufficient for those who remained.

# CHAPTER 11

## COLGADO

**Rose**

It's fear at first, fear of violence, fear of a strange place, fear of something worse happening. And then it's custom, routine. Maggie said it became enjoyment, a job with good money. I could never see it like that but the routine is a treadmill that you walk, your mind as closed as possible to the destruction of your inner self. It is like walking in a barren land, a flat, dry emptiness.

Within weeks, I was used to the routine: the drinks in the evening for the men, the visits to a room upstairs, on quiet nights, one or two but on busier nights, three or four. And always, whatever mask I wore, I was shrivelling inside, becoming numb, losing any feeling. With each day, I felt more worthless – that's all I'm fit for, I would say to myself, echoing Annie's da. Could I ever love a man now, I wondered? Could a man ever love me? Was there such a thing as love or was it just sex, the smell of sweat, the fumbling, the breathing, the cursing, the heaving flesh?

I could still see James, my sweet man, when I closed my eyes as I lay in bed after the evening's activity. His arms held me and his voice was soft in my ear. Kisses, velvet kisses, he would lay on my cheek, on my eyelids and I longed for him to be real, lying beside me. I allowed myself to believe he would come back as he had said. I told myself he need not know what had become of me and I fashioned a future where this nightmare present did not exist.

It was Lent – Easter was very late in 1889 – and I felt that I was in a kind of wilderness too, preparing for death, the death of my soul.

Shame was the result of eating the forbidden fruit in the Garden of Eden. As a child, I had understood the Tree of Knowledge to be about knowledge of good and evil. But now I realised it was more specific; it was the knowledge of sex, it was the awakening of desire, it was the shame that came with it.

Why was Eve shown as the temptress? Why did the serpent approach her first? It was, we were told, because women are weak, but they also have a power over men, the power to tempt with their bodies. How wrong can things be? Why should us women take the blame when it was the man's desire? I had done nothing to tempt Ramirez or Calvo or the others. If my looks, my hair were a temptation, they were given by God himself.

It was fear and routine then that kept me at Placer House though there were other attempts to reconcile me to the life. At the end of March, Ma called me into her little private sitting room. "Now, Rose, I can tell you what you've earned thus far. Come and see." She had a big ledger spread in front of her. My name was at the top of the page and then each day was listed with amounts against them. From where I stood, I could not of course read anything other than my name and I noticed she did not invite me to look closely. "Now, these are what the gentlemen are paying for you but of course I have to take off what it costs to run the house, provide drink, feed you and so on and so forth. I'm paying you 130 pesos a week, that is one pound. Now how is that?"

I looked at her. One pound a week was as much as my father earned. "Thank you." I did not know what else to say. I wanted to say I didn't want money earned the way it had been but I thought of Maggie and her sending enough money home to buy the farm.

"I'm sure I'll be paying you more when you become better at your job and then of course there may be gifts from the gentlemen." Her sly eyes looked keenly at my face. "Maybe not so bad now, is it?" It was bribery of course but I knew I had no choice. Ma would turn vicious in a flash if she thought she was going to lose the earnings I made and she would set Michael on me like a brute of a dog on a rabbit.

I said nothing so she went on briskly. "Now I imagine you'd like to send some money home. I'll give you a little now for your spending money and you can tell me how much you want to send home. I'll then arrange a postal order and you can write a letter to go with it. Of course, you may want to wait a bit but you have four pounds. That's a lot of money for a young girl to be earning. So, what would you like to do?"

I thought quickly. I'd rather send as much home as possible and get it out of her keeping. I did not trust her but I had to admit she seemed to be honest with the money. I thought I'd never see a penny. "I'd like to send three pounds ten shillings home and I'll just have a couple of shillings for spending."

"That's very good of you, Rose. Your parents will be pleased. Now, you write a letter, put the address on the envelope but leave it open and then I can pop the postal order in when I get it and send it off."

I couldn't help feeling she was disappointed and would like to have kept more of it. Mind you, she could easily have paid me less. Apart from asking the other girls, I had no way of knowing what the men paid or what I should get. I would tell Annie and see what she thought. I asked Ma about writing paper and envelopes and she told me I could use what was in the drawer in the sitting room.

The clock ticked heavily in the rich furnishings of the sitting room as I thought about what kind of letter I could write home. I could not of course tell them the truth but, as a child, I had been stamped with the need not to tell lies. I wanted to write a cheerful letter full of the excitement of Argentina and how well things were going for me but I knew I didn't have the heart to string a story like that. Should they ever find out the truth, they would be devastated. I decided not to sound too enthusiastic, to tell them about the house but of course say nothing about the men and what went on.

As I wrote, I could see the excitement in the household when my letter arrived. My mother would hold it up in the kitchen, standing in front of the fire, to show everyone and my father would say, "Well open it then, why don't ya?" All my younger siblings would crowd around saying, "What does she say? Does she ask after me? Will she be coming home soon?" And my mother would open the envelope and hand the letter to my sister, Mary, who would begin to read. Each word I wrote must be carefully written to comfort them, but without lies. It took a long time to write.

Ma would of course read my letter. I was sure that was why she had offered to get the postal order but there was nothing in it she could object to. Perhaps she thought I would tell my parents everything and they would rescue me. There was no chance of that. If I told the truth, they would be sick with worry but powerless to help. I thus presented a story that would cause them no alarm. I did not actually tell any lies, I simply did not tell them everything. It seemed like the best thing to do.

On the Saturday that followed my talk with Ma, Molly asked me if I'd like to see the tango dancers in the city. I was suspicious but any chance to get out of the house was welcome. We would go straight after lunch to see the dancers and then I would go to confession. Apparently, there were dancers in a particular square every Saturday, starting soon after midday and going on long into the evening. Molly was being friendly but it seemed an artificial sort of friendship, as though she had been told to be nice. The money and now this ... they were parts of an attempt to persuade me to be reconciled to this life. That would never be.

I could hear the music before we reached the square, the insistent rhythm of the drum and a strange sound, not quite a violin. It was a squeezebox I discovered when we entered the square. People stood or sat, forming a large circle in which the dancers strutted. Immediately, I was mesmerised as I had been when Molly danced a few weeks before. It was a dance of passion, of sexuality, a smouldering tension between man and woman, inviting and then repelling, a drama played out in dance. Couple followed couple. Some were better than others inevitably, but all had that fiery spirit, almost an aggression, at least disdain. It was not the man dominating the woman, though it suggested an attempt to. It was a constant tension between desire and rejection.

"Is this where you learnt to dance the tango?" I asked Molly between dances.

"It is. Wait now a bit and you'll see how I started."

I did not know what she meant but after the next dance, one of the women stepped into the circle and shouted to the crowd in Spanish. "Y ahora es tu turno de bailar." She strolled around the circle, smiling.

"What did she say, Molly?"

"She said, *and now it's your turn to dance.*"

Then both men and women dancers were walking around the circle, pulling people from the crowd. A young man stopped in front of me and smiled. "Senora," he said, taking my hand.

"No, oh no ..." I stammered but he ignored me and pulled me out into the circle. I noticed Molly was with another man. The woman who had shouted out initially was now giving instructions which I did not understand. The young man I was with, gently but firmly moved my arms and my head until I was in position, close to him, our heads almost touching. No music played but suddenly we moved, short jerky steps backwards, first for me, and then forwards again. Then to the side one way and back again. The woman demonstrated how the feet should go, the second foot following the first on each beat.

The music started and I could feel it within me but I could not abandon myself to its rhythms. It was as if it was an alien sound that found no resonance in me … at first … but then I started to feel it, and I started to move my body in the way I had seen the other dancers do. By the time the music had stopped, I was flushed. "Muy buena, señorita, eres una hermosa bailarina."

I smiled at him but had no idea what he was saying. "Thank you." He bowed and left me for another partner.

"He said you were very good and you're a beautiful dancer." I had not realised Molly was so close. "I saw you … you started to feel the rhythm, I could tell. It's like what we do, you know, dance in a hot, steamy way with the gentlemen." She smiled again. "Come on, we'd best get you to your confession."

Molly did not go to confession. She said the church had done nothing for her so she saw no point in it all. She waited outside, sitting in the sun. This was the first time I had come to confession since that first week. Each week, I told Ma I was going and Michael would follow me as usual. I would kneel in a pew, trying to summon the courage to go into the box. How could I tell a priest what I had done? "Forgive me, Father, but I have sinned. I've had sex with several men, more than one each night." The priest would probably have heart failure.

I dipped my finger in the bowl of holy water and made the sign of the cross. The church was quiet and dark inside, the occasional foot knocking a pew echoing in the empty space. I genuflected and went into a pew, noting who was waiting before me. Kneeling, I tried to pray. The words sounded hollow in my mouth, insubstantial, meaningless. I felt a shiver of fear. If I could not pray, how could I ever inherit eternal life? The messages from childhood were engraved in my mind. Today I was determined to go. I needed that feeling of release, the lifting of the burden of sin from my shoulders. Father Thomas Dolan was the name on the box.

When it was my turn, I forced myself to stand, to walk to the confessional box, open the door and kneel down. This was a different priest to the one who had heard my confession that first time, not the lovely old priest who had also taken mass that first Sunday. It was a cold voice, a hard voice, one that would judge and judge harshly. I stammered but could not say the words that would condemn me as a fallen woman. I told him the usual trivial things, therefore, and my penance was three Hail Marys and an Our Father. I said my penance kneeling in another pew in the side aisle but I felt no release. How could I? I had not confessed. I left, carrying the guilt and shame with me, the failure to confess an additional burden on my shoulders.

I thanked Molly for taking me to the square to see the dancing. "What you said, Molly … about the dance being like what we do … it isn't at all."

"That's because you've not freed yourself from all that crap the nuns and priests talk. When you're free from that, you can enjoy your body and the attentions of the gentlemen, and you can enjoy your power over them, leading them on then denying them, teasing them."

"I suppose it feels like freedom if it's a choice. But I haven't chosen this life, it was forced on me."

"And neither did I choose it at the start. But now I would. I have money, no worries and just the occasional fella who wants something I don't really like. I can put up with that."

I said nothing more. It seemed that Molly and I would never agree. We were different. I did wonder whether she was really as happy about it as she claimed. Had she become so hardened by it that she no longer realised what her life was? That was it, I supposed, and part of me felt sorry for her. Would she wake one day and realise that she was being used, that she could never respect herself? I felt suddenly tired. Would that be my future? Gradually, one's resistance crumbles, it becomes all one knows and you start to believe that it's all you're fit for.

I did not see Annie that week as we had to go back for our bath to be ready for the evening but I did see her most Saturdays. She was my one relief in that dark time. Always, Michael's grinning face was there watching me from the shadows but slowly I learned to ignore him. As long as he did not come near me, I was fine. One time, I had to stop Annie from marching up to him and giving him a mouthful. "That won't solve anything, Annie."

"No, but 'twould make me feel better."

I asked Annie about the money. She said it was a good sum but she asked me if I was sure Ma would buy the postal order and send the letter. I was surprised. "Why wouldn't she?"

"Oh, just a thought. I suppose I don't trust anyone. It's better that way."

I looked at her and put my hand on her arm. She turned to face me. There was no self-pity in her eyes just a hardness. I knew without asking her that the life she had endured since childhood had given her the view that everyone was out for themselves, everyone would exploit you, abuse you. It was a bleak view of the world but I was coming to realise that it was probably accurate. I hated my life, I hated what had become of me and I hated the way I was losing the will to fight against it. Before long, I would accept it like Annie, Molly, Maggie and Sheila and all the other girls in our position.

I suppose I still hung on to the idea of escape but it was increasingly a dream into which I could slip only fleetingly for a few minutes in the blissful solitude of my bed before exhaustion overcame me. It was a dream in which James came to me although his face was becoming indistinct, a picture gradually fading. Some nights, I could not summon him at all and then fear gripped me. If I lost this dream of rescue, of escape, I would have nothing.

Easter came and went and the long winter settled on us like a grey fog seeping into every crack, a serpent slithering into my soul. Things were busier then, men coming in the late afternoon as well as the evening, and each of us would have to entertain four or even five each day. The season seemed to bring out the animal in them. There was a sense of thinly hidden violence, a roughness in the way they treated us – I was sure it was the same for all of us. Some wanted to do things that filled me with disgust but, when I protested, it seemed to make them more determined. I was not a person, I was just a body to be used as they wished.

One day, I was folding the washed and ironed sheets with Maggie. She seemed a little distant, pre-occupied. "Are you alright, Maggie?"

She smiled briefly as if suddenly becoming aware of where she was. "I'm fine."

"Maggie, do you get men wanting to do things you don't want to do?"

She looked at me, perhaps deciding whether to be truthful or not. Her voice was quiet. "Of course …'tis not what I'd choose to be doing, Rose, but how else would I earn the same money? Besides, I'm too far in it now to do anything else."

"It isn't like you said before, then … something you come to enjoy."

She looked sad. "No, Rose, 'tis not. I'm sorry but I knew Ma would force you to stay and so I thought it would be better if I said that to help you deal with it."

"I'm not angry with you, Maggie. I think I've gone beyond that now. I'm not sure I feel anything."

"That's the best way to be in this job, Rose. But you have to try to keep the idea of yourself alive inside you. Let them use your body, but don't let them destroy your mind."

"I think they already have." I placed the folded sheet on a pile and Maggie came towards me. We hugged then as sisters would, the first real closeness I had felt since the day she had shown me the tools of the trade.

"It will end, you know, Rose. It'll end when we become too old for the punters to want. And then we take the money we've put by and we start a new life somewhere far away from here."

"And by then, we'll have ice for a heart and no love to give anyone, no prospect of marriage, no chance of children, discarded like an empty bottle. Was that what we were born for?"

"I no longer think of such things, Rose. I suppose I've accepted the way it is – no use fighting something you can't overcome."

I tried to hold onto who I was inside. Perhaps the revulsion I usually felt when hands roamed my body without a by-your-leave, when they thrust themselves inside me, when they wanted other unspeakable acts was a sign that I was keeping a part of myself alive. I'm not sure that was the case; it always left me feeling worthless, numb, beyond even anger. That conversation, that small and rare piece of honesty on Maggie's part, did make me feel closer to her. I felt I had someone in Placer House who understood me, as well as Annie outside, even if both were resigned to the life they had.

I waited for a letter back from my parents but none came. I thought of my younger sister sitting at the table to write the reply they wanted to make. I thought of the pleasure they must have felt at receiving the money and wondered why I had not had an answer. It had been several months since I had handed the unsealed envelope to Ma for her to put in the postal order. I knew of course that the post from Ireland would be a long time coming and there was always the possibility of something getting lost. I hoped my letter with the postal order had not gone astray. I had written again at the end of May but had said to Ma not to put any money in as I wanted to be sure the first had arrived. She looked pleased.

By the end of July, I had still not had an answer to any of my letters. I wondered if replies were being taken by Ma but I was usually downstairs first in the morning and, more often than not, picked any post up from the hall where it had fallen through the letter box. I decided I would try one more time but this time I would post the letter myself. I wrote it and asked Ma for my money, explaining that I would go to the post office myself and buy the postal order.

"Well, Rose, I don't have that much cash on me at the moment."

I looked directly at her. "How much can you let me have?"

"I think I have about one hundred and fifty pesos."

"What happened to all the money from the men last night?"

Her face suddenly hardened. "That's none of your business. I look after the money and sometimes the gentlemen pay in advance, sometimes in arrears. I keep a careful account. It so happens that I banked it all yesterday and last night there was no cash handed over. Satisfied?" The last word was spat at me in a vicious spurt of anger.

"I'll take what you've got then."

She went to her cash box which was locked with a little key and took out the money. She made no move to come across to me so I went to her, my hand out palm upwards. Before she released the money into my hand, she spoke slowly with threat in every syllable. "You may think you'll get the better of me. But you'll not. You're no better than the rest of us. You're a whore now and I know how to deal with you. Watch your step or you'll know about it."

I left without a word but I was shaking. As soon as I had fetched my coat and left the house, Michael was there, walking close behind me, much closer than usual. He dogged my steps to the Post Office where I was able to exchange the pesos for a postal order and buy a stamp for my letter. I posted it there and prayed it would get home. I longed to hear from my family. If they had not had my previous letters, they would fear I had died. The thought of their grief was a thorn in my heart.

That day, I went to the church to pretend to confess and afterwards met Annie. I told her about the letters and the conversation with Ma. "Well, like I said, don't trust anyone."

"But I have no choice, Annie. She takes the money and I never see it. I could be doing all this for nothing at all. I mean, will she ever give me what she's keeping?"

Annie thought for a while. "She may do, Rose, but she may not. That's the truth."

"I can never be happy doing this but I have consoled myself with the idea that my family may benefit. If that doesn't happen, there's no point. I may as well be dead."

Annie put her arm around my shoulders but said nothing for a good while. "I wonder, Rose ... would you ... if I told you what to put ... would you write a letter to my mother for me?"

"Of course I will." I wondered whether to say anything. "Is it that you can't ..."

"That's right. I can't read or write. I think one of me little brothers can but I hardly ever went to school. There was always work to be done to put food on the table."

"Annie, I'd do anything for you. I would not be alive now were it not for you."

We arranged that I would bring writing paper and an envelope the next Saturday and we would sit under the arches around the square to write the letter. I felt happy that I would be able to do something for Annie at last and we both became more cheerful. There was something that I had wanted to ask Annie for a long time and now I thought I would.

"Annie, you know when the men come at night, I hate it and it gives me no pleasure. Is it ever a pleasure for a woman to have sex."

Annie turned to look at me. "What's brought that on?"

"I've just been wondering. People talk of sex in marriage as a great gift to each other but it seems the gift is all one way. The fella has all the pleasure."

"It's a rare thing to find a man who gives a tinker's curse about a woman's pleasure! There's been one or two who've tried to and succeeded. You know your sensitive part down there? I've had one or two men use their tongue. That's a great thrill and then you might come."

"Oh. That's not happened to me."

"No. It's very rare. But you can of course do it yerself with your fingers. Have you done that?"

I blushed, whore though I was; 'twas not easy to talk of such things. "I have touched myself there."

"Ah but have you kept going long enough 'til you felt a great rush of pleasure?"

"No ... I don't think so."

Suddenly she stood up and grabbed my hand. "Come with me." She led me out of the square and along a street until we reached a park where there were trees and bushes. She giggled as she led me into a clump of shrubs and told me to lie down. With no explanation, she lifted my skirt and petticoats and pulled down my underwear enough to allow her hand onto my private parts.

"What are you doing? Michael will see," I hissed urgently.

"He'll not see and if he does, 'twill give him a thrill. Maybe we'll invite him in and get his dick out. Now just relax. This won't work if you're all het up."

I lay back my head and closed my eyes. She had wet her fingers and I felt her hand gently massage my private area. Slowly, slowly, her hand moved in a circular motion and I felt desire stir within me. I could feel my breaths shortening, my heart beating, my nipples hardening. The pleasure was intense and I did not want her to stop. I could see James, his lovely eyes on me, his hand there instead of Annie's, and I wanted him, I wanted him inside me. I felt the rhythms of the dance, the tango, the passion, the abandon, the fire and suddenly a flood of pleasure so intense my body shook, again and again, convulsing.

This was what the men experienced. I understood now their urgency and the shuddering of their bodies but they took their pleasure with no thought for ours. I propped myself up on my elbows. "Annie, that was wonderful."

"Any time you need to feel you're still alive, do that to yourself."

"But is it not sinful? The nuns …"

"Forget what the nuns told you, Rose. If it were sinful, why would God have given you that thing between your legs that gives you such pleasure?"

"I s'pose. Will I do that for you now, Annie?"

She was surprised but pleasantly. "You don't have to."

"I want to. You've been so good to me." She now lay back and opened her legs and, with my fingers wet, I began to rub her slowly as she had done. "Will I use my tongue now?" I surprised myself but I wanted to give her the pleasure she had given me.

"Only if you want."

I did and Annie's back arched. She moaned quietly and laid a hand on my head softly. And then it was her turn to convulse and cry out with pleasure. We lay there for some time, giggling and talking quietly about nothing at all. It was the closeness, a joy shared. I loved her then in a way that I had not loved anyone. This was what it should be with a man. This is what it would be with a husband … with James.

When we left the bushes, we saw Michael rushing to and fro on the other side of the park. He had lost us and was clearly in a state of panic. "Come on quickly, before he sees us." Annie grabbed my hand and we ran out of his sight and then out of the park, giggling. I had not laughed so much for months. We walked back and, after hugging tightly, I left Annie at her door.

It was the last time that I saw the spirit and fun that for me characterised Annie. After that, she became increasingly withdrawn, dull, lifeless.

I made my solitary way back to Placer House. It loomed before me like a dark tower, a place of constant sorrow. I wondered what horrors awaited me that night and the next and the next …

# CHAPTER 12

# ABRAZO

**Patrick**

March 1890. I recorded in my journal that we had gathered a reasonable harvest. It should have been a time of joy and celebration but the loss of friends, fathers, mothers, children, especially the children, hung like darkness over us. The sun dropped lower in the sky and we celebrated Easter as best we could, trying to make it a special time for the remaining children. The only comfort was that we should have enough food to last the winter but the shortening of the days, the darkening of the nights, the threat of the long winter months to come brought a weariness that could not be shifted.

It was late one afternoon when the June sun was low on the horizon that Signor Sanchez came roaring into our compound, banging on my door. "Violó a mi Gabriela. James violó a mi Gabriela." He was breathing heavily, his fists clenched by his side. "You get him now and I kill him with my hands."

I was perplexed, not knowing what he was saying. "James? What has he done?"

"He make fuck with Gabriela. She no want him to. I kill him."

"Whoa, whoa, slow down. Come in and tell me what happened." He came in the door of my hut still shouting. I had one chair but he would not sit. I thought I understood what he was saying but I suppose I hoped it was not true. This was beyond my experience. It is one thing to listen to the sins of humankind in the confessional box, but to be confronted with this anger, here, far from any structures to deal with it …

"We get him now. I batter his head."

"Juan, Juan, you must calm yourself. If he has done wrong, he must pay the penalty but it will be after a fair trial in court. Now calm down and tell me what has happened."

"I go into the barn and I hear sounds, sounds of struggle. I look around the … divider … how you say? Wood …"

"Partition?"

"Is right … I look around partition and I see him there on Gabriela on the straw. When he see me, he run away and Gabriela, she's crying." His eyes bulged. "Is not right. He a monster. I kill him."

I could feel myself trembling; I was horrified. If James had done this, he would have to be punished but I could not conceive of James, kind, considerate and always willing to help, doing what Juan had said. Looking back, I should have been surprised that such a situation had not arisen before. We had so many young, unattached men with no prospect of meeting young women, the frustration was bound to build. And Gabriela was a very attractive girl, with a lovely warm nature that could easily be mistaken as an invitation. But rape? The very word filled me with dread. It was only ever darkly suggested in the seminary as a grave sin, not a mortal sin, but one that would attract a heavy penance, as well as punishment under the law.

"Wait here Juan. I will find James and see what he has to say." As I walked away from my hut, I dreaded what truth I might discover. Could I have been so wrong in my judgement of James? How could he do such a thing when he had the prospect of Rose to return to? Gabriela was a lovely girl but could it be that her very beauty, her vivacity, had unleashed that dark force that all men know lies within them? I was sickened at the thought that her loveliness could have been so abused. I knew the men would be out on the fields, preparing more ground, and I trudged across the softening soil towards them.

I came upon Will first. "Is James about?"

"He's just over there. You can see his bum sticking out." Will grinned and bent back to his digging.

"Tell me, did James leave the field at all this afternoon?"

"Don't think so. If he did, I never saw him."

I approached James and asked him how the digging was going. He stood up and looked around. "Pretty well, I'd say, Father. We've got a good bit extra dug already."

"Good." I was looking at his face and eyes as he had spoken. If he had recently done what Juan Sanchez accused him of, he was a very good actor. There was no shadow of guilt there, nothing different to the James I knew. "James, there's been some kind of misunderstanding, I think. Would you come back with me now so I can sort it out?"

We walked back, James chattering about the various things to be done and making suggestions for improvements. I made no comment. When we reached my hut, Juan Sanchez was standing outside, his arms folded, his eyes still blazing. "James, this is a very difficult situation but Signor Sanchez's daughter, Gabriela, has made a very serious allegation. I suggest, Juan, that the three of us walk over to your house now and ask Gabriela if this is indeed the man."

James was alarmed. "What am I s'posed to have done?"

Sanchez was about to explode with accusations and I stopped in front of him, shaking my head. "Say nothing, Signor." We walked in tense silence until we reached the house. Sanchez barged inside and after a minute or two led Gabriela out by the arm, accompanied by her mother; Gabriela was understandably distressed.

"Is this the man?" Sanchez pointed in a theatrical manner at James.

She looked up, giving James a fleeting glance from lowered eyes. She shook her head. I had not realised how tense I had been and I breathed out. The alarm left James's face but he still looked concerned. Sanchez was talking rapidly to Gabriela. He turned back to me. "She says he is smaller man with dark hair … he walks with head down. He has bent teeth and she says maybe he is no clever."

James and I looked at each other. "That may be Jimmy," he said. I nodded.

"I think, Signor, we may know who it is so I will send James back to his work. Before I fetch him, I think I must ask Gabriela exactly what happened."

He immediately turned to Gabriela and spoke rather harshly to her in Spanish. I interrupted and said I would like to speak to her alone. He sneered. "So you can persuade her nothing happen?"

"I am a priest, Signor. If there has been wrong-doing, I will see it punished but the man Gabriela accuses is a quiet, shy man who keeps himself to himself. There may be, shall we say, a misunderstanding."

He was not happy and was all for storming off across the fields to find Jimmy. I recruited his wife, Martina, to keep him calm and to wait until I had spoken with Gabriela. We went into the house and sat in the quiet and warmth of the sitting room where Paloma had already lit a fire, flames dancing in the grate. Gently, I coaxed the story from Gabriela and, without putting words in her mouth, arrived at what seemed the truth. Jimmy had been passing the house on his way to one of the new wells and Gabriela called to him to lift something down for her in the storeroom. He did so. She had then began to flirt with him, teasing him. "It was just fun because … you know … he not clever." She blushed.

She had teased him by pulling her skirt up and sliding the top of her dress off one shoulder. She led him into the barn where she kissed him and told him to put his arms around her. She stopped but

I could sense she went further, perhaps deliberately arousing him. The next thing, she said, he was lying on top of her on the straw. He had lifted her skirt completely and pulled down her underclothes and … I told her to stop.

"I'm sorry to ask this but it is important … did he … was his … did he enter you?"

She shook her head. "My father, he come in before …"

I breathed out. "When your father came into the barn and Jimmy ran away, did you tell him how it had started?"

She lowered her head and shook it. She began to sob. She had been wrong, foolish, but that was her inexperience. I felt for her. She had released the animal in Jimmy, poor, limited Jimmy who was too shy to look anyone in the eye and especially not a woman. At least she had been honest. She had not accused Jimmy out of wickedness but from the fear of having to tell her father she had invited it. I explained carefully to her that we had to tell her parents. If we did not, Jimmy would be arrested and charged with rape. That would result in a long prison sentence. "Is he guilty, Gabriela? Should he go to prison?"

Again, she shook her head. I blessed her then and said I would fetch her parents. I spoke with them at length outside before bringing them into the room. Martina consoled her daughter; she understood what it was to be a girl testing out how attractive she might be to men. She understood that at seventeen, situations can easily get out of hand as one does not have the experience to deal with them. Sanchez was angry, his anger now turned on Gabriela. I spoke to him at length and mollified him a little but I feared what may arise when I left.

I went to find Jimmy. He was already standing outside my hut, his eyes darting everywhere with fear. I brought him inside and sat him on the chair. Calmly and carefully, I extracted from him his account of the incident. He was blubbering as he told me, ashamed, frightened, almost unable to understand how a walk to the well had turned into this nightmare. His account tallied with Gabriela's and when he was calm enough, I said we should walk over to the house. He walked with me, in fact slightly behind, like a dog trailing its master.

The sun had by then slipped beneath the horizon and we walked towards the lights of the Sanchez house. I wanted Sanchez to see the man his daughter had accused. Jimmy stood with lowered head, wringing his hands and muttering 'sorry' continually. Gabriela confirmed it was Jimmy and Sanchez thrust his face close. "You touch my daughter again and I kill you. Understand?"

Jimmy nodded. "Sorry, sir … I didn't mean to …"

Gabriela stood up and approached Jimmy. Her face was determined and I thought she might slap him. But she did not. She stood in front of him and said gently. "I sorry, Jimmy. I flirt with you. I was wrong."

Jimmy looked up briefly into her face. She smiled, a lovely warmth returning to her eyes with no hint of flirtation. He smiled back, quickly, averting his eyes from hers. "Thank you, ma'am. Thank you."

"Well, Signor Sanchez, you must now decide whether to report this to the police and have Jimmy arrested."

He looked uncertain but Gabriela intervened. "No … no police." She turned to face her father. "Was my fault."

I hoped that would be the end of it; Gabriela left soon after to live with her aunt in Bahia Blanca. Jimmy seemed even more cautious around people, even more shy, and I felt for him. I wondered that night and often since whether I had done right. Perhaps I should simply have had Jimmy arrested and let the police sort it out but I suppose some instinct told me that Sanchez had not been given an accurate account to start with.

Justice is not easy. The law pretends it is: one person is guilty, another innocent. Perhaps we were all at fault. Perhaps Sanchez and his wife should have considered sooner that their daughter needed a different place to finish her growing, somewhere she could mix with people her own age, where she could meet young men to flirt with in safety. Perhaps she was at fault because, even at seventeen, she should have been able to judge the kind of man she was dealing with. Jimmy was at fault but perhaps only because he was a victim of his shyness and inexperience around women. And I was at fault for not foreseeing such a possibility and guarding against it.

I asked Jimmy to come to my hut the next evening. I needed to make sure he understood how he had sinned and how to avoid such situations in the future. I also wanted to ask him about himself, show some interest in him. He struck me as a young man with no self-worth. "I think, Jimmy, that you are not so much to blame for yesterday as Gabriela, and she was generous enough to say as much. However, do you understand that you have sinned? The act of sexual intercourse undertaken before marriage is a sin …. even if you did not …"

"Yes, Father," he mumbled. I could see the misery in his face and he would not look me in the eye. "I didn't know what to do, Father."

"I'm sure you did not. Temptation comes to us all and 'tis a difficult thing to deal with. I'm sure it never entered your head to have … relations with Gabriela when you went to the well. I'm sure it jumped out at you from nowhere. That is how the devil works. That is what we must always be prepared for."

He made no response for a few moments, then he said, "Do you want me to go away, Father?"

"No, Jimmy, no." The idea of Jimmy trying to make his way on his own anywhere was perturbing but here, in a strange land with a foreign language, he would not stand a chance. "Why did you leave

Ireland, Jimmy? Why did you come on this voyage?"

"Me ma said I should. She said she'd had enough of me."

It was the matter-of-fact way in which he put this that horrified me most. I could picture it: a mother, probably weighed down by the task of bringing up other children and realising that Jimmy would never be off her hands, packing a suitcase for him and sending him away. But how could any mother do that to her own son, knowing he would not cope on his own? The inhumanity appalled me.

"I think it would be a good idea to make your confession now, Jimmy."

He knelt on the ground and I sat on the chair. "Bless me Father for I have sinned and 'tis nearly a week since my last confession. I took an extra potato at dinner the other night, I thought bad things about Mikey when he called me a name …"

"Is there anything else, Jimmy?" He said nothing so I prompted him. "Perhaps something that happened yesterday?"

His face contorted. "I did … bad things with that girl."

I gave him a penance and said the words of absolution. He did not rise from his knees. "You may go now Jimmy and say your prayers."

"Father, am I … am I damned to hell now?"

I put my hands beneath his elbows and raised him from the ground. "No, Jimmy, you are not. You are, I know, genuinely sorry for what you did and God's forgiveness is infinite to those who make a good confession. You are forgiven. Jesus has taken your sins away and paid for them with his suffering." I watched him leave, not sure that he really understood what had happened or what I had said. Sin and forgiveness are difficult ideas for the brightest of minds. I prayed that Jimmy would be safe, that he would gradually understand enough of the world to have a decent life.

I remained anxious for him, however. He became even more

withdrawn than previously and I had to speak firmly with some of our women who were laughing at him and calling out as he passed. 'Come and show us what you've got in your trousers, Jimmy,' and 'You've been snuffling like a pig in the bush.' Those were the kind of things and Jimmy's head went down even further, his face anguished. I asked a few of the more reliable men and women to keep an eye out for him, to stop people taunting him. I am sure they did what they could but one cannot watch a person all the time.

Every night, Rose's image came to me, gliding with the poise and natural elegance I remembered, and I confess that my thoughts were not pure. I longed to hold her, to kiss her soft face, to feel her hair on my naked shoulder. I knew these thoughts were wicked and I did try to dispel them for her sake, for James's sake, for my sake. Eve offered the apple but Adam was a willing accomplice. Those dark forces that lurk within and stir in the flesh between one's legs are powerful, too powerful sometimes to resist. Why did God make us like that? Why does he punish us daily with something we cannot satisfy. "I am a priest," I repeated to myself. "I have vowed celibacy," and I knew that celibacy is not just refraining from the action, it is curbing the desire; I was failing.

The long winter at last began to lighten and, in late September, we began to sow again. It brought a lightening of the mood though I sensed in some that the cholera deaths had sapped their enthusiasm. There were three more children born during that spring and this felt like a new beginning – perhaps. However, we did not see even the first shoots rise above the ground before the rain came. It started in October, deluge upon deluge of water. Juan Sanchez said he could not remember a year when it had rained so much in spring. Some days it would be a steady downpour, sometimes it would be heavy showers, and sometimes it would fall softly like a gift from God, but always it added to what lay on the ground.

Gradually, water smothered the fields, first in puddles, then small lakes until, eventually, most of our cultivated land was under water. In places, it would come almost to your knees, elsewhere it barely covered the soil, but everywhere the ground softened into a slippery mud beneath the rippling surface. There were days when wind drove the rain almost horizontal and being outside was impossible. It beat against the huts in which we cowered, howling round them like a banshee, threatening to come in or to destroy our dwellings. We longed for stone houses and warm fires.

Only the land on the rise was free of the lying water. We watched the crops shooting out of the ground, driven by the rain to stretch upwards. With increasing anxiety, we watched for shoots to appear above the water on the flat but nothing came. This seemed like a biblical flood to us and we knew that our precious seed may well rot in the ground before it could germinate. When the rain at last abated, we waited for the floods to subside. We waited. Nothing appeared save for a few miserable shoots. We had no other seed to replace what had been destroyed unless we used the grain we stored for food.

I stood with a group of the men, looking over the sea of mud. "Father," Big Pat said softly. "The crops on the rise are very good and we will share what we have."

"Thank you, Pat, and God bless you. But that'll not keep us all over the long autumn and winter. We have enough to see us through the summer from the last harvest but we'll not survive beyond that."

No one said anything to counter my words. They all knew I was right. We stood in silence, each of us considering what options we had. Signor Sanchez joined us. He shook his head. "I very sorry. Is not good."

"No, it is not."

"I think you must contact Buenos Aires again for more money and food when the stocks finish."

"I can't ask again, Juan. There are thousands of other immigrants arriving every month who need support. There is only so much they can do for us." In my heart, I knew it was over.

As we stood in dismal silence, we could see a solitary, female figure hurrying towards us, lifting her skirts to avoid the mud. When she drew closer, I recognised Paloma, the Sanchez maid.

"Señor, su esposa dijo que debe venir rápido," she gasped, looking at Sanchez.

He looked at Paloma and said he had to go. Paloma said something else to him and indicated myself. "You must come too, Father."

We followed Paloma back to the Sanchez house and round it to the barn. As we entered it, Paloma made the sign of the cross. My stomach lurched. What would we find? When I saw him, I sank to my knees. *Why … why?* My voice was strangled but it thundered in my head. It was a cry of anguish that had been building for two years. What kind of God could allow so many sorrows to fall upon us? What had we done to deserve this? I looked up. His body was hanging limp like a rag doll, his head lolling to one side away from the rope that tied his neck to the beam, the rope from which the pig had been hung.

"Who has done this?" I shouted, rising to my feet. "Who could do such a thing?" I whipped my head round to Sanchez.

He did not flinch. Instead, he pointed to the wooden crate that had been kicked over and lay on its side. "He has done this himself I think."

That was worse. If Sanchez had exacted his revenge, I could understand it. I would condemn it of course but – this was the hard part for me – I would have been relieved of the responsibility. But this … it was firmly my lack of care. I knew Jimmy was vulnerable. I could protest that I had taken steps to ensure he was safe, that I had kept an eye out for him but I knew that I had failed. Again. Over and over, from the start, I had failed in my ministry. What kind of priest must I be that I could allow such things to happen?

Sanchez called two of his men and we lowered his body carefully to the ground. I went to organise some of our men to carry the body to the communal building where the women would prepare him for burial. It was a silent procession: James, Will, Big Pat and Arthur carrying Jimmy's body on a board with myself in the rear. He was laid on the table in the building and we left the women to their sad task.

The four men hovered outside. James spoke first. "Why did he do that?"

"Perhaps he was driven to it. The comments did not stop and he would have felt the ridicule, the humiliation. I daresay some did not realise how fragile he was."

I left them to be by myself. Not for the first time, I wondered how it was that some brush away their own wrongdoing as if they have no conscience – like those two agents who had brought us all to Argentina – yet others carry the punishment for their misdeeds inside them, eating away at them until they can take no more. I thought of the priests who taught us at the seminary, intoning sins, and their punishment like a funeral bell. Suicide is a mortal sin, they said, for it is despair. It shows you have no faith in God and that is the one thing God cannot forgive.

It seemed very simple at the time. Why would we question it? We had no expectation of ever being in such a state. We had no reason to doubt God's goodness. We had not been tested. How could a man be condemned to hell because he was that unhappy, had so little prospect of anything good coming his way that he took his own life? Surely, a loving God would reach his arms around him, lift him from the despair that swamped him, carry him to a better place? I saw the wooden cross Monsignor O'Rourke had given me beside my mattress and I picked it up, feeling its smoothness and the way it nestled in my hand. Oh, it was comfortable alright. But it was a lie. God had abandoned us and no amount of clinging to this piece of wood could change that. For the first time, I thought of flinging it away … but I didn't.

Someone asked if he should be laid in the graveyard with all the others, being a suicide. "He will be buried with the others," I said firmly without hesitation. "He was as much one of God's children as anyone else and his soul should now rest in peace. It was our sin, the sin of neglect, that brought this to pass." I am sorry now for that rebuke but I wanted to forestall any complaint of that nature.

The next day, we buried Jimmy in our graveyard – the one hundredth grave – one hundred wooden crosses accusing me of failure. Everyone stood in silence as I said the requiem mass, standing on the steps of the communal building with his body on a table in front of it. I wanted to express my anger at his death, anger at the people who had driven him to this with their comments, anger perhaps even at God. But, of course, I did not. I made a reference to the barbs that had driven him to suicide and I noticed some heads bow.

Jimmy's death was a clear sign to me that we could not remain.

Two days later, I called a meeting in the late afternoon whilst there was still plenty of light and a good day's work had been done. I explained the position we now faced and the decision I believed we had to make. "My friends, we have to decide what to do. We do not all have to do the same thing … there may be other options to explore. Some may want to stay here and try to make it work, others may want to try to find work in Bahia Blanca; some may want to follow those who went to Balcarce, but I believe that most of us must now face the fact that this place cannot support so many of us. Most of us must return to Buenos Aires. We do not, of course, have to make a decision today but I think we must be clear what we mean to do by Christmas."

I looked around at the faces – troubled, downcast faces, lined with hardship and struggling against a cruel land. "I myself intend to return to Buenos Aires. Whether I stay there or return to Ireland, I am not sure."

There were plenty of questions over the next few days. If we left, what would we do about the fishing boat and nets? What would happen to the tools and equipment we had? What about the animals? A large part of me no longer cared about such things. I wanted to leave this place and return to something more like civilisation but I knew that I could never abandon these people. I had decided to come with them to support them in their search for a better life. I had been a leader to them thus far and I needed to complete the task. After that, I could relinquish the responsibility, the constant pain in my chest.

Sanchez said if we decided to leave, he could use a couple more men on his ranch. Big Pat and most of the others who had plots on the higher ground decided they would stay. About twenty decided to try their luck at Balcarce and half a dozen decided to go to Bahia Blanca to find work. If they failed, they would return with the rest to Buenos Aires.

It was with these that I set off once more to Bahia Blanca. We walked in the fresh morning of early December, the summer sun already warm on our backs and the track away from the compound once more dry. When we arrived, I showed them to the labour office and explained to the clerk what they were seeking. He sent them off in various directions and I arranged to meet them all at six o'clock. "You'll have no difficulty with the time; you'll hear all the clocks striking."

I went myself to the Post Office to telegraph Canon Peter one more time. *Leaving La Viticola for good. Will arrive Buenos Aires in early Feb. About 100.* I hoped he would understand what kind of condition we would arrive in. From there I went to the bank, closed the account and took the little that remained in cash.

The harbour was my next port of call. I sat on a lobster pot, looking out at the sea while I waited for the Keenans to come in from fishing. Bahia Blanca meant *white bay*. It was indeed white. The shoreline was encrusted with salt, the sea under a clear sky, a cold turquoise. It seemed idyllic sitting there, small waves gently washing against the harbour wall, but I knew there would be hardship here too. Gulls wheeled above my head, calling and screeching, always on the lookout for easy food. Easy food!

The Keenans were still buoyant with their lives as fishermen. They had heard of course about the failure of our crops and they listened in silence while I explained what would be happening. "What about the boat, Father? We've not enough money to buy it from you."

"I'm not expecting or wanting that, Frank. You can keep the boat if you'll continue supplying fish for as long as they want it to those staying at La Viticola."

"Will you take the train to Buenos Aires?" Mike's question was tentative.

"No … there's nowhere near enough money for that. We'll walk, and the little we have will buy what we need along the way. We must trust in God."

We were silent for a while, looking out at the benign sea and listening to the squabbling gulls. Then Frank said, "Father, we have saved some money. I know Mike will agree when I say you should have that to ease your path to Buenos Aires."

I protested at first but they insisted and gave me several thousand pesos. I thanked them, blessed them and returned to the labour office. All six had found jobs and would be able to start in a few days. I thanked God for that: a few less to worry about.

# CHAPTER 13

# CASTIGADO

**Rose**

The letter lay on the kitchen table. My eyes were misted with tears …
joy, regret, grief all struggling within my breast.

*Dear Rose,*

*It was grand to receive your letter. We had feared the worst when we had
heard nothing for so long. Mary is writing this for me – she has lovely
handwriting. It was kind of you to send the money which will be very helpful with
the younger ones growing and eating us out of house and home! I don't know what
can have happened to the letters you said you sent and postal orders in them, too. I
wonder did someone steal them or perhaps they got lost on a ship over?*

*Mary has been working in service as you know with an English family living
here, but the family are moving back to England. They have asked Mary to go
with them which is nice but I don't want to lose another daughter. I wonder will
you ever get the chance to come back to Ireland?*

Late September. It had been a long time to be without any news
of my family. I was overjoyed to have it, to know that they were all
well but it made me feel alone, so alone in this hostile place. Would I
ever see them again?

I was glad of the early morning and being on my own. Memories
crowded my mind: the delight and pride on my mother's face when
Monsignor O'Rourke recommended me to Miss O'Leary. "The nuns

tell me she is quick to learn, can read and write and will be an excellent employee," he had said while I blushed and looked at my feet and she stood beaming with happiness beside me. She would feel no pride in me now.

I re-read the letter several times, recognising my sister's hand; four years younger than me and the oldest of my siblings. It grieved me to think of my parents losing a second daughter to a foreign land but at least Mary had a job to go to and was not thinking of joining me in Argentina. England was so much nearer home; one had the chance of return.

There were some little bits of news about my other brothers and sisters but the line that they had heard nothing and feared the worst drew my eyes again and again. I felt a deluge of guilt. What had I put them through? It was not just me who was suffering as a result of my foolishness in coming to Argentina. I longed to wallow in thoughts of my home and family; I had not paid them enough regard when I had them and that was perhaps part of my punishment. The paper on which the letter was written carried the faintest smell of the peat fire, threatening to hold me in an ecstasy of homesickness.

I returned it to its envelope and placed it carefully, tenderly in the pocket of my apron. Wiping my face with my handkerchief, I forced myself back to reality. Why had my previous letters not arrived? And what had happened to the money? It grieved me to think that all that money had been lost. But then I thought about it. The letter I had posted myself had arrived along with the small amount of money I had sent. My mother's reply had arrived. Maybe the other letters had never been sent. I felt a stir of anger, something I had not felt in a long time.

I waited until breakfast was done and asked Ma if I could speak to her privately. She led the way into her small office with its polished wooden desk, turned and faced me.

"I had a letter this morning from my mother." Her face remained set, no flicker of guilt; that made me nervous but I was determined to press on. "She says she received the letter I sent at the end of July – that was the one I posted myself – and the postal order inside it but did not get any of the other three I wrote. Those were the ones you posted with the postal orders of my earnings."

She shrugged. "The post is unreliable. Someone along the way may have opened the letters and seen the postal orders inside them. There are thieves everywhere." She turned away and started fiddling with the papers on her desk.

"Maybe … or maybe they were never posted. Maybe there were never postal orders put inside them. Maybe you've kept my money."

She whirled around. "Are you calling me a thief? Is that it?" Suddenly she advanced towards me and grabbed my hair, twisting my head sideways. "How dare you? How dare you?" She gave my hair a twist and I cried out. "I take you off the street and give you a safe home. I feed you, I clothe you, I give you make-up and perfume and you call me a thief?" She pushed me violently away and I crashed into the wall. "You listen to me, you little bitch! One word more from you about this and I'll thrash you and then I'll put you out on the street where any thug can have his way with you for nothing. D'you hear me? Now get out of my sight!"

I was shaking. The sudden violence shocked me and I knew that she would have no qualms about carrying out her threats. I was sure she had never posted those letters and was keeping the money I had earned. I wanted to demand all of it so I could send it home but I could not go back into her then. I was frightened.

Later that day, I had an opportunity to ask Maggie about the money. She said she had been able to send a lot home already but then she was older and wiser and Ma perhaps had decided not to try it on with her. "Leave it for a bit, Rose, and I'll see if I can have a word with her."

I did leave it and avoided Ma as much as possible. That night (it was a Saturday), Ramirez was one of the men who called. I saw Ma take him aside when he arrived and talk with him. His glance flicked across to me once but I thought nothing of that. He would often catch my eye when he arrived. I brought him a drink but his usual playful manner was absent. His eyes were hard and impenetrable like dark stones. I busied myself with other customers until he came across to me.

"Rose, I like you to come with me."

I nodded and went with him up the stairs to one of the rooms. When I opened the door and walked in, Ma was there. I hesitated in the doorway but Ramirez, who was behind me, pushed me firmly into the room. Ma told me to sit on the bed.

"Now, Rose. Ma tells me you have been disrespectful." He struggled with the pronunciation of the word. "Ma has given you many things … you are in good house. Is important to be grateful for these things." He was taking off his leather belt as he said this. "Perhaps I give you a lesson."

He walked up to me and lifted me by the arms from the bed. He twisted me round so he was behind me. I felt a strong hand on my back and I fell onto the bed, face down. Ma was on the other side. She grabbed my hands and pulled them towards her so I was spread out. Suddenly there was a stinging pain on my back and a sharp smack as the leather hit me. Then another and another. I lost count after five. I think there must have been ten. I was sobbing. I lay on the bed, burying my face in it. My hands were released.

I heard the door open and close and then I was being pulled up and turned again to sit on the bed. Ramirez put his face close to mine. "You will do what Ma tells you. This was nothing. In the police, we have many ways of making sure people do as they should.

You understand?" His hand was gripping my chin. "Never make me do that again. Alright?"

I said nothing. All I could do was sob. My back ached and I hoped it was not cut. This was just a warning, then. I had no doubt they would kill me if they needed to but there are many things worse than death. Then he was pulling my dress undone, roughly, removing most of my clothes while I stood with my eyes down, unable to resist.

"Now, you little whore, I fuck you." The violence had excited him, driven him on to treat me with such disregard. He took me from behind, bent over, my hands gripping the footboard of the bed. When I thought he surely must finish, he spun me round and thrust me down onto my knees where he put his member in my mouth and finished his business.

I had suffered much mis-treatment in my time at Placer House but this was an extreme which I had not previously experienced. I sat on the floor as he dressed. The face he turned on me before he left was pure cruelty, the thin scar of his moustache and his sharp features accentuating the vicious gleam in his eye. "Remember, Rose, be grateful for what you have." He turned away and left the room.

I was like a dog who is beaten by its master yet cannot run away. And, like such a dog, I cowered and tried to lick my tormentor's hand. I could do nothing, say nothing. I tried to keep a low profile but I could see Ma watching me in the days that followed, making sure I smiled at the customers, fetched them drinks, satisfied their lusts. Maggie did speak to me about the money after a couple of weeks and said Ma should let me have what was due. She did but now I was only worth ten shillings a week, apparently. I knew I could not argue and accepted it. That amount was still a good wage for someone my age and would allow me to send some home. Ma and I never discussed it again. She gave me the money at the end of each month and I took it to the Post Office.

As for Annie, she never did receive a letter of reply from her mother. As the weeks passed, I stopped asking until one Saturday I asked her if she would like me to write again.

"There's no point. Oh, I'm sure they were glad of the money I sent but they don't care about me. They'll have forgotten I existed."

It was the way that she said it that saddened me. There was no anger, no bitterness … a lack of feeling as though it was what she expected. "You and I are sisters, Annie. I love you like a sister, anyway."

That was when I noticed her sliding into a sort of living death. The two of us would sit on a bench, for the most part in silence, like two old women. But instead of the memories that fill the heads of old women, there was an emptiness. I sensed it in Annie and felt the dread of that happening to me. I knew I was well on the way but Annie seemed far worse … drowsy. Eventually, it was sometime in early November when the parakeets were chattering in the trees, the sun blazed on the flowers in the park and the air was pungent with the scent of lilies, she said the one word. "Laudanum."

"Annie … what d'you mean?"

"They gave me laudanum and now I can't do without it. It was great at first. It took away all the pain but … now there is no feeling, just this drowsy state …"

"Annie, you must stop taking it."

"Ha! If only … I need it Rose, I can't do without it. I crave it and if I have none, I cannot rest until I get another little bottle. That's where all my money goes now."

"Annie, Annie … what have they done to you?" I thought back to that first time in Placer House and wondered if the drinks I had been given had been laced with laudanum. Perhaps.

And so, the summer grew. We still met, Annie and I, usually every week, though she was increasingly remote. I still went to church every Saturday, before we met, more to get out of the house than anything as I did not go to confession. I went to mass every Sunday morning but I had not taken communion since that first week. No confession ... no communion, that's how it goes. December 1889 came bringing a strange Christmas in the heat of the city. We decorated the house, there was a party atmosphere, plenty of customers but it was for me a heartless time.

Summer gradually faded into the autumn and on into winter 1890, the cold winds of June blowing off the sea. The treadmill turned, endless weary steps leading nowhere. James came to me in the privacy of my bed and sometimes I touched myself, making believe that his hand caressed me there. I felt his kisses on my face and longed to wake in his arms. Every day, I woke to harsh reality.

In July that year, Ma took me on one side. "Now, in case you have any ideas, you should know that the little friend of yours who you meet left her house and was picked up by the police. She's in jail now. Arrested for drug offences. I'm sure she'll be treated well." She smiled at her own sarcasm, a smile that was triumphant, vicious, a clear warning to me.

"Annie? I must visit her, I must help her!"

"Leave her be, Rose. You don't want to go getting mixed up with all that."

I had another idea. The following night, Ramirez was there. I had been wary of him since the beating; he had used me since but without that level of violence and neither of us had ever referred to it. Now I made a point of being extra diligent in serving him drink. I fluttered my eyes. I used all the little tricks I had picked up from the other girls and then I whispered in his ear. "I wanted you to know that I learned my lesson all those months ago. I've never been disrespectful to Ma again and I'm very grateful."

He smiled. Perhaps even a crocodile can be flattered into kindness. "Excellent. You know, Rose, it was for your good."

"I know. Perhaps, Signor, we could spend some time together tonight. I could do something special for you …" I looked at him from lowered eyelids, that seductive look no man can resist. Part of me was ashamed for acting like that but I knew it was essential. I would do almost anything to help Annie. Later, I led him up into a room and close to the bed. Before he could do anything, I dropped to my knees and undid his belt and the buttons on his trousers. I pulled them down enough and then took out his member. Everything in me was revolted at what I was doing but I forced myself and took his member in my mouth. I could see he was in ecstasy. I gave myself to him in different ways until finally he exploded over my face.

"That was wonderful, Signor. Thank you."

"Rose, my leetle Rose. You now make the best sex. I want you again and again."

I made him sit on the bed and I kissed him, gently rubbing him until he stood erect again and then again I used my mouth. When he had finished, he lay back on the bed breathing deeply. I lay beside him and stroked his chest.

"Signor, I have a friend … her name is Annie. She's been arrested. I'd like to visit her in prison."

He sat up slowly and his shrewd eyes looked at me. "Ah … that's what this was about?"

"No, no … I wanted to give you a good time. You're very handsome and you're a great lover." Even as I said it, I hated myself for the lie.

He laughed indulgently. I realised how much I had learned about men. They like nothing so much as to be reminded of their own power and to be congratulated on their prowess. "And what has your friend done to end up in prison?"

"I'm not sure. Ma told me earlier. 'Tis probably a mistake."

"My officers no make mistakes. You come on Monday to my office and we'll see. What did you say her name is?"

"Annie Boyle."

"Annie Boyle … Yesss, maybe I remember her. I ask the officer in charge. Come on Monday at eleven o'clock."

"Thank you, Signor. You're a good man."

He spread his hands and smiled in self-congratulation. He was being magnanimous. I was careful to say nothing that would change his mind. I helped him dress, told him again how handsome he was and how much I enjoyed being with him and then kissed him full on the lips when he was leaving at the front door. He held me for a moment and smacked me playfully on the bottom.

I ran straight to our room where I washed my face and rinsed my mouth with water. I was full of self-loathing. There have been many times since when I've asked myself whether I did the right thing. The answer has always been that I did. When the life of one so dear to you is threatened, you will do anything. A drowning person will clutch at a piece of driftwood, a starving person will eat the hay intended for the cattle. This life gave few choices … the choice to help or not, to survive or not. Things are not simply right or wrong; circumstance is everything.

At eleven o'clock on the Monday, I walked cautiously into the police station and asked to see Signor Ramirez. The officer at the desk corrected me: 'Chief Superintendent Ramirez.' He looked at me as though I had crawled from under a stone but he asked my name and sent a young officer into the bowels of the building. After a few minutes, the officer returned and took me to Ramirez's office.

He was standing behind his desk in an impressive uniform, looking stern. A flag hung limply from a pole in a corner and there were two armchairs by a small table to one side. He waved the young officer away and then relaxed, his face breaking into a smile. "Rose, how nice to see you. Sit ... please sit." He gestured to a comfortable chair and sat in another close to it.

I sat on the edge of my chair nervously. "Thank you. Did you find ...?"

"Annie ... Annie Boyle? Yes, I found her. She is in prison for a serious offence. She was on the street in a drugged state. My officers cannot allow that. Of course, we know that it happens – plenty of people take opium – but we do not allow it in a public place. Therefore ... she is here."

"How long will she ... I mean, has she been sentenced?"

"Not yet. We usually keep them until they show no effects from the opium but of course as soon as they get out, they're back on it."

"Can I see her? Will she have to pay a fine?"

"Perhaps you will be able to see her ... perhaps there will be a fine." He smiled, calculating, amused, disturbing. Then he stood up suddenly and went to the open door. He called to someone outside in Spanish and then closed the door, locking it. He strolled back to where I was sitting and stroked my hair. I had to stop myself shrinking away from his touch. Instead, I turned my face to him and smiled. "Perhaps all things can be sorted out when we have had some time together. I enjoy very much our time on Saturday."

Then he was in front of me and unbuttoning his trousers. I knew what he wanted and I did it, fighting nausea. Afterwards, he said that the fine would be only five hundred pesos, almost four pounds. It would take me two months to earn that. "I will pay the fine, Signor, but I have to get the money from Ma and I earn only about 250 pesos per month. Can I pay later?"

He seemed surprised when I mentioned my wage. "That is not how it is usually done, Rose. A person stays in prison until the fine is paid."

"But that would be two months away. Please, Signor, can't you do something?" I went to him and placed my hand on his chest rubbing it gently and looking up into his eyes.

"You like to see Annie?"

He called an officer to his door and spoke rapidly to him. The young officer led me through the building towards the back where we came to a locked door made of bars of iron. He called and a jailer came, jangling a bunch of large keys. Again, there was a rapid conversation in Spanish and the iron grille was swung open with a screech of protest. I was led down an echoing corridor with cells either side. An unpleasant smell – damp, rot, human excrement – hung in the cold air. The jailer stopped and unlocked another iron grille. He gestured me inside to a small, gloomy cell. For an awful moment, I thought I was going to be locked in on my own but, as my eyes adjusted to the feeble light from the little window high in the opposite wall, I saw a form huddled in the corner.

"Annie … Annie?"

The door swung closed behind me and I heard the rasp of the lock being turned. She looked up. Her eyes were vacant, her hair straggling down her face. She looked dirty. I stepped over to her and crouched in front of her, putting my arms around her shoulders and pulling her to me. I held her. She did not cry as I wanted to do but I felt her hands creeping around me until she could hold me also. We stayed like that for a while until my crouched position became too uncomfortable.

"Annie, I'm going to get you out. I've spoken with Ramirez and I'm going to pay your fine. I just don't have the money at the moment but I'm going to work something out."

"Thanks … thank you, Rose." A few sobs did escape her then and I helped her up to sit on the hard bed.

"Do you want to talk about what happened?" She shook her head.

"Have they treated you right in here?"

She turned to look at me, her eyes set in hollows, betraying no emotion. "I'm a whore, how d'you think they've treated me?" Again, there was no bitterness; it was a simple statement.

"Do you need anything, Annie, before … before I can get you out?"

"Hah! I need laudanum but they'll not let you bring me that."

We sat together on the solid bed, hardly speaking. My arm was around her and I hoped the touch would give her some comfort. The jailer appeared and unlocked the door. He barked a few words in Spanish and gestured for me to leave. "I've got to go, Annie. I'll come again when I know I can get you out. Don't give up, Annie. I love you."

She lifted her head and smiled. That one smile brought me much relief. "Thank you, Rose. I love you too. You're my sister, my only family."

I could not stop tears rolling down my face. I hated leaving her there in that dark, squalid place. The jailer took me through the iron grille and the young police officer was waiting to take me back to Ramirez. I tried to wipe my face as we walked. Ramirez was at his desk. I was shown into the office and I stood before him. He looked up and then stood and walked around the desk to me.

"Rose, you've been crying." His fingers gently brushed my cheek; he leant over and kissed me. The unexpected kindness brought further sobs. "Why you cry?"

"Seeing Annie like that. They've treated her badly. She said they used her. I must get her out as soon as possible."

He shrugged as if it was to be expected that police officers would rape arrested girls. "It is not a good place … what can one expect from prison? But I hate to see you sad so I tell you what I do. I pay the fine for her and you can pay me back. Then she can go very soon."

"Really?" I searched his face to see if this was another piece of cruelty – raising hopes only to dash them.

"Yes, really. Now you come back the day after tomorrow, Wednesday, and you take her away. But we will warn her not to be in that state again on the street."

I flung my arms around his neck and kissed him on the cheek. "Thank you, thank you, Signor."

He laughed and removed my arms gently. Then he kissed me on the cheek. "You see, if you treat me well, I can make things happen."

I was very happy as I made my way home. I even waved at Michael who still followed me whenever I left the house. I had hoped by now that Ma would trust me but clearly not … unless it was Michael's decision to stalk me like an incompetent hunter might stalk a deer. As I walked, my mind was churning with thoughts that veered between guilt and triumph. Part of me was horrified at how I had used sex to manipulate Ramirez but part of me was glad. It was like using his own weapon against him. Perhaps we could hold some power by granting or withholding the satisfaction of desire.

Annie was duly released and my next two months money was paid to Ramirez. I knew that prison would not have enabled her to free herself from the laudanum and I was right. Our meetings were largely silent, her eyes lost in a hazy world with no sensation. I mourned the loss of the Annie I had met on the boat, the vivacity, the sparkle, the energy, the sense that she could never be bowed or beaten.

The dark of winter gave way to spring, the sun climbing higher each day and warming us when we sat on a bench in the park or in the square. I loved to see the flowers blooming. It gave me some hope that life could return though increasingly it felt as though they bloomed for others not us. One plant in particular fascinated and horrified me. It was a bush with leaves like tongues and, when the blooms came, they were like open mouths, yellow at the higher, narrower part and red-brown lower down. They had a white section in them that the birds would peck at. It always made me feel as though the mouth would suddenly snap shut, trapping the head of the bird which the plant would slowly devour.

And so, it seemed, for myself and Annie. I could see no escape. I longed to get away from this city, this country, to take Annie with me and get her away from the poison that had destroyed her mind and would surely destroy her body over time. But escape was a dream that I no longer really believed. I comforted myself with the image of James each night but I could no longer be sure I remembered him, his face, his eyes. I loved someone I had to create each time.

It was in November that it happened. I had clothes to wash in the scullery that morning. Ma and the other girls had all gone into the city to choose fabric for new dresses. I think they wanted them to make Christmas a bit special. I had said that I would make dresses for all of us but I was happy for them to choose a fabric for me. It was, therefore, just Michael and me in the house. I thought he was out the back, chopping wood for the fires or something.

I was bent over the tub, scrubbing a chemise when I became aware of him behind me. I turned to look over my shoulder as I was always nervous when he was around. His stooped, hulking figure said nothing but he grinned at me. "Hello, Michael. D'you want something?"

"No." He laughed and I carried on with my work.

I felt a hand on my bottom and I spun round. "What d'you think you're doing?"

"Nice bottom."

He was close to me and I put my hand on his chest to push him back. It was like pushing a solid weight. I remembered his strength when he pulled me from the door that first morning. "You may not do that, Michael. You're not a customer. Go away and leave me do my work."

He grinned at me but did not move. I thought it best to continue working in the hope that he would go. Suddenly, he grabbed me from behind and I felt his hands come round to my breasts. I could hear him laughing and felt his body pressed against mine. "Get off me, get off!" I shouted and dropped the chemise in the water. I tried to pull his hands away from me but he was too strong. He took one hand away and I could feel him pulling up my skirt and my petticoats despite my attempts to hold them down.

"No, no, no!" I screamed, not sure whether it was aloud or just in my head. Then he pushed me forward, bending me over the tub and I had to grab its sides to stop my head going in the soapy water.

# CHAPTER 14

# ELEVACION

**Patrick**

We had quite a feast on Christmas Day, killing one of our own pigs for the dinner, but it was tinged with sadness: the loss of those who lay in the graveyard, the loss of those who had already left and now this final separation. "Ah 'twill be quiet when you've all gone," Big Pat had said to me as he stood in line for the dinner. I nodded. My heart was too heavy to risk speech.

Sanchez, his family and workers joined us after the dinner for dancing but there was none of the energy and spirit we had enjoyed the previous Christmas. I noticed that Gabriela was with her family, having returned for Christmas. She appeared beside me, gliding up silently. "Hello, Father. Feliz Navidad."

"Happy Christmas to you, too, Gabriela." Neither the greeting nor my response had been spoken with any conviction. Happiness seemed a long way off. "You're not dancing."

She shook her head. I thought she began to speak but she coughed and we stood side by side for a few seconds in silence, watching the dancers. Then she said, "I hear about Jimmy."

I turned to look at her. I could see she was fighting tears. "Very sad. Such a waste."

"Is my fault." She turned to me, her watery eyes pleading. She wanted a denial, she needed comfort.

I touched her arm lightly to turn her more towards me, speaking to her in an earnest whisper.

"No, Gabriela. Many of us must share in the responsibility for his death but, above all, it was a tragedy that may have happened at any time and in any place. Jimmy was a sad man who was ill-equipped to deal with the world."

"But he no do that if I no …" She sobbed once, a racking sound that convulsed her.

"It was a factor, Gabriela, but it was more the way he was treated afterwards. I did not look out for him as well as I should have."

"Paloma say it was where he … we … why there?"

"I understand what you are saying but it was there because that was where the rope was still hanging … that was where the pig had been hung. I am sure that is why it was there." I am not sure she was convinced; I was not fully convinced myself but it was the least I could do to save her distress. Some would no doubt argue that I should not have tried to reduce her part in Jimmy's death but, where there is clearly contrition, there is no need for condemnation. A person of conscience will punish themselves every day and far more than anyone else can punish them.

I laid my hand gently on her head and blessed her. She started to sob again and she put her hands on my waist, pulling herself closer. "Thank you, Father, thank you."

And then she was gone and I was saddened that I would never see her again, never see her grow into womanhood, take a husband perhaps and raise children. I knew, however, that she would always bring kindness and understanding to everyone whose path she crossed. I could not help thinking of Rose. There was goodness, loveliness in the world, even in this bleak place.

On St Stephen's Day, we stood awkwardly in the compound to say our goodbyes. Big Pat and those staying were waiting in a group, and Juan Sanchez, his family and his men were all there too. Those who had found work in Bahia Blanca had already left as had those who were heading for Balcarce. I had asked them to stay so that we might all share Christmas day together but, understandably, they had wanted to be on their way.

Juan had insisted we take an ox and cart for the luggage and food and for those who became weary. I tried to pay him but he would have none of it. We had put on the cart some of the tents we had used when we first arrived and a couple of spades in case we needed to fill potholes. We were taking two goats as they would provide milk on the journey and, eventually, meat. We had flour for bread, potatoes, a barrel of salted fish and some other foodstuffs but we would need to find food once these stocks were exhausted. That would not take long given our number: ninety-four. It was a huge number to look after on such a long journey.

Three hundred and ninety miles, Juan had said. It seemed daunting but, if we could cover about ten miles a day, it would take us forty days, the time Jesus spent in the wilderness, I reflected. That might prove a better comparison than any other such as the flight from Egypt. I was no Moses leading the chosen people to a promised land!

I looked around the assembled group. My task now was to lead them all safely back to Buenos Aires. Hopefully, there would be others there who could take over the responsibility. I shook hands with Big Pat and all the others staying.

Maggie O'Keefe held my hand firmly and looked me in the eye. "Thank you, Father, thank you for what you've done."

That made me feel miserable. "I've done nothing, Maggie ... I've not been able to ..." I stopped, feeling the smart of tears in my eyes.

"Where would we have been without you, Father? You're too hard on yourself. 'Tis not your job to sort everything out and look after everyone."

"Oh, but it is Maggie, it is and I ..."

"Think of what would have happened without you. That's what's important."

"You're very kind, Maggie. Thank you and may God be always with you and everyone here."

Juan Sanchez similarly shook my hand for far longer and with much more warmth than I expected. "I sorry, Father, I sorry …"

"Juan, it was not your fault. You did your best and you did more for us than many would have done. I thank you for that and I am sorry I bullied you at times." I smiled at him.

He laughed briefly and then his face became serious again. "It was too many people, too many … we were not ready … we did not know there would be so many…"

"No, I know. I hope those staying will be alright now."

"I make sure, Father. I look after them as if they my own children."

I nodded. "Thank you, Juan, thank you."

Will set the ox moving and the heavy cart rumbled over the stony ground. There were waves and shouts and the long line of people gradually stretched out behind the cart as it made its way along the track. Not quite two years we had been here, two years marked by misery, hardship and pain. None of us could ever be whole again, leaving as we were so many in the harsh ground of La Viticola.

At first, we made good speed but the sun grew hotter each day and we chose to rest in the early afternoon. There was rarely any shade but we were able to use coats and a few sheets to escape the heat of the sun. At night, we pitched the tents which were allocated to the women and children; the men from those families slept in the open or under whatever shelter we could find. Fortunately, at that time of year, there was little rain. I estimated that we covered about fifteen miles in most of the first ten days. We had plenty of food and there was a desire to complete the journey.

The plan was to head north and eventually follow the main railway line which passed through Azul. There I hoped we would be able to refresh ourselves and buy more provisions. It would not be quite halfway. Many of us had to carry our luggage as there was not room on the cart for it all but we knew that, as we used the food, there would be a little more space. The youngest children rode on the cart as their little legs were not up to the distances we were covering.

The land we passed through was unvarying for those first days, an endless grassy plain with which we were so familiar. The long grass hissed as light breezes blew through it, creating a ghostly sound, and the monotonous chirp of cicadas was a constant companion, a chorus of derision. Bright yellow butterflies flitted over the grass, sometimes settling, oblivious to the dry heat of the day. At night, the lonesome sound of wild cats shrieking in the grass troubled our sleep.

Much of our food had gone by the end of that ten days. There was discussion about killing one of the goats but I was reluctant. They were still providing milk and they were no trouble to feed as they ate whatever grass and scrub was available. But the consumption of our rations necessitated it and so we stopped for an afternoon, set up camp and boiled one of the goats in pots over open fires. The other goat looked on with no apparent concern. I wondered what passed through its brain. Perhaps it was thinking, 'I'm next!' The meat restored us a little and we pushed on.

It was Mary and Finbar McCarthy's son, Peter, who was first. He had always been a weak child, no surprise given the poor diet and hardship his mother had endured during pregnancy. This journey, the return to a poor diet, the relentless sun during the day, sometimes the difficulty of obtaining water, proved too much for him. He became weaker, would not eat and lay listlessly on the cart as it bumped along the track, his mother walking beside him with anxious eyes.

I prayed hard that he would not die. Losing one child was bad enough but to lose another would be devastating for the McCarthys. But I found myself once again kneeling beside a child as he drew his last breaths. I said the usual prayers and watched with his parents into the depths of the night when his little body ceased to move.

"He is with God now," I whispered, placing my hand on Mary's bent back. She was not crying nor wailing; she stared with disbelief, horror – I'm not sure – at the lifeless body.

Suddenly, Finbar exploded. "God? God? What kind of God does this? I'll hear no words about God!" He stormed out of the tent and off into the scrub. I could hear him railing against God and I felt it best to leave him until his anger subsided. I spoke quietly to Mary and saw the hollowness of her eyes. It was as if a light inside had gone out, as if the spirit had already left her body. I feared for her then, that she may simply give up the struggle and so join her children.

In the morning, I asked a couple of the men to dig a shallow grave by the side of the road and we buried Peter there in the middle of nowhere. At least there was a community where Ellen and all the others had been buried, but here there was nothing but the dry grass whispering, the occasional call of a buzzard and the emptiness of the vast sky. That evening, when we had eaten what little we could spare and everyone was at rest, I walked out into the scrub to be alone.

I knelt on the ground and prayed. I asked for help, I asked for strength to endure this ordeal, I asked for the wisdom to guide all these people who still depended on me and I prayed that Finbar and Mary would find solace somehow. I paused in my prayers and listened. Nothing … save the barking of a fox or some other wild animal hunting in the darkness. I closed my eyes and tried to feel God's presence. Nothing. I tried and tried but I had no sense of God at all. He had surely abandoned us.

I felt for the cross in my jacket pocket and clutched it, bringing it out in front of my eyes. I looked at it carefully. Perhaps I would see the face of Jesus, full of pity, full of love. I saw nothing. "What use are you?" I said aloud, "When I need you most, you're not here." I felt an aching emptiness within me. Could it be that I had lived a lie all these years? Could it be that God was just a creation of mankind desperate for some kind of guardian?

I stood up. I could feel tears forming in my eyes. I reached back my arm and started its motion forwards, intending to hurl the cross into the scrub. But when I should have let go, I didn't. The cross was still there. I did not even have the courage to discard this redundant symbol. I was too weak to let go. With a heavy sense of failure, I slipped the cross back into my pocket and plodded slowly back to join the others.

Weariness now set in with the daily walking, the poor food and the death of little Peter. There was no singing, no talking even, as we trudged along the dusty track, a long straggling line of fragile people. I watched carefully for signs of particular weakness, anyone who may need extra help but everyone was the same, eyes down, drawn faces, blank expressions. I knew in my heart that we would have more deaths but I could not prevent them by giving extra rations to the weakest as I could not identify them. I made sure that the children had the milk from the one remaining goat but each had a meagre ration only every three days.

It is fascinating how different people react to the sight of desperate people. Some took pity on us, gave us clean water, bread and other food, but they were not wealthy people and were giving *us* what *they* needed to survive. Others closed their doors, even ran from us in fear. One man came out of his hut with a shotgun and shouted at us to move on. This was the pattern everywhere, whether in towns or in the country; some helped us but most did not. We passed through Azul, watched from behind twitching curtains. I was able to buy food but the shopkeeper I bought from looked suspiciously at the money I offered him as though it might be forged.

After twenty days of walking, I estimated we had covered about two hundred and fifty of the three hundred and ninety miles and was pleased with our progress. I admit, I was desperate to reach Buenos Aires as I knew the longer we were travelling, the more likely we were to have people die. Perhaps I pushed too hard. Perhaps it caused more weakness than a slower pace. More did die, children, women, men, no one was safe. With each death, we dug a shallow grave and I took a funeral service, not a full requiem mass as this would have delayed us even more. As it was, each death really cost us a day. I hated myself for thinking like that but I needed to lead these walking ghosts to safety.

And we were like ghosts, waif-like, no smiles, no light in our eyes. Any words of encouragement I spoke sounded hollow to my own ears and must have had little impact on those who heard them. We had become automatons, placing one foot in front of the other, no longer sure why we were doing so. It was an endless plain that we crossed, a vast flat wilderness. Thirteen souls we had lost by the time we reached San Miguel del Monte on the thirty-second day of our journey; it was a small town and one that had only been established twenty-five years before.

I discovered that we were now in Buenos Aires province and only some seventy miles from our destination. I made sure everyone knew. Seven more days would take us into the city where I hoped we would be given food and shelter. There is a large lake at San Miguel and we washed ourselves in its waters, luxuriating in the warm sun and feeling our skin renewed. We slaughtered the second goat there as its milk had all but dried up; it would give us a little energy for the remaining miles.

On the second day after leaving San Miguel, in the late afternoon as we were setting up our camp for the night just off the road, we heard the thud of horses' hooves. Three horsemen were riding around the encampment and in between the tents, shouting to each other and grinning. They stopped in a group, the horses pawing the ground and shaking their heads as if keen to run. All three dismounted and started shouting in Spanish to a group of our people. I walked over to them.

"Can we help you?" I was making gestures but had no idea if they understood.

"Dinero!" The speaker grinned at me and put his finger and thumb together. He seemed to be the leader of the trio.

"I'm afraid we have no money." I imitated his gesture and shook my head.

He pulled a knife from a sheath on his belt, a long vicious-looking blade that glinted in the evening sun. I stood my ground. Thoughts raced through my mind. If I were killed now, it would not matter as we were nearly at Buenos Aires. If I were killed, it would not matter as I felt there was no value remaining in my life. If I were killed, it would be a release.

His face sported a moustache and a beard growth of a few days. His eyes glinted in the dark face and he sneered when his eyes fell on my clerical collar. I suppose I had assumed it would offer some protection but clearly not. He stood unmoving, staring at me, an amused expression in his eyes. He lifted his hat, fanned his face briefly and returned it to his head. He walked away from me slowly, looking at each of our people who were grouped around. They returned the stare, without hostility and without fear – they were a long way past feeling that by then.

He stopped in front of Kate O'Mahony and looked her up and down. I could see his eyes settle on her breasts. In normal times, she would have been a very attractive woman though now her beauty had been tarnished by poverty and the rigours of our journey. Her husband Tom stood beside her; he was not a strong nor dominant person, rather quiet, in fact. The bandit's two colleagues, holding the horses, started grinning and said something to each other.

Suddenly, the leader reached out his hand and squeezed Kate's breast. I moved forward and was aware of figures beside me moving too. The bandit laughed and grabbed Kate's arm. He began to pull her back towards his horse.

"Let her go this instant!" I shouted and a chorus of shouts echoed mine.

"Tomaremos y tendremos sexo con ella," he laughed and continued to pull her.

I stood in front of him, blocking his path. "Let her go!"

He stared at me, menace in his eyes, and spat on the ground. Kate tried to yank her arm from him and, unable to do so, hit him on the shoulder with her free fist. He did not flinch. She and the other women started to scream. I grabbed the arm that held Kate and tried to pull it away. Suddenly, a knife flashed in the corner of my eye as he withdrew it for the strike. I braced myself as it came towards my stomach but it did not connect. James was pushing me aside and he and Will were wrestling with the bandit, one in front and one behind. The bandit let go of Kate and managed to wriggle free of James and Will.

He stood glaring at them, his knife held at the ready. "Te mataré si vuelves a intentarlo."

I did not understand the words but his intention was clear. "Go!" I shouted.

They mounted their horses and, just before the leader turned his animal to ride off, he pointed the knife at me. "Nosotros volveremos."

Again, I did not know what he had said but assumed it was a threat of some kind. We watched them ride off in a cloud of dust, no doubt to look for richer pickings elsewhere. Kate and her husband came up to me to thank me but I shook it off. And then I noticed James. Blood was coming from his side, seeping into his shirt.

"James, you've been injured."

"Ah, 'tis nothing, Father … a scratch is all."

"We must get that wound cleaned." I lifted his shirt and looked carefully. He was right, it was not a deep wound, fortunately. Kate and another of the women took James to a tent where they washed the wound and bound it with strips of cloth from a shirt.

We arranged a watch overnight so we should not be taken while sleeping if the bandits returned. I did a spell with Will in the hour before the sun rose. It was the coldest part of the night, though that was not a problem in January. The light gradually strengthened, shapes becoming visible, and the sky turned crimson in the east melting across the sky to a deep purple in the west. The birds welcomed the new day, calling in the sweetness of the early morning. The sun crept over the horizon, filling the sky with an orange light and, despite the dull plain on which we were camped, transforming that uninspiring landscape into a beautiful and remarkable world. One could believe in those moments that there was a divine purpose but what was our place in it, crawling as we were from one disaster to the next?

James assured me he was not badly hurt. He tried to smile but I could see him wincing as he walked and I suggested he rode on the cart. He would have none of that, allowing no weakness in himself. By the end of that day, however, he looked more tired than usual and was clearly struggling to keep up. I asked the women to look at his wound and they washed it with water before binding it again. It did not seem to be healing, they said.

Next day, Will came to me in concern. "Father, James seems very weak."

I went with him to the rough canopy that had been rigged under which several of the men slept. He was propped against a tree and breathing hard. "James?"

"I'll be fine, Father … just feel a bit weak at the moment."

"You must ride on the cart today, James, until you get your strength back."

He refused at first but very soon it was clear he could not keep up and he allowed himself to be lifted onto the cart. It was not a comfortable place for an injured man, the jolting as the cart bumped over the rough track causing his face to crease with pain. At the end of that day, Kate O'Mahony and her husband said James should sleep in their tent and, although at first he declined, he was prevailed upon to do so.

As the sun started to fall in the late afternoon, Kate came to me. "Father, James is bad, getting worse, I'd say."

I nodded and went with her to the tent. James had gone a deathly pale and he had his hand on his wounded side. His breaths were short and his voice frail. "Father, you must leave me here and I'll catch up with you when I'm back on my feet."

"We're not leaving anyone behind so put that idea out of your head. Another night's rest and you'll be on the mend. 'Tis only three days to Buenos Aires. Then there will be rest and nurses to see to the wound."

He did not look convinced and nor, for that matter, was I. That look I had seen on too many faces: the grey pallor, the bleary eyes, the skin slack and lifeless. I left him for a while and returned as the sun was a giant golden ball sitting on the horizon. When I saw him, I knew without doubt that he was not long for this world. Kneeling beside him, I began the last rites. I asked him gently if there was anything he needed to confess.

He looked directly at me and I could see he knew that this was the end. He spoke in short gasps. "Nothing ... as far as I know ... just one promise that I'll not ... be able to keep. Finish the prayers, Father ... and I'll tell you about it." I did so and he spoke again. "I promised Rose – you remember her – that I would come back for her … be rich with me own farm … huh! Find her … tell her I tried … tell her I would have loved her … and, Father, will you see she's alright for me?"

"You'll be able to tell her yourself, I'm sure." I did not believe it but whilst there's life and a will to live, there is hope.

He smiled weakly. "Promise me, Father, you'll see she's alright."

"I will, I will, to be sure, I promise. I'll not forget." I sat on the ground beside him and watched him, his breathing becoming more laboured, more faint until … he lay still. "No, no," I hissed, "not James, not good, kind James." I stood and walked out of the tent to where the O'Mahony's were about to lay down. "He's gone," I said simply and Kate nodded to me. She knew what had to be done.

I stumbled far out into the scrub, the darkness from the east now creeping across the vast sky, though there was still light aplenty in the west. I sank to my knees. Lifting my head, I shouted at the crescent moon, "Why, why, why?" I thought of James, always cheerful, always optimistic, always willing to shoulder the most difficult burdens, and of Rose, that gentle, kind young woman who would never again see the man she had started to love. My mind became confused then, chasing an endless train of thought that was like a serpent in my brain. Here was I tasked by a dying man to care for the woman he loved, the woman that I loved too. For the first time I acknowledged my feelings for her. James had taken the knife wound that had been intended for me. It was as if I was being deliberately freed to take the woman he loved. That was the ultimate punishment, the guilt of knowing that James's death was convenient to me.

This was not a benign God, this was a scheming, evil, punishing God. Why would I worship such a being? How could I be a minister of a religion that deified such a force? I stood up, anger burning in me, taking my left hand from my pocket. I had not realised but I had been gripping the small wooden cross tightly, squeezing it as if I could crush it. "It's a lie, it's a lie!" I repeated over and over and then, "There is no God, there is no God!" I took the cross with my right hand, preparing to fling it this time into the scrub but I could only stare at my left hand. The shape of the cross was printed on my palm, the skin white where I had been gripping it. *"I will not forget you. See, I have engraved you on the palms of my hands."* The words from Isaiah were a distant voice echoing in my head.

I stared at it. It was only where the blood had been forced from my hand; it meant nothing. My eyes were fixed on my hand as the image slowly disappeared and the skin of my palm resumed its usual grimy colour.

God was fading from me.

I tried to raise my right arm to hurl it away but I could not, I could not throw it. I put it back in my pocket and looked around me. I may be branded with the cross but I knew I could no longer be a priest. I could no longer lead people in a faith I did not have myself. I would lead these poor, good people back to Buenos Aires and I would tell Canon Peter of my decision. I thought then of the plans that had filled my mind as I walked back from the discussion with Monsignor O'Rourke the day I had agreed to come to Argentina. It seemed a lifetime ago. How could I have been so ambitious, so naïve, so full of pride? Well, that was all gone. I had failed in everything; I had failed in my ministry as a priest.

The following morning, we buried James in a shallow grave. As part of the service, I read the end of Psalm 38, more for myself perhaps than for James or for the rest: *"Forsake me not O Lord; O my God be not far from me. Make haste to help me, O Lord my salvation."* Despite the words, I felt abandoned.

We set off in silence to complete the final thirty miles to the city – so near and yet so far for James.

# CHAPTER 15

# BARRIDA

**Rose**

Afterwards, I slumped in a chair in the kitchen, unable to cry or move, staring at the floor. The daylight, penetrating the grimy window, seemed to shatter on the flag stones. I don't know why I felt it to be worse than any other of the abuses I had endured every night for nearly two years. Maybe because he was not a customer, maybe because I was in the scullery and not in a candlelit bedroom, maybe because it was him … animal-like, bestial, taking me from behind with no preliminaries. I knew I should not feel that way about another human being but I could not help it.

Ma and the others found me there, staring into nothing and slowly coaxed from me what had happened. Ma's face set into that hard, thunderous look I had seen on a few occasions. She said nothing but walked through the scullery and out the back.

"Bad," said Molly. "Still, we're all used to it, aren't we?"

Maggie laid her hand on my shoulder and spoke gently. "Did he use a rubber?"

"I … I don't think so."

"Where are you in your cycle?"

"What d'you mean?"

"You know … when was your time of the month?"

I struggled to bend my mind to the task of remembering. "About two weeks ago."

Maggie nodded but said nothing more. Faintly, we could hear a sound from outside, a regular dull thud and an occasional yelp. We all listened and then Sheila led the way through the scullery and out the door at the back. Ma was wielding a leather belt above her head and Michael was cowering in front of her. She was frenzied, out of control with rage, her voice lashing him as hard as the belt.

"You're not to touch the girls. I made that clear." The belt whipped through the air and smacked into his bent back. "How dare you … you animal? You're no better than a dog."

"Stop, stop!" It was my voice. I leapt forward and lifted my hand to grasp Ma's. "Stop, Ma. This will do no good."

"I would've thought you'd be pleased to see him beaten."

"He did wrong but beating him will change nothing."

She looked at me and then at Michael, still cowering in front of her. "It damn well will change things. Don't you dare do that again! D'you hear me?"

Michael whimpered his assent and we left him there. I was sickened by Ma's violence as much as I had been sickened by Michael's rape. Did he, I wondered, know what he had done? What level of understanding was there in his strange mind? Maggie put her arm around me. She said nothing but it was a gesture of support which I needed and I loved her for it. Perhaps she too thought Ma's aggression was wrong. She led me away and up the stairs to my room.

"Lie down there for a bit until you feel better," she crooned, and her gentleness brought a tear to my eye. Like my mother, she was then, and me a child again, being comforted, the hurt being soothed away with kindness.

"Thank you, Maggie, thank you." I closed my eyes and tried to rid myself of the image of Michael's leering face but could not. Pale sunlight entered the room and cast a weak square of light on the wall opposite the window. I could hear people passing on the street, the rumble of a heavy cart on the cobbles. It seemed distant, as if I had no part in it. It was a life that was lost to me – the everyday business of living. All I had was this endless abuse, men with an insatiable appetite for a woman's body. Even Michael, poor damaged Michael, whose needs had finally overcome him.

He would not have dared do that to Molly, Maggie or Sheila. Why was that? What was it about me that had invited his desire? Was it my fault or just that he knew I would not be able to belittle him as the others would do? Perhaps I was too kind and that made men want to take advantage of me. And so, my mind twisted and turned through endless possibilities, returning always to the same sense that I was worthless, it was somehow my fault. It was the sound of waves breaking against the heavy timbers of the dock, ceaseless, unrelenting, until they were worn down and cracked.

I missed my next monthly time. There was nothing. I confided in Maggie and she told me I might just be late. After a week, still nothing. "You can miss a whole month and it means nothing, Rose," she said but I knew deep within me that something was happening.

There was no joy for me at Christmas. It was yet another play acted on a stage, lines that were by then faultless, well-rehearsed gestures, the same, inevitable finale. The men were in good spirits as they had been the previous year. We were busy in the weeks just before Christmas. They were treating themselves and would then, no doubt, spend Christmas Day with their wives and families, the good husbands that they pretended to be.

I sat in church on Christmas Day, the cool of the building welcome relief from the sun blazing outside in a cloudless sky. This baby, born to save the world, had no meaning for me anymore. All I could think about was the baby I knew was growing inside me. I was sure of it. This baby would not even save me. Would Ma throw me out? She certainly would not be happy to have an infant crying in the house and needing feeding and me unable to entertain the men. But it was a baby nevertheless, my baby, new life, someone who would need me as a mother. How different to be loved and needed for the care one could give rather than merely for one's body?

When I missed my next time, I told Maggie again and she said we would need to tell Ma. The look on Ma's face was one of irritation, another problem to solve. She looked me straight in the eye. "It happens. I'm sorry for it but there's a good woman I know will take care of it."

"What d'you mean? I'm not giving up my baby."

She looked puzzled. "Giving up? I'm not suggesting you have it adopted."

"What then? What do you mean by this woman taking care of it?"

"She'll make it go away, Rose, that's what I mean. You can't have a baby. If you have that child, you're finished here and there'll be nowhere else you can go."

"You mean … you mean?" I stared at Ma, horrified.

She said nothing but as she turned away, she said, "I'm not ready to give you up yet Rose. You're too good for business."

"But 'tis a sin – to kill a child in the womb, an abortion, is a sin. I'll be damned to hell."

"Ah, for God's sake Rose, quit that nonsense now. There's plenty has had abortions before now and nothing happened to them. There's plenty more will do so in the future, too. We've all had at least one." She glared at me.

"I'll not do it. You have damned me already but I'll not do that just so's you can make money from me being fucked every night." I had never used that word before and I could see she was startled by it coming from my mouth.

"You think about it, Rose. Think about it very carefully. Ask Molly, ask Maggie, ask that friend of yours, Annie, if she has a brain left to think with. They'll all tell you the same. You're better off without it."

I asked Molly first as we were going to bed. The glow from the oil lamp cast her shadow huge on the wall. "Yep, I've had two. There's nothing to it. Ma'll give you a little something and the woman will sort it out. You'll hardly feel it if you do it soon and … the problem'll go away."

I was not willing to accept such an answer. "But Molly, how can I just kill a child like that? It's another human being."

"Ah, 'tis nothing of the kind. It's a wee little thing that can't see, or hear or think. It's not even shaped like a human being. 'Tis just a bit of mess."

The picture she painted was revolting and I could not agree. The sanctity of life had been always stressed by the nuns at school and Monsignor O'Rourke in his sermons. To kill the infant in the womb was a mortal sin. Whatever the circumstances, it had been placed there by God and to destroy what God had created was a rejection of him.

"I can't do it, Molly … I can't."

"D'you want to give birth to a creature like Michael? After all, he's the father." I said nothing. Of course I did not want to give birth to a child who suffered with Michael's shortcomings but there was no reason why it should. Molly continued. "D'you want to be like Ma, having a thing like that for a son?"

"Like Ma? Son?" I stared at her stupidly. "Do you mean …?"

She nodded, a smile of satisfaction spreading across her face. "Yep. Michael is Ma's son. She made the same mistake as you're about to do. She decided to keep him … and look what she ended up with. Is that what you want, is it?"

I could say nothing. I had not realised but it made sense. Why else would Ma employ Michael? The frenzy with which she had beaten him was not just because he had done wrong, it was her bitterness at keeping a baby who turned out to be less than a mother would want. But that was not the point. He was one of God's children anyway. He needed love like anyone else. He should be cared for, even more than another child, as he could not fully care for himself. Perhaps, had I shown him more kindness, more interest, been less suspicious, less frightened, he would not have done what he did. Perhaps.

I lay in bed that night, unable to sleep for a long time, my mind once again churning over this latest revelation and re-visiting my conduct to Michael over the last two years. I had never spoken ill to him but I had certainly thought of him as less of a human being than myself or others. Ma had not let him in the house since he had raped me and I felt that must change.

Next morning, I sought him out. He had slept in the shed where the tools were kept on an old straw bed covered with sacking. It was the kind of place you'd keep a dog, dirty, smelling of old timber, musty. "Michael, I have not spoken to you since … since you did that to me." He was fidgeting with his hands in front of him, his head lowered, wondering I suppose what further punishment would befall him. "What you did was wrong, Michael, though God knows the men who come each night do things just as bad, but I want you to know that I forgive you."

His head lifted a little and his eyes shot me a glance before dropping again. A grunting sound came from him but I had no idea if he understood what I was saying. "Do you understand what I mean when I say I forgive you?" He said nothing and I stooped a little to try to see the expression on his face. "I mean, Michael, that I don't hate you for it." I put my hand on his and gently separated them. I then shook his hand for I did not know how else to signal my forgiveness. He looked up and grinned sheepishly; I think it was my gentle tone of voice that reached him rather than the meaning of the words I spoke.

"Michael, you and I are going to have a child." I laid my hand on my belly. "You can't feel anything yet but this child came from what you did to me. You must help me look after it." He looked completely bewildered; I realised that he could not understand and, even if he did, there was no way he could help with the raising of a child. I rubbed his arm softly and left him. I spoke with Ma and told her I had forgiven him and she must allow him back into the house. She looked doubtful but I noticed him going about some tasks indoors later that day.

I did ask Annie what she thought about my pregnancy when I next met her towards the end of January. She looked at me, her eyes swimming and distant as though in another world altogether.

"No babies," she said, shaking her head.

"Annie, do you understand what I'm telling you? I'm with child. Ma says I should get rid of it but 'tis a sin to do that."

She turned and faced me at last, dragging herself into the present. "Get rid of it. I've done it a couple of times. 'Tis no problem. No baby ... you don't want a baby."

The more I heard that advice, the more determined I became. I would keep the child though I felt a chill of fear at what my future would be. Ma would turn me out, that was certain, so where would I go? How would I keep myself and the child alive? I thought of the streets, dark and cold in winter, hot and dusty in summer. Was it possible to live on the streets? I knew the only way I could get money would be to offer myself. It was a frightening prospect. At least at Placer House, there was some sense of security in numbers, there was comfort, degrading though the life was. But a baby ... how could I commit a mortal sin and kill an unborn child?

It was laudanum or something similar they used, a few days later. They laced my tea with it and then, already drowsy, forced me to drink more. They gave me plenty of it so that I was barely conscious. Everything was like a mad dream, faces swimming in front of me and sounds, disembodied, floating around the room. I had no sense of what was real and what was part of this nightmare. I remembered the ship coming over, Annie's face, her eyes bright and mischievous, that nice priest by the old man's bed, and James's face, looming in front of me and receding. I heard the slap of Ramirez's belt on my back, I saw Ma's malicious smile, Michael's leering face, Molly dressed as a nun or a nurse, smiling her 'now you're not so grand' smile.

I was dimly aware of being half carried, half led upstairs to one of the rooms and being laid on a bed. The room spun and I sank into a sort of pleasant oblivion. There was someone pushing up my skirts and removing my underwear but I could not raise my head to see which man was about to poke his member into me. I remember thinking that I did not care anymore. I had no understanding of what was happening to me. Then I drifted into sleep and remembered nothing more until I woke, feeling strange, low, so low as if a weight pressed on my heart. I understood why a person would crave more laudanum, to escape that black despair.

I remembered what Annie had said … how they had given her laudanum and now she could not do without it. Poor Annie. I must not let that happen to me. I must fight it for the sake of my baby. Slowly, I sat up and waited until my head stopped swimming. I managed to splash some water on my face which helped a little and then I stumbled down the stairs, clinging onto the banister with each slow step.

I found Ma in the kitchen, preparing food for the dinner. "You gave me laudanum didn't you? Why?"

Her face was hard. "We did. 'Twas for your own good, Rose."

"You had no right. 'Twill harm the baby."

"There's no chance of that, Rose. The baby is past harming."

"What d'you mean?"

Her voice was like a lash. "There is no baby, Rose ... not anymore."

I stared at her blankly, my fuddled brain trying to make sense of what she was saying. "No baby?"

"No. 'Tis all gone. Problem solved. No need to think about it at all. And *we* did it so you can't think of it as *your* sin."

I slumped on a chair, unable to speak. I wanted to scream. My hand was on my stomach as if trying to feel for life. "What have you done?"

"We've done what needed to be done. Now get yourself sorted out and ready for tonight." She flung the peelings into a bin with the same disregard she showed for the life of my unborn baby.

"I cannot escape it ...'tis *my* sin, 'tis *my* sin. I should have left this place before! You have damned me to hell! What kind of woman are you? What kind of monster?"

Suddenly she was holding the top of my dress and her fierce eyes were burning into mine only inches away. "Now you listen to me, you stuck up little bitch! There's nothing, nothing that has happened to you that has not happened to me and worse. It's happened to Molly and Maggie and Sheila. Just get used to it. You're still alive, damn you!"

She shook me and released my dress, turning back to what she had been doing. I stood and left the room. The tattered remains of my mind were trying to frame what I should do now. Should I try to leave again? But where could I go? What would become of me? I wished I could cry – it would bring relief – but this was too bad for tears. I felt drained, empty; the last part of me had been flushed away with that tiny, growing infant. It could only be that I was wicked, that this was my punishment. Why else would I have been reduced to this?

The next day was Saturday, the first Saturday in February. I think it was the seventh. I walked to the church in the afternoon, determined this time to make my confession. If I failed again, I would surely be damned. The church seemed more imposing than previously, a vague sense of doom in its echoing interior. I knelt in a pew and tried to clear my head, working out like an actor learning lines what I would say when I got in. I pleaded with the figure on the cross above the rood screen to give me the strength this time to unburden the weight that lay on my heart, to fill me again like an empty glass filled with wine.

I was shaking as my turn approached. The door to the little confession box opened and an old woman came out letting the door swing closed behind her. I stood and walked as if in a nightmare towards the box. Even at the last moment, my hand upon the handle, a voice inside me said it was not too late to pull out, turn away and not face the ordeal that lay ahead. But, like an automaton, I opened the door and knelt inside in the dark closeness of old wood and the hint of incense. This felt better – more protected than the open space of the church.

"Bless me Father for I have sinned. It is two weeks since my last confession."

"And what is it you want to confess?"

The voice was hard, the younger Irish priest to whom I had confessed my little sins before. It was a voice that spoke of rigid laws, of rules that must not be broken, of judgement. I opened my mouth to speak but could not say the words I had rehearsed. How could a man like this begin to understand the life I led, let alone grant forgiveness? In that moment of hesitation, I resorted to my usual catalogue of minor demeanours. He gave me absolution and the usual penance.

I took a deep breath. "Father, I have a friend who … who is with child … but she's not married. She may be thinking of having the child … removed." I could not think of what word to use. "Would that be murder?"

"Of course. To kill a child whether born or in the womb is a mortal sin. The sixth commandment: *Thou shalt not kill.* The child in the womb is a gift from God and only God can take away that life. To murder that defenceless child is a rejection of God's gift, a wicked act and it is a mortal sin. It cannot be forgiven and hell awaits those who sin in such a way. You must tell your friend that she should not go ahead with that plan. Fornication outside marriage is a sin, but murder is a mortal sin. Even thinking of doing such a thing is sinful."

I mumbled my thanks and started to rise from my knees. I had known what the answer would be but was desperately hoping there may be another. I was damned, there was nothing for me. There could be no life for me in the future. I felt even more empty than before. I sank back on my knees. "Father, she has also talked of taking her own life. I suppose that is just as bad?"

"Despair is the work of the devil. Taking her own life would be an act of despair, it would be a terrible lack of belief in God's goodness and forgiveness. It is for God to decide when a life should end. Your friend must not take her own life. If she does, she is damned."

"Thank you, Father."

I walked from the confessional and out into the sunlight without saying my penance. What was the point? I was damned as a murderer for not protecting the life I held inside me. There was no forgiveness, there was nothing. I was damned for breaking the sixth commandment and I would be damned if I ended my life. What was the difference? If I were damned anyway, enduring this daily suffering was pointless.

I was not aware of where my steps were taking me, so lost was I in my thoughts. I found myself in the harbour walking towards the empty dock where our ship had landed nearly two years ago. The sun glinted on the surface of the water when you looked across the bay, a picture of peace and beauty, but close by it was grey. The waves lifted and died against the vast old timbers, endless and unchanging. How many unfortunate souls had stood on this spot wondering about the future? But the sea and the dock were unaware, unconcerned – we are ants upon this land, one minute scurrying busily to and fro, the next dead. What purpose did it serve?

I stepped closer to the edge and looked down. The day was warm but the sea looked cold. It would not take long … in my dress and petticoats, I may float a short while but I could not swim and the water would seep into those garments, dragging me down. A moment of horror and then oblivion. My soul would go to hell – that was certain. I dreaded the torments I would suffer but could it be any worse than this?

I thought of that priest in the confession box and wondered if he had ever been in a position of temptation or sin. Had he ever had to endure what I and countless others endured – abuse, violence, poverty, hunger? Probably not but he was certain nonetheless about what would damn you to hell. It was what we had been told as children, sitting open-mouthed at our desks as the nuns described the torments of the damned souls, the fires or extreme cold, the tortures. They terrified us so much with those accounts that we would never sin. That was the intention anyway but I had fallen. What was it about me that had led me to this?

The faces of my family floated in my mind. Would they grieve or was I already lost to them in a far-off land? My parents, faces creased with worry, loomed large, their eyes full of reproach. I had probably devastated them by leaving home; if they were ever to find out what had become of me, it would definitely destroy them. They were better off without me.

Perhaps I had expected too much when I'd boarded that ship,

perhaps I thought only of myself; perhaps I was greedy for wealth or adventure. And now I was being punished. My thoughts became confused and all sorts of memories crowded my mind. Welling up inside me, obliterating all those memories, was an overwhelming sense of despair. I could not endure the sunlight, nor the people bustling past, going about their business. The thought of yet more days opening myself to voracious men sickened me. This life was unbearable.

I stepped to the edge of the dock and looked down. The water was rising and falling like a monster breathing, waiting ... waiting. I was floating, my head swimming, crying out inside myself to find the courage to take another step. If there is a God, I thought, a God who forgives, a God who loves, surely now he will send angels to lift me from this broken world. Perhaps ... please ... as I fall, golden hands will grasp me.

I lifted one foot and moved it out from the edge. All that was needed was to lean forward and it would be over.

# ACT III

# CHAPTER 16

# PARADA

**Patrick**

It was mid-afternoon, two days after we had left James in that shallow grave. We were still a couple of miles from the city, our pace seeming to slow with every step. The track ahead quivered in the heat rising from it, making everything seem unreal. I could not be sure that my eyes were seeing things as they were. A tree ahead blurred and the trunk seemed to separate. When we drew closer, I realised it was a stranger who had stepped out from the tree's shade.

He stood in front of me and I stopped, wondering what misfortune would now befall us. "Father Gilligan?" he said in heavily accented English.

"Yes. What is it?"

"I ride to Canon Peter and tell him you come. Everything is ready."

I could scarcely understand those simple words. "Please ask him to send a cart, for some of our number are very weak."

"Carts, si. I go now. Is not far for you. No give up now." He grinned and turned back to the tree where his horse stood in the shade blinking flies away. He mounted and with a wave galloped off, dust rising from the hooves, quickly obscuring him, leaving an empty track when it drifted away, still shimmering in the heat.

I turned to Tom O'Mahony who had been walking close behind with his wife, Kate. "Did I hear and see that right?"

Kate answered. "You did, Father. I think we're nearly there." She smiled. "Thank God."

I said nothing but told them to walk on. I stood by the side of the road and told each group in the straggling line as they stumbled past. There were some smiles but mainly blank expressions as though they did not believe it or they could not understand what I said, so worn were they by the endless walk. This would be no triumphal entry into the city but a slow procession of the barely living.

And then there was dust again ahead of us and soon the rumble of cart wheels. There were shouts of greeting from those with the carts. They loaded one with the luggage some of us had carried all the way from La Viticola. There was room in the second cart for the weakest, many of whom were children. We set off again, the carts coming behind us so we didn't breathe in the dust from their wheels. The buildings of the city appeared, at first a just few and then more dense, until we were on cobbled streets and there was little space between the houses. We walked behind one of the men and finally he stopped outside the Hotel de Inmigrantes.

Canon Peter stepped out from the building, his face creased with anxiety. I lifted my hand to signal to him and he sought me out. "Father Gilligan, Patrick, 'tis good to see you." He shook my hand. "God, man, you look half dead. Now you're not to worry about anything. I have everything arranged … accommodation for everyone, and food. The nuns and the volunteers will direct everyone to where they should go. Some can stay here and we've places for you all."

I stared at him. I felt my legs weakening and then his arms were around me, holding me up. "Thank you, Father, thank you."

"You'll stay at the presbytery. Bernardo will take you there." He called a man over who looked at me with consternation. He took me by the arm and led me away."

"But I must make sure …"

"You come, Father … everything is good."

At the presbytery, I was given food by Emilia, Canon Peter's housekeeper, and she showed me to a room. There was water for washing and she said I should sleep a little. The luxury of that bed and that room felt almost sinful. As I lay down, I realised how exhausted I was, physically, emotionally and spiritually.

For two days, I did little but sleep and eat. Canon Peter gave me positive reports of the situation for all the others who had walked from La Viticola and told me I need have no worries. After two days, slowly I began to tell him of the things that had happened, our struggles to survive, the decisions I had made, my failures. That evening, Father Thomas Dolan, Canon Peter's assistant priest, was invited to dinner. He was a little younger than me and had come out after I had left for La Viticola. He was not a man I took to – his views were strong and by the book. His heavy, dark features seemed to emphasise that and I ate mainly in silence as he talked about what people should and should not do. He had quarters in the convent and one of his duties was chaplain to the nuns.

After dinner, we went into the sitting room. He walked ahead of me and I noticed how short he was and how he strutted like a cockerel, his chest puffed out. I smiled to myself at the image of him as the cockerel and the nuns as the hens. I wondered what they made of him.

When we were sitting cradling cups of coffee, I told Canon Peter of Jimmy and asked him was I right to bury him in the ground I had consecrated. Before he could answer, Father Dolan cut in. "The church teaches that the sin of despair should prevent a body being buried in consecrated ground. It sounds as though he was an unpleasant fellow. A man like that should not be rewarded with consecrated ground."

Canon Peter let a silence hang in the room after Dolan's remark. I studied his face anxiously, fearing he would also tell me I had done wrong. At last, he spoke. "The church has its teaching on many things and we are told that taking one's life is a sin, a mortal sin. It is despair of God's forgiveness, a lack of trust in God. But … I have learnt through my long life, that a priest must make judgements based on the exact circumstances. What may be right in one case, is not right in another. It sounds to me as though Jimmy would not have understood such notions. He perhaps should be regarded as a child and not responsible for his actions. Besides, God's forgiveness is infinite, God's love for every one of his children is unequivocal. I would have done the same as you."

"That's not what we were taught at the seminary." Dolan's voice was hard, full of judgement.

I breathed out slowly. I had not realised how much I had been wanting Canon Peter's affirmation. I ignored Dolan's comment and turned to Canon Peter. "But his death was my failure, Father, one of my many failures."

He gave a short laugh. "Success, failure … these things are not important." I looked at him surprised. "Oh, I can see they are to you but they should not be. God is not interested in success or failure. All He requires is that we use the gifts we have been given and strive … we strive to do good every day. Some days we will succeed, others we'll fail, but we must never stop striving … the only failure is the failure to try."

That stayed with me but I could not quite accept it. I had set out to lead that group of people to a better life and I had brought them back – not even all of them – because I had not achieved it. I could see that Dolan did not understand me at all; he had not experienced the trials of my last two years and I wondered how he might fare in similar circumstances. I was glad that Canon Peter did not invite him again.

I think it was on the fourth day that I ventured out into the city. I needed to find out how the others were faring. I went first to the Hotel de Inmigrantes and was relieved to see, in the courtyard, some of the children running around in the sunshine. Their parents were sitting in the shade, looking on and chatting. They greeted me with waves and shouts. I could not believe the transformation. I went round shaking hands and asking after everyone. The food had been good, they had taken baths – luxury they said – had been given new clothes and boots, the rooms were comfortable and the beds? Oh to lie down on beds! There were so many comments, so much life restored already, I felt enormous relief. Perhaps now these good people could start to rebuild their lives.

I spent time with the people there and then sought out others staying in places around that part of the city. I walked to the convent where a few of the families were living, the men of course having to sleep in the outbuildings but even these had been made comfortable. The Reverend Mother, an Irish woman, showed me around, a twinkle in her eye. Nothing would disturb her; she had seen every form of human suffering and knew how to respond. I thanked her with tears in my eyes.

"I think you've been sorely tested," she said quietly.

"I have, Reverend Mother, I have … and so have *all* the people who went to La Viticola. We lost a hundred …" I could not finish the sentence.

She nodded. "But they are not lost, Father – they are with God."

I stared at her, trying to make sense of that simple statement. Was it true or was it just something to soften the blow? "It feels like … I feel that …"

"Of course you do but sure God will help you through, I promise you. Hold on to him, Father Patrick, hold on to him."

I heard the words she spoke but no longer had any confidence that God would come to my aid. He had abandoned us out there in that hostile plain, left us to fend for ourselves when we needed him most. After our evening meal, I sat with Canon Peter in his sitting room. I had to tell him. "Father, I have come to the conclusion that I can no longer be a priest."

He said nothing for a long time but nodded slowly. At last he said, "And when did you come to this decision?"

"It has been growing for a long time. I suppose doubt has been seeping into my mind with every failure – I know you say failure does not matter but it does when your failure results in the suffering or death of others. Three days out from Buenos Aires on our long journey back, a young man called James O'Neill died. He had been injured by the bandit's knife whilst protecting me. I suppose the wound became infected and in his weakened state, he could not fight it. After he died, I went out into the grassland to pray but my words seemed to stay with me … I felt nothing, I heard nothing but the occasional call of a bird. I knew then that we had been abandoned by God and I could no longer lead people in a faith when I had such doubt."

Canon Peter sat in silence. I looked up. His eyes were on me, full of pity, full of love. If only I could feel that I deserved love. "Patrick … you must not give up on God. Think. Imagine a young child falls and hurts her knee. She cries in pain and horror at the sight of her blood spilling from the wound. Her father rushes to her and lifts her up in his arms, full of love. He tries to shush her, to calm her but she cries the louder. She does not feel his arms around her, only the pain in her knee. She is alone with her pain … but … but her father has lifted her and carries her home where her wound will be dressed and heal."

I did not understand him at first. How could a child's injured knee be compared to the suffering we had endured? "I could do nothing for James, that was the point."

"You did what you could and, when you could do no more, God lifted him from his suffering and took him to himself." He watched me. "But God also lifted you and carried you even though all you could feel was the pain you were suffering."

"I didn't feel Him with us, Father."

"No … but Patrick, do not give up on God yet – please. You are exhausted, you have been through it. Give yourself time to rediscover your faith."

We sat for a long while then in silence, the daylight through the window darkening. Emilia came in, tutted and lit the gas lamps. Their soft glow bathed us in yellow light, bringing warmth and safety. "Tomorrow, Father, I must try to find a young woman. In his last words, James asked me to find her, explain why he could not return to collect her as he had promised, and make sure she is alright. I don't know how to start looking."

"Her name?"

"Rose … Rose Kelly."

"Would she come to church?"

"Probably if she's stayed local but I've no idea where she might be. She has lovely long, auburn hair; one could not mistake her."

"I don't recall seeing a young woman of that description. You knew her before I presume?"

"She was on the boat on the way over. Lovely she was. When an old man called John took sick and was dying, she tended him with gentleness, as if he was her own father."

Canon Peter nodded and smiled. "Seek and you shall find," he said quietly.

The next day – it was Saturday – I spent the morning again visiting those who had returned with me from La Viticola but, as I walked around the city, my eyes were searching every alleyway and by-way, hoping to see a flash of her hair. A few times, I thought I saw her and dashed off in pursuit only to find no one or a woman who looked nothing like her. It was hopeless I realised. She may not even be in Buenos Aires anymore. I decided I must be more systematic and find out what I could.

I went to the Ministry of Immigration, the same place I had been on that first day, trying to get accommodation for the *Dresden* passengers. I asked the clerk – the same one at the desk as two years ago – if they kept records of immigrants and where they went. "Sometimes …" He shrugged.

"May I look at your records please?"

He shrugged again, showing no interest at all but went into the office behind the desk. He returned with three huge ledgers which he thumped down without a word on a table in the foyer. I began the search, discarding the first as too early. The ledgers recorded the date of arrival and the name of the ship but it was clear they were incomplete. I found a few people who had arrived on the *Dresden* the same day as I had but not many. These had apparently gone to an area about two hundred miles west of Buenos Aires but Rose's name was not among them.

After a fruitless hour, I thanked the clerk and left the building. In something of a daze, unsure of where to look next, I walked slowly to the docks. I suppose in a dark recess of my mind, I thought I should start where I had last seen her. As I wandered aimlessly through the docks, the sights and sounds of that arrival day came back to me. I remembered the chaos, Italians from the other ship, no one to tell people where to go. I remembered then the flash of auburn hair in a carriage as Rose and that other girl, what was her name? – Annie – were driven away. Where had that carriage taken them? Perhaps somewhere in the city.

I stood and looked out over the waters of the harbour. There were no ships in the dock where we had landed. A mass of gulls was squabbling over scraps from a fishing boat further down the quay and then flying up into the air, screaming in triumph or defeat. They rode the air for a while and then dived to the harbour wall to snatch a morsel from a competitor. I looked along the dock and then froze in shock. Were my eyes playing tricks or was that a cascade of auburn hair?

I moved closer, slowly, as if any sudden movement would make the image disappear. It did not move. I was only yards away when the figure lifted one foot slightly from the ground and put it forward as if to step over the side of the dock. I gasped in a sudden realisation of what she was about to do and lunged forward, grabbing an arm in each hand. For a horrible moment, I felt myself being pulled forward and I thought she would drag me over the side into the water but I put my foot against the raised edge of the quay and pulled her back.

## Rose

"Rose, Rose!" A shout close to my ear, a sudden pull backwards. I struggled to turn around and free myself. A voice from another time, a face I did not recognise. All I could think was attacker or saviour? Attacker or saviour?"

"Rose, it's me. Patrick Gilligan. Remember … the boat, the *Dresden* … I was the priest."

I looked at him, baffled at first and then with slow recognition. He had changed. His face was gaunt, drawn; he was thinner and his eyes spoke of suffering. What did he want with me? What interest could a priest have in me? "I must go … leave me go … please."

His mouth dropped open and I left him standing there. I walked quickly and did not look back. How could I face him? I started to remember him as I walked hurriedly back to my place of torment.

Curiously, it now seemed almost a refuge … a refuge from the dark thoughts in my own mind, a return to normality, however repugnant. I walked without noticing anything at all, images flooding my mind of that journey on the ship, the way he had protested to the captain and the agents about the conditions down below, the way he had taken John to the empty cabin next to his, the way he had tended him in his last days, the lovely words he had spoken as the body slipped into the cold sea.

He was a good man and what could a man like that have in common with me … a whore, a murderer? Part of me hated him for pulling me back from the edge of the dock to face this life of torment but part of me recognised something else. I had hoped that angels would catch me when I fell and take me from this life. Was he God's angel? Was he sent to save me? Or was it a cruel coincidence, him there on the dock at the very moment I had decided to relinquish my life?

I did not go to church the next day. I had failed even to say the small penance I had been given for the trivial things I had confessed. But in truth, it was because I felt shame, a shame so intense that I could not risk seeing him again. I had no place there amongst those who lived lives of decency. Perhaps that was why Molly and the others did not go to church, though I thought they had rejected it as having no relevance to them rather than staying away from a sense of disgrace.

On Monday morning, I was in the little room stitching garments that needed repair when Molly stuck her head round the door. "There's a fella here to see ya. He's odd. I don't think he's a customer … well, not the usual sort anyway."

I stuck the needle in the garment and laid it carefully on the table. "Should I go up and change?" It was very unusual to have a client in the morning.

"I'd see what he wants first if I were you."

Molly had shown him into the smaller sitting room and he was standing in the middle of the floor. The priest looked uneasy. When I entered, he turned quickly to face me. "I'm sorry, Rose, if I startled you on Saturday – at the dock. I didn't mean to but I thought …" I dismissed it with a small wave of my hand but I said nothing. "Rose, I need to give you some news – about James. I think we should sit down."

I shrugged and sat on the edge of the armchair where I had perched that first day we had arrived in Buenos Aires. He sat on the armchair next to mine, turning his body slightly towards me. "Rose, things didn't work out in La Viticola where we went from here two years ago. James was with us. We had to walk back – we arrived on Wednesday last. But James … I'm afraid James died a few days before we reached the city – on the Sunday before we arrived."

I stared at him then; his eyes looked sorrowful, a genuine grief in them that I knew could not be false. I had finally lost James from my dreams a little over a week ago. I felt numb. A year ago, I would have cried, I would have felt devastated. Now it was as if that was only to be expected. Why should someone like me have any happiness? James would not have wanted to know me now anyway.

"I'm sorry for that."

He looked directly at me. "I thought you'd be upset, Rose. I thought there was something between you … he seemed to think …"

"Oh yes, when we left the boat, he said he would come back for me and take me to that wonderful farm he would establish. It was just dreams … the kind of thing young people say."

"He cared for you, Rose. He had not forgotten you nor his promise. His dying wish was that I should find you and tell you he was coming back for you … though sadly without the farm he promised."

"How did he die?"

"We were set upon by bandits and when one of them thrust a knife at me, James pushed me out of the way and took the blow. He saved my life ... such a good man."

As he talked, I realised that he, James, everyone had endured awful suffering. Why was it that we immigrants should be treated so badly? It jolted me a little out of my own world. I had assumed everyone else except Annie and I had made a success of the move to Argentina. Clearly that was not the case. "What happened in the place you went?"

He let out a huge sigh. "Nothing was ready. We struggled for two years against hunger and illness but ..." He found it difficult to speak of it.

"I'm sorry, Father. Please do not distress yourself by remembering those things. It is perhaps best forgotten."

"I'm no longer a priest, Rose. I have lost my vocation – if I really ever had one. Maybe my faith, too. I'm not sure. I'm not sure of anything anymore. Just call me Patrick."

That was what had confused me. He was not wearing his clerical collar. He sat hunched in the chair, a poor version of the man I had met on the boat. We sat in silence for a good while, lost in our own thoughts, gazing at the window.

Then he spoke again. "Are you settled here in Buenos Aires, Rose? This house seems substantial and well appointed."

I stared at him. He didn't know. "If I could get away, I would."

He looked around quickly and his face softened from surprise to concern. It must have been the look on my own face. I could not meet his eyes. "You're unhappy." It was a statement, not a question.

I nodded and turned my face away lest I reveal the desperate state of my mind. "I thought you would know what kind of house this is."

"What kind of house ... what do you mean?"

I felt a savage desire to hurl the truth at him. "It's a brothel, a house of ill repute, and I'm a whore. Every night I fu..."

"No, Rose, don't say it." We stared at each other for a few seconds and both turned away.

"You'll be going back now to wherever and you'll not want to know me. James would not have wanted to know me had he lived so perhaps 'tis better he didn't."

"How ... was it your choice?"

I laughed then, a short humourless bark. "Choice?" I wanted to shout at him about the drugs, the violence, the threats, the fear of arrest ... but I said nothing.

"Rose, I want to get you away from here. I need to be honest. Even though I knew James and you had some bond, I have not been able to keep you out of my mind."

"Well, I'm sure what I've just told you will do the job."

"No, Rose ...'twill not."

"I suppose you want to save me, is that it?"

He turned to face me and I looked at him. I had become used to feeling hopelessness and sorrow in my own breast but to see it mirrored there in his eyes was a shock. He looked like a lost child, defeated, broken. I felt a stirring in me and rejoiced that I had not entirely lost the ability to care for another's suffering. I laid my hand on his arm.

His voice was little more than a whisper. "It is not that I want to save you, Rose ... I'm hoping you may be able to save me ... maybe we can save each other."

"I don't think I can be saved ... I'm too far gone. I've been to confession nearly every week for the last two years but have never been able to tell the priest my real sins. How can I be saved?"

"I don't know, Rose, but perhaps Canon Peter will guide us."

Patrick asked me to meet him the next day but I explained the impossibility of leaving Placer House. He asked me to come to church on Wednesday evening as it was Ash Wednesday. "We can talk some more," he said. I was doubtful after not feeling able to go to mass on Sunday but he persisted. I agreed, provided Ma would let me. Our meeting ended abruptly when Ma came in and told me to return to my work. She showed Patrick out the door and I heard him say, "May God forgive you." She laughed and slammed the door shut.

"Who was that?"

"He's a priest," I said simply not wishing to elaborate.

"I didn't think he was a customer."

I told Ma I was going to the Ash Wednesday service the next day. She grumbled and said I was to be sure to be back in time for work. I suppose that act of going to church was like a drowning woman gasping for a final breath of air. I had no real hope it would do anything for my soul nor my well-being. In truth, I was drawn by Patrick. What had he endured that had turned him from the priesthood, perhaps from his faith altogether? I could not remove from my mind the image of him turned towards me, the look of the lost child on his face, his eyes bewildered.

The sun was already falling towards the tallest buildings of the city when I set out next evening for church. The air was still warm, the long heat of summer seeming to radiate from the masonry. There is a softness to the sunlight in autumn, a hint of mist in the air, giving the evening the look of a painting. Purple shades of darkness would soon creep from the east, dispelling the light, chasing it down below the horizon, an eternal battle.

The church was already nearly full when I arrived. I recognised a few faces from the boat – they must have been those who had been with Patrick at La Viti … whatever it was called. I knelt in a pew near the back. In the pews immediately in front of me was a group of nuns. I had only very occasionally seen them in church – they normally worshipped in their own chapel, I supposed, but today was a special service. They sat in silence, their long veils crisply white, falling past their shoulders. The one at the end of the pew nearest the aisle had a different colour veil; the Mother Superior no doubt.

I wondered what I should do when the congregation was called up to receive the sign of the cross in ash on their foreheads. Could I do that, not having confessed my sins? Was I a child of God? The nuns in school had taught us that was the meaning of the ashen cross but it was also a sign of repentance, the start of the forty days of Lent. Slowly the people filed out of their pews, starting at the front and waiting in a long line down the centre aisle. The nice old priest was making the sign with that Father Dolan next to him so the queue split in two as it reached the chancel step.

Then the nuns rose as one and the Reverend Mother stood in the aisle smiling as her nuns passed her. I was the first in our pew and she glanced at me, still sitting down. She smiled and gestured to me. For a split second I thought I would refuse but then my legs lifted my body. It was something in her that made me stand – perhaps the old respect for religious authority that childhood had instilled in me, perhaps the kindness of her gesture, I'm not sure, but I stepped out into the aisle and she ushered me before her.

I was glad for some reason I cannot explain that I went to the old priest. He seemed as though a long life had given him understanding. I closed my eyes. His finger was gentle on my forehead and, when I opened my eyes again, he was looking directly at me. "Remember that thou art dust and unto dust thou shall return. May God bless you, my child."

I felt lighter. I could not explain it but the ashes on my forehead felt like a kind of purifying power. When I knelt in my pew again, I prayed that I would one day have the strength to confess the horrors of my life.

At the end of the service, I knew I should not linger but I wanted to find Patrick, if only to show him that I had come. When I stood, the Reverend Mother was already in the aisle watching her nuns file past. I waited for them with my eyes down. The last one passed and I stepped into the aisle and genuflected. Rising to my feet, the Reverend Mother was smiling at me.

"May I know your name?"

"Rose … Rose Kelly, Reverend Mother."

Her eyes sparkled with kindness. "You are troubled, Rose, but trust in God … He will take care of you."

I could not say anything for a while but gaped, open-mouthed at the unexpected intrusion of her remark. For a moment, I wanted to tell her what I was, what I had allowed to be done … that I was damned … that God would condemn me. She put out her hand and laid it gently on my arm. "Sometimes it's good to talk. You can find me or one of the sisters at the convent just along the road at any time. You do not have to be alone, Rose."

"Thank you, Reverend Mother."

To my relief, she moved away and I stayed where I was for a while to make sure I did not have to talk with her any further. It was not that she was unkind but that I could not begin to unburden my heart to a nun. How could they understand with their sheltered lives? They had never been with a man, let alone suffered the abuses that I had.

Patrick was standing near the door and I walked slowly towards him.

# CHAPTER 17

## OCHO CORTADO

**Patrick**

She approached shyly and to be honest I was not sure what to say to her. She had come as I had asked and I saw the ashen cross on her forehead. "You came."

"I did, as you can see, though I'm not sure why."

"No. There is a pull, though. I suppose it's what we've known since childhood that draws us back."

"Maybe. That Reverend Mother said I am troubled, not even that I *look* troubled."

"It's plain to see, Rose, as I'm sure 'tis with me. We're a pair, I think." She said nothing but watched people filing out of the door onto the street. I could hear the urgency in my voice as I dropped it to a conspiratorial whisper. "I'm going to get you out of there, Rose. I can't bear the thought of you there."

"And how do you propose to do that? I think you don't realise what you're dealing with."

"Maybe, but I have to try. I promised James." My mouth opened again but I did not speak immediately. "It's for me too, Rose, I have … feelings for you."

"For me? Why would you have feelings for me? You know what I am."

"I know what you have to do, Rose, but 'tis not who you are." Again, she said nothing but her face was slightly flushed. "It was on

the boat. I was a priest then and you and James were together but …
your gentleness with old John, your intelligence, your gorgeous
smile…"

"Stop, stop. You're still a priest remember … once a priest, always
a priest. And if you do really give up, there's lots of good young
women who'll make you a lovely wife. Me … I'm broken, I'm
destroyed, I'm empty."

"Rose, you may be now, but you can be restored, you must believe
that."

"Maybe. But you need to know that Ma, my jailer, will not let me
get away while she can make money from me. I have to go now. I
hope you find yourself again. Don't waste your time on me … I'm
too far gone."

And then she was out the door and hurrying along the road back
to her torment. I didn't follow but I knew what I was going to do. I
walked back to the presbytery deep in thought.

Next day, I asked to speak with Canon Peter. We sat in
comfortable chairs in his study. "Father, I need to get a job. My plan
is to leave Argentina, probably for America, so I'll need money for
the ticket and for when I arrive."

"You've had no income for the last two years, have you? The
church owes you something, the kind of money you would have had
from the Christmas and Easter collections if you had been in a
parish. I'll ensure you get that at least."

"Thank you, Father, but I'm not looking for charity and whilst I'm
under your roof but not as a priest, I want to work to pay my way."

"You're a determined young man, Patrick, I'll say that for you. Let
me see what I can find for you in the way of a job."

"I'll do anything. There is another reason I need money." He smiled
knowingly. "I need to get the young woman I told you about to a place

of safety. I'm going to ask her if she'll come to America as well."

"Tell me more about her."

I told him of how I had seen Rose on the ship that first evening as we left Queenstown, watching Ireland recede into the evening light. I told him of her loveliness in tending John and, at last, I told him of the place she was now.

"I'm going to get her out of there. Why in God's name the police have not done something about it before now, I don't know."

"They can't. It is shameful but prostitution and brothels were legalised in Buenos Aires back in the last decade – 1875 I think it was. You'll probably find the police use their services as much as any other kind of men."

I was horrified. "Well, then I'll simply remove her and bring her to a place of safety until I can get tickets to America."

He was silent for a while. "You care for her, don't you, Patrick?"

The directness of the question startled me but my voice was firm. "I do, yes, Father."

"And when did your feelings start?"

"I'm not sure … her face used to come to me at night, especially when things were bad."

He nodded. "When you first saw her on that ship … that's when she will have entered your heart." I looked up, startled again. "It is no matter. That is the way between men and women. It's something we cannot put a name to, that feeling, that joy we cannot explain when we see that person."

"You speak with great … understanding."

"I was a young man once, Patrick. In the parish where I was curate, there was a young woman. She was virtuous, a good person and lovely as the finest spring morning. I loved her Patrick. It was as simple as that. But I had taken my vows as a priest so I did nothing, just wrestled every night when her smiling face entered my mind. When my curacy was over, I told the bishop I would like to work abroad and I came here. I thought I would be able to put her out of mind."

"What became of her?"

"She married, had children … I hope she was… is happy. Me, I never lost her image, though now she will be much older. I have often wondered if I made the right decision. Perhaps I should have renounced my vocation and asked her to marry me. She may have said no of course but … I didn't. Not a day has passed since when I haven't thought of her and the life I may have had. I have no real regret. I made my vows and I am proud that I stuck to them but … the love between a man and a woman is a gift from God, as valuable as a vocation. We should never think of it as less worthy." He leaned back in his chair as if exhausted by this revelation.

"I had no idea …"

"There's no reason why you would and I know, Patrick, that I can rely on your discretion. Now you must make a decision about your future. If it is to be with this young woman – if she'll have you – God will bless your union. If not, I pray that you will be restored to your ministry."

I thanked him and left his study in something of a daze. I had expected him to be suspicious, to tell me I was a priest for life but he had an insight into the human condition culled from long years of ministry that enabled him to understand without explanation, to bless without conditions. He had freed me from my duty in a way I had never expected. I determined to carry out the first part of my plan without delay.

It was early afternoon when I arrived at Placer House. I was let in by a young woman but not so young as Rose. She said her name was Molly and did I want to spend time with her now? I didn't realise at first what she was asking; I stammered and flushed as I declined. Her eyes mocked me but I would not be deterred from what I had to do. I asked to see the madam of the house. I waited in the same room as before, standing awkwardly as I had done on my previous visit.

"So, 'tis you back again." She stood with her hands on her hips. "What is it this time? You want to see Rose again?"

"No. It is you I want to see. I want you to know that I will be taking Rose away soon and I'll not stand for any resistance."

She laughed. "You're just going to take her away, are you? And what does Rose say about this?"

"She doesn't know … yet."

"I think you'll find she does not want to leave. She is safe here, she is fed, has nice dresses to wear. She's part of our family here. That's more than can be said for many of the girls that come over."

"Safe? Safe? How can you say she's safe when every night those men do things to her? Can't you see they've broken her? She was a lovely, virtuous young woman and you've destroyed her."

"Ah, yes. Virtuous. She had to grow up sometime and it may as well have been sooner than later. What are you proposing? You're a priest. You can't marry her and even if someone else does, what d'you think they'll do to her? Have her skivvying all day and then spreading her legs at night!"

"You soil everything you touch. Do you not have any conscience?"

"Conscience? The likes of me can't afford a conscience. Oh, 'tis all very well for priests to talk about conscience when they get everything provided and never have to grapple with the real world."

I spoke quietly. "I have seen more of the real world in the last two years than many see in a lifetime. But that's beside the point. You need to know that Rose is finished here … as soon as I can get her to a place of safety."

"Well now, if you're so determined, you can of course make me an offer. You should bear in mind though that I make good money from Rose. She's popular with our gentlemen because she is pretty and has a lovely nature. Men like that. So, what will you offer me?"

"You want me to give you money?" I was horrified.

"You didn't think you could just take her away, did you? I want compensation."

"She is not a cow to be traded in a market. You don't own her."

"Oh, but I do and I'll look after my own." She stared straight into my eyes, no shame, no concern, nothing but greed.

"When I'm ready, I will take her away ... no money ... nothing."

"Well, you can try but perhaps you should think about that carefully. You see the Chief Superintendent of Police is a regular customer of ours and he is very fond of Rose. I don't think he'd take kindly to her being abducted. I'm sure he would take action against anyone who kidnapped her."

"Kidnap? You twist everything round. 'Tis you have kidnapped her."

"Try telling that to the policemen who arrest you. Try telling that to the judge when there'll be witnesses aplenty to say how well looked after she was and how happy to be at Placer House. Now, I have things to do. I'll see you out."

I was speechless and followed her out to the front door. "You've not heard the last of this," I said lamely.

"Oh, I think I have. Don't come here again if you know what's good for you." She slammed the door in my face.

I walked away, contemplating my next move. This was not going to be as easy as I'd thought. I needed to see Rose again but knew that I could not go to Placer House. I would have to hope that she went to confession on Saturday or church on Sunday. I wandered slowly back to the presbytery, deep in thought. Perhaps this was a hopeless mission. Something I had convinced myself I needed to do when it was simply a way of rescuing my own self-esteem, a success to be dragged from the ashes of the last two years.

That evening at dinner, Canon Peter announced that he had found me a job. He repeated his view that I had no need to take a job as I was welcome to stay at the presbytery rent free and I would receive a payment from the church for the last two years. I insisted, however. I had renounced my ministry, so I must support myself. It was as a clerk in a bank run by two Irish men. Most of the employees, Canon said, would be Irish by birth and most of the customers too. Next morning, I set out, was duly interviewed and hired. I would be trained as I worked in the back office but the salary was enough for my purposes. In a few weeks, I would probably have enough for one ticket at least.

After work that day, I went to the presbytery via the docks and called in at the office of the main shipping line for America. I was delighted to find that a ship would sail on Easter Saturday. That would give me the whole of Lent to earn money. That would be Rose's release, provided I could get her out of that place.

I was strolling back in better spirits than I had been for a long, long time when I was stopped by two police officers. "Signor, you're papers, please." The one who had spoken held out his hand for the papers and stared, unsmiling, into my face.

I pulled out what I had – the certificate of entry I had been given on that first day when we arrived on the *Dresden*. I handed it over and the officer gave it a cursory glance. "Thank you, signor. And where are you going now?"

"I'm going back to the presbytery where I'm staying. Why do you need to know?"

"Where you come from?"

"What, just now?" He nodded. "I've been to the shipping office to make enquiries."

"You are leaving Buenos Aires?"

"When I have the money for a ticket."

"You'll go alone?"

"Hopefully not. I'm not sure."

He smiled, a hint of malice in it. "You go alone, signor. Don't make plans for another person ... for a young woman ... bad things happen to people sometimes."

"Are you threatening me?"

"Of course not, signor. I just warn you that bad things happen sometimes. You not want anything bad to happen, huh?" He turned to his colleague and they shared a knowing smile.

He gave me back my papers and I walked on, inwardly fuming but also feeling sick with fear. This was what that woman at Placer House meant. She had moved quickly. Now I understood what Rose meant about the difficulty of escape. Those police officers had found me easily; I assumed they were not acting alone. Ma O'Shaughnessy's claim to have influence with the most senior officer was clearly not empty. He liked Rose and would abuse his power to keep her at Placer House for his pleasure. I needed to think carefully about my next move. I must not arouse suspicion but I was determined to see Rose and persuade her to come with me.

## Rose

"That fella was here again. Is he a priest or is he not?"

I was washing clothes in the scullery. Ma's tone was aggressive and put me on alert. "Who d'you mean, Ma?"

"That fella that came the other morning to speak to you. I don't know his name."

"Oh, Patrick Gilligan. He was a priest but he says he is no longer."

"Well now, you listen to me. He's trying to make out he's going to take you away from here. But don't think I'll let that happen. I'm not done with you yet." The menace was plain in her voice.

"Take me away? But he said nothing of the sort to me. Why would I go away with him?"

Her eyes narrowed, assessing how much she could trust my surprise. "Remember, Rose, Signor Ramirez. He would not want you to leave and he'll do what he must to prevent it."

"I know that Ma. I remember …" I did indeed remember the lashes with his belt on my back, the way Annie had been picked up and flung in prison to be used by the junior officers. "I'm not going anywhere. Surely you know that by now?"

She stomped off. I would need to do everything I could to reassure her in the coming weeks. I had not been watched by Michael since the rape and I didn't want that back again … not that Michael would do anything to me now.

I went to confession as normal on Saturday afternoon. I wondered as I walked to the church whether I would now be able to confess the life I lived, having told Patrick. I had watched his face closely when I'd told him. He was clearly shocked at first, but to his credit, he recovered quickly. I wondered what experiences he had endured to make him lose his vocation. When he had spent a few weeks in a more civilised place, he would probably find it again.

I was unable to tell the priest in the confessional box about my life. It was the same young priest I'd had before, Father Dolan, who liked to sit in judgement. He was the voice of the church, ready to condemn and punish. Where was the understanding? Where was the forgiveness? I said the penance this time and left the pew. I noticed

Patrick then, standing at the back of the church. He smiled and moved towards the aisle so that I could not avoid him when I reached that spot.

"Hello, Rose. May we talk please?"

"Yes, but not for too long. Let's sit outside."

We left the quiet gloom of the church and sat on the shaded base of a pillar in front of the building. The sun was bright on the street, though without the full heat of summer. "You saw Ma the other day. She reminded me of what would happen if I tried to leave. I told her I had no intention of doing so."

"I hope I have not caused you difficulty, Rose. I thought I would just have to make clear that I was taking you away from there but …" He hesitated before continuing. "… she wanted me to pay her money for you. I was horrified and told her she was treating you like a head of cattle."

"That's what I am!"

"Rose you must not accept their view of you. You are a person, a lovely, kind young woman. But I now know how difficult things will be." He paused. "I was stopped by two policemen. They made it clear what would happen if I took you away. That madam called it kidnapping you."

"Well, you haven't actually asked me if I want to leave."

He looked at me startled. "But surely …"

"Oh yes, I'd like to leave but not at the risk of being flung in jail and raped by every police officer in the city. They are ruthless – Ma, Signor Ramirez, the police." I had thought of using a harsher word than rape but his being a priest stopped me. I softened my tone – after all, he was trying to help me. "D'you remember Annie?"

"Annie? I don't …"

"I met her on the boat over and spent a lot of time with her. She looked after old John too."

"Annie … yes, I remember her. Lively, dark-haired young woman with a bit of cheek … an attractive cheek, I should say."

"She's in a worse way than me. She works in another house, rougher she says. They gave her laudanum at some point and now she's an addict. I see her most Saturdays after confession but she's in a bad way. She's accepted her lot and has no fight left." He said nothing and I sat in silence for a while, remembering the things Annie had told me. "She had a terrible childhood, you know, in Dublin. The things that men do to girls."

He nodded but said nothing. When I looked at him, his face was grief-stricken, his eyes dark, brooding. "Not all men, I hope," he said quietly. "Surely there is some goodness somewhere … but so much suffering – why so much suffering?"

"I don't know. I'd like to hear more about what happened to you and the others who were with you over the last two years."

"I will tell you when I can. All I can say is that I failed all those people. They set out to find a better life and I couldn't even keep them all alive."

"That's not your fault surely? 'Twas not your responsibility to keep them."

The look of appeal in his eyes was frightening. "I wish I could believe that. One day maybe I will but not yet. It feels like a huge weight on my heart, a pain inside that I cannot remove."

We sat in silence for several minutes, watching passers-by going about their business, oblivious to the serpents in our thoughts. The question that always twisted and coiled in my mind appeared again. "Did God choose this life for us? If so, why did he want to punish us?"

"I no longer feel able to answer that, Rose, or anything to do with

God, for that matter."

"When we were on the ship, you said God had led me to be there to bring comfort to John. It was all part of his purpose, I think you meant."

"Perhaps. But what purpose can we be serving? Why should we be destroyed like this?"

"Why are some born into luxury, comfort, riches and others into poverty, toil and pain? Why is it that one person becomes a great leader, famous, admired and another who strives just as hard achieves nothing? There seems no justice in that."

"I have no answer to that." His voice was no more than a whisper, his eyes cast down.

Again, we sat in silence until I said, "I have to go … to see Annie."

"There is a ship, Rose, leaving from here on Easter Saturday … in a few weeks. 'Tis bound for America and I intend to be on it. I want you to come with me. We can start a new life …" My face must have betrayed surprise. "Oh, I don't mean … unless you'd want that. I know I do but I'm not assuming … Will you come?"

It was that desperate appeal in his voice that meant I did not dismiss it. This was no attempt on his part to be the noble saviour but it was a hand reached out to me from one who was drowning too. "I'd have to get away somehow from Placer House."

"We'll find a way, Rose. It's the only way I can think of to get you to safety."

"Thank you … I'll think about it." It was a lame answer but I was touched. It was perhaps a mad scheme but he had thought of it to help me … the first time really anyone had suggested helping me since the day we landed on the quay. I leant forward and laid my hand upon his shoulder. "You're a good man, Patrick. I knew that when I first met you. Be kind to yourself … you've suffered as well as me." He looked up and I realised his eyes were watery. He lifted his hand and laid it on mine. The touch was gentle, no suggestion of possession in it, just thanks. Perhaps I was not in such a bad state as he was. Perhaps he was right … I could save him.

I walked a little way along the road and looked back. He was watching me and raised a hand in farewell. He smiled, a sad, shy smile and I returned it, raising my hand too. I went straight to the square where I usually met Annie. She was already sitting on our favourite bench. I kissed her cheek and sat beside her. She mumbled a greeting but nothing more.

"D'you remember the ship over here, Annie?"

She turned bleary eyes towards me. "I do."

"D'you remember there was a priest on board who did his best to make things better for us? Remember that old man John whom we looked after in the cabin until he died? The priest had him brought to that cabin and looked after him with us." I watched her carefully and slowly saw a memory light in her eyes.

"I remember him … handsome fella … wasted as a priest." She grinned. I was so pleased that she had remembered. There was still hope that her brain could be recovered from its state of stupor.

"I've just been talking to him. He had a terrible couple of years with a group from the boat who went to some place … can't remember where. Now he's back here and he's working to save enough money for a ticket to America. He wants me to go with him."

"America? Nice."

"Annie, Annie, don't you see? You could come too. We can get out of this place. You can get better again without that stuff you take."

She looked across the square, her eyes not focusing on anything. "You go, Rose. I'm sure 'twill be good. But will you marry the priest?"

"Marriage doesn't come into it. He'll not look at me because of what I am and what I've done. I want you to come too, Annie. Please say you will. There's a ship leaves on Easter Saturday."

"I'll stay here, Rose. What good would it do to go to America. 'Twould be the same thing there for me. 'Tis all I'm fit for."

"Annie, Annie, you mustn't talk like that. You're a good person, a lovely person and you can be well again, get a proper job." I heard myself echoing some of Patrick's words but I didn't care. I didn't think I could go and leave Annie in this place in the state she was in. "Please say you'll think about it."

"If it'll make you happy … I'll think about it." She gave a weak smile and seemed then to lapse again into her drugged state.

I realised that the brief discussion with Patrick had raised a tiny flower of hope but, as I walked back to Placer House, I felt it shrivel and die. Perhaps Annie was right. Perhaps starting again somewhere else was just a dream. Once he knew the full truth about me, he would not want to know me. What decent man would?

That evening, Signor Ramirez was one of the customers. He sought me out as soon as he arrived; I was hovering as I usually did at the edge of the room trying to go unnoticed. "You have a new friend I hear, Rose."

I genuinely did not make the connection at first and frowned. "A new friend?"

He smiled, his slightly dangerous smile, his eyes amused. "A priest, I hear."

"Oh him … Father Gilligan. He's not a priest any more, he said. He was on the ship coming over that's how I know him. He's not a friend … just someone I know."

"Ah I see. I thought perhaps you leave Buenos Aires with this Gilligan, maybe marry him."

I feigned shock but I doubt I was convincing enough to fool Ramirez's sharp eyes. "Not a bit of it. He's still enough of a priest not to be thinking of such things. Anyway," I added with a twinge of malice myself, "what would he want with a girl like me ... a whore?"

"Does he know what you do?"

"Yes."

"But he still talks to you?"

"Yes. Perhaps he wants me to confess my sins."

"Perhaps." He smiled again. "We will spend a little time together later." He put his hand on the small of my back and let it slide onto my bottom. I let it rest a moment before gliding away.

Before I had to climb the stairs with Ramirez, Molly danced the tango with one of the customers. She did not do so every Saturday by any means as there were only a few men she thought could dance well enough to partner her. She always wore the red dress, the one with the split that revealed her stockings. The eyes of all the men were fixed on her as she danced and you could sense their excitement growing. Molly loved the attention. I suppose it was a kind of power over them, the power to seduce, to excite, but it was deadly as one or two, maybe three or four, would later exact a perverse revenge on her.

She seemed to see that as part of her triumph. The dance no longer excited me as it had done at first. It was, I decided long ago, a perfect image of our slavery not the freedom that it should have been. Molly had tried to persuade me to learn to dance the tango, but I had resisted. I did not want to raise that level of anticipation in the customers – they were already demanding enough.

Ramirez that night certainly wanted his pleasure. He treated me like a rag doll, pulling me into different positions and pumping away as if trying to prove his virility. I was well used to it from him and the others. It was about domination, showing the power a man has over a woman who is there just for his pleasure. There were another two customers that night, too; both had been excited by Molly's dancing and wanted to exert their power. One grabbed a handful of my hair and pulled my head towards his member.

As I lay in bed, I shuddered at the memory. I had lost the ability to cry a long time before. I was numb but I still felt the humiliation. I thought of Patrick, a gentle, broken man. Did he really care for me? He had said he had feelings for me. I longed to believe there could be escape, a future. But how could I tell him about the tiny soul who had been flushed from my womb? How could I tell him I was a murderer, damned to spend eternity in hell?

# CHAPTER 18

# CADENCIA

**Patrick**

That night, after our evening meal, we sat as usual in the sitting room with cups of coffee. It had become our custom and I suppose Canon Peter sensed I needed time to talk, to unravel the strands of thought that had become twisted into an impossible knot. Emilia had lit a fire earlier as the evenings were already becoming a little chilly. The temptation to banish all the thoughts that troubled me, those memories that haunted me, was huge. It crept into me with the warmth of the dancing flames, the ruddy glow the coals cast on the room with its faded but comfortable armchairs.

"Today, Rose asked me was it God who determined that we should have lived the lives we have done over the last two years. Was it God, she was asking, that decided she was to be a prostitute."

"And what answer did you give her?"

"None. I no longer have answers. I know what I would have said two years ago – I would have said something about free will and predestination but, if I'm honest, I'm not sure I really understood it then. St Thomas Aquinas always baffled me a little. How can a loving God allow such things to happen to those who believe, who want only to do good?" I know the hurt and sense of betrayal I felt was evident in that anguished question.

Canon Peter thought for a minute before responding. "So many people have the notion that God is like a puppeteer, pulling strings, making each of us do this, that or the other. I struggled with it myself for many years. Does God control the seas? If so, why does he send the storm that destroys the ship?"

"You struggled with it too, Father? You always seem to be sure in your beliefs."

"Surer on most things than I was when I was younger but never completely sure. I accepted many years ago that understanding God is the work of a lifetime and even then one may not be sure. But let me offer you my thoughts and you must decide whether they make sense or not. I believe that God does not control everything at first hand. He moulded the Earth with the forces of creation and destruction in balance. He made each of us with a set of gifts which we must use to manage our lives in the world he created. Thus, the captain of the ship has the knowledge and ability to see the storm coming and to operate accordingly. He may not always succeed but he tries."

He stopped again and looked into the fire. I followed his gaze and stood to put on another log. It flared with tiny sparks when the new log hit the red hot embers and started to add its warmth to the room.

"When I was at the seminary, we had a retreat at Dunbrody Abbey in County Wexford. Do you know of it?" I shook my head. "Next to the Abbey is an old castle – not really a castle at all – and in the grounds there is a maze. That's a strange business, trying to find your way to the centre. There was a bit of a wooden tower in the centre which you could climb if you could get there. But, here's the thing, you'd be taking paths that led you all over but not to where you wanted to go. But from the tower, you could see people deciding which path to take and you could let your eye trace that path and see where 'twould lead."

We both looked into the fire, watching the flames curl over the new log, darting up and dying only to spring up again. There were so many colours within them, so much richness in the destruction by fire of that simple piece of wood. It had been part of a thriving tree, it had once had life, the sap rising each spring to burst joyously into leaf and then to close down each autumn, waiting for the cold to pass and life to start again.

"It was many years before I thought the maze could help us understand that mind-teasing conundrum of free will and predestination. Imagine God was on that tower. He sees the decisions we are having to make but that does not make it easier for us – we still have to make the decision. But he knows what we will decide and where it will lead. We have the freedom of choice yet, at the same time, our destiny is known. And whatever we choose, there is love ... always there is love. Perhaps that will help you, perhaps not."

I looked at Canon Peter. His old eyes held wisdom and not a trace of pride. He offered me this in humility, one person lost in that maze to another, struggling to reach the centre. I thanked him quietly. I knew that I was having to start again, rethink all that I had once thought I understood. It was my autumn, the closing down, the cold of winter to come, but perhaps there would be a spring, a new rush of life, a new understanding.

And so as Lent progressed, I worked in the bank by day and looked forward to those evenings with Canon Peter. We told each other of our lives, how we had found a vocation, how I had lost mine. Each evening, he would ask me something about La Viticola and I would tell him, wrenching those sad days from my memory. I knew that it was a therapy for me. He understood that I would only be able to restore myself by unravelling the past, coming to terms with it, identifying where I could have acted differently.

And every Saturday, I waited for Rose to come from confession and we talked. We spent longer with each other each week because she said Annie had so little to say now. She told me of how she had come to be at Placer House, how she had been very excited and pleased at first before she discovered what her fate was. She told me how she was drugged that first time but she never told me of the things that had been done to her by those men and I did not ask her. I felt that there was something else she wanted to say but it was always left hovering in the air between us.

I knew how she felt. She asked me about my time since arriving in Argentina and I repeated the sad stories I had already rehearsed with Canon Peter. It was painful for both of us but my love for her grew as I saw her concern. She was especially interested when I told her about Jimmy. I suppose that episode reflected things she had endured. I think she began to care for me a little but I did not want to make assumptions. She seemed to me like a wild creature, shy and vulnerable, that would dive for cover as soon as she sensed any danger.

One evening in the week before Palm Sunday, Canon Peter said he had been in the city, catching up with the situation of the others who had returned with me from La Viticola. Many had found places outside the city to start again, but this time with loans and decent land to farm. Those who wanted to had been offered the money for tickets to America or back to Ireland. Some of these had found work whilst they were waiting to leave, others were given enough to live on as well as the money for the ticket.

"I was speaking to a couple of single men. They're planning to return to Ireland on the next ship which leaves a week after Easter. I asked them about La Viticola and, as you'd expect, they told me it was terrible. But then one said, "Thank God for Father Patrick. He was the only true friend we had. Were it not for him, we'd have all died."

"That was kind but I don't see it like that. What was his name?"

"Arthur somebody, I don't remember his surname."

"Arthur? Are you sure? Was he a surly looking fella with dark hair?"

"He was. Why so surprised?"

"Arthur was my fiercest critic I'd say. He questioned and criticised all the decisions I made. He really said that?"

"He did. One never really knows the impact one has on the lives of others. Perhaps you judge yourself too harshly … more harshly than others judge you."

I was amazed. Arthur! Arthur who had criticised my decision to buy the boat and just about every other decision I had made. Could it be? He had no reason to say it but, knowing Arthur, he would not say something he did not mean. That evening was the first time I felt the stirring of hope. I became even more determined to get Rose to safety. I owed it to James, to her and to myself. The pay packet I received at the end of that week gave me enough, along with what Canon Pater had given me from the church, to buy two tickets for America. Escape was no longer a dream. I longed to tell Rose.

I met her next day after confession as we had done for several weeks, sitting as usual on the base of the stone pilar outside the church. The day was cloudy, a harbinger of the coming autumn, warmth still in the air but not lasting long after the fall of the sun. Across the street, a poor man was squatting on the ground, trying to sell a few scrawny vegetables. No one seemed to buy from him but he sat motionless, as if he expected nothing else. Perhaps that is how we should be … expecting nothing, accepting everything.

I told Rose of my intention to buy two tickets in the coming week, that we had only to think of how we could get her out of Placer House and onto the ship and then we could start again in a new country, far from this place. She looked startled, almost fearful.

"You speak so easily about me leaving Placer House. How can I do that when they watch me and the police would find me very quickly. They'll arrest you as well."

"I'll think of something, Rose. We'll succeed, trust me."

"And my friend Annie. I don't think … I can't leave her here on her own, in the state she is. But she won't come, I already asked her."

"I don't have enough money for a third ticket but if we can find enough, I'll be happy for her to come."

"I have some money, only a little, from February's earnings, which I have hidden. I have sent it in the past back home but this month I kept it … for…"

I smiled at her. "That was a good idea." Three weeks ago, then, she had allowed for the possibility of coming with me.

"I can bring that to you. It won't be enough for a third ticket but, as I say, I don't think I can persuade Annie. 'Twill give us a little for the first days, though. I should have a little more for March but I'm not sure I'll get that in time. I don't want to arouse Ma's suspicions by asking for it early."

"Bring what you have to church tomorrow. I'll take it into the bank and have it changed into dollars. If you get more, all well and good. If not, we'll manage." I smiled encouragement to her. "This will work out, Rose. I feel it in my bones."

"Let's hope your bones are right then!" She laughed briefly, the first time I had seen her laugh since the early days of the voyage over. I wanted to kiss her but held back, afraid that such an act would frighten her away. She was like a deer who has walked out of the forest into the fields to graze; the slightest sound would startle her and send her back into the cover of the trees.

I felt that we had drawn closer, imperceptibly, without words being spoken or any commitments made. It was because we had both suffered, both needed to leave Argentina, both needed to start anew. I felt it as a bond stronger than any vow and I began to hope that she felt it too.

## Rose

At the end of the service, I left the pew and was looking around for Patrick. I shuffled with the departing congregation to the back of the church and hovered behind the last pew. A voice close by startled me. It was the Reverend Mother.

"Hello, Rose. I'm glad you could come. 'Tis a special day for us, is it not?"

"Hello, Reverend Mother. Yes, it is. Palm Sunday."

"Special and joyous but very sad. To think that he rode in triumph into Jerusalem and within a week was nailed to a cross. Such is betrayal. So many are betrayed … let down … used by others."

"Yes …"

"Rose, I want you to know that we, myself and my sisters, are here should you ever want help."

"Thank you, Reverend Mother but I don't think …"

"You don't think we can help?"

"I wasn't going to say that. I don't think … you would want to help … someone like me." I was mumbling by the time I finished the sentence.

She leaned forward and spoke quietly, her eyes softening as if they could fill me with gentleness.

"I know people have strange views about us." Her eyes shone brightly in the filigree of creases that surrounded them and then returned to liquid. "We devoted ourselves to the service of God, to spend our time and energy helping those in need. That is what we do."

I felt a surge of anger almost. Did she not realise what I was? "I think I'm beyond help."

"No one is, Rose. No one. Which house is it you work in?"

I was startled by the question. "Placer House."

"Ah yes. Ma O'Shaughnessy. 'Tis well known to us. We have helped a couple of girls from there in the last years." I blushed and dropped my eyes. I felt her hand take my own. "Rose, 'tis not your fault. I daresay that you have been made to do what you do. We can offer you a safe place to be but 'tis you must decide whether to come to us."

"They'll stop me. I've already been threatened with the police."

"We would act carefully and swiftly so you need not worry about that. But I know how the life you lead traps you. 'Tis not just the fear of the consequences, it is the way they make a prison inside you so that it is yourself who keeps you there."

I looked up and stared at her. She was right but I had never been able to formulate the thought. It was true for me and for Annie and probably for Maggie, Sheila and even Molly. We could not be free until we had broken those prison bars inside our own minds.

"You know where we are, Rose. St Joseph's Convent. Ring the bell at any time, day or night, and ask for sanctuary. We will not let you down."

And then she was gone and I stood dazed. I could not imagine the nuns at school being so matter-of-fact about the life I had. Reverend Mother seemed to know all about it without me telling her. I was still trying to understand what had just passed when Patrick sidled up to me.

"I see you were talking with Reverend Mother. She's a great woman is she not?"

"She knew … about me. All I told her was where I live. She said I could go to the convent but …"

He smiled and said something about her working in Buenos Aires for a long time. "You could do that, Rose. Even if it was on

Thursday or Friday after mass. Just go to the convent not back to Placer House."

"I don't think ... 'tis not that I don't trust the nuns. 'Tis the police ... they could search the convent. They'd arrest me."

"I'm sure they wouldn't do that."

"I've seen what they can do."

I gave him the money then, not much but I wanted to contribute something to my ticket. He took it and put it in his pocket swiftly as if he did not want anyone to see. "I may be able to get the money for March before we go but ..."

"It's no matter, Rose. I have enough. I'll get the tickets this week. You'll come to the Maundy Thursday service, won't you? I can tell you I've got them then if I get them Wednesday or Thursday. We'll then talk about how we're going to get you out if you won't go to the convent."

"It will be better if I just leave very early Saturday morning, before anyone is up and then I can keep out of sight somewhere ... here or at the docks. What time does the ship sail?"

"Eleven o'clock in the morning. We must be on board by ten o'clock and can board any time from nine."

"That should be fine. The only person who might hear me if I leave very early is Michael. He sleeps in a room off the scullery. But if I go by six, he should still be asleep. You will come, won't you?"

"Of course. Why would I not?"

I said nothing but in my mind was the awakening he may have, realising that he was giving up his vocation for a prostitute, a murderer. I knew I had to tell him. It would be wrong to let him do this for me and not know what I was. And then there was the pull of the church. Would Canon Peter let him sail off into the sunset without stopping him? I doubted it. They would at least try to persuade him to stay and pick up his ministry again. So much uncertainty, so much doubt, so many ifs.

I walked slowly back to Placer House, going by the street where St Joseph's Convent nestled, its old stones held between two more recent buildings. I looked surreptitiously at the doorway, the bell pull beside it, as I walked slowly by. Did safety lie within its old stones? I was tempted to walk across the street and pull the bell, throw myself into their care but … it was true. The prison bars were within me. Would I be able to free myself on Saturday morning? I must not allow the fear of discovery to prevent me from opening the door of my prisons, both the physical house and the one in my mind.

I wondered then whether I should walk by Annie's house and try to see her, try one more time to persuade her to leave with me. I decided against it just in case Annie should blurt it out to someone. I could afford to trust no one. But I could do that after church on Thursday perhaps so there would be less time for the whisper of my flight to drift around the city before I left on Saturday. Would there be time then and money to obtain a ticket for her? Probably not. I would have to accept that I would leave Annie behind. I grieved then for her. What could I do for her? Reverend Mother had said they could only help if a girl came to them. Annie would never do that but perhaps…

Sundays were usually quiet at Placer House, only a few men escaping wives and families in the evening. That night was no exception. There was one fella, Signor Roberto I think his name was, who usually went with Molly. I was, as usual, hovering at the edge of the room when he arrived. Molly went to him and started sliding up against him, her hand travelling down his shirt front and lingering tantalisingly on his belt. She fetched him a glass of brandy and sat on his lap in an armchair. I could see his eyes roving around the room and he smiled at me a couple of times. I, of course, smiled briefly but turned my eyes away as soon as I had done so.

Other customers wanted my attention for drinks and I was surprised when Signor Roberto was suddenly beside me. I looked for Molly. Her face spoke of fury and I wondered what could have happened. Then his arm was around me and he was smiling down into my face.

"I think I'd like to spend time with you tonight. I want change from Molly."

"Are you sure? You usually go with Molly."

"Si, I sure. Molly I have spent plenty time with."

"I just need to speak to Ma and then I'll be back." I left him with a toss of my hair and he chuckled. I spoke urgently and quietly to Ma. "That Signor Roberto says he wants to go with me tonight …but he usually has Molly. What will I do?"

"You'll go with him, of course. That's what you're here for."

"But what about Molly?"

"What about her? She can go with someone else."

Molly gave me such a look as I left the salon with Signor Roberto. I could say nothing but I hoped she could read the apology in my eyes. Clearly, she did not or if she did she chose to ignore it. As I was preparing for bed, the door burst open and she gave it a fierce push to close it so the slam made me jump. I turned to look at her. She advanced towards me.

"I suppose you think you're the queen of the place now, taking Signor Roberto?"

I shrank before her anger, stepping backwards. My lower legs hit the bed and I sat down suddenly. "Molly, I did nothing. I even asked Ma what I should do. I know he always goes with you."

"Oh yes … you're Miss Goody Two Shoes, aren't you?" She put on a child's voice. "I did nothing, I just stand there looking pretty." She bent towards me, pushing her face close to mine. "Oh, you think

I don't know what you do? I know alright. You toss your long red hair and put on your sweet little smile and they come flocking. I'm not good enough anymore even though I know far more about how to pleasure a man than you do!"

She turned away and I said nothing, trembling as I sat on the bed. I had done my best to avoid getting on the wrong side of Molly for two years and now it had happened through no fault of mine. I waited until I thought she had subsided. "What could I have done, Molly? I had no wish to spend time with him. Ma said I had no choice."

"You could have taken your pretty face and gone somewhere else. I knew you'd be trouble ... I told Ma you would be. Well, I'll not let you take away all the business from me. They won't want you with your hair cut off and a scar or two on your face."

"Molly, please. I've done nothing to deserve this. I never wanted this life but Ma won't let me go."

"Of course she won't ... you're worth too much to her."

What a perverse compliment that was. I would gladly be worth far less to her, so little in fact that she would let me go. I stayed awake, Molly's threat ringing in my ears. Perhaps the loss of my hair and a few scars as she put it would be enough to release me. I thought I would gladly endure those things to get out. But then I thought of Patrick. If he was true to his word, there was the chance of a new life. My hair would grow but would he want me with scars on my face? Molly's anger had done one thing. It had renewed my determination to leave on Saturday morning and I had no regrets about leaving without a word. Molly could have been a support to me those past two years but she had marked me down as a rival and there was no sisterhood between us.

When I heard Molly's deep breathing and knew she was asleep, I allowed myself to drift off but my sleep was plagued with dreams which, at least twice, were so vivid I woke in a sweat.

# CHAPTER 19

# BALDOSA

**Patrick**

"Will you be one of the twelve then on Thursday evening, Patrick? I'd like you to be."

"Father, I cannot let you wash my feet."

"Why ever not?"

"I should be washing your feet ... you have done so much for me."

Canon Peter looked at me. He smiled and then looked serious. "Is this pride, Patrick, or humility? I can't decide."

"I think I've been cured of pride. 'I am not worthy...' is, I think, the reason."

"Perhaps so. But you are worthy, Patrick, and you must learn to allow others to help you. 'Tis not you that has to be always the one who sorts everything out. You're like Simon Peter when Jesus wanted to wash the feet of the disciples."

I looked at him, surprised, and then coloured. Could one take pride in one's humility? Of course. It is always down to motive but I felt that I was not being falsely humble. I had a deep sense of my own unworthiness. But it would have been churlish of me to refuse. Jesus washed the feet of the disciples before the last supper to show them that all should serve others but that also meant we should allow others to serve us. "For I have given you an example, that you should do as I have done to you. The Gospel of St John, I think."

"Precisely." He smiled again. "So that's settled. Be sure to wash your feet beforehand and wear clean socks!"

I arranged with the manager at the bank to start work early on each day during Holy Week so I could finish at lunchtime on Maundy Thursday and get to the shipping office. Several times that morning, I checked the money I had and put it carefully in my wallet which I put in my jacket pocket. When I stepped out of the bank after lunch, I did not feel the excitement I had expected. Part of me wondered if Rose would actually come and part of me was nervous about the police. What if I were seen buying two tickets at the shipping office? Would they put two and two together and arrest me then and there?

I walked quickly, flicking glances over my shoulder until I was down at the docks and close to the shipping office. As I approached it, I saw two figures sitting on the ground in the grime at the side of the road and with a shock I realised it was Mary and Finbar McCarthy. I would have preferred to give them a quick greeting and hurry on but something in their demeanour stopped me. Finbar was slumped on the ground, a bottle clutched in his hand whilst Mary, also sitting on the ground, looked across the harbour with vacant eyes. Their clothes looked dirty and Finbar had several days growth of beard. Tentatively, I asked them how they were.

"Fine, Father, fine," said Finbar. I could smell the drink and his speech was slurred. I looked at Mary.

"We're not fine at all." She did not look at me. "How much does a body have to endure?"

I felt a surge of anger at Finbar. I could see what the situation was. He was drinking any money they had and now they were destitute. And then the anger passed and I thought of him walking out of the hut at La Viticola when little Ellen died, demanding why God had let her die. I thought of him on the road back to Buenos Aires when Peter, the child Mary had borne at La Viticola, also died. If I had suffered that, would I not turn to drink? My heart went out to Mary, though. She had watched the two children she had carried in her womb pass away and now she was left with a husband who was filling with drink the space that hope had left.

"Mary, tell me how you come to be here," I said gently.

"They said we could go somewhere else in Argentina and have a loan or we could have money for tickets to go back home or on to America. We chose to have the money for tickets to America. Much of it has gone on drink … and now there's only enough for one ticket and we have no place to stay."

She spoke without anger. I think she had gone beyond that, so hopeless, so worn down that she had no capacity for any emotion. I made a decision. "Stand up, please." Mary did so, holding the wall and rising slowly like a woman twice her age. "And you, Finbar."

"What for?" He raised sullen eyes to mine.

"You're coming with me."

"Why?"

I did not answer but bent down, took the bottle from him and tipped out the contents before laying it at the side of the street. I grabbed him by the collar and heaved him up so he had no choice but to stand. He slumped against the wall and I put my arm through his. "You'll find out." I marched him along the street with Mary walking beside me. I had to help him up the steps into the shipping office. It was a large office with two openings in a long wooden partition at which the clerks sat. My steps were hard on the stone floor and reverberated in the space beneath the high ceiling. Mercifully, there were not many people waiting at the desk. I dragged him up to the counter, asking Mary who had the money. She rummaged in her pocket and took out a small wad of notes.

The clerk in a crisp uniform looked suspiciously at us and especially at Finbar. "I'd like two tickets for the ship that's leaving for America on Saturday." Mary started to protest but I shushed her and gave their names to the clerk. We watched in silence as he filled in forms and took a large stamp which he thumped down on the tickets and on his record. Mary flinched at the first stamp as if it were a gunshot. When all the formalities had been complete, I gave the tickets to Mary. "Now look after those. You and Mary, Finbar, are to wait over there until I'm finished." I pointed to a bench seat at the edge of the room.

I bought a single ticket in Rose's name as I did not have enough money left for two. My heart sank at the thought of sending her off alone. I would not tell her until I had walked her to the boarding ramp. I would tell her that I would come on the next ship and find her in New York. I knew I was doing the right thing – I had no choice as I saw it. Finbar and Mary had suffered enough; I could not leave them on the streets of Buenos Aires while Finbar drank the remaining money and they starved.

I joined them at the bench and leaned over Finbar as if I were a schoolteacher reprimanding a naughty schoolboy. "Now you listen to me carefully, Finbar. The ship leaves on Saturday morning. You and Mary will be on it – you've to board by ten o'clock but get there early so there's no problem. D'you hear me?"

He mumbled a reply but Mary spoke. "Thank you, Father, thank you. He doesn't deserve it but…"

"He didn't deserve to lose both his children and nor did you." I spoke directly to Finbar. "There'll be no more drinking until you get off that boat, is that clear? You have a lovely wife but the drink will drive her away. Then you'll have nothing. Now come with me the both of you."

I knew that my officious manner was partly a way of avoiding the sadness that lay in my heart. Rose would go to New York and by the time I was able to get there, she would have disappeared into that vast city or perhaps beyond and I would have little chance of finding her again. I must think of a way of getting her to leave me a note of where she went. My mind was churning this over as I supported and half dragged Finbar along the road to the Hotel de Inmigrantes. Mary trotted beside us, carrying the few possessions they still had in her bag.

In the hotel, I had enough money to pay for two nights for them. Mary was again effusive in her thanks and Finbar managed to mumble some gratitude. "Perhaps I'll see you in church this evening or tomorrow afternoon?"

Finbar looked at the floor but Mary said she would be there. I left them with a reminder to Finbar about avoiding drink and arriving for the ship in good time. I felt tired as I trudged back to the presbytery, trying to deal with my disappointment. So near to being with Rose and now so far. Would she turn up for the voyage? I was still not sure. If she did, would she refuse to go on her own? Possibly. I felt too drained to think that through – I would have to deal with that if it happened. Fleetingly, I thought that if Rose did not go, I could use the ticket but I dismissed the idea immediately. I could not leave her alone in Buenos Aires to endure the life she had.

As I entered the presbytery, Canon Peter was emerging from his study, whistling softly. "Ah Patrick. Did you get the tickets? All set, are you?"

"Yes…" I mumbled, not looking him in the eye.

I could feel his shrewd eyes on my face. "Then why so glum?"

He would understand of course so I told him, simply. "I will not be leaving Buenos Aires yet, Father. I must earn more money for my ticket. Hopefully they'll keep me on at the bank." I told him of the McCarthy's and reminded him of what they had suffered.

"Will Rose leave on her own?"

"I don't know, Father."

"Come in here." He led me back into his study and I stood awkwardly at the door while he unlocked the little cupboard on one side of his desk. He took out a metal box and put it on the surface. "How much do you need for the other ticket?"

"No, Father … I can't take money from you. You've already been very good to me. I'll work for the other ticket."

"How much is it?" He looked at me sternly and I realised resistance was futile. I told him and he thrust out his hand towards me with several notes in it. "That'll cover it." I did not take it from him but he did not withdraw his hand. When he spoke again, it was softly, not with anger, nor chidingly, but with care. "For I have given you an example that you should do as I have done for you. I have taken your example, Patrick. You gave money you needed to help that poor couple and now I give you money to help you. If I am in trouble, someone will help me. That is what Jesus wanted us to do."

I put out my hand slowly and took the notes from him. "Thank you, Father, thank you from the bottom of my heart."

He waved the words away and replaced the metal box in the desk. "You have determined to save that young woman from a life of suffering. That is a wonderful thing. If you save her, you save the world."

"How so? 'Tis a poor creature I am that can save only one person. Indeed I cannot save the world"

"Fortunately, that has already been done." He smiled. "But Patrick, if you save one person, someone else will save another, and someone else another and so on because they will follow your example. And so, you will save the world. Now you'd better get back to that shipping office before it closes."

## Rose

The church was almost full when I arrived and I found a place in a pew near the back as I usually did. The nuns were, as before, in the pew in front of me. I looked cautiously around the church. I saw him at the front, standing and talking with some other men before I lost sight of him when he sat down. The service started and I stood and knelt and stood again with everyone else though my mind was not on what I was doing. The last supper, the night of betrayal. Would I be the betrayer or the betrayed?

The time came for communion but I could not go up for it or even for a blessing. I sat and watched the file of people moving confidently towards salvation; I was not among them and would never be. I felt the weight of my sin upon my heart then, the sin that could not be forgiven, the attempt on my own life, unsuccessful, but the intention had been there and thus the guilt. I noticed that Patrick did take communion. He had found some kind of faith then … perhaps it would not be long before he found his vocation again and he would lose interest in me.

He was having his feet washed, cleansing all the grime of the last two years. If only I could wash away the last two years so easily. I realised as I sat there that I could never leave with him unless I confessed my sin both to him and to a serving priest, one who could give me absolution … or damn me. How could that be? Confession was on Saturday afternoon and the ship sailed in the morning. He was still a priest though he had given up his ministry. Once a priest, always a priest was what they said. Perhaps I could confess to him and he could give absolution. It was all so difficult. I felt tired, drained. I began to think I no longer cared.

It was not until Reverend Mother had disturbed my thoughts that I realised the service had ended. "Rose … you're lost in thought."

"Yes, Reverend Mother. Hello! I was miles away I'm afraid."

"At this time of year, 'tis hard not to think deeply. Our Lord about to be betrayed and go through that suffering."

"Yes, 'tis a sad time."

"There is so much suffering in the world, much of it unnecessary. Why don't you come and see us, Rose? We could just talk ...."

"I ... I don't think I need that at the moment but I have a friend for whom I worry." She looked at me with interest and her kind eyes invited me to go on. "Her name is Annie ... Annie Boyle. She's in another house ... worse than mine ... and they got her onto laudanum. She hardly knows what day it is. I wanted her to leave with me but she has accepted her lot. 'Tis not right, she must fight it." I stopped suddenly, realising that I was babbling. That is always the problem with talking; as soon as you open the gate a fraction, the flood bursts through.

"That's a hard one but we may be able to help if she will talk to us."

"I fear she'll not ... she seems to have a poor view of priests and nuns ..."

Reverend Mother smiled. "Many do I'm afraid. Where is her house?"

I rummaged in my pocket and thrust a piece of paper forward. "I've written her name and address here but we usually meet after I've been to confession on Saturdays in the little square by the church of San Martin. D'you know it?"

"I do. You wanted her to leave with you but she won't?"

"That's right." I coloured, suddenly realising I had revealed the plan to leave. "Please say nothing, Reverend Mother. If Ma finds out, she'll have the police arrest me."

She held up her hand. "Don't fret, Rose. I'll say nothing at all. So your friend has a poor view of us."

"I think she has had bad experiences back home with …"

"So many people think that we become priests or nuns to escape the world. Perhaps some have that idea to start with but one soon finds out that the world is in many ways an easier place … not for everyone, of course, because terrible things happen. But a nun has to decide to devote herself to the service of God and God calls us to do all sorts of things we would rather not. Now I know that the nuns in schools in Ireland may appear very simple minded. But how can you explain to children such complicated things as one encounters in adulthood?"

I looked at her. She was eyeing me keenly as was her wont, judging what impact her words were having. I did not know if she was expecting me to speak but I remained silent.

She turned her face towards the altar and then back. "My sisters and I made a decision when we took our vows that we would give up certain things… the love of a man, the pleasures of the body … and there are pleasures, Rose, though it may not seem like that to you. That is a hard thing to do." She studied the tiles on the floor before looking up and continuing.

"When I was young, before I became a nun, I loved a young man, Rose, and I am sure he loved me. It was a precious thing. I think I may have broken his heart when I told him I had decided to devote myself to the service of God. I had many agonised hours over that decision but it was right for me."

I looked at her carefully, as if I had not seen her before. Beauty still lay in her face and especially her eyes, enhanced by the delicate lines that age had etched. Any man would have found that face attractive.

"He did find someone else and I am sure he was happy so I was freed from the guilt of that separation. I do not regret my decision because I know God called me. If He is calling you to love a man …

a man who needs that love to restore him as you perhaps need the love of a good man to restore you, that is a precious calling. Accept it my dear as I accepted my calling and you will find happiness. We will do what we can for Annie."

And then she was gone, re-joining the sisters and leaving the church. She knew, then. How, I wondered? It made no matter, I would be gone. I watched Patrick making his way towards me, stopping to talk with many people, those I suppose who had been with him in that place. He was a good man and one who did need the love of a good woman to restore him. But was I a good woman? Could he love me when he found out what I had done?

"Rose, I have the tickets. We need to talk about getting you out of Placer House. I was thinking could you give that fella Michael a good few slugs of brandy or something on the Friday night so he won't wake early next morning? I could get you the brandy and give it to you at church tomorrow."

"I could but I don't think that will be needed. I'll leave very early before even Michael is awake … and I'll stay hidden somewhere near the docks until you come. 'Tis best if we are not together until the last minute."

He nodded slowly. "As long as you're sure. We don't want him stopping you."

"I'm sure of nothing, Patrick, but there is a risk that he'll make a fuss and then I'll be discovered. He'd want to know why I was giving him brandy."

"Let's meet on the dock road by the Hotel de Inmigrantes at say nine thirty in the morning. Would that be alright?"

"That'll be fine." It still seemed an improbable dream; he was yet to hear the extent of my past. We stood awkwardly together and then a woman came up to him.

She seemed uncertain, fragile. "Father, I want to thank you again for what you've done for us. Finbar has not touched a drop since and he came with me tonight to church. I think he is ashamed and that's why he would not come to speak with you now."

"It is nothing less than you deserve, Mary. Get a good night's sleep tonight and tomorrow and be ready for the journey on Saturday."

She thanked him again and left us. He explained what had happened, the loss of her children, finding them earlier that day, the husband drunk. "What did you do that made her so grateful," I asked.

"Oh, nothing in particular." He looked away but I could see he was embarrassed so I didn't pursue it. It was clear to me the high regard in which he was held by the people who had been with him in La Viticola. He had told me much about it but I suspect he had underplayed his own part, his attempts to improve their lot. I remember when he tackled those two crooks on the ship over, about the food and other provision for us in steerage. I had an image of him coming down the steps to the deck on which James and I sat and I said to him that he demanded too much of himself. That is often the cruellest thing – what we demand of ourselves rather than what others demand of us.

I walked back past Annie's house. I thought of calling to see her but I would already be late and that would set Ma's antennae twitching. I stood for a while on the opposite side of the road. Two men were approaching, arm in arm, shouting and laughing, staggering a little. They looked like sailors or fishermen or some such – rough anyway. I thought of poor Annie having to deal with them. My heart ached for her. Could I do this? Leave her here without a word of farewell? But what if she did say something and word got back to Ma? I couldn't risk it. I hoped that Reverend Mother and the sisters would be as good as her word and seek her out. I felt confident that they would and that they would not give up easily. Perhaps they could persuade her where I had failed.

I walked slowly on, not wishing to return to my own form of hell. I was better off than Annie, there was no doubt about it, and I had to keep telling myself that. It is strange that, as the end of something approaches, it seems further away. I remembered once walking out of Cork city with a friend when I was working at Miss O'Leary's. When we turned to come back, the triple spires of the newly built Anglican cathedral, St Fin Barre's, were clearly visible. It looked as though you could reach out and touch them. But as we walked back into the city, they seemed to shrink and recede so you'd think you could never arrive there.

And so it felt now. The prospect of escape from this life in two days made the time in between doubly painful. The hours seemed to go more slowly and it felt as though time would stop altogether before Saturday morning came. Outside Placer House, I paused to compose myself. I must give nothing away, must be completely calm as always, must smile and smile and let them do what they wanted. 'Twill not be long, I told myself, but I think I was trying to convince myself. So much could go wrong in those hours remaining.

# CHAPTER 20

# APILADA

**Patrick**

"And so we come to the darkest day … Good Friday." Canon Peter had climbed wearily up the steps to the pulpit and was beginning his reflection on the day. I looked around the church, the statues shrouded in purple cloth as they had been during the whole of Lent. There were no flowers, nothing to distract the eye and the mind from the passion of Jesus.

I had not lost my faith entirely but I was filled with uncertainty, doubt. I was no longer sure what I believed; my only anchor was the tenderness I felt whenever I thought of Rose, which was most of the time. Save one person and you save the world, Canon Peter had said. I had no wish to save the world, none of the arrogant, presumptuous ambitions that had filled my head when I walked away from Monsignor O'Rourke's that day … a lifetime ago.

Canon Peter's voice was anguished. "Why did Jesus have to suffer so much? It is a question I have often asked myself. The easy answer is to say he suffered to pay for our sins. But I think it is more complicated than that. The answer lies in the suffering that we see daily in our own lives, suffering that no one should endure. And I have seen a great deal of that, as have many of you. God is showing us that even his own son, as a human being, was not exempt from the suffering caused by other people. It is easy to condemn them but have not we all been guilty at some time of demanding retribution on a person we think has wronged us? Have we not all been guilty at some time of washing our hands of the suffering of others?"

He looked around the church and I tried to think through the last two years. Had I been guilty of those things? Had I done enough for poor young Jimmy? Had I done enough for the hundreds at La Viticola who were half starved most of the time? No, I had not … one can never do enough.

He continued. "Some will say that suffering is necessary to experience the joy when it is over. To the drowning woman, one breath of clear, pure air is joy, to the starving man, one mouthful of wholesome food is ecstasy and to the sick child, the hour she wakes free from the fever is heaven." He paused, looking along the rows of faces.

"Does God want us to suffer then? I say no, he does not, but he created the world with a balance of life and death. The forces of life are strong. The child grows to be an adult, to have children him or herself, but within us all are the elements of our own ageing towards death. Think of a parent whose child grows to adulthood and goes out into the world to make their way. The parent cannot protect them from everything, may even be distant from them, may be unable to help them. But does the parent feel any less the suffering their child might endure?" He looked around again as if expecting the congregation to respond. "No, of course not. Any caring parent would happily die to save their child one minute's pain. And so it is with God."

The congregation was transfixed, all eyes on the pulpit. Canon Peter's voice was tired but full of gentleness. "God cannot prevent our suffering but He weeps at every blow we feel. He longs to gather us into His arms and carry us to a better place. And, if there is no other solution, that is what He does. He takes the sick child to himself to save its suffering, He lifts the wounded soldier in his arms, He carries us, the broken, the damaged, the despairing to a better place for He has given his son to pay for our transgressions."

But I had not felt lifted nor cared for out on that barren plain when James had died, when all the others had fallen ill and passed away. I had felt abandoned.

"People often say to me that when they are at their lowest, there is no sign of God. It feels that way. And so, we cry out, 'My God, my God, why hast thou forsaken me?' It is the cry of anguish from Jesus on the cross, when God appears to be nowhere near, the lowest point we can reach. But God has not abandoned us. We must keep faith and His spirit of goodness will fill the heart of someone who will bring us help. And if that cannot be achieved, He will take us to himself. In nomine Patris et Filii et Spiritus Sancti, Amen."

I watched him descend the steps slowly and my heart went out towards him. He had been that other person filled with the Holy Spirit who had come to my rescue. I had felt abandoned but a few short days later, he had done what was needed to care for us, all of us. He was filled with goodness, with humility, with love. If only I could be like that.

At the end of the service, people filed out silently as was the custom. I hovered as usual at the back of the church to see Rose. I saw her walking towards me slowly, her head down. "Rose? Are you alright?" I whispered, conscious of the need for silence.

She nodded and then looked up at me, a fear in her eyes I had not seen for some while. "I need to make my confession. Can you still hear confessions?"

"Technically I can but it wouldn't be right for me to hear yours … there is too much between us … on my side anyway."

"I want to make my confession before we leave tomorrow but the ship will have sailed by …"

She looked miserable. "Well, all I can suggest, Rose, is that we find Canon Peter and ask him."

She nodded again and we walked slowly up the aisle to the chancel and then into the vestry. The altar boys were just leaving and Canon

Peter was on his own, derobing. The heavy old furniture seemed to exude the smell of incense. "Father, thank you for that reflection."

He looked up and shrugged. "I'm not sure if it made anything clearer. 'Tis a difficult one that … suffering. Life would be easier without it." He smiled at Rose. "I take it this is the young lady who has turned your heart. I can see why you would, my dear."

"Father, Rose would like to make her confession and I wondered if you could hear it now."

"Of course. Just give me a minute. You go on out there, Patrick, and Rose will join you after."

"No … I'd like Patrick to hear it too … it's important he does." Her words startled me.

Canon Peter lifted his eyebrows. "That's unusual but … if you're sure?"

"I'm sure."

He dragged a prie-dieu from the side of the vestry next to his big old chair and motioned Rose to kneel. "Now, is this alright for you here, Rose, or would you prefer to go into a confessional box?"

"This is fine, Father." She knelt and put her hands together resting them on the surface of the prie-dieu. She looked like a child, angelic, untouched, but I shrank into the shadow at the edge of the vestry, made fearful by her manner of what she would confess. Her head was bowed slightly, her eyes lowered. "Bless me, Father, for it is two years since I have made a full confession … I never felt able to say what was in my heart."

"Well, my child, 'tis a good thing you feel able to do that now."

"You know Father that I am a prostitute." She laid the word before him in all its ugliness, but with no trace of bitterness. "I did not choose this life but I have been unable to bring myself to get away from it. I know I should have sought help, perhaps from the nuns, but it was as if I was in a prison in my mind. But there is something worse. Before Christmas, a man took me when I was not on my guard and I became pregnant. I had already felt that new life growing within me and it was washed away."

She stopped. I realised tears were silently trickling down her face. I wanted to hold her in my arms, tell her that I loved her the more for her suffering but I was frozen in horror at what she had endured but had never been able to talk about. Her voice continued, quietly, hesitantly, pausing, and I had to strain to hear the words she uttered.

"And then, Father, when it was flushed from my womb, I could not confess my sin and … I was going to throw myself into the waters of the harbour. Patrick stopped me. I have committed murder and the mortal sin of despair."

"And you have carried this burden within you, with no one to take it from you?" His quiet voice held the wisdom of the ages.

She nodded and clutched a handkerchief to her face. "I am damned, Father, am I not? Can I – can I be forgiven? I am not worthy …" The watery eyes she lifted to him were pleading, every abuse she had suffered in the last two years contained in that broken sentence.

Canon Peter stood and turned to the cabinet in which his copes were held. On top was a brass crucifix which he lifted and placed on the surface of the prie-dieu. Rose leant back, removing her arms to make space. "Look at this figure, my dear. 'Tis so familiar to all of us that we forget its meaning. Look at the eyes in that face. Even in the moment of death, they are full of compassion, full of love. You are forgiven, Rose, even before you committed any sin, as Jesus has paid for all our wrong-doing. You are as much one of God's children as anyone else and you are loved more than you can ever imagine." He put his hand gently under her chin and lifted her face. "Lord, I am not worthy but only say the word and my soul will be healed. All we have to do is ask." Canon Peter said the words of absolution and then, "Now will you pray with me?" She bowed her head as did I.

"Hail Mary, full of grace, the Lord is with thee. Blessed art thou amongst women and blessed is the fruit of thy womb, Jesus. Holy Mary, Mother of God, pray for us sinners now and at the hour of our death, Amen."

He put the crucifix back on the top and put his hands under her forearms. "Come, my child, stand." He looked in her eyes, tears still welling from them. "Tell me ... did you want the baby to be aborted or did you want to keep it?"

Her body crumpled as if she would fall but Canon Peter's arms held her still. "I wanted to keep it. I could feel that life inside me but they ... they gave me laudanum so I couldn't resist."

He shook his head. "Why do you think you have sinned?"

"Because I should have known that was what they intended and I didn't get away. I thought I would just tell them I was keeping the baby and that would be that."

"And did you want to become a prostitute?"

She looked at him incredulously and her voice was full of anguish. "Of course not, Father. They drugged me the first time and threatened me with violence, with the police if I tried to get away."

"My child, you cannot be held responsible for what others do to you, even though I know you feel shame, you feel degraded."

"I do feel shame, Father. I feel that I must have done something wrong in my life to be punished in this way."

"No Rose. You are not being punished ... you are the victim of people who have done evil. Think of Mary Magdalene. Did Jesus reject her because of the life she had led? No. You are washed clean; you have no sin on your soul. Wanting to end your life is understandable. It shows how much you cared about what had happened. You say Patrick stopped you?" He turned to me and smiled as if he had been proved right.

"What is my penance, Father?"

"Penance? There is no penance, child. You have not sinned and you have done the penance already for the sins that were committed against you. If only everyone had your conscience. Some punish themselves every day of their lives with remorse for their actions, others never seem to give it a thought. But which of these will enter heaven? For one must repent and be forgiven to find that state of grace."

"Thank you, Father," she whispered.

"Tell me, Rose … what of the man who made you pregnant without your consent?"

"He is Ma's son though I did not know it at the time. He is a poor creature whose mind is not complete."

"And did you report it to the police?"

"No, Father … there was no point. I found Ma beating him like a dog. I stopped her. I forgave him, though it was weeks later; I could not do so immediately."

"You are a good person, Rose. There's not many could forgive an act such as that. But forgiveness is important for ourselves as much as for the sinner. It frees us from the anger of being wronged and allows us to flourish. 'Forgive us our trespasses as we forgive those …' You know the words right enough."

I struggled to look at Rose. I was filled with powerful emotions. I wanted to hold her, to tell her I would look after her, and a tenderness so great possessed me. But she would not look at me, as if she was too ashamed and dared not meet my eyes. What was she thinking? She had wanted me to know what had happened to her. Why? Would it not have been better to leave me in the dark? Had she wanted me to hear because she wanted to repel me?

"Rose …" I got no further. She thanked Canon Peter again and accepted the kiss he placed on her cheek. Then, with a small wave of her hand, she glided from the vestry, her eyes never lifting to meet mine. I thanked Canon Peter hurriedly, intending to go after Rose but he detained me, asking me about when I had stopped her jumping from the dock.

When I got away, she was nowhere to be seen. I was in an agony for the rest of the day and much of the night. I had wanted to tell her that I loved her even more now I knew the extent of her suffering. I had wanted to reassure her, hold her, convey my love for her. But she had gone without a backward glance. It could only be that this was her way of saying she would not be coming with me on the ship. And yet she could easily have said so.

Emilia had prepared a supper of fish as was usual on Good Friday. We ate in near silence, Rose's revelation hanging in the space between us, my departure on the morrow unspoken. I thanked Canon Peter for the kindness and understanding he had shown to Rose. He shrugged as if it was nothing.

"Forgiveness … 'tis a hard thing," I ventured.

"For us, yes."

"Much easier of course if there is genuine repentance on the part of the wrong-doer. Those two agents who brought everyone over here on the *Dresden* with a pack of lies showed no remorse. I suppose they're comfortably back in Ireland, living off their ill-gotten gains. I know I should forgive them, but I cannot find it in my heart to do so."

"And yet Rose found it in her heart to forgive that poor creature who wronged her. God knows it is a hard thing to do … she is a remarkable young woman. Learn from her example, Patrick … free yourself by forgiving."

After supper, we both retired to our rooms to pray and reflect on the meaning of the day. At least Canon would have done so. I sat looking out of the window as the city shrunk into the night, the sounds gradually falling away, some lights flickering on but the clear shape of the buildings fading.

I slept fitfully, rising several times to try to quiet the turmoil in my mind. I gazed out of the window and thought of Rose somewhere not too distant. I hoped her work for the night had been brief and I shuddered at the thought of some man using her. I wished she had taken up the offer from Reverend Mother to stay at the convent. It was too late for that. I thought of her going to her bed. Would she be able to sleep? Would she be planning for the early morning? Or would she have dismissed me and the idea of escape from her mind?

When the first light of morning broke through the curtains, I rose and splashed water on my face. I dressed and sat on the bed, unable to do anything. I had already put my few possessions into my old suitcase. I noticed the cross that Monsignor O'Rourke had given me sitting on the bedside table. I had put it there when I first arrived from La Viticola. I had not carried it in my pocket since. I decided I would leave it there. It had done nothing for me when I had needed it most, despite what both Monsignor and Canon Peter said.

Breakfast was a little strained. We made small talk, avoiding the subject of my departure. It was of course more than a departure from Buenos Aires; it was a departure from the priesthood too. I think Canon Peter hoped that I would at last change my mind and take up my duties as a priest again. But I could not do that while Rose needed help. Would I do that if she chose not to come? I did not know.

And then came the time of my leaving. I brought my suitcase down from my room, my overcoat draped over my arm. Canon Peter was in the hall. "You're off then, Patrick?"

"I am Father. 'Tis time to move on."

He nodded slowly, deep in thought. "You will always be welcome back again … you know that, don't you?"

"I do, Father. I cannot tell you how grateful I am to you for everything you have done. I wish I were half so good…" I choked, feeling a sudden rise of tears.

"Oh 'tis the other way round, Patrick. What you did for those people, what you are about to do for Rose, is the work of God. I am truly blessed to have met you."

I couldn't help it. I dropped to my knees. "No, Father. I am nothing but may I have your blessing?"

"Of course." I felt his hand laid gently on my head. "May you find fulfilment and love on this Earth and may you feel God's love with you always wherever your steps may lead you. In nomine Patris et Filii et Spiritus Sancti. Amen."

I stood. "Thank you, Father … thank you."

"And now you must go."

Just then, there was a clatter on the stairs and Emilia was hurrying down holding something in her hand. "Father … Father … you forget this." She held out her hand and on her palm nestled the cross I had decided to leave behind.

"I … I … was going to …"

Canon Peter looked at me keenly. "Take it, Patrick. Take it and hold it in your hand and God will always hold you in his hand in return."

I reached out, took the cross and slipped it in my jacket pocket. I had tears starting in my eyes again, I did not know why. I shook hands with Emilia and then Canon Peter. I looked him in the eyes one last time, eyes that had seen so much, eyes full of love, understanding. I walked away from the presbytery completely uncertain as to what the morning would bring.

# FINALE

## EASTER SATURDAY 28<sup>TH</sup> MARCH 1891

**Rose**

I look up from my hiding place between the stacks of crates. There is a strip of blue sky, and lazy white clouds drifting across it. I want to reach up and grasp them. It is like another prison with just a glimpse of a better life beyond the bars. If I could see more, the sky would be pastel shades of blue, pink and yellow, merging imperceptibly, retreating from the sun. I hear the cry of the gulls, wheeling and diving to snatch morsels of food. The sounds of the dock remind me of the lives that continue, oblivious to the tiny drama that plays in my head.

The game we played as children comes to my mind, plucking each leaf from the head of a daisy, he loves me, he loves me not. Now the refrain is "He'll come, he'll not come, he'll come, he'll not" over and over again like the breathing of the sea, the waves endlessly washing against the harbour side, the rise and fall of the sleeper's chest, the thrust and withdrawal – these, the most basic elements of life.

I did not dare look at his face after making my confession. He was silent except for saying my name once as I left the vestry. What did he mean by that? Had the sentence continued, would he have said he was sorry but he could not leave with me, knowing what had befallen me? Or would he have said that he loved me nevertheless? He'll come … he'll not come."

Canon Peter – what a lovely man – such kindness, such understanding. Perhaps if he had been taking confession the times I tried, things would have been different. But the mind is unfathomable. Even though he had said I had not sinned and I was washed clean, I did not feel it. It was this uncertainty. God may not condemn me and that was a comfort but I would be condemned by the world. There is no sympathy for the prostitute. It is assumed she is a bad person and deserves whatever comes her way. Would Patrick be one of those? Would he condemn me despite Canon's words?

And if he does not come, what then? I will not return to Placer House – I cannot go back there to that life. I will go to the convent and ring the bell. I will devote myself to saving Annie from the drug that is killing her, from the life that has destroyed her. Perhaps that's what I should do anyway, instead of pursuing my own chance of escape.

Perhaps … perhaps … so many uncertainties, so many decisions, so many turnings that might be wrong. How can one ever know how to reach sanctuary?

I look out from my hiding place and I am suddenly cold. Two police officers are strolling down the road by the quay. Are they looking for me? Am I to be so close and yet be taken? They seem to be looking for something or someone. They are peering behind the piles of fishing nets and crab pots. I hear myself whimper. How long before they reach me? I creep to the back end of the crates nearest the water and peek out from that end, cautiously, leaning forward so only my head is visible. I pull back my head and wait a few seconds then lean forward again only to jerk backwards. I cannot see them; they must be moving towards my crates and out of my sight.

Easing myself out again I stand between the crates and the edge of the shore and then I remember my bag, sitting where I left it between the crates, ready for them to see. My heart is thumping and I lean my head the other way now to peer between the crates. I cannot see them but I must retrieve my bag. I take a deep breath like a diver about to plunge and I rush towards the bag, bashing my elbow on a crate. Snatching the bag, I rush back to breathe, leaning against the rough wood and looking out over the grey water. Slowly I turn my head to left and right … no one is in sight.

I wait for what seems a lifetime but really only a minute or two before looking again between the crates. The gap at the end is too small. I glide slowly towards it, ready to leap back if I see them. I can always jump in the sea, I think. Better that than be taken to prison. I look out first to the right – they are not in sight – and then to the left. They are walking away from me.

They return the occasional greeting to a docker or one of the street vendors. They are smiling, they are relaxed. It must be just a routine patrol but I shrink back between the crates just in case. What or who are they looking for? I realise that I have been holding my breath as if that would make me invisible. Suddenly there is a commotion from where I last saw them, shouting in Spanish, a woman's voice. I peer out again. They are holding a woman, dirty, in ragged clothes and dragging her away. She is yelling. One of the policemen slaps her hard across the face and she stops shouting.

I know what she is and I know what will happen to her. There are tears in my eyes. Are they for her or for me? That could be my fate if he does not come.

The clock has not yet struck the half hour … at least I have not heard it. That will be the time of truth. He will be here or not. How long should I wait if he is not here at the appointed time? Perhaps ten minutes. I feel as though I have been waiting for two years so ten minutes more should not be a problem but time seems to be crawling very slowly as if it has stopped. I think of the candle I lit in the church. It would still be burning but would already have shrunk to a flickering stump. Would it last until the clock struck the half hour? It feels important, as if my life is dependent on its lasting until then.

The people for whom I lit the candle drift into my mind like apparitions – my parents. What agonies had they suffered about me in the last two years? Would I ever see them again? I would write as soon as I reached New York – if – and Annie, her lively spirit broken. If I ever reached New York and safety, I would write to Reverend Mother, I would come back for Annie … perhaps. I allow myself to imagine myself as a wealthy woman married to Patrick who makes his fortune in some enterprise. I imagine returning to Buenos Aires, staying in one of the big hotels, marching boldly into Annie's house and demanding to see her. I would take her in my arms and then walk out the door with her.

And the child that had formed in me. Was that little soul already in heaven? I would light a candle every year on the day of its death and pray, pray that heaven has welcomed him or her, that we will meet sometime in the life hereafter.

I look out again and scour both directions as far as I can see. No sign of him as yet, no sign of the policemen, no sign of anyone from Placer House. Ma would be up by now, though still bleary-eyed and dozy from the night before. Michael would be out chopping wood. Ma would at some point notice that the salon had not been cleared of glasses and tidied – my job first thing. She would think nothing of it until Molly came downstairs, rather grumpy, and then Ma would ask her about me. Molly would look puzzled and ask if she had not seen me.

They would become suspicious and start to look around the house – the little room where I did the sewing – the bedrooms upstairs. What time would it be before they realised I was nowhere to be found? Nine thirty? Would Ma send someone, Maggie perhaps, to the police? That would take some time and then it would be more time before the police got a message to Ramirez unless he was working on Saturday. He would then have to organise a search. It would be well gone ten before all that could happen.

So if he does not come, I will need to be at the convent before ten o'clock. I start to feel nervous. This nightmare may not be over.

The sounds of a drum and an accordion drift across to me, coming from a gap in the quayside buildings. It is the rhythm of the tango – probably musicians practising. I hate it and I love it. My body starts to move, imperceptibly. It is more a movement inside, the rhythm creating a sinuous feeling in my very bones. To give oneself to the dance, to give oneself to a partner completely must be a wonderful freedom and yet it is tainted with the memories of the last two years, a travesty of love, a corruption of the God-given union.

Tomorrow, it will be Easter Sunday, the rising from the dead, the rebirth of goodness. Or so it should be. Bells will ring, the purple coverings will be thrown off the statues in church and spirits will lift. How cruel it will be if I am still here, if the promises of a new beginning are empty ... empty again as the promises made two years ago. What possessed me to come on that ship? The promise of a better life, work, comfort, adventure? I no longer know and I realise that it is useless now to worry. I am here and what has passed cannot be changed. What is important is tomorrow.

The clock strikes the half hour. I peer out from my hiding place, looking first in the direction of the ship further down the quay, not the direction from which he will come. No sign of the policemen. Slowly, holding my breath again, dreading the sight of an empty street, I turn my gaze the other way ... and I see him, walking towards me, his suitcase in his hand and his coat over his arm. He is looking around anxiously, checking every nook in every building, his brow furrowed. I lift my bag.

I step out from the crates into the sunshine. I am startled by a gull screaming close over my head but I keep my eye on him. It is not until he is a few paces away that he sees me. His brow straightens and then forms an expression of surprise as if he did not expect to see me. He takes two paces towards me, slowly, and, just as slowly, I move towards him. He places his case on the ground as do I and his mouth opens. But no words come out. Suddenly, he flings his arms wide and I feel them surround me, pulling me tight as my arms circle his neck. I feel my feet leave the ground and our lips meet.

My heart lifts. There is hope, there is redemption.

# POST-SCRIPT

The Dresden Affair, as it came to be known, brought an abrupt end to Irish emigration to Argentina. In 1889, Thomas Croke, Archbishop of Cashel and Emly, wrote: "I most solemnly conjure my poorer countrymen, as they value their happiness hereafter, never to set foot on the Argentine Republic however tempted to do so they may be by offers of a passage or an assurance of comfortable homes."

Emigration to Argentina from Ireland did not resume until the early twentieth century and then at a reduced rate. Numerous Irish people had emigrated successfully in the 1800s and did so again later, so the Dresden Affair does not reflect the experience of many. Argentina is believed to have the largest Irish diaspora of any non-English-speaking country; some 500,000 are known to have Irish heritage and some say the figure is closer to one million.

# ABOUT THE AUTHOR

Photo by Dominic O'Regan

Kevin's parents came from County Cork in Eire, his mother just before the war and his father just after it. Kevin took a degree in English Literature at Exeter University, followed by a PGCE, and then taught in maintained secondary schools for many years, becoming a headteacher and afterwards an educational consultant. He left his career in education early to develop his vocation as a musician and writer. Kevin is an award-winning songwriter who performs across the UK and abroad, solo, as a duo and with his band.

As well as *The Dresden Tango*, Kevin has written a young adult trilogy and an historical crime novel set in World War II.

If you would like to know more about Kevin, please visit his website:

www.kevinoregan.co.uk

https://www.facebook.com/profile.php?id=100085039475922

Printed in Great Britain
by Amazon

11987488R00181